The Patriot Spy

Yankee Doodle Spies series

S. W. O'Connell

Twilight Times Books
Kingsport Tennessee

The Patriot Spy

Paladin Timeless Books, an imprint of
Twilight Times Books
P O Box 3340
Kingsport TN 37664
http://twilighttimesbooks.com/

First Edition, July 2012

Library of Congress Control Number: 2012941871

ISBN: 978-1-60619-252-8

Cover art by Damon Shackelford

Map by Cate Scovel

Printed in the United States of America.

For my Father

The Patriot and citizen soldier

Who introduced me to
The gallantry of the men from Maryland
On a day long ago in Brooklyn

To him and all the citizen Soldiers

I dedicate this tale

Acknowledgments

Some talented people helped me in the development of this story. Paul Harpin, former military history professor at the US Army Military Academy at West Point, and Teresa Whitehead, former Department Head for Counterintelligence at the US Army Intelligence Center and School provided much insight and many thoughtful suggestions. Michael Varhola, whose encouragement helped keep this tale from the dustbin. Cate Scovel, whose map will help orient the reader to the setting. Finally, to those who for the sake of security, as well as mystery...must go unnamed.

"...Send Me, Lord..."

Isaiah 6:8

Prologue

In the summer of 1776, Great Britain had almost two thirds of its army and half of the Royal Navy in North America. Their mission seemed straightforward: crush the nascent American rebellion and assert Royal authority in the wayward colonies. After a prickly rebel army forced them from Boston in 1775, a reinforced British armada carrying almost thirty thousand men made its way down from Canada into New York Harbor and seized Staten Island in order to use it as the springboard for a campaign to wrest New York from the rebels. Doing this would establish a central strategic position aimed at dividing the rebelling colonies. To counter the British move, Lieutenant General George Washington moved his army of twenty thousand men from Boston to New York City by overland marches. Washington immediately put his ill-equipped and underfed army to work digging entrenchments and building fortifications. These covered the approaches to lower New York Island—as Manhattan was then known—and, later parts of Long Island. There, he concentrated about one-third of his army in a defensive cordon near a Dutch farming village called Brooklyn.

On August 22, 1776, the British Army came ashore at Gravesend, a sandy area just to the east of the Brooklyn narrows. The campaign for control of New York and the central position in the colonies had begun.

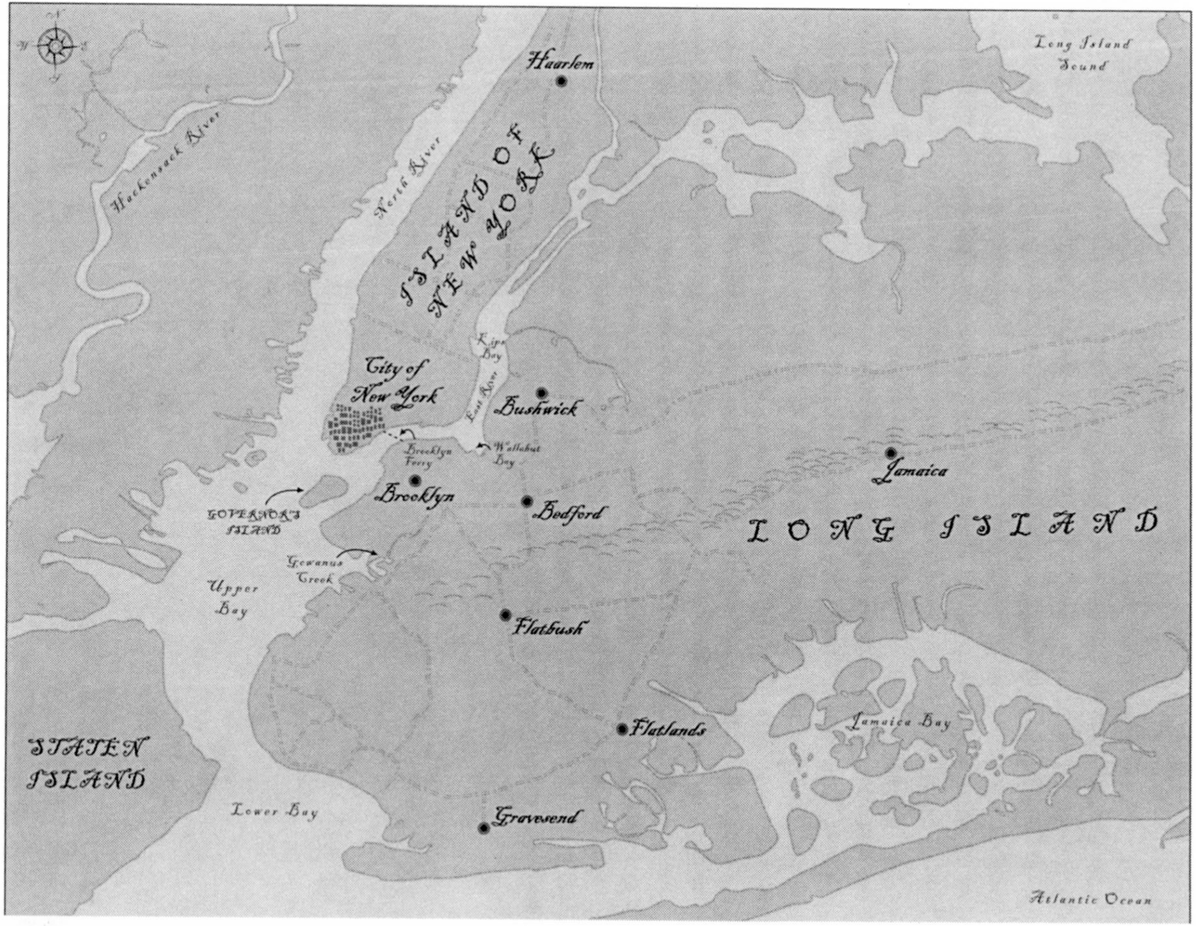
Long Island Sound
Haarlem
Hackensack River
North River
ISLAND OF NEW YORK
Kips Bay
City of New York
East River
Bushwick
Brooklyn Ferry
Wallabut Bay
Jamaica
GOVERNOR'S ISLAND
Brooklyn
Bedford
LONG ISLAND
Gowanus Creek
Upper Bay
Flatbush
STATEN ISLAND
Flatlands
Jamaica Bay
Lower Bay
Gravesend
Atlantic Ocean

Chapter 1

New York, July 20th, 1776

Colonel Robert Fitzgerald finished his letter to the commander-in-chief. As George Washington's intelligence advisor, Fitzgerald had engaged in an unending stream of talks over the past several weeks with the general. The subject was their enemy, the largest force ever to descend on the continent. Both Fitzgerald and his commander-in-chief agreed on one thing: they needed a superior intelligence arm to win. Fitzgerald decided to put his thoughts on paper, both for his own purposes, but also to influence Washington. They agreed on broad principles but could not agree on how best to achieve their aims. The British had a long history of using their "secret service" to great effect and had agents and Loyalists up and down the east coast. They had a powerful navy, which could dominate and control the coastline, ports, and coves. They had tremendous influence over the Indian tribes throughout the north and west. Moreover, they had gold to buy plenty of spies and informants. To counter all this and thwart the British would take extraordinary efforts—and extraordinary people.

80C3

New York
20th July 1776
Commander-in-Chief
Continental Army

Your Excellency,

After great Rumination on the subject so often discussed between us, I have come to some Thoughts that I felt best put in writing, so that our mutual Understanding with regard to this Enterprise brooks no confusion or hesitation. Our greatest Resource is our People, both our Soldiers and the Patriots who support the Cause. Of these, we must find a special Group who are loyal and dependable and will endure much for little or no recognition. They must be intelligent, remain undaunted in the face of adversity, and exhibit calm resourcefulness under pressure.
And they must be brave...
As for the Organization, it is of secondary importance but of course, relevant. A small organization is better, operating clandestinely wherever possible. They may be organized as part of a "regular" unit, but their true role must be known to only a

very few. Such a unit, made up of Men who can both spy and counter enemy spies, is indispensable if we are to obtain necessary Intelligence in a timely manner.

Very Respectfully,
R. Fitzgerald

An orderly knocked on the door. "Sir, I have a note here for you."
Somewhat peeved by the interruption, Fitzgerald looked up. "Who is it from?"
"I don't know sir. A lady delivered it. Said she worked for a Mister Smythe."
Fitzgerald cocked his head quizzically. "I cannot recall knowing a...'Mister Smythe.' Very well."
When the orderly left, Fitzgerald sliced open the envelope with his jackknife and read the contents. The message startled him. Written in block letters so as to disguise the handwriting, it contained a simple message.

My Dear Colonel Fitzgerald,

Things may go badly for the Cause if the British come to New York. In that event, you will need Information. I may be of some help.
Meet me at the corner of Ryndert and Bayard at noon. I shall be taking a midday stroll near the Deep Pond. I will wear a dark blue hat and a dove gray suit. Do not be surprised at my appearance...for Appearances often deceive.

A Patriot!

Fitzgerald read the note several times as his mind raced with speculation on the possibilities this offer presented. How did this person know of him? Could this be a Loyalist trap? Should he inform Washington? Although Washington and his staff remained buoyed with confidence at repulsing the anticipated British invasion, Fitzgerald himself felt that if the British acted boldly enough they would drive the rebel army from New York with ease.
Fitzgerald decided to keep the matter to himself. If there was a Loyalist plot behind this it would be better to keep the commander in chief distant from it until after. He would attend the meeting and decide what it meant, and what to do based on his assessment of the "Patriot."

ഇൗ

The midday sun turned an already sultry day into a steamy cauldron that suffocated and stifled any unfortunate enough to be out in it. Dust from the occasional passing cart or rider swirled in plumes and then gently hung in the air that choked the pedestrian foolish enough to neglect a kerchief. Fitzgerald rode slowly north on Nassau Street, his lanky frame on the small horse giving him a comic appearance. He passed neat houses of brick and mortar interspersed with the occasional wood frame house with shutters. The city seemed cleaner, more livable to him once he got north of Wall Street. The crisp mountains and meadows of his Pennsylvania home seemed so far away now.

Fitzgerald looked about fifty although he was ten years younger. He was tall, just over six feet, very thin and wore steel-rimmed spectacles that usually lay perched at an angle on his long thin nose. His white hair was tied in the back with a queue. His dark blue uniform did not quite fit, hanging loosely on his thin frame.

When he reached the northern edge of the city, he tied his horse near the intersection of Ryndert and Bayard and walked west towards the pond. The unbearable weather had kept the usual strollers indoors; this "Patriot" had chosen the time and place wisely. Fitzgerald walked south and then west around the pond. A few stray sea gulls had winged in from the harbor and now flew low across the still water in search of a quick meal, their shrill calls the only sound to break the noon silence. Nobody was in sight. He walked for another fifteen minutes, his officer's sword clanking clumsily against his boots. The sweat oozing from pores had already made his dark blue woolen tunic a soppy mess. Fitzgerald did not wear a uniform very well.

The trail around the pond wended through a stand of shrubs. When he cleared them, he saw a slender figure in a gray suit, wearing a blue hat. He stopped and grew at once nervous and suspicious. Could this indeed be the "Patriot"?

"A fine day for a stroll, although it could be a bit warmer I suppose...Mister?" Fitzgerald fumbled for the words.

"Smythe...rhymes with blithe. 'Mister Smythe' it is. You read my note?" The stranger replied.

Fitzgerald nodded. "Yes but...This is all very...unanticipated...and new to me."

"To me as well. I do not often correspond within an intelligence officer and offer my services as a spy. You read the note. I think I may be of assistance if things go badly—as I fear they will."

Fitzgerald looked left and right to see if anyone was watching. He saw nobody. "You offer information on the British if we are forced out of the city. That presupposes many things...."

"Is that not your job, Colonel? To presuppose many things?"

Fitzgerald glanced behind him. There was no one there. "How do you know of me? And...my duties? I am a simple staff officer, unfit for a line command. A glorified clerk at best."

"Quite simple, Colonel. The press, *Rivington's* specifically, announced the arrival of General Washington's staff and conveniently published a list of his key officers. You were identified but not as a Commander, Aide de Camp, Adjutant or Quartermaster. I surmised your role to be something special. Something more discreet. The British and Tories have many spies, colonel. You must beware what you allow the press to release. Make them earn their keep."

Fitzgerald put his hand to his head and laughed. "Your prescience and sagacity impress. Now what exactly do you propose to do, Mister Smythe? Assuming we do wind up evacuating this lovely island."

"I sense from your tone you are less than impressed with our fair city? Well, I cannot promise very much help—only that I will assist when and where I can. Should the British arrive, I will likely have access to information and perhaps to some of their officers. Through connections that I will explain, so that you will know the source and value of any information that I glean."

Fitzgerald tingled all over. He knew immediately that this was not a Loyalist provocation. A Loyalist would promise anything to get Fitzgerald's interest. Mister Smythe...this "Patriot," was refreshingly circumspect. He regained his composure and began a long stroll along the pond with Mister Smythe. They had much to discuss.

∞ဆ

Paulhus Hook, New Jersey, August 20th, 1776

The First Maryland Continental Line regiment began crossing the North River in barges from a point in New Jersey known as Paulhus Hook. More than two hundred miles of marching had brought them to what seemed to the simple men from Maryland to be the edge of the earth.

Private Jonathan Beall beamed with excitement as he gazed south onto the great bay of New York. The expanse of water was blocked by the green hills of Staten Island but past it they could see the silver beaches of Long Island and the Jersey Highlands beyond. "It is fantastic, is it not? Have you ever seen such a sight Simon?" He asked his cousin, Corporal Simon Beall, who was the acting Company Sergeant.

Simon Beall frowned. "Not recently, Jonathan. Not since Baltimore anyways. Besides, we came to see the backs of the British, not the sights of New York."

An older private of thirty named Thomas Jorns removed the pipe from his mouth and spat out into the salty water.

"Just because we came to kill some British doesn't mean we cannot enjoy the fruits of this place."

The rest of the company laughed. Jorns had the reputation of the town rake back home. "I hear there are some really nice sights at a place these New Yorkers call 'the Holy Ground'.

More laughter and a few whistles followed. The "Holy Ground" was the euphemistic term for New York's largest red lamp district.

Although excited by the new sights and sounds, each man secretly nurtured fears. Fear of the enemy. Fear of death. Fear of a wound so horrific it made death a pleasure. Fear of disfiguration. Fear of capture by the hated lobster-backs or the more hated Tory Loyalists. Trained and drilled by their commander, Lieutenant Jeremiah Creed, they had confidence in what they could do. But even Creed had warned them that no amount of drill could remove the nausea felt at impending battle, or the sick feeling as the enemy closed on you and your friends began falling to the earth screaming in agony and desperation. However, their greatest fear was that they would fail: fail in their duty...fail their commander...fail their comrades and friends.

Creed sensed the tension behind the men's banter. "Come now lads, every large city has its 'Holy Ground,' although none a finer one than Paris. Or so they say..."

The men laughed again, even the taciturn Simon Beall.

Simon then turned serious. "Where do you think the British will land when they come, sir?"

"Why, they could land nearly anywhere, Corporal Beall. You see, the British are experts in warfare on land and at sea. We will have to match them on both to win our liberty. However, if I were Billy Howe I would start right there."

Creed pointed at Staten Island. "See that island? It provides a perfect base for action against New York, Long Island or points north. The British know that General Washington can likely defend any one place but he will have a devil of a time defending everything."

Creed eyed the harbor while fingering his rosary beads, out of a curious mix of nerves and piety. Sometimes he did not know where one ended and the other began. The island of New York seemed quite defensible—if the army gathered up enough troops and cannon to cover the numerous landing points. Creed watched his men banter as the salt sprayed around them. He was proud to command such a unit, this elite infantry company. To lead these men in battle appealed to him more than anything but he shuddered at the thought of what they would soon face. He knew his men were up to the task. He had trained them. The question was - could he face the challenge himself?

The bosun suddenly stood at the stern. "Prepare to debark!"

Twenty stout oarsmen heaved in the locks and the barge slid effortlessly into the slip. Minutes later, Creed was leading his company north along the Broadway. They were to be quartered north of the city near an area called the *Bouwery*. The Dutch settled New York more than a hundred and fifty years earlier, and their influence still dominated the area, most noticeably by the many quaint names derived from their language.

As they tramped north they all gazed in wonder at the sturdy brick and timber buildings. Jonathan Beall could not control himself and marveled aloud. "What fine houses these Dutch New Yorkers build...I wonder if we will get to sleep in one?"

Jorns eyed a buxom Dutch housewife busy watering her front garden. "It's not one of their houses I want to sleep in..."

"Enough of that rubbish from you, Jorns. And you too, Private Beall! No talking in the ranks!" Corporal Simon Beall cried.

Simon Beall exercised his rank with a firm authority. His men were some of the toughest in the regiment, perhaps the army. And he made sure that none could accuse him of favoring his younger cousin. Their closeness was well known as most of the company came from the same small town. Now they were brothers in arms serving a great cause—the cause of liberty.

They arrived at their appointed bivouac, a large meadow north of the *Bouwery*. Across the lane sat a picture-perfect house. Not the sturdy brick and timber house of the Dutch but a pleasant English-looking house of solid wood frame painted neatly and adorned with flower boxes at every window. The sign above the veranda announced it as the "Stanley House."

In short time the men had set up tents; foraged for firewood and found the well near the house to draw cool water to quench their thirst. The army was under strict orders to quarter themselves outside the homes in New York. The rebellion was driven in part by the British custom of forcing soldiers on the civilian populace and Washington aimed to avoid that. Officers were another matter. Despite that, Creed decided he would sleep with his men and near his horse, Finn. Yet, he had tired of the army's coffee ration and allowed himself the prerogative of inquiring if the fine house possessed itself of any tea.

Creed knocked at the door and removed his neat black tricornered hat, which he tucked formally under his arm. The door opened and Creed came face to face with the most beautiful young woman he had ever encountered.

"May I be of any assistance...Captain?"

A mature and well-read woman of nineteen, Emily Stanley was on the tall side with long limbs, a narrow waist and the widest eyes of a shade of bright blue green. The fairest and finest skin Creed had ever seen complimented her finely-shaped nose and high cheekbones. She wore a simple blue dress with a white apron and her dark honey colored hair was tied up in a fashion that highlighted her stunning features. It took Creed a few seconds to compose himself.

"Uh, um, that would be lieutenant, not captain, missus. Lieutenant Jeremiah Creed. I command the unit camped across the lane. Part of the Maryland Line."

"Maryland? You are quite a long way from home, Lieutenant."

"Indeed. Several weeks of hard marching for the lads. Not including the long march from Frederick. We are from western Maryland."

"I watched the boats bringing the army across. The men look determined. The city is all abuzz with excitement."

Creed's lips tightened a bit. "War is a terrible thing. It begins with excitement but too often ends in a whimper, with little but grief in between. Still, the lads appreciate the show of support from the people. We thought New York was Tory."

"It largely is," Emily said. "However, the Patriots here are very dedicated and make up in ardor what they lack in numbers."

They stopped speaking and for a brief moment just stood there, taking each other in.

Creed broke the silence. "I should not be troubling you, but I have a terrible craving for tea and was wondering if I could buy some. The army coffee...well...I have had my fill of it, missus."

Emily giggled with delight at the handsome young officer who appeared before her door so magically.

"That is miss, not missus. You talk awfully funny, Lieutenant Jeremiah Creed. You are not from around here, are you?" They both laughed—his accent guaranteed he was not local.

"No missus...I mean miss. I told you, we are from western Maryland."

"I heard you the first time, Lieutenant. That is not what I meant."

"I know, miss. Tis all I'll allow, however. Does my manner of speech reveal me?"

She laughed. "Just a little. Although I sense a trace of something else there as well, Lieutenant. But I will allow you your privacy."

Creed bowed his head in assent. "But sure I am now at some disadvantage miss, as I don't have your name."

Emily's smile melted him. "I do beg your pardon. My name is Emily Stanley. I operate this boarding house for my father."

Creed looked around, exaggerating each turn of his head. "And where is the good Mister Stanley?"

Emily arched her eyes, but then smiled gently. "Not Mister Stanley–Doctor Stanley. Father is away, with the army."

"And which army is that, might I ask?" Creed grinned.

Emily frowned, and then smiled. "I am sorry. The British Army. They need surgeons. But enough of this. I run the house now. Please come in and I shall see if we can brew you up some tea."

ᛒᛖᚳᚷ

Creed's company remained in bivouac for two days. During the mornings the men drilled. In the hot afternoons, they took what shade they could and cleaned and oiled their weapons and equipment. At night, they sat in camp, fighting the mosquitoes and gnats while listening to the crickets. Some stole time to write home or play cards but most just slept, never knowing when the next opportunity would present itself.

On the second evening in bivouac, Jonathan Beall took some time to continue work on the letter to his family back in Maryland. He worked against the waning daylight, carefully crafting it just as his mother had taught him back on their Maryland farm. Although they could not send him to formal school, his parents made sure that each of their children could read and write, as well as do basic numbers.

The March north had most of the boys staggering from heat and the burden of our Packs. Most of the Srgnts pushed the men along with Curses and Oaths. Frtuntely for us, Simon is our Srgnt. He moved us along with a firm but decorous hand. As for Lieutenant Creed (I wrote of him in letters past), he marched along with us, sometimes in front, sometimes alongside the column. And always with a smile or a joke. So unlike the other officers. Not that he does not love his horse. Finn is a fine animal. Simon says one of the best he has seen. Bred in Maryland, you see. Most times, Lieutenant Creed allowed some of the Sick and lame among us to ride Finn, in turns.

We have camp'd here north of New York. They have not allowed how long we shall remain here. The Homes are lovely but the Weather is hot. So sticky that I marvel the ink hasn't run off the Paper. We have tolerable food...on rare occasion. The water here is cool and sweet...until it spends ten minutes in our flasks. Lieutenant Creed drinks tea...boys have noticed him sneaking over to the nearby boarding House where they say...a lovely Mistress attends him with tea and cakes and such. But none of us begrudge him that...he is our officer and we are blessed by God to have him.

While Jonathan wrote his note, most of the men tried to sleep before the ants, spiders, flies and mosquitoes circled in on them. The Continental Army quartermaster did not include nets for poor infantrymen like them.

Creed finished rubbing down Finn and decided to pay a visit to the Stanley House and inquire about a spot of tea. He walked through the flower garden under a trellis of rosebuds. On a whim, he plucked a small one and nearly skipped to the back door, facing a large neat stable.

A servant answered his furtive knock. With her creamy cocoa complexion, she had that look of indeterminate age: she could be thirty...or fifty. Her hair was thickly coiled, dark and glossy, and she had large eyes. She had a figure well-rounded, but not plump. He had heard Emily call her Nancy. Creed removed his hat and bowed. "Good evening Nancy. I was wonderin' if I could trouble you for a spot of tea. We drilled all day with little but water to wet the whistle. My tongue could use a change in refreshment."

Nancy's smile gave her round face a golden tinge. "Why come right in, sir. I think I could boil up something. Step into the parlor. Miss Emily is gone into the city on business but I do expect her back soon."

Creed followed her in and before long, was sipping weak but very tolerable black tea with a couple of biscuits to go along.

"Does Miss Emily go into town often?" Creed asked as Nancy moved about.

"Yes sir. Quite often. We have many fine boarders here and they need things. Miss Emily has many connections in the city."

He noted her West Indies accent, she was likely the result of a transient sailor's dalliance with one of the African slaves working the plantations or the bordellos.

Nancy beamed at her mistress' importance but she sensed Creed's discomfort. "Not what you might think, sir. Miss Emily has no beau. Not that many—very many—have not asked. Her daddy's being a British officer and all..."

Creed nearly spat his tea. "A what?"

"She didn't tell you? He is a surgeon with the British Army."

"A surgeon yes. An officer, no."

"Does it make a difference?" Nancy asked.

"To some. Not too me, at least." Creed replied.

"Many folk, if not most, here 'bouts are loyal to the king, sir. Just the way it is, sir. Myself—I'm not political."

Creed nodded. "I understand too well the divisions caused by the rebellion. You know, Nancy, like yourself, I am new to this land. "

Suddenly the back door flew open and they could hear Emily enter the kitchen. Nancy hurried back to help her with her bundles and Creed followed like a puppy wagging its tail.

"Lieutenant Creed, what a pleasant surprise. I hope Nancy provided to your needs. Unfortunately, I had to go down into the city and purchase some goods."

Creed bowed and stammered. "I...I simply came by to purchase a cup of your lovely tea, Miss. I did not mean to be a bother."

Creed followed Emily back into the parlor. They sat together on a small calico divan near the window. They both stared out at the garden and watched the shadows lengthen against the chestnut and maple trees. Across the lane they could see movement, outlines of the soldiers who moved about the camp at dusk.

After some time Creed turned to Emily and fumbled until he produced the rose. "I plucked this for you. Truth be told, it came from your own garden but I thought it would look lovelier on you then a...stem."

She giggled. "Why thank you, Lieutenant. I have not received one of my own flowers before...nor any at all for that matter."

He blushed, as did she. The veiled insult was not intended.

"What I meant...it is very thoughtful of you. Thank you." She placed the rose in a button loop on her dress, which had a wide V shaped front revealing her fine neck and upper bosom.

He looked at her wondered how anyone so beautiful and lovely could be Loyalist and a Tory.

"Nancy says your da' is with the other side. Does the same hold for you?"

She marveled at the question. Most of the men who visited her cared not one whit about her political thoughts...or any of her thoughts for that matter.

"Well, father was born in Derbyshire, England. He was a prominent physician there but came to the colonies to serve in the Royal Army in the war against the French and Indians. He served under General James Abercrombie as well as Geoffrey Amherst but then took sick himself and missed the grand battle on the Plains of Abraham. That is one reason he volunteered his services, once more, to the Crown."

Emily did not have to tell Creed that her father was quite well off thanks to his boarding house as well as his years in a successful medical practice. Creed could tell from the look of the home and its furnishings that Reginald Stanley was among the more prominent residents of the city.

Creed nodded. "Once more taking up the surgeon's knife on behalf of the King. I understand that political conviction might conflict with duty, especially when enshrouded by a sense of honor."

She shook her head. "No, father is indeed a Tory. He believes that many of the grievances of the colonies are justified, especially with regard to self-governance and self-taxation. Nevertheless, he is loyal to his King and still had a strong attachment to the Royal Army."

He sipped at the dregs of his tea. "And you agree?"

Emily placed her hand pensively to her temple. "I believe the one thing worthy of rebellion is a crown. But I keep my innermost thoughts a secret. Even father remains unaware. I felt it safer that way, for both of us."

Creed nodded. "I am honored at your taking me into your confidence, Miss. It shall not be misplaced, I assure you."

Emily beamed at him. "I knew that the moment I met you, Lieutenant Jeremiah Creed."

છૠ

On their third day in bivouac, Creed was suddenly called to a meeting at regimental headquarters. The eight company commanders assembled at a small tavern on the Post Road. Major Mordecai Gist, the second in command of the regiment, stood before them at the end of an oak plank table in the tavern's back room. Two Continentals guarded the door.

Gist, a ruddy faced man, aged thirty-four, was from the Baltimore area and the son of the famed explorer and pioneer Christopher Gist, who had saved George Washington's life during the French and Indian War. Earlier in the rebellion Mordecai Gist had helped reorganize Maryland's militia and later was instrumental in forming the Maryland Continental Line. For that, the governor appointed him the second ranking officer in the regiment. Now, as they faced their battlefield initiation, he was in sole command.

Gist leaned over the table and addressed the officers in a somber voice. "Something urgent is afoot, gentlemen. The British are landing at Long Island, even as we speak. Although His Excellency fears a deception, he has decided to reinforce General Putnam. We are among the regiments selected for this task. We leave at once. Assemble your companies for a march south towards a place called Peck's Slip where we will board ships. Prepare your men for the worst."

Creed spoke. "They say Long Island is a beautiful place, sir. We should enjoy the viewing of it."

The other officers laughed at Creed's remark but Gist seemed unimpressed. "Colonel Smallwood is to remain in the city until his court martial duty is finished. I am in command of the regiment until his return."

One of the company commanders, a captain named Walter Runyon, spoke up. "Do we know our destination once over, Major? I understand we are building strong defense works around the heights near Brooklyn. We might need our heavy picks and shovels and such."

Gist shook his head. "The boys must travel light, Walter. We are going forward of the defense works. Therefore, we will not have time for our baggage to cross."

A murmur went through the group.

"What? Where are we going?" asked Runyon.

Gist replied. "Beyond the village of Brooklyn. We shall help defend the passes and block the British advance from their landing place. Somewhere near a village called Flatbush."

Chapter 2

Long Island, August 27th, 1776

A twig snapping...just a soft double crackle was all it took. Jeremiah Creed turned to his left and saw the Hessian soldier moving quickly, bent at the waist, his short hunting rifle slung tightly across his back. He recognized the uniform—a Jaeger, one of the elite Hessian light infantry trained and equipped to move and shoot through forest and brush and typically used to either patrol or screen a main body of troops. Creed needed to discover which, as that would determine his next move. The Jaeger's dark green jacket and hunting cap blended with the dark foliage and made him barely visible to even Creed's practiced eyes as the man slowly worked his way through the underbrush using his short sword to cut aside leaves and branches. The thick thorn bushes to Creed's front left started rustling. He saw that more Jaegers moving up the slope through the heavy under-brush. Creed knew he had to act quickly—this was likely the advance guard of a larger force. Against this, Creed led a patrol of just four men, albeit handpicked members of the Maryland Continental Line. Farmers and shopkeepers from central Maryland just weeks earlier, they now faced hardened professionals from across the ocean, part of the greatest military force in the world.

Creed and his men had rehearsed and drilled the plan—simple, but dangerous and difficult to execute—so often over the past few months. They would take out the lead men; enfilade the advancing forces from the flank; and then harass them in firing pairs, before returning to friendly lines. Surprise, stealth, discipline, and speed were the key. Their mood was tense when they stepped out on this, their first patrol. Although a powerful fear coursed through them, each of Creed's men fought to stay composed, none wanting to disappoint their officer or fail their comrades. None of Creed's men had ever been in combat, so he did not yet have the measure of their mettle—nor they, his. All that would change in minutes, amidst the erstwhile serene woods and pastures of Long Island.

The sultry morning air had grown silent once more but for the nervous whistling of a bird high up in a nearby chestnut tree. Creed turned to his men and signaled twice with two extended fingers - the signal to form two pairs. He then motioned left. Creed moved with Jonathan Beall following closely behind him. Simon Beall led the other pair. Simon Beall and his partner, Thomas Jorns, were to provide cover for Creed, now in ambush position not more than ten yards from the Hessian's flank. When Creed was in position, Simon Beall and Jorns quietly worked their way to the front of the patrol and blocked their advance in a classic ambush. Everything was set and now there was no time for fear or even doubt—just time to act.

Simon Beall launched the attack, surprising the lead Hessian with a bayonet that pierced the man's chest. The Hessian's eyes widened and he fell backward as the corporal plucked his bayonet from the body. An easy first kill, but he suspected the next would prove more difficult. Fortunately for the Americans, the Jaegers had advanced with unloaded rifles to prevent an accidental discharge warning the rebels. The Hessian light infantry, expert with the sword-bayonet, did not expect a challenge from colonial rabble in arms. Now, seeing their lead man killed by a rebel, anger took control of their judgment.

Three more Jaegers, spewing guttural blasphemies that broke the morning's silence, stepped through the brush and rushed Simon Beall and Jorns. Beall parried the first man's sword thrust and stepped past him, tearing open his side with a bayonet slash. A sudden gleam to his right warned him in time to deflect another Jaeger's blade and crush his assailant's jaw with a butt stroke that sent blood and teeth flying in all directions.

The German stood his ground and looked at him defiantly with blood dripping from his mouth. Beall hesitated a second, then ran his bayonet into the enemy's heart and withdrew it with a sucking sound that made him sick. Just a few feet away, Jorns was down on one knee and bleeding from a wicked three-inch gash in his leg.

"I could stand some help here, Simon!" Jorns cried in panic, his usual bravado suddenly gone.

Jorns was frantically fighting off another Hessian who stared at him the way a village butcher looks at a fatted calf. Jorns' bayonet had snapped. Now brandishing a broken blade, only eight inches long, he felt hopeless. The Hessian frowned mercilessly and raised his sword-bayonet to finish him with a downward stroke. Anticipating the blow, Jorns drove his musket butt into the Jaeger's groin. The blow bowled the man's torso over Jorns who, in reflexive desperation, stuck the jagged blade upwards and into the Hessian's gut. The Jaeger fell off Jorns and then rolled lifelessly into the tall grass.

In a glade not far away, Creed and Jonathan Beall had surprised a squad of Jaegers rushing to help their comrades. The first two Hessians went down amid curses and cries, but the other four surrounded the Americans. Creed and Beall now stood back-to-back, fending them off with desperate parries and thrusts. The Hessians also worked in pairs, one lunging high while his partner went low. They remained silent and dispassionate throughout, just another day's work for them, it seemed. Creed felt it just a matter of time before the Hessians overcame them. Realizing they might need more weaponty, they each took a short hunting rifle, powder, ball, and sword-bayonet from two of the slain Jaegers.

Suddenly, a series of huzzahs echoed from the tree line. It was Simon Beall, followed by a limping Jorns, who now surprised the Hessians from the rear. Soon, the last four Jaegers lay dead from a series of well- placed thrusts. His tired band huddled around him. They sipped warm water from their canteens. Their chests heaved and stomachs knotted as heat, fear and exhaustion began to grip them. Creed feared his men had had enough. He needed to keep them moving and motivated.

Creed whispered encouragement. "Lads, these Hessians failed in their mission—to push through the woods silently and eliminate our pickets. Likely their officers told them that rebels would run on first sight. Overconfidence proved their undoing. We must avoid the same. Never fear your enemy, but always respect him."

To the Hessians' misfortune, the men they faced this hot humid morning were not militia, but members of the First Maryland Continental Line's Light Company, and although no one realized it at the time, it was the best unit in Washington's army.

But it had been exhausting and bloody work for the colonials. Creed quickly considered what lay ahead and pulled Simon Beall aside. "We must to warn the defenders at the passes but we have to try slowing the enemy advance to give our lads time to prepare."

They could see a large body of Hessians advancing from the wood line down the slope.

Creed pointed at the line of blue forming. "We must act quickly if we have any hope of stopping them. Are the lads up to it?"

The corporal nodded. "Jorns is badly wounded but he is willing and able to fight. It will give him tales of valor to impress the doxies."

Creed wiped the sweat from his brow with his dirt-stained sleeve and paused for a moment to give his final instructions. "Alright lads. Form a tight skirmish line two yards apart. At fifty paces, fire three volleys. After the third volley, Corporal Beall will take Jorns back to our lines and warn them of the attack."

Simon flushed. He did not want to leave his cousin or the fight. "Will our volley not provide enough warning, sir?"

Creed looked at Jorns, now pale in the face with blood oozing through his makeshift bandage. He knew the brave man would not see nightfall.

Creed shook his head. "You must get back and tell Captain Runyon that a major attack is imminent. And then get Jorns to a surgeon."

Creed turned to Jorns. "A few days' rest and some food will have you back on the front soon enough."

Jorns nodded. "Missed my better parts, at least. I'll get better and rest–then enjoy some time at the Holy Ground."

Creed placed a hand on his shoulder. "Don't tire all the doxies, Private Jorns."

Creed looked at Jonathan. "You and I must continue to delay their advance. Now, remove bayonets so we can fire and load more quickly."

Simon said. "I'll return here with the rest of the company, quick as I can. So please don't kill them all, sir."

Creed forced a smiled and then shook his head. "No need to rush back here, Corporal. Stay with the company until I return. Before this is over, we will all have the chance to kill and be killed. Now let's greet these butchers like men from Maryland."

Creed's words inspired them so despite the heat, fatigue, and fear–they flushed with anticipation.

The four moved over the crest of the hill and took up positions some ten feet down the opposite side. They checked their primers. Their muskets were British made and of good quality, but relics from the French war almost twenty years earlier. Still, they could fire a three quarter-inch lead ball eighty yards with some accuracy and mass volley fire a hundred yards with great effect. At fifty paces, even in the dense woods, the surprise and shock effect of even just four muskets would wreak havoc–or so Creed hoped.

Creed whispered, "Tis our last chance to use our water bottles–there is more hot work ahead and we will likely have little chance to slake our thirst."

The men gratefully sipped once more at the warm, grimy water. In the growing morning heat, it tasted better than a cold mountain spring.

Simon whispered to his cousin. "How are you doing, Jonathan? I have a little water left if you need it."

Jonathan shook his head. "No thanks Simon. But check Jorns. I think he slipped some rum in his bottle last night. His thirst must be fierce by now."

They looked over at Jorns. He looked pale and tired, but worked dutifully on priming his weapon.

Simon said, "Take some of this, Jorns. I'm done with it."

Jorns looked askance at the usually officious corporal. He nodded and took a sip of the warm, slimy water. It refreshed like the waters of paradise.

"Obliged," was all he said, but to Simon's surprise he had left some of the liquid for the burly corporal.

"That is sapping your strength," Simon observed. "Let me take your extra gear. Just keep your musket and a few cartridges."

Surprised, Jorns handed his pack, canteen, knife, and tomahawk to Simon Beall. "Much obliged, Corporal Beall." Then he grinned slyly. "More strength I save now...the more doxies I can chase later on."

Before long, the head of the Hessian column appeared at the foot of the slope. They moved four abreast, although staggered and scattered by the rough vegetation. Still, the formation was compact enough for what the Marylanders had in store for them. At seventy-five paces, they could make out the uniforms and insignia, the blue coats—more Hessians.

Creed spoke. "Look lads, these are soldiers of the line. Hessians call them musketeers. Not as powerful as grenadiers or quick as Jaegers but professionals, trained and experienced, none the less."

Jorns gasped to Simon Beall in a hushed voice. "How the hell can he tell which of these pox-ridden scum we have to fight?"

Creed spoke again, as if he had heard Jorns' complaint. "See, they are wearing tricornered hats, not the tall miter hats of the grenadiers."

Jorns muttered. "Damn them anyway."

"Watch how they move lads," Creed said, somewhat more loudly, "they are hot and tired as we are. Fatigue saps all men of courage, even these Hessians."

At sixty paces, Creed ordered, "Present. Remember your training...Keep your muzzles low, aim at their knees. The recoil will compensate."

They aimed for the center of the formation. The men fought the urge to run, each struggling to keep his heavy musket steady...and low.

Creed called out loud enough for the attackers to hear, "Fire!"

The volley rang across the defile and two of the Hessians tumbled into the rocky grass. The two nearest Hessians returned fire but missed. The column struggled to deploy through the heavy underbrush. In the confusion, the Marylanders let two more volleys rip. They hit five more Hessians, two mortally, including an officer who clutched bug-eyed at a belly wound that sprayed his waist coat with gore.

"Let's go! Follow right behind me, Jorns!" Simon cried.

He and Jorns pulled back through the thick woods towards the American lines with the Germans' fire spraying wildly over their heads, tearing leaves from maple and chestnut trees high above. As they ran, they could hear a mix of guttural voices and scattered musket shots from the confused attackers.

Creed and Jonathan Beall had moved to a new firing position before the Hessian fire could zero in on them. After a few rounds of blind fire into the wafting gun smoke, the Hessian infantry reformed to attempt another advance. This gave Creed time to make his next move. They carefully loaded their newly acquired weapons and then reloaded their muskets.

Creed whispered. "We'll each fire in turn. While one fires, the other reloads. These German rifles take a bit longer to load so we will use our muskets now... save the rifle for later. After two shots, we change position. Just follow my lead. Do you understand?"

"I think so." replied Jonathan. "But what if they flank us?"

"As we drop back we'll move around their flank, as a boxer circles his opponent."

Now the Hessians were less than eighty paces away, advancing up the slope. The heavy underbrush and rocks of the American woods and forests was vastly different from the dark, pristine manicured forests of central Europe. The Hessians struggled to keep their bearings and their footing and moved forward tenuously. Creed and Jonathan each got off three shots in a minute. They moved from vantage point to vantage point, firing a round each before moving again. Each time they dropped at least one of their assailants. The Hessian return fire had grown hesitant. They were European line troops trained for mass volley fire and bayonet attacks, not skirmishing.

Beall grew more nervous. "Shouldn't we leave now, sir?"

Creed nodded. "Patience, lad....It will take your cousin thirty minutes to get to our lines and return with help. We must play out this game a bit longer."

For twenty minutes Creed and Jonathan Beall played a cat and mouse game that lured the Hessians a quarter mile away from their original line of advance. They gained precious time for the American defenders and more than a dozen Hessians now were casualties.

"How much ammunition left?" Creed panted. The heat and humidity were stifling.

Beall checked his ammo box. "Six balls, not enough powder for four..."

Creed wiped his brow again, he realized they were finished. "Then double load, volley fire, and move toward our lines. These German rifles fire better than our old British muskets. Let's take them and leave these damned antiques!"

Smooth bore muskets were almost five feet in length and weighed more than eleven pounds. A double load meant two musket balls rammed down the barrel. The smaller hunting rifle of the Germans, just over four feet long, weighed less than ten pounds, making it much easier handling in close quarters and skirmish fighting. Creed correctly surmised they had much of that in store.

Their last volley struck down one more Hessian and stopped the advance long enough to make their escape. Before they did, Creed decided to risk all....

Beall watched awestruck while Creed rushed in a crouch toward a place along the Hessian lines, where he had spotted an enemy soldier cowering behind a tree without his weapon. Not quite six feet, Jeremiah Creed had the build of an accomplished athlete and moved like one. He covered the forty yards quickly, rushing from tree to tree, unseen in the smoke and confusion. Creed grabbed the soldier, a boy no more than seventeen years old, and dragged him by his belting as they retreated toward the American lines.

They struggled though bushes and rocks with their captive.

Beall asked. "Why did you risk yourself to capture one of them?"

Creed panted out his reply. "Our generals have little idea what is happening right before them...I suspect...this is...part of...a major British attack. He might provide some...information. "

Creed's words proved correct. Among the American defenders, from the lowest private to the highest general, confusion reigned.

ဢ)

Major Mordecai Gist, still acting commander of the First Maryland Continental Line, had just received word of British infantry advancing near the Red Lion Inn, a half mile to the south west.

The previous night, Gist's command had joined the American forces screening the Flatbush pass of the Heights of Guan, also known as the great moraine, a low ridgeline of wooded hills running east to west along the length of Long Island. This ridgeline, rarely reaching more than 120 feet in elevation, provided a natural barrier of steep rocky hills thick with deciduous trees, rocks and underbrush. By holding the few passes with troops behind fortified positions, the Americans hoped to blunt any British movement toward the main American positions located several miles to the north near the town of Brooklyn. Gist and the First Maryland Line were three miles to the southwest. They covered the main approaches from the vicinity of Gravesend Bay where the British had landed several days earlier. Creed's light company, plus one line infantry company had been placed under the command of Walter Runyon in order to reinforce General Sullivan's inexperienced militia regiments. Realizing the gravity of the situation and in anticipation of a major battle, Gist wanted this detachment to return immediately.

When they returned to the American lines, Creed questioned his captive and was soon able to ascertain the trouble facing them. According to the prisoner, to their front was a large force of Hessians and Scots Highlanders under the German General Von Heister. Creed had heard of him, a skilled and ruthless professional. The young soldier was not privy to any military secrets. Instead, he provided his regiment's name and identified his immediate commanders. He talked of seeing redcoats and cannon. He described the Scots Highlanders accurately enough to Creed, fierce looking men in kilts and war bonnets who vowed to take no prisoners.

Before long, the weary soldier revealed something of great importance...a third column existed! The prisoner had seen what he described as "many thousand" redcoats–infantry, with horsemen and cannon, moving northwest towards an area the Dutch called the Flatlands. He assumed they were part of his column and would join their assault at Flatbush.

Creed, however, suspected otherwise. He lacked a map of the area, and if he had one, it would probably have been inaccurate. Nevertheless, he knew that another pass lay to the northwest at Howard's Tavern near Jamaica–where the British planned to turn the American left flank. This would cut the forward deployed Americans from the defense lines to their rear, near a village named Brooklyn.

Finished with his prisoner, Creed interrupted Jonathan Beall's rest, "Turn this man over to the militia. I must get a message to Major Gist."

Before doing either, Creed discussed the information with Runyon.

"Yes, Lieutenant Creed, it makes perfect sense that the redcoats would try to ensnare us from behind. They learned their lesson about frontal assaults on Breed's Hill." Runyon spoke as if he were a master strategist. Before the war, he had been a shopkeeper in Annapolis. Now he was the senior officer at a time and place of grave peril for his new nation.

He gripped Creed's shoulder tightly. "Place Corporal Beall in command of your men. You must return to regimental headquarters and inform Major Gist of what is happening here. Tell him I will return with the detachment as soon as possible. Our place is with Maryland."

But as Runyon prepared to march his detachment back to the regiment, Brigadier General John Sullivan approached them on horseback, red in the face and panting with excitement. "Runyon, where do you think you are taking your men? Your place now is here at the Flatbush pass. I need your Continentals to help steady the line!"

"Sir, Lieutenant Creed has just questioned a prisoner taken from the enemy's advanced guard. A British column is moving to our northeast. We now face encirclement. Our place is with the First Maryland."

Sullivan frowned and rubbed the sweat from his forehead with a soiled handkerchief. The mid-morning heat descended on them upon them like a kettle on a slow boil. Sullivan was a brave and experienced officer from New Hampshire who had commanded the ill-fated attack on Quebec the previous year. He also served with some distinction during the siege of Boston. Now he, along with Brigadier General William Alexander, the self styled "Lord" Stirling, commanded the forces deployed forward by General Washington in a desperate attempt to stop the British from getting through the Long Island passes.

Sullivan shook his head and pounded his fist on the pommel of his saddle. "The ravings of a single prisoner do not make for good intelligence. Until we know for certain what the British intend, we must hold this pass! I have damned few troops assigned here who are up to the task. I need your support, Runyon. You may send one of your companies back—but the other remains here."

Runyon bristled, "Dividing my detachment is not something I think advisable to do at this juncture..."

Sullivan abruptly cut him off. "There is little chance the British could move a large force around our flank in so short amount of time. They would be too far from their base. Look about you, Captain Runyon. The woods are thick, and there are few passes through this ridgeline. You have your orders...detach one company...the other must hold here at all costs."

Saluting with disdain, Runyon turned and gestured to Creed. "Your company is ordered back to regiment. When you arrive, report everything to Major Gist. If your suspicions prove correct, Creed, this army faces disaster."

Letting his Cork brogue come through more than usual he nodded, "I am telling you only what I know from observation of the facts before me, Captain. God willing, I may be incorrect in my assessment, but God help us if I am correct."

Runyon answered tersely. "I fear God has little to do with this day's work, Creed. Now go!"

Creed saluted and returned to his men.

He grabbed Simon by the shoulder. "The company is returning to the regiment. You will command its movement back. I must go on ahead and report the situation to Major Gist. What of poor Jorns? "

The corporal replied. "He has lost a lot of blood, sir. He could never make the return march. I left him with the other sick and injured. He's usually so cocky. Hard to picture him lying there with the fever setting in."

Creed lowered his head. "Jorns will be gone by dusk, poor lad...but so may we all. We are down to twenty-five men. Very well. Have two of the lads stay with him. If we hold out, they can move back with the other wounded. Now I must go. Get the company moving and stay low along the ridge. I shall meet you when you return to the regiment. Quickly now! The trap is closing."

Creed retrieved his haversack and refilled his canteen from a nearby water barrel, then ran off ahead of his company to report to regimental headquarters. His mind raced as he thought of the disaster facing the army. He felt that Gist would understand the danger too. Perhaps he could reason with Sullivan—although it might already be too late to cover the left flank. The Hessians' actions clearly indicated an imminent attack. Creed now realized that General Washington and his generals had little understanding of the situation. The idea of entering battle and fighting so blindly vexed him.

Just as Creed started back, cannon fire erupted from two sides: behind him, from the Flatbush pass and before him, near the Gowanus Bay, where the Americans had thrown up hasty defense works over the past few weeks. He could distinctly hear the boom, followed by an eerie whoosh and thud as each iron ball fired, sailed over the lines, and then plunged downward, slamming into trees, earth and rocks. The attack through the passes has begun.

The defenders at the passes counted among their number the First Maryland and First Delaware Continental Line, possibly America's two best regiments. Comprised of highly motivated men, they were better equipped and trained than most of Washington's army. Several months earlier, Congress, at the request of General Washington, had organized and equipped Continental Line regiments along professional lines. They served long-term enlistments and could deploy outside their state. In contrast, the poorly equipped militia units, led by local political leaders, enlisted for short periods, usually no more than a season. Militia units did not normally fight far beyond their state borders and often formed only for local defense purposes. However, neither the Maryland Line, under Colonel William Smallwood, nor the Delaware Line, under Colonel John Haslet, had any combat experience. Moreover, both regiments had just arrived on Long Island without their esteemed colonels, who were currently serving on Courts Martial duty back in New York City.

Moving alone, Creed arrived at headquarters well before his company. The enemy artillery fire had increased in intensity, though the occasional ball whooshed overhead or pounded a tree trunk to splinters; it never came close enough to harm him.

Creed spotted Gist standing on a bluff with "Lord Stirling," observing the British gunners at work in the wood line across a narrow field. Stirling talked loudly to Gist, supplementing his words with violent gestures that needed no interpretation.

"That damned artillery will not move our men from their positions—and neither will those bayonets forming behind the guns. The likes of them will not drive us off this ridge. Not without a bloody fight."

Before Gist could reply, Creed reported in. He saluted Gist smartly, then removed his hat and wiped the sweat and grease from his forehead. Creed wore a black tricornered hat and the simple hunting frock of a continental light infantry officer. Its light straw color had faded after only a few months in the field, and his white britches and leggings had streaks of green and brown from crawling through grass and dust.

Creed quenched his parched lips from his water bottle before he spoke. "Sir, I have good reason to suspect that British forces have moved to a pass near Jamaica with the aim of severing us from the main army."

Stirling said, "Why, I shall lead two regiments north and thrash them before they know it."

Creed shook his head. "To make matters worse, General Sullivan has substantial numbers of Hessians and Highlanders facing him at the Bedford pass and cannot disengage. I believe this pass is next."

Gist glared. "Where is your company?"

Creed replied. "Right behind me. They shall arrive in within the half hour. Captain Runyon ordered me to report events directly to you. However, General Sullivan refused to release his company back to the regiment. They are making a stand at Flatbush."

Gist was not pleased to learn that half of Runyon's detachment was still with Sullivan's forces, but he also understood that if there was a third force approaching Jamaica, then Sullivan was already outflanked and outmanned. He would indeed need the extra troops.

Gist turned to Stirling. "Sir, I suggest we send a message back to General Washington and prepare to withdraw into the main defenses before the British encircle us."

Stirling exploded. "Withdraw from these passes? Nonsense! With the Maryland and the Delaware troops, we should give these British a trouncing. I shall hold the bastards right here. I do not believe your lieutenant's report. The British would not divide their forces thus in the face of the enemy. Besides that..."

Stirling's rage did not stop Creed from correcting him. "Sir, General Sullivan's Brigade is prepared to hold both the Flatbush and Bedford passes—but a forced march by the British toward Jamaica was not anticipated. We have little time left to act."

Creed's blunt reply calmed Stirling, but just barely. "Thank-you Lieutenant, but I command here and my instincts are always correct. We shall beat the damned British on this ground."

Then Stirling turned to Gist. "Prepare your regiment to stand and fight. We shall show the damned lobsters what real men are made of!"

Gist looked at Creed in resignation. "Go find your company and place them on the right flank of the regiment. We are along the trail down below. Go quickly, Mister Creed."

Creed looked up at the steadily rising sun and adjusted his hat. "The heat sir, make sure the men drink copiously. Things will be even hotter by noon."

He saluted Gist, turned smartly on his heel, and took off to find his men. Creed was tired of the bombast of the generals. He decided at that moment that he would focus on the company and try to lead it as best he could through the maelstrom he knew they surely faced. Just then, the sound of cannon fire from the Flatbush pass increased and the rattle of musket volleys and rifle shots erupted, a major engagement was now underway. The fledgling nation's first battle had begun.

Chapter 3

Frederick, Maryland, April 7th, 1776

When the recruiting officer, Captain Abraham Cushing, first came to Frederick in March, he had no difficulty finding the sixty good men needed for the Light Company, First Maryland Continental Line. Western Maryland had plenty of men who were good shots, as good as anyone could be with the flintlock muskets they had. Moreover, most men from the frontier were in top physical condition, used to hard work but well-fed and robust. Cushing talked to each prospective recruit, attesting to their loyalty, intelligence, and initiative—three critical attributes for members of the elite Light Company. Of the three, Cushing considered initiative the most important, as the Light Company would often operate in small units, squads or files of ten men or less. Their unique role required them to screen the regiment from the enemy and to conduct patrols, primarily for scouting or reconnaissance.

Who, however, should lead such a unit? The regimental commander, Colonel William Smallwood, had authorized one officer's commission, in addition to two sergeants and six corporals. The sergeants and corporals were easy enough to fill, the most literate or those clearly most popular among the rank and file. However, unlike ordinary militia units that elected their officers, the Maryland Continental Line, as a professional force, would not be officered by the most popular men, but the most capable.

The lanky, middle-aged recruiting officer was staying in a room above the Great Oak Tavern, which he also used as his recruiting office. The tavern was a large stone building with a great room trimmed in oak beams and a floor of oak planking. More than a dozen pine tables made it the largest "Ordinary" in Frederick. Cushing seated himself near the window so he could more easily deal with potential recruits, giving him also a fine view of the main street of Frederick. The wood and timber homes that lined it, he noted, were simple, sturdy, and clean.

"Ale, barman, if you please!" Cushing had just finished appointing his last corporal and sergeant, but still had to select the company commander. The tavern keeper placed a pint of ale at Cushing's table. It was between normal meal hours so the two of them and the serving girl were the only people in the tavern. He also set down a small dish with pickled herring and bread on the side. Cushing spent a lot of his off-duty time in taverns and inns—usually at the bar. He found many a tavern keeper and barman to be shrewd judge of men, having to deal with all sorts of folks coming and going.

"So tell me, confidentially, if you were in my shoes, which one of these lads would you select as commander?"

The tavern keeper crossed his arms over his ample belly as if to draw his answer from there rather than his brain.

"Well Ralph Smith or Simon Beall would do fine. Smith is well educated and teaches school. Beall is strong and reliable, but also intelligent and organized. Most of the larger land holders here are good men but probably not up to things physically, certainly not in the sense you describe."

Another patron suddenly entered and sat himself at a table in the corner. He moved with almost a martial gait, dressed in a simple but well cut gray coat, britches and knee-high riding boots. He had removed his hat revealing dark hair to match his dark eyes, in striking contrast to his light, but not pale skin. At five foot eleven, he was above average height, had long legs, and a sturdy, but not brawny, build.

"Who is that gentleman?"

Cushing asked the question softly. Something about this man caught his attention. He seemed different somehow. "Ah now, that is 'squire' Creed."

"Squire?" The appellation surprised Cushing.

The barman chuckled, "Well not really, I merely call him that. Jeremiah Creed he goes by; arrived from Ireland by way of Baltimore some six months ago. He purchased several hundred acres outside town, near the Monocacy River. Now he is clearing it to establish a farm. He has built a nice stable so far, but no house yet. He lives in the stable with his horses and a couple of laborers he hired in Baltimore. They are Irish as well. Too many of them moving out here, some say. Prefer the Germans myself, if we are to have foreigners amongst us. Anyway, the 'Squire' comes here each day for the mid-day meal, occasionally on a Sunday evening."

Ignoring the tavern keeper's prejudice, Cushing asked, "Is he Whig or Tory? No blather now, man."

"I told you, he is Irish." The barman laughed again.

Cushing grabbed his arm firmly. "Now hear me well, there are plenty from Ireland who will stand for the King if it suits their personal interest, or their purse. Is he one of them? Or one of us?"

The barman winced. "Well I doubt he is one of them. Although I cannot say for sure, I suppose he is a man who believes in freedom and independence—perhaps a neutral politically but with Whig leanings, I would say."

Cushing released the barman's arm. "Would you please introduce us?"

After a few short introductions, Creed agreed to share a meal at Cushing's table. Few people came in over the next two hours and the tavern remained relatively quiet. Cushing did little probing as to Creed's personal background but talked politics in a general and was careful to avoid offending him in any way. Many folks in the colonies were extremely circumspect with regard to their politics. Tensions were running high between Whigs and Tories, the former wanting a new status for America and freedom from royal interference, the latter being loyal to the king, almost to a fault. Many people remained neutral or had leanings that shifted with events. For many, caution controlled their passions. It was a survival mechanism. Moreover, it usually worked.

Not long into their conversation, Creed sensed Cushing probing his political leanings and became suspicious. Although new to America and Maryland, he learned quickly that Yankee political discussion could quickly escalate into altercation. When the barman introduced Cushing as a recruiter for the Maryland Continental Line, Creed had understood that the officer had met his quota for this area...so he could not be seeking another soldier...or was he?

Sensing some duplicity of purpose, Creed decided to toy with Cushing a bit, throwing out ideas and comments that would mark him as a Tory, then as a Whig, and he argued passionately for each. Devotion to king and country was the paramount duty of every civilized man. Liberty is every man's God-given birthright. The king is king by God's will and damnation to those who oppose the will of God. God made men before he made kings, kings serve their people, and when they do not—the people have a right to put them aside. England's benevolence and protection made America great, and the colonies owed the mother land allegiance in return. Neither the British king nor parliament has the right to dictate terms and taxes to a free and independent people. And so it went for more than an hour.

By his third ale, Cushing began to realize that Creed was having fun at his expense. His eyes began to show his exasperation, not to mention the effect of the alcohol.

"Mr. Creed, in the name of God, what is it that you actually do believe? Your thoughts appear as promiscuous as a Baltimore harbor slut!"

Creed broke into a hearty laugh.

"My dear Captain, one must play the devil's advocate to truly understand the devil. When I decided to leave Ireland, I had the pick of any land in the world as my future home. France, Italy, Germany, even England. South America and even India were also possibilities. I chose America. And why sir? Because I can hear. And I can see. Because I listen and I read. Moreover, I think and understand. Although my family has prospered, the King and his agents have beaten Ireland to a pulp. The people are exploited in every conceivable way. The land suffers from oppression and bigotry of all sorts. I have read much about the American colonies and talked with many who had visited or lived here. I have read the speeches and pamphlets of some of your great thinkers and writers, Thomas Paine, Patrick Henry, John, and Samuel Adams to name a few. I reckoned these colonies were the one place in the world where men could be free and live in peace. It had the natural resources, the quality of people, and a standard of living that was the envy of the world. But most of all it had the idea that freedom and the rights of free men were the basis for a civilized society. So here I came."

"Why Maryland then, of all the colonies?" asked Cushing, wiping foam from his lips.

"Well, I am Irish, and Catholic, although not always the most devout practitioner thereof. Nevertheless, I felt that if a colony gives succor to the Catholics it is most likely an accommodating place in other ways. And although Catholics here no longer enjoy the succor I had hoped to enjoy, I have not been disappointed by her other charms."

Cushing was impressed with the young man's eloquence, his obvious intelligence, his knowledge of things political and otherwise, and his enthusiasm for America. It occurred to him that perhaps the "squire" would make a good officer for the Light Company after all. But did Creed have the manly attributes necessary to lead a group of these rough frontiersmen?

At that moment the door to the tavern burst open and six men wearing cloth masks over their lower faces and brandishing cudgels ran in and rushed at Captain Cushing.

Crying, "Long live the King," they flailed at Cushing, who drew his saber and parried their initial blows.

"Damn you, Loyalist curs," he cried. Despite his obvious danger, he made an effort to avoid slashing or stabbing any of his assailants. Naively hoping that they were just blowing off steam, he vainly countered bravado with bravado.

The leader, a middle-aged man, larger than the others by a head, replied. "Down with all rebel scum!" He smacked his cudgel down across Cushing's shoulder, breaking his clavicle with an awful crack. Cushing went down in agony, nearly passing out from the pain. The tavern keeper made no effort to help, no doubt for fear of reprisal. The men of western Maryland lived in a world of passionate violence and relentless vendetta.

Cushing's saber fell to the floor with a clang and skidded across the room. Creed glanced at the barman who stood secure behind the bar, impassive, Creed had to decide quickly whether to intervene or not. The decision was made easily. Creed's instinct and background drove him protect the unprotected. He picked up the saber and with the flair of a master fencer, waved it twice to gauge its heft and balance.

"It will do," he muttered. Then with a wry smile on his lips he rushed to Cushing's defense. He placed his body between Cushing and the Guardians, who continued laying blows on the downed recruiting officer's head, back and shoulders.

Cushing cried in pain, "Do your worst!"

Another blow struck him, then another.

"Damn you, scoundrels!" Cushing cried. His voice had grown weak.

Creed spoke out in a soft but commanding voice, "Stand back and depart. You have done your worst to this officer."

Creed raised the saber into the *en Garde* position.

The Guardians' leader laughed. "We have no need of traitors imported from Ireland either, Creed. We know who you are. Hiding out there on your farm will not protect you from the King's justice."

The big man stepped forward and raised his cudgel. Two others circled around Creed. The room grew silent for a second. Creed calmly marked his targets—then he struck. He feinted back a step, but while doing so he lunged right and jabbed the attacker trying to circle around him from that side. Creed's sudden move caught him off guard and the thug staggered backwards towards the bar with a cry.

Creed spun the blood-stained blade, barely in time to block a downward blow from the lead man's cudgel.

The big man bellowed triumphantly. "I'll crush your damned skull like an egg, Irishman!"

Creed pushed hard, but the man, stronger than Creed, pushed back harder and grabbed his throat. Creed realized the man was an experienced brawler—something Creed was not. He knew he had to end this quickly or he and Cushing were dead men. Creed raised his knee into the man's groin and kicked out violently with his right boot sending the man sprawling backwards and tumbling across a table and chairs, scattering ale and food across the floor.

The third attacker now moved in, but Creed side-stepped the blow, which missed his head by inches. Creed twisted his wrist with a flick and slashed the man across the arm, cutting him to the bone. The attacker screamed in pain and dropped his cudgel. He stepped back in tears, grasping the arm.

"Damn you rebel, I am done for!" He cried shrilly. Weeping, he grasped at a checkered blue and white tablecloth to staunch the bleeding.

Maintaining a cold silence, Creed turned back to face the large man, who now charged at him like a bull with the other assailants behind him. With the door behind them closed, Creed knew he had no escape route, not that he ever thought to flee. He could not leave Captain Cushing to their mercies.

Creed shoved a table in front of them with his left hand while moving forward, saber at the ready. The table caught his lead assailant a glancing blow to hip, which proved just enough to throw him off balance for a vital half-second. The big man's cudgel came down hard, but his blow went wild and missed.

"You rebel bastard!" he huffed, now nearly out of breath from anger, excitement, and fatigue.

Creed ignored the man's false bravado. He faked a parry, stepped quickly under the man's follow-on blow, and ran him through to the hilt. The large man's eyes bulged and blood foamed from his mouth as he collapsed in a heap. The burly leader tried to cry out his defiance but a short sucking sound resulted, followed by a gurgle, and then his death.

Creed now turned for the next Guardian, a tall thin man with a long scraggly beard and equally scraggly long hair, but he and his companions broke and ran, leaving their erstwhile leader in a puddle of ale and gore.

As Creed checked to ensure his assailant could do no more harm he saw that a pool of blood was already oozing out from under his large, lifeless form.

He then turned his attention to Cushing. "Are you alright, sir?"

Cushing's face had a gray pallor. "I think he broke my shoulder. The pain is tremendous."

Creed grinned and nodded, "But better pain than the alternative."

Cushing grimaced and glancing at the assailant's body, nodded.

"Who were those men, and why did they attack us?" Creed asked.

The barman spoke. "They call themselves the Guardians, members of a self-appointed action arm of the local Tories and that battle with Whigs and Patriots. They claim to protect the privileges of the crown. Because the acknowledged allegiances in this part of Maryland are murky affairs, most activists are discreet even when they act openly, hence the masks."

"They may have hidden their identities," Cushing rejoined, "but the anger in their eyes was plain to see."

The barman nodded. "Though I am in sympathy with your plight, I have a business to run. I think you need to leave, gentlemen. If you will settle up your bill, I will summon the Constable after you depart."

Creed paid him for the meal, damages, and two bottles of rye whisky, the preferred drink of the western fringe of the colonies. He helped Cushing to his horse and took him to his farm, "Blackwater."

Not a word was spoken during the twenty-minute ride to Blackwater, Creed's 500-acre land holding along the Monocacy River. The farm was situated in a mixture of rolling hills, lush meadows and verdant woodland, watered by a gentle river along its southern exposure. They entered through a primitive cut rail gate bearing the farmstead's name painted in simple white letters. They continued riding past the orchard, over a gurgling stream, and into a large whitewashed barn with a gently sloping wood-shingle roof.

After applying cold-water compresses to Cushing's shoulder, Creed carefully wrapped it in linen and let Cushing rest. Despite the pain, it did not take long for the injured recruiting officer to lapse into a deep sleep.

Cushing awakened a few hours later to a throbbing shoulder and a great thirst.

Creed saw the older man stirring and handed Cushing one of the bottles of whisky.

"This will help dull the pain."

"I certainly aim to give it a chance," replied Cushing, grimacing despite his own humor. "Thank-you, for your gallant defense, Mister Creed. I am not so sure they would not have but left me for dead."

"I am sure they would have done so. Once the bloodlust of such rascals is up it is a very hard thing to control." He felt guilty not coming to Cushing's defense before the scoundrels could harm him. It never occurred to Creed that he was a civilian while Cushing was the soldier and that it was Cushing who should have defended him.

Creed shook his head ruefully. "I have caused the effusion of much blood and the death of a man, deserving though he was. Now the question is whether the local authorities pursue a Tory or a Whig course."

"Fear not, but regardless, the tavern keeper would speak in your defense, as will I."

"I appreciate that, sir, but I think I may have to depart the area for awhile. There are two kinds of justice going on around here. If one does not get me, the other just might."

"Indeed," said Cushing. "You might want to take a holiday until things quiet down here. You know, Mister Creed, you fought to defend a commissioned officer of Maryland. Why not make it official?"

Creed gasped, spitting out a swallow of whisky from his lips, "What? Join the rebellion?"

Cushing nodded, "I believe you just did—by your actions at the tavern. I mean, now all you need do is to make it official. That will ensure that you are clear and free from the law and make your actions unambiguous to those Tories who might seek revenge. It is one thing to fight as a civilian, quite another to do so as a commissioned officer of Maryland."

"But I am not..."

"You could be. I am authorized to commission one officer from this region to command the Light Company of the First Regiment of the newly constituted Maryland Continental Line. You could be that officer. If you will sign on, I will date the commission today, and as far as anyone is concerned, you acted as one officer of the state in defense of another. Besides, you acquitted yourself quite smartly with that saber; I reckon you have some experience that you are holding back."

"My past is my past and tis nobody's business but mine," replied Creed. "But your offer is intriguing. What is this 'Continental Line'?"

"Congress has authorized, requested is more accurate, that each state raise a permanent body of troops trained and equipped to fight for the duration of hostilities with the British. The local militias and levees are not professional enough and often as not disappear once their enlistment is over, often sooner. We cannot plan sustained military operations without a core of reliable forces. There will still be more temporary militia regiments and local companies and such but the bulk of the fighting will be done by the Continental troops, which will be prepared to move anywhere in the colonies."

Creed took a sip from his bottle of whisky. It had a harsh bite. "So Captain, tell me more about this Maryland Regiment."

"We hope that there will eventually be as many as four regiments from Maryland. We are recruiting the First Regiment under the command of Colonel William Smallwood. He is a native Marylander, and has military experience as an officer in the war with France. We have recruited nine line companies from the areas around Baltimore and Annapolis. Colonel Smallwood decided to recruit the Light Company from this western region as the men of the west have more experience in shooting and ranging through woods and mountains."

Cushing winced as he raised the whisky bottle to his lips. He had drunk almost half the bottle and was finally beginning to feel the effects of the alcohol.

Creed stared long and hard into the crackling fire, which struggled to ward off a damp early-April chill.

"Let me think about it. I will sleep on it tonight. You had better get some sleep as well. I will have one of the men keep watch in case those Tories decide to come renew the fight."

Both men awoke the next day with heads pounding from drink and the intensity of the previous day's events. They discussed the future over hot oatmeal and biscuits with eggs washed down with hot tea. When the meal was finished, Creed silently left to tend his horses and check on the hands, leaving Cushing to rest beside the fire.

৪০৪

Creed had reluctantly decided to accept the offer of the commission. He based his decision out of a feeling of patriotism for this new and strange land, but in his inner mind, he could not rule out some self-interest in avoiding legal trouble. He figured he would go to war for a few months; it should be over by the year's end, next spring at the latest. He thought the Congress would eventually come to terms with the British—that the Crown would resolve things through allowing colonial self-rule, individual rights, and a special status within the Empire. It was to prove one of those rare instances where Jeremiah Creed's strategic thinking missed the mark.

Creed spent the next few days preparing for deployment and in arranging things for his absence from the farm. He drafted a contract that granted his workers fifty acres each upon the proviso that they continued to improve his remaining acreage so that there was at least 100 acres of farmable land and 100 acres of pasture. Creed would permit them the use of the barn until they could construct suitable shelter on their own share of property. They also had full use of his tools and implements but needed to maintain the barn in his absence. Creed packed two changes of civilian clothing in addition to the hunting jacket, britches and boots he would wear until he received his uniform.

After packing the essentials: toiletries and some liquor, Creed produced a five foot-long trunk from under his bed. It was red maple with fittings, hinges and a lock of highly polished brass. He opened the trunk as Cushing watched. To Cushing's surprise, the trunk had several high quality weapons wrapped in oil-cloth. There were two French cavalry pistols, elegant and with quality fittings of finely milled and polished metal as well as a cavalry carbine, also French and obviously of top quality. There was also an assortment of blade weapons. Creed selected two of them, a light cavalry-style saber with very fine trimmings, and a heavier dragoon saber with a blade almost three feet long.

"So...you have had some military experience?" Cushing asked with feigned surprise.

"We shall not go into my past Captain, let us just say that I have had some experience using such equipments, and leave it at that."

Cushing chuckled at his good fortune in finding an experienced military man to command the company.

"Well, we shall leave it at that then."

ಬಂ

The company formed in a small meadow just outside of town, along the Baltimore Post Road. Captain Cushing thought the location outside the town would be less provocative to Tories inclined to avenge the death of a senior member of the Guardians. Cushing had straightened out the legal matter with the

Constable. His statement attesting to the nature of the assault and the fact that Creed acted as a duly commissioned and sworn officer of Maryland was all it took. A small payment to the tavern keeper helped allay any possible confusion as to Creed's status at the time of the incident.

"Men, I present your new commander, Lieutenant Jeremiah Creed, First Maryland Continental Line. A man of honor, skill, and courage, I can attest to that personally."

The men smiled in assent as Captain Cushing addressed them; they had heard the full story of the incident in the tavern and the drubbing Creed had given the Guardians. Cushing was wearing his full uniform with blue jacket, white breeches, and black riding boots. His tricornered hat was black felt, trimmed with a black, red, and yellow cockade, the colors of Maryland. Since the Light Company did not have a guidon, the small flag used by line companies to guide the formation, Cushing presented Lieutenant Creed his own sword in a symbolic display marking his assumption of command. After accepting it and saluting the captain, Creed turned about smartly and saluted the men who had formed up in three ranks.

He addressed them briefly, "I accept this command with pride and a commitment to do my best to bring you back alive and drive the British and their sympathizers from our soil."

He asked Company Sergeant Jedediah Hudson to step forward.

"Sergeant, take charge of the company and route march to Baltimore."

Hudson attempted a salute and then got the men moving. They were un-drilled, wearing the civilian clothes they had and carried only whatever personal weapons they possessed, a motley mix of old muskets from the last war, some fowling pieces and the ubiquitous tomahawk or hunting knife. The famed Pennsylvania long rifle was relatively unknown in western Maryland but almost all men were above average musket shots and handy enough with knife or tomahawk.

The company marched hard, but only for six hours each day. They spent the extra four hours beginning the rudiments of military training, mostly commands and formations, to prepare them somewhat prior to joining the regiment. Cushing conducted all the training while Creed observed, took notes, and then partook in the drills as company commander. Finally, they arrived at the regimental camp just south of Baltimore, in a place called Jansen Town, near the Elk Ridge Landing; here they were issued uniforms and weapons, and received their general orders.

Next came eight weeks of intense training in maneuver, field craft, use of musket and bayonet, and the additional skills required of the Light Company. The latter involved such things as patrolling, scouting, skirmishing, and screening.

They were the eyes and ears of the regiment. It was obvious to many of the regiment's officers and even some of the enlisted men that this Lieutenant Creed, with his subtle accent, either was a quick learner or had some prior military experience. Nobody dared to ask however, and Creed never volunteered much information about his past. So it remained one of those mysteries from which military organizations build the unit's élan.

One night around a bivouac fire, Jonathan Beall brought up the subject of their new officer. The cool night air seemed a tonic after warm days of marching and training. The men liked to sit up late into the evening to reminisce, boast of future deeds, and just plain gossip.

Beall said. "I heard from someone in Second Company that Lieutenant Creed had once been a pirate, and captured a huge treasure chest from the Spanish. It is how he bought his farm."

Sergeant Hudson guffawed. "Pure fantasy, boy. He was a merchant sea officer, grew rich from honest trading."

Simon Beall disagreed. "No, my take is he was either a naval officer, or had served in the British Army. He knows way too much about soldiering."

"Maybe a marine, then." opined Thomas Jorns. "Bet he knows a thing or two 'bout doxies."

Hudson nodded. "His accent seems strange—not quite Irish, not quite French."

Jonathan Beall chimed in. "He might really be a Canadian of some sort. What do you think, Simon?"

Simon Beall scoffed. "And what does a Canadian sound like, Jonathan?"

Jorns interrupted. "Half-French, half-Indian is most of them. And randy as hell if you ask me."

Hudson scowled. "No one's asking you, Jorns. And that's enough speculating for one night. Hit your hay. We move north in a few hours."

Musket training for the Light Company was more intense than for the line companies whose only task was to load quickly, point the musket at an enemy formation, fire on command, and go through the routine again. The muskets, all of them smooth bore, were accurate only for massed volley fire. The light companies learned to volley as a basic skill but received much more ammunition to practice skirmish fire and individual fire at point targets. With practice, a trained sharpshooter could actually hit an individual man at eighty or even a hundred paces with some accuracy, depending on the wind, quality of the powder, and the amount of time he could take. They learned to skirmish in pairs, one man firing while his partner reloaded to keep up the rate of fire on the enemy.

However, the Light Company's primary day-to-day mission was scouting ahead of the regiment, screening its flanks or front, and patrolling. They did this as a company, in files of ten men, called squads by some, or in platoons, made up of two or more files. Patrols seized key objectives ahead of the main body, conducted raids on secondary objectives, or harassed opponents to determine their intentions.

Creed displayed an understanding of how to organize, equip, and conduct such actions, in addition to his skill at drill and weaponry. What Creed lacked, however, was knowledge and experience in the heavily wooded and rugged American terrain. To make up for it, he turned to his sergeants and corporals for advice and guidance. This partnership created a very special bond and trust between the young officer from Ireland and the rough men from Frederick. He trained them in the skills of a light infantry soldier and they taught him the skills of tracking, trailing, and surviving in the back woods. By the end of the eighth week the Light Company, First Maryland Continental Line was arguably among the best companies in the Continental Army.

Chapter 4

Long Island, August 27th, 1776

The Americans now faced a grave military situation and, worse, General Washington was unaware just how grave. Political as much as military necessity forced him to establish a hasty defensive position on Long Island. He had divided his small army but maintained most of his forces at his center of gravity, the Island of New York, sometimes referred to as Manhattan. In a tremendous miscalculation, he initially ruled out a British movement toward Long Island as anything but a ruse. Then, finally conceding the British would land there first, he placed nearly two-thirds of the army on Long Island under the command of his most able subordinate, Brigadier General Nathaniel Greene.

The highly competent Greene, a former businessman from Rhode Island, decided to defend the obvious approaches to lower Manhattan, the Brooklyn Heights, a small stretch of high ground opposite the city. With six regiments, he built a mile-and-a-half series of fortifications just east of the town of Brooklyn, stretching from Wallabout Bay to the Mill Dam at the head of Gowanus Bay. These defensive works consisted of a series of forts and redoubts connected by rough earthworks and trenches. Anchored at both ends by salt marshes, they ran through a picturesque landscape of rolling hills, woods, and farm fields. However, in a stroke of bad luck, Greene came down with fever just at this critical juncture in the campaign.

His replacement, Major General Israel Putnam, not nearly as able as Greene, now faced a very threatening situation. If the sudden British arrival on Staten Island with thirty-two thousand troops did not achieve strategic surprise, the movement in strength against Long Island certainly achieved a tactical one. Moreover, despite having more than fifteen hundred troops and forty guns on Long Island, Washington still feared General Howe might have enough strength to risk a move on Manhattan. He no longer underestimated the British strength on Long Island, but he still miscalculated their intent.

༄༃

Earlier that morning, Major General Charles Cornwallis had watched anxiously as his column of British cavalry, infantry, and artillery deployed through the Jamaica pass. The successful night march brought a quiet and quick movement of troops, horses, and guns around the American flank, then a march toward the Flatlands of Brooklyn and a sharp turn north in the direction of the village of

New Lots. An extremely competent and aggressive officer, Cornwallis reveled in helping lead this surprise move on the rebels.

A mounted officer trotted up to Cornwallis and saluted. He wore the dragoon's scarlet tunic and white vest, but with buff breeches and brown boots. Most British dragoons of the day wore knee length black boots and white breeches. However, Major James Drummond dressed differently, not so much to make a fashion statement but to fit better into the woodland environment in America. For this his fellow officers—and behind his back, his men as well—called him "Sandy." At thirty, Sandy Drummond was an experienced officer who entered the service a decade after his father died at Quebec, the final battle of the campaign that drove the French out of North America more than twenty years earlier. He rose quickly to command a squadron of dragoons, his father's old regiment. Everyone considered him, while at times tempestuous, in fact, a finer and more professional officer than his father.

Cornwallis returned Drummond's crisp salute. "So Major Drummond, what brings you back from the vanguard? I thought by now you would have your troopers watering their horses at the Brooklyn Ferry!"

"Sir, your compliments are duly noted. But Colonel Thorne requested I report to you that the rebels had merely a squad of pickets at the pass and that they were quickly dispatched."

"Did any get away?"

"Sir, our horses are bred in Ireland and our troopers England. Even the most frightened American cannot out run that combination. We did take some prisoners and one talked straight away."

He spoke with neither a boastful nor a gleeful tone. Drummond was a through-and-through professional and this was all business to him.

"From him, we learned that the rebels had stripped many of their best troops, this so called Continental Line, from the defenses before Brooklyn to cover the passes. If we press the march straight up the Jamaica road we could overrun the rebel defense works before they know that we are here."

Cornwallis replied, "True enough, Sandy, but our immediate objective is to drive the rebels out of the passes and prepare for a deliberate move on the works. I will advise General Clinton to send a courier back to General Howe."

Drummond protested, "But sir, the time to strike is now."

Cornwallis cleared his throat for effect. "So it is indeed, but not without orders. Tell Colonel Thorne to proceed quickly but with due caution and vigilance."

Drummond replied anxiously, "Milord, this next phase of the battle will provide an opportunity such as is only dreamed of and taught at military academies the world over. Another Cannae! The rebel forces are thrice divided. One third remains in New York, whilst the other two-thirds here on Long Island are further divided. Why, Washington has foolishly pushed several thousand forward of their main defenses at Brooklyn. We should exploit that now!"

Cornwallis removed a heavy leather glove and slapped the side of his mount with a nervous energy. His face grimaced as his thoughts raced with the consequences of his next move. The rebels had pushed forward a division to provide a forward defense force at the passes through the ridgeline that bisected the island.

Cornwallis replied adamantly. "We have two columns deployed at those passes to pin the Americans and keep them in place. One is under General James Grant, who although pig-headed in nature, has vast experience fighting in America. The other under that Hessian Von Heister includes some of the most ferocious soldiers in the world, even if they are hirelings..."

Drummond pleaded. "Milord, This column has accomplished one of history's most remarkable night marches. Thanks to my informant, we have seized the one unguarded pass from the rebels. If we advance at all speed it will complete the encirclement of the forward deployed Americans."

Reluctantly, Cornwallis nodded in agreement. "Very well, Sandy. But proceed with caution...move slowly. I will inform Clinton. He can inform Howe."

Though normally aggressive, Cornwallis was suspicious of a trap. He did not share the same confidence Drummond had in his spy. And he knew that any failure due to audacity would meet with grave censure by Howe and be exploited by Clinton, his rival. The unspoken rivalry among the three top British generals simmered like a stew, never quite bubbling over but slowly burning away until it left a meal that lacked both taste and nutrition.

Drummond saluted crisply, reined back his horse and cantered down the road with a cloud of dust soon obscuring him from Cornwallis' view.

ಬಂ೮ಡ

At first, the cannon fire had minimal effect on Sullivan's dispersed forces. However, as the fire increased in tempo his casualties started to mount. Not too many, but enough to disrupt his effort to maintain a strong line and to keep the Americans' heads down as the Hessians advanced, and advance they did. At first, there was desultory rifle and musket fire from the advanced guard, the element that Creed's men had checked, but the fire picked up as the morning progressed.

Then everything happened in a blur, or so it seemed to the American defenders. The British artillery fire stopped as suddenly long columns of blue clad Hessians, led by tall imposing grenadiers in their brass-plated miter hats, emerged from the woods in columns of four. They deployed methodically into a three-deep line that stretched across the entire front, and without pausing they charged the American defenders. Almost half the defenders broke and ran back in panic toward the main American lines. Those who stood their ground offered minimal resistance to the savagery of the bayonet. A desperate Sullivan rode up and down the remnants of his line exhorting his men. "Steady boys, steady now. Use your firelocks as at Breed's Hill. Aim low. Make each shot count. The boys back at the heights wish they could be here."

But the fight went out of most of his men very quickly. Knowledge that the Hessians were eager for a bloodletting and took no prisoners mattered little and many resigned themselves to a grim fate rather than resist. The Hessians, who hazarded untold discomforts on their journey to this strange land, unleashed a butchery never seen on this scale in America.

The Americans attempted a few sporadic volleys but most of them lacked bayonets and had to use their muskets as clubs for self-defense. The Hessians butchered many—whether the defenders resisted or not. Americans were pinned to trees by long bayonets. Surrendering bands of Yankees were gut shot, sabered, or clubbed to death. Many stood like sheep and faced the slaughter meekly.

There was one exception to this: Walter Runyon kept his Maryland company in good order, two men deep and thirty across. Men were stationed one-yard apart—not enough for concentrated volley fire but enough for sweeping volleys or concentrated independent fire. Moreover, unlike Sullivan's other units, his men had bayonets. For that reason, Sullivan had posted the company at the intersection of the Porte and Flatbush roads. This vital junction lay behind the Bedford and Flatbush passes and formed the yoke of a letter Y with each arm diverging toward the main American defenses. The Porte road turned toward the salt marshes of Gowanus Bay while the Flatbush road swerved right and led straight to the center of the American lines.

"Double load and be prepared to fix bayonets!" Runyon ordered. Besides his sixty-odd strong company, he had nearly the same number of stragglers who had fled the heights of Guan at the first Hessian onslaught whom he organized as best he could. He positioned them on either wing of his force although he could hardly rely on them. He paced the lines in front of them and loudly barked out commands himself, as he did not have time to single out officers, sergeants, or corporals. To this mixed band of men, desperate for leadership, the untested Runyon stood with the command presence of a senior veteran of war. To himself, he was not so sure, but he intended to give his all for the cause and for his men from Maryland.

"Give me two volleys, if you please. That is all I ask. Let the enemy get to eighty paces before firing, and damn it, aim low! After that, fall back and reform in a line 100 paces behind my men. We will fall in on you if the enemy overwhelms us. We have trained with these bayonets. It will be good to put them to good use."

The Hessians advanced just as Runyon posted himself at the center of his company. He suddenly seemed unsure of himself, despite the outward bravado to the troops. He had no experience in combat, no right to lead these men under these circumstances.

"Hold fire, till my order!" His voice cracked, partially from a dry thirst, but mostly from fear.

Runyon could see that the stragglers on either side of his company were nervous. A few began to look back as if plotting their escape from this man-made hell. Even if they stayed, the question that racked him was, could they hold fire long enough?

Runyon stepped out along the line to steady the men. He looked into their faces and saw a strange mix of fear, determination, and hope. He realized that they had given over their trust to him. His men's demeanor suddenly flushed all doubts from his system and renewed his self-confidence. "Boys, I have complete faith in you. Hold fast like Marylanders and the day is ours!"

They did. At eighty paces, he gave the command to present and fire. The volley had a better effect than he had hoped. To his amazement, more than a score of Hessians fell sprawling like scarecrows suddenly plucked from their stands. A few men doffed their hats and cheered.

Runyon tried to regain control of the line. "Corporals attend, reload, and present!"

He could see now that the Hessians were fatigued from a night of marching and fighting their way through thick underbrush in the heavy August heat. Most, now out of water, also felt the debilitating effect of thirst and dehydration. The Hessian line slowed and grew ragged as they traversed the thick shrubs and rocks strewn across their path. Their discipline, enforced by merciless noncommissioned officers, kept them coming and now there were at least 300 more behind them.

Despite the growing enemy numbers, Runyon's confidence grew. Then disaster struck. After the first volley, the stragglers on Runyon's right broke and ran, only half forming up to the rear as he had ordered. His company completed two more volleys, while the stragglers on his left could manage just one more. Another dozen Hessians fell and their assault stopped forty paces out. He hoped for a retreat but the enemy quietly straightened their lines and, once they were "dressed," reinforced their ranks. Then with a snap, snap, snap that evinced their discipline and inspired terror, they calmly and methodically went through the entire loading manual. As the Americans watched in awe, the Hessian infantry performed fifteen precise moves, which finished with the snap of five hundred bayonets sounding as one.

Suddenly, General Sullivan appeared from their front left leading a group of twenty men. He was on foot and minus his hat but looked undaunted. His men had maintained an orderly withdrawal from a formation of redcoats wearing kilts and Highland headgear that were in hot pursuit amidst guttural cries and swinging claymores.

"The Scots! By God, so it's by my own people that I shall go down," Runyon said softly to himself. He knew then that defense was hopeless. Runyon's forbearers were from the low lands of Scotland.

Sullivan approached Runyon, sweating and breathing heavily. "We shall make our final stand here," declared the general. Runyon just stared at him. He fought off thoughts of home and family. He sensed he would never see them again. He only hoped his grave would be marked.

The last of the stragglers, now mostly junior officers and sergeants, quickly formed a line behind the Marylanders. The rank and file that had not run back to the American lines lay skewered by the Hessian and British bayonets. A few minutes later, the skirl of the bagpipes began as the Highlanders aligned themselves on the right flank of the Hessians.

Runyon shook himself from his sense of fatalism. "Alright boys, drink what water is left you, load a last round and fix bayonets."

Suddenly the blue and red lines surged forward towards the anxious Americans.

Runyon gave his last command when the Hessians were less than twenty paces out, "Fire!"

At point blank range, even the Continentals' dated British army muskets could devastate a formation. Nearly a score of Hessians fell but relentless, they pressed home their charge with a wild "Hurrah", just as the Highland infantry force crashed into the left of the American rear guard. Men yelled—but none for mercy. This was a fight to the death and both sides knew it. Farmers and shopkeepers, greatly outnumbered and with inferior weapons against the best-trained professionals in the world. Bayonets slashed throats and speared open breasts. Musket butts crushed skulls and close musket fire ripped open bellies, disgorging entrails and offal. In a few minutes the once pleasant green ground became a morass of limbs, bodies, blood and gore.

The outcome was never in doubt. A file of elite Highland grenadiers rushed Sullivan. They had orders to capture him alive and would not be denied their quarry. Runyon himself stepped to Sullivan's aid, but a grenadier parried his saber as another stabbed him in the thigh. His head swimming with anger and frustration, Runyon turned and slashed the second grenadier in the face while firing his pistol into the breast of the first. However, a third grenadier stepped forward and finished him with a blow to the head. Runyon died cursing the land of his ancestors.

Three more Highland grenadiers joined the fray and took Sullivan prisoner. The Maryland line and the remaining militia fought valiantly, but the fight was over in less than fifteen minutes. In all, more than eighty lay dead or dying. Sullivan and a few officers marched as prisoners toward Gravesend Bay and the British prison ships. The Hessians and Highlanders lost almost 100 men, killed or wounded. However, they held the passes and the vital road junction, and it was not yet noon. The King's hirelings had smashed Sullivan's weak brigade from its indefensible position. The road to Brooklyn lay open, and this attack was merely a diversion.

৪৩০৪

Brooklyn, Long Island

Jan Braaf folded the stiff white parchment and sealed it with wax. He used a generic seal, not the one he normally used in his law practice. Braaf's family had immigrated to Dutch New Amsterdam over one hundred years earlier, just before the British seized the prosperous colony and renamed it New York, in honor of the King's brother, the Duke of York. Braaf had a comfortable house in town with a small plot of land. At forty-five years of age, he was a large, portly, and balding man who prospered through a variety of business ventures, not the least of which was a successful law practice in a small fieldstone building near the town square. Braaf was also prominent in the local Whig faction. Whigs were a minority on western Long Island, which was a Tory bastion. Throughout New York and even New Jersey, many Dutch settlers at the time remained loyal to the crown or cloaked their beliefs in neutrality. The Whigs, the party that advocated for the rights of the colonies and now the states, was the American counterpart to the British Whig party, which stood for limits on Royal power and the preeminence of Parliament. Ironically, many of the British officers serving in the colonies were Whigs.

Braaf had a seventeen-year-old son, also named Jan, who had recently joined the New York Continental Line and was now somewhere with the forces defending Brooklyn. He also had a daughter, Krista, aged eighteen, slender, fair and beautiful.

Braaf locked up his writing materials, and after folding the envelope into his vest pocket, he left his office, and walked towards the East River. He had several business matters to attend to before he dropped in on his close friend, Cornelius Foch, owner of a small shipping firm. Foch's "office" was on his flagship, a brig called the *Red Hen*. Foch was the head of the Whig group to which Braaf belonged and had asked him for a discreet meeting to discuss the Whigs' plenary session scheduled for the next evening. The subject at hand: how to support the rebellion if, or when, the British arrived.

Braaf made slow going toward the waterfront. Brooklyn was now an armed camp. Hundreds of soldiers seemed to march back and forth between the Brooklyn Ferry and the defense works to the east of town. Braaf occasionally had to step aside to avoid a file of militia or the occasional courier galloping with orders for some regiment. The heat and humidity stifled him and, being large and on the heavy side, gave him trouble breathing. When he finally reached his friend's boat, his suit was soaked with sweat and dust from the road. Even the water of the East River provided no relief from the heavy air.

Foch greeted his friend with a mug of apple cider, made in the Dutch style, heavy and slightly sour with a low alcoholic content.

"So Jan, any word from beyond Brooklyn? I hear the sound of firing—it must be the English have begun their attack, no?"

The Dutch of the new world referred to all British as well as the British colonists as "the English," a legacy from the days of Peter Stuyvesant, New Amsterdam's last governor. It could be considered a derisive term, depending on the tone used.

"*Ja*, Cornelius, it has started...... The army is rushing men from New York and marching them to the defense works. The English attack has begun, I fear."

Foch gritted his brown-stained teeth on his meerschaum pipe. "Did you expect less?"

Braaf downed the last of his cider and wiped his lip and then his brow with a handkerchief. "Somehow, I never thought it could come to this. What will we do?"

Foch grimaced. "I am not sure. However, we must organize the men and prepare. The Tories will exact revenge if we make any overt move to support the rebellion. Yet, the army expects, and needs our support. You go home to your family now, and give my warm regards to your lovely wife. I must be off..... I have some important affairs to attend to this evening."

Braaf gave his friend a surprised look. "Affairs...this evening? What sort of mischief are you involved in now, Cornelius?"

Foch glowered, and then gripped his pipe tightly and a stream of smoke wafted out. "You lawyers are all the same...you ask too many questions and have too few answers."

"I think we should wait this out, Cornelius. The affair has become serious."

Foch eyed his friend. "It has been serious for some time, Jan. Now, it is merely dangerous."

ಜುಡ

Braaf arrived home at mid afternoon to find his wife Marta setting the afternoon meal on the table. Because of the heat, the normally extravagant Marta kept the fare to a simple meal of cold lamb, bread, and cucumbers. She was pouring cider for the three of them when her husband walked in.

Marta Braaf, almost a decade younger than her husband, was widely regarded as one of the most beautiful women in Brooklyn. At thirty-six, she was still very shapely in the Dutch rounded way, dark haired and dark eyed with soft, pouty lips. Many thought she looked young enough and pretty enough to be Krista's sister.

Jan sat himself at the table and with hardly a pleasantry took to his food. "Where is Krista?"

Marta was used to her husband's diffidence. "In the barn, milking the cow. We did not know when you would return, Jan. So she decided to eat later. When it is cooler."

Braaf nodded, barely looking up at her. "Good for her. I finished all my business early and hurried back. I worry now, even though the gunfire has stopped."

His wife looked at him distantly. They had long ceased to be intimate, but she did love and respect her husband, who was a good provider and a good father to Krista and their son Jan. "Will the army fight the English here? I hope they do. I fear if the English come to Brooklyn...Jan, you are eating too quickly!"

Braaf swallowed his last mouthful and drained the cider in one gulp. "I am sorry, Marta. I must leave again on business. I have a client who wants to prepare a new will, in case the English come and there is violence. I will be back after dark...very late...do not wait up."

Marta knew that Jan was active with the Whig faction and his nocturnal business often involved things he kept from them for safety's sake. Marta preferred it that way, having little interest in things outside the household.

She nodded dolefully. "I understand. There is no reason for me to wait up."

Chapter 5

Long Island, August 27th, 1776

Mordecai Gist made a last inspection of the regiment, making sure that each company commander understood his orders and had his men prepared. Although well-drilled and motivated, none of them had seen action before. Without Runyon's company the First Maryland's actual strength was now significantly fewer than four hundred officers and men. The increasing musket and artillery fire coming from the direction of Bedford Pass did not bode well. Gist wondered if Runyon's company was lost for good.

Gist inspected the Light Company last. He did not know much about Creed. A small landholder in western Maryland, somewhat new to America, that was about all he knew for sure. Irish he claimed, but his accent seemed different than most men he had encountered from the Emerald Isle. There were not many Irish in America, which was largely viewed as a place of Protestant refuge where all popery was held in contempt. Still, the Irish had begun to immigrate to America—mostly to Pennsylvania and Maryland. Gist supposed some came to Maryland because it was once a Catholic colony, founded by the Calverts. Gist never inquired as to Creed's religious affiliation. Nevertheless, he seemed a decent and courageous young man. Gist felt fortunate to have him in the regiment.

"Mister Creed, is your company ready?" Gist asked.

Creed was loading his new Jaeger rifle, replying while he rammed the ball home wrapped in its oiled-cloth patch. "Indeed, sir. I had them fill water bottles, clean and load muskets. Tired as they are, they want to fight."

"Well that is the important thing, isn't it?" replied Gist, smiling for the first time that morning. "Holding the right of the line is crucial as the British may try to work around you and into the swamps to flank us. Stirling is determined that we stand and give them a fight. Frankly, I would have pulled back to our main lines. There are several thousand British just a few hundred yards from us. Most of Stirling's militia units do not even have the bayonet. Without good breast works this could be some bad work we are facing. However, I am convinced the regiment will do its duty."

Creed nodded as he checked his flint. "These are good men sir. Best men in the army. Sure I want to fight as much as the next man, but squandering troops like this...for nothing...borders on reckless."

Gist gave him a knowing look and moved on to talk to some of the privates and corporals. After a few minutes of discussion, he returned to Creed. "Look for my signal. I will be between the two center companies. If we redeploy, your company will move first and anchor the next position. I do not know where or when that will be, mind you. That, unfortunately, Stirling will decide. He is a brave officer, but not very subtle or sophisticated in his line of thought, if you know what I mean."

Gist smiled at his own wit, another of his rare smiles.

Creed smiled back. "Well, sir, he is a Lord."

The drums began beating and the companies prepared for action, emerging from the thick woods and marching smartly to take battle positions along an open field of tall grass. They formed three deep, their blue coats and white leggings making a colorful contrast to the militia, who wore a motley combination of faded blue, brown, or red. The sun was approaching noon but it steamed rather than burned. Both sides would suffer much from the heat and humidity.

The British artillery picked up the tempo. Most of the heavy iron balls sailed over the Marylanders' heads, usually bouncing harmlessly off rock and loamy soil, but occasionally crushing an arm or leg of some poor unsuspecting straggler in the rear. The men stood calmly behind some very quickly prepared abates, stacks of fresh cut pine strewn with jagged pieces facing the enemy. A cannon ball ploughed through the company on the left taking off the head of a young soldier and crushing the arm of another. The wounded man screamed in pain and horror as a mate helped him to the rear. That was the hidden danger, Creed thought. Under the stress of combat men sought all sorts of reasons to get out of harm's way, and helping a wounded comrade offered the perfect convergence of service and preservation. However, it depleted the ranks as quickly as well placed musketry.

Creed stood in front of his company with his hat on as straight as if he were in a parade, ignoring the artillery fire.

Jonathan Beall turned to his cousin, who stood silently at the rear of the formation. "Simon, is it wise for the lieutenant to make such a target of himself?"

The corporal replied. "No, not wise, but necessary. You and I have seen action, but most of the other boys face their first fight. An officer, especially one like Lieutenant Creed, must provide an example to the men. That is why they have more privileges when we are not fighting."

Jonathan quipped. "Like visiting the lovely lady's house while we were at bivouac?"

Simon scowled. "Enough of that."

Creed took this last chance to address his men as a group. "Lads, the recent act of Congress has us now fighting for a nation, not merely a political cause. The stakes are higher now than when we joined the regiment, but they are now higher for those people, as well." He motioned toward the enemy lines.

"But the British are the paid mercenaries of an unjust king. You fight as free men and for the right to be citizens of a free nation. God has not given me the chance to fight for the land of my birth, but I am grateful to be able to fight for my adopted land and lead such fine men as you."

Creed then raised his hat over his head and bellowed as if to drown out the sound of the artillery, "For liberty, for Maryland, and...for America!"

Simon Beall led the company in a chorus of huzzahs as Creed took his place in the formation. From across the large Dutch farm field advanced a line of red coats, drums beating and moving smartly—and in step. The Continentals rarely did that under parade conditions, and the militia, never. It impressed the Marylanders, whose constant drilling enabled them to marvel at such discipline in combat, even from an enemy.

Creed called out, "Fire at my command, aim low. After the third volley load your fourth ball with buckshot and fix bayonets. Since you are light infantrymen, the last shot is yours to take."

"That's right nice of him. Thank-you Lieutenant," Jonathan Beall remarked aloud and the entire file broke into laughter.

"Enough of that, boys. We have serious work right now." Simon Beall called from behind the ranks.

The British advanced two regiments abreast. Each numbered around 400 effectives in ten companies. The lines were two deep, covering the entire field in a sea of red from end to end with the sparkle of sunlight off bayonets and sabers adding to the impressiveness. Although the Marylanders could not see them, another two regiments formed up behind the first echelon. This was the spearhead of General James Grant's column of 5,000 men. Grant was a cold professional who had served with Washington in 1758 at Fort Duquesne. He had little regard for colonial troops, like most of the British officers. He now outnumbered Stirling's Brigade by more than four to one.

The British closed to just under 100 paces from the Americans and then halted to dress ranks. Many of the Americans took that as sign of contempt, not military necessity, and jeers and curses erupted along the lines.

"Damn you lobsters!"

"We came to fight men, not dance with a gang of strumpets!"

The enemy grew closer but the Americans stood silently now. After what seemed an eternity, Gist shouted the order they had waited patiently to hear, "Commence fire!"

Creed responded, "First rank, fire!"

They fired by rank, or line of men, although they formed three deep rather than two like the British whose extensive training and drill afforded them the advantage of forming two deep, thus covering more frontage with fewer men. Forming three ranks narrowed the frontage covered but provided more dense and concentrated fire, essential for effective volleys. The Marylanders fired in order, first rank stepping back, second stepping forward, and followed by the third. Each rank re-loaded as quickly as possible, normally a twenty-second drill.

The British advanced at a slow march, sixty steps per minute, moving to the rhythm of the drums. Clouds of smoke now hung across the front of the Americans but the British marched into it like a Sunday morning stroll. They covered the first eighty paces under a withering fire that despite the blinding smoke dropped almost two score men from the first echelon. At twenty paces out, they lowered their firelocks from shoulder arms to the ready—a wicked line of steel points now aimed at the bellies of the defenders. As one, they gave a shout of "Huzzah" and charged with bayonets at the ready.

They fully expected the Americans to break and run as they had in earlier engagements. Once they broke, it would be a simple affair to chase them down, bayoneting those who did not surrender. But the formation did not advance fast enough and the Americans fired individually as the British veterans attempted to close on them. The defenders shot down most of the British and bayoneted the few who got through. Now it was the British screaming for mercy as the Marylanders surrounded individual soldiers and took them down with a slice of cold steel or a crushing musket blow to the head.

The first British echelon fell back fifty yards to recover and the second echelon regiments pushed through. This time, instead of closing, they halted sixty paces out and commenced a volley fire. For almost fifteen minutes the Marylanders, and the Delawares to their left, exchanged intense fire with the British. Lead balls seemed to fly every direction. On both sides, men keeled over screaming as bone and flesh rent apart from close-range fire. The gun smoke hung heavy and obstructed their line of sight so the fire became less effective with each volley. Creed's company had lost six men in the short firefight and all along the American line the toll was beginning to show.

Gist turned to a sergeant standing just to his left rear. "Tell Mister Creed to move his company 250 yards north to the high ground and cover the regiment's movement."

The sergeant made his way through smoke and fire to find Creed's position. Creed knew it was time, and gladly withdrew his two platoons one after the other, in alternate bounds, firing a volley each time to hold back the British. The broken ground and small stands of trees to their rear provided good cover and few men were hit.

Once on the high ground, he walked among the men, providing encouragement and instilling confidence.

"This is good ground, lads. From here we can provide cover for the rest of the regiment. Form ranks, two deep. Drink one half cup of your water, no more. Reload and prepare to receive infantry."

It then occurred to him that he had not used his new toy—the German rifle. He scanned the smoky battlefield for a likely target. At almost 300 yards out, he spotted a juicy one: a British officer riding along the line as if on parade in Hyde Park. Stung by the stout American defense, the British had moved forward slowly to fill the gap where Creed's men once stood. He had never fired one of these rifles before so he carefully aimed high and to the right to adjust for wind. The bullet went short by half the distance.

Creed looked over at Jonathan Beall, himself the owner of a rifle. "Private Beall, it seems the effective range this German firelock is double the musket—150 yards. Very well then, we will let them get closer."

The Americans now began to fall back all along the front, some in orderly fashion by companies or platoons, but others with a haphazard desperation that belied the valor they so recently displayed. Several of Creed's men began to waver, a few looking rearwards for a line of escape. One young man from Poolesville felt the crack of a ham-like fist across his ribs. He bent over double and the same fist grabbed his neck and stood him up.

Simon Beall stared him down. "Planning on a personal retreat, Jenkins?"

"Just seeing who was behind us was all." The man looked down ashamedly.

Beall glared and bellowed for all to hear. "Nobody goes but where Lieutenant Creed orders! Now stand tall or I'll ear box all of you!"

Lord Stirling rode along the line exhorting the troops. "Keep your formations, lads. We are going toe to toe with them and we are smashing them right well."

He had just received detailed word that Sullivan had been defeated at Flatbush and he had an unconfirmed report that Cornwallis had reached the Gowanus Road, a little more than a mile to his rear. The Maryland detachment he sent to aide Sullivan could have been better used right here. He faced a hopeless situation but Stirling determined to give as well as he got.

From the east came the curious mix of heavy fire, bagpipes, and drums. The Hessians and Scots from the Flatbush and Bedford passes were now engaging his left flank. With Grant pressing his front, even the bombastic Stirling had to admit the enemy had him in a tight vice that would soon crush them.

Stirling summoned the commanders of the Maryland and Delaware regiments. "Gentlemen, we are in a real kettle. Lobsters are now a mile to our rear on the Gowanus Road, at Cortelyou House. We cannot hold our front much longer. Sullivan and his brigade no longer exist. Now our left flank is threatened. We are on our own now. "

"Do you suggest surrender?" Gist asked.

"No. Your two regiments must hold a while longer while the remaining militia break up into detachments and try to get back to our lines. The Gowanus salt marsh will channel them toward the British. Some may be able to swim or find drift wood to cross. The rest will have to fight their way through the British. But Gist, a detachment of your men will remain with me."

Gist stared with a bewilderment that soon turned to anger, then despair.

Stirling looked at him and a sly grin crossed his mouth, "Glory! We will give the British a taste of their own medicine and use the bayonet. We shall drive straight north at the British blocking our way and fight through to General Washington, or die in the attempt. At the least, this will buy time for the rest to get back to our lines."

Gist looked incredulous. "Sir, your proposal is a shade short of suicide. There must be several thousand British between us and General Washington."

"And so there are," answered Stirling smiling grimly, "and so there are. We move out immediately. Gist, form your detachment on me. Have them turn about and form in line of companies. Once we move out, Lieutenant Colonel Smith here will hold the line near the Red Lion Inn with his Delaware lads before pulling back."

Smith nodded. "Would only that Colonel Haslet were here for this."

Within minutes, drums were beating and orders shouted up and down the line. The Delawares and remaining militia engaged the British, now pressing from the south and east, just long enough for Stirling to move his unit north toward Cornwallis' forces. The Maryland detachment, now little more than 250 effectives, deployed in echelon and with flags flying high and drums beating, moved north toward the Cortelyou junction. Once clear, the remaining forces broke up into small packs of soldiers and headed north and west toward the American lines in a frantic race for safety. This soon turned into a rout as over a thousand men left musket, kit and comrade to attend himself. Those wounded or simply not swift enough became easy pickings as the British and Hessians completed their days' work with butchery as yet unknown in the war.

A column taking sick and wounded back to the American lines was stranded along Porte Road. The chief surgeon and a few aides walked among wounded and sick who had been thrown helter-skelter into carts and wagons for the hot and bumpy ride back. Moans of pain and thirst, cries for home, God, or mother drowned out sounds of war that grew increasingly closer. Most of the drivers had abandoned them when the British attacked. Now the surgeon had but a few volunteers from the ranks to assist. Private Jorns lay in one such cart fighting a fever. His leg had stopped bleeding but had grown swollen with pus and fluid that made the slightest movement painful.

Suddenly a group of three New York militiamen trotted up the road minus their weapons and hats. The surgeon called to them. "Hey there, boys—I need help moving these sick and wounded."

A small, skinny man waved him off. "Forget them, sawbones. Run for your own life—the lobsters is right behind us!"

A pop, pop of musket fire erupted from the wood line and a platoon of twenty kilted Highlanders emerged. Roaring and howling like madmen, they charged towards the line of carts along the road.

The surgeon raised his hands in supplication as the line reached him. "Nothing but sick and wounded here, we are at your..."

A grinning sergeant swung a broad claymore down on the surgeon, slicing the surgeon's head open like an apple. Before the body tumbled to the ground the sergeant and his men were among the wagons, bayoneting and stabbing the hapless invalids and ransacking the corpses for loot. Men yelled for mercy and a few tried to resist but most were resigned to their fate and meekly submitted to the slaughter.

Two Highlanders reached the cart where Jorns lay trussed-up against the corner holding his haversack flush against his side.

One barked at Jorns while eyeing his haversack. "Must have the King's jewels in there, eh? Alright man, give it up and we'll be quick about it."

Jorns' anger abated his fever just enough for him to smile back at his assailants. "Fine talk for someone wearing a dress now, ain't it? Well, come take it and do your worst, you damned lobsters."

The Highlander frowned. "Why, I'll skewer you good, Jimmie rebel."

He lifted his musket high over his head to drive its seventeen inch blade into Jorns. As he his arms came down, Jorns opened his sack and grabbed the pistol he had stolen from an officer back in New Jersey. Before the blade could strike, he pulled the trigger and the lead ball slammed into the Highlander's chest, sending him tumbling backwards and dropping his musket onto Jorns' lap. The pain caused by the impact on his infected leg nearly caused him to pass out but he gathered the weapon and fought off the angry slashes and stabs of the other Scotsman.

"Damn you, rebel!" He cried. "You have slashed me!" Blood oozed from a wicked bone cut to the soldier's arm. Jorns pulled the trigger of the musket and the weapon discharged into the face of the Highlander.

Jorns never saw the sergeant approach the cart. The claymore came down in a ferocious strike that sent Jorns' head skipping along the dusty road. The rebel hospital had fallen to His Majesty's forces.

ಞ ೮೩

Lord Stirling led Major Gist and the Marylanders north toward the Cortelyou House to strike Cornwallis' troops. There would be no time for volley fire. Each man had one musket ball loaded and his bayonet fixed.

"Forward! And give them cold steel!" cried Stirling shrilly, his voice cracking not from fear but from thirst and excitement.

Gist signaled his men forward, up a narrow sunken lane lined with fruit trees. Simon Beall breathed deeply and caught the scent of apple buds just springing into bloom. For a fleeting second the scent flooded his mind with a thousand thoughts of home. The sounds from the hell waiting up ahead snapped him back to the grim world that currently held him.

Gist's force moved up four companies strong and fanned out into line of battle. Jonathan Beall marveled at how this resembled a parade drill with lines of men and stirring music. Then the rolling British volleys drowned out the music except for the constant beat of the drums. Creed's company now anchored the left of the Maryland line, which was two deep and over five score across.

They advanced at a brisk pace, the regimental flags now cased, but officers out front, non-commissioned officers to the rear. To Creed this fight seemed more like a battle on the plains of Europe than the typical skirmishes in thick woods and deep forests of America. The rolling farmland of western Long Island looked more like southern England or parts of France than most of the rugged new world.

They had less than a mile to cover to reach Cortelyou House. However, before they went half the distance a pair of cannon bombarded their flank while skirmishers opened fire across their front. Men began to drop, clutching frantically as British musket balls tore through their limbs and bodies but mostly heads. Few who fell would ever rise again. Still, the formation kept moving right into the jaws of the awesome fire.

Behind them they could hear Grant's column overrunning the few Americans still holding the line. Creed began to think through the situation. They were a forlorn hope, but he determined that he would get his company through it somehow. His mind raced to come up with a solution and, as he scanned the field towards the northwest, he came on one.

Creed's company was closest to the American lines—which lay to the north and west, just over Gowanus Creek. If they could manage to break through the British near Cortelyou House there was a chance they could fight their way back. However, two regiments of crack British infantry blocked their way, making his solution a risky one at best.

The musket fire grew more intense and the smoke mixed with the sticky air to choke each man and making eyes redden and tear. Controlled volleys had ended. Now both sides resorted to individual fire. Musket balls cracked and whizzed randomly across the front, tearing through branches, leaves and men.

To Simon Beall's front, one of his best men turned to signal something. Beall saw the man's eyes widen and a torrent of blood gushed from his breast. He twisted in a slow spiral that sprawled his lifeless form across a gray boulder. Beall's stomach turned at the sight. He had been a close friend back home but in the shock of combat, he could not recall his name. When Beall passed him, he looked down into his friend's once cheerful face now staring blankly into the blue sky.

"Jonas!" Beall exclaimed. He felt guilty that at the moment of his friend's death, he had forgotten his name.

The British had deployed their forces to take advantage of the terrain along a slight rise with small trees and split rail fencing. Despite the growing cloud of gun smoke, their colorful red coats, white belting, glistening halberds, sabers, and bayonets made them stand out against the green and brown background of the hills. At eighty paces, more Marylanders began to drop from the British fire. Gist ordered the detachment to halt and return fire. To the surprise of the British defenders, they did so in a cool and professional manner, then, with fixed bayonets and against all odds, the men rushed forward. Direct fire at point blank range tore holes in their ranks but the mighty British infantry fell back 100 yards to regroup from the ferocity and determination of the Marylanders' attack.

"Reload and dress ranks," ordered Gist.

The men jostled over dead and wounded comrades to tighten the lines. The snap and rattle of a hundred ramrods competed with screams and the boom of cannon fire. Stirling then gave the order to charge again and without a word the stalwart men from Maryland ran headlong at the British positions only to be forced back again by a fire even more intense. Wounded and dying were strewn across the field, many supine with arms stretched out as they begged for water or a bullet. Fortunately, for the Americans, pockets of smoke now obscured much of the ridgeline. This protected them from the specialty of British infantry—long-range volley fire.

Creed called out to his men. "Alright lads, reload—this time ball and buckshot. Drink your water now; share with your mates."

Creed thought this would be the last drink for most of them, perhaps all of them. Many were in fact out of water already but refused to take from their comrades.

A third and then a fourth charge went the same as the first two, advance forward thirty yards, fire a ragged volley only to fall back under heavy British fire. Creed's company was down to nineteen men. Simon Beall was still with him as was his cousin Jonathan and both seemed willing to continue. Creed marveled how they could fight through the heat and terror of all this after the early morning fight with the Hessians.

The noon-time temperature was at once searing, sticky, and stifling. The previous day's thunderstorm had done nothing to break up the weather. Many of the men could barely breathe and white chalky sweat stains covered their blue tunics. They were low on water and ammunition.

Even Lord Stirling realized they could manage only one last charge. He strutted before them as they prepared for the final attack. "This time we shall break them, lads—do not load your muskets. Bayonets only. Let no man stop until he has stained his with British blood. Kill them where they stand or send them running back to the beaches!"

Creed knew the last charge would finish them.

While Stirling exhorted the men he quietly spoke to Simon Beall. "Tell the lads to prepare for a separate maneuver. We will move to the left to...distract fire from the main body."

Beall looked at Creed. "Leave the regiment, sir?"

Creed stared at him. "Support it from a different position."

Creed also felt pangs of guilt for leaving the main body at this critical juncture but he wanted an even playing field for his men from Frederick. He owed them a chance to survive and perhaps fight again rather than perish in another of Stirling's frontal attacks. He scanned the ridge and saw that the British had reinforced the line by several hundred more and now numbered well over a thousand, plus several cannon.

Lord Stirling raised his saber and swung it in tight circles like a *berserker* from the dark ages of warfare. "Attack the lobster-backs! They are ours! Forward!"

"For Maryland!" cried Gist, now resigned to his fate.

"For Maryland!" answered the men. With loud "huzzahs" they charged forward as musket balls whined around them. Most had dropped their packs and many went hatless; the constant back and forth took a toll on their military appearance, but not their discipline or will. A cannon near a red brick farmhouse at the end of the ridge pounded them with iron balls that ricocheted through the ranks, crushing bone and tearing limbs. That was followed by devastating grape shot, which shotgun-like, tore the unit apart. The survivors, however, reached the British lines ready to avenge their fallen comrades. Screaming with blood-lust, each man fought with fanatic determination that few British expected from American soldiers. However, the attackers were too few to break the British line and the assault dried up like a powerful ocean wave hitting a broad expanse of beach.

While the Marylanders under Stirling launched assault after assault on the British, small groups from the other American formations desperately fought their way back to the lines. Many died trying to get to safety. Still, many made it back, although most were weaponless and all completely demoralized by the sheer terror of the British onslaught.

Near Cortelyou House, Creed was the first to reach the British lines. Three enemy soldiers rushed him but using the short German rifle with the sword-bayonet attached, Creed was able to stay under their musket thrusts and quickly dispatched all three. The longer blade and shorter radius of the weapon enabled him to strike, extract the blade, shift weight, and strike again before they could react. Creed tore open throat, belly, and breast in a whirl of precision cuts that surprised even him. He felt neither hate nor remorse. This was cold work.

To the right, Creed saw a short, stocky redcoat fire directly at Jonathan Beall. As luck had it, the musket misfired. Even a few rounds of firing could cause black powder weapons to foul and jam.

The redcoat and a companion closed on Beall with their bayonets lowered, screaming "Rebels die!" Creed saw Beall meet the first man head-on, parry his blade, and thrust his sword-bayonet into the soldier's chest. Beall then rammed his rifle butt into the chest of the second redcoat, cracking his breastbone and collapsing him backwards over a hedge. Sweat and tears poured down Beall's face as he realized he and his cousin would die at this place. Around him, he heard curses and screams for quarter mixed with the sound of steel on steel. The British began to fall back as the desperate Marylanders pushed ever so slowly forward. Before long, the men began to waver from exhaustion as the British committed another two hundred men into the melee.

Now desperate, Gist ran along the line ordering each company commander to do "what he could" to get his men to safety. As Gist attended his unit Lord Stirling plunged into the noise and smoke of combat. Stirling wielded his saber like a pirate's cutlass, cutting and slashing as redcoat after redcoat rushed him. With bloodlust up, his screams and curses rose above the din of the fight. Small groups of Americans attempted to rally around him but as they did, larger groups of British closed on them and, one by one, they went down. Finally, the red wave rolled over Stirling like an ocean of blood and Gist lost sight of him in the smoke and confusion.

Gist reached Creed last. "To continue on with this would border on arrogance. I instructed the other commanders to break free with what men they can. Stirling fought like a wolf. I saw him personally down five British soldiers with his sword, but now he is gone. I fear him dead or captured."

Creed indeed saw the other companies breaking up into small groups. Most dropped back, but some tried to fight through the British lines, where most would perish.

His face showed composure. "Sir, stay with my company, we are going to make our way through to the west and safety. Corporal Beall, have the company move in double file, on me."

Creed moved at a near run, bent over at the waist as British musket fire began to close in on them. Gist was right behind him, followed by Jonathan Beall and the remaining members of the light company. As corporal, Simon Beall covered the rear. He had no idea of the plan, but he began to have a strange sense of confidence in his officer. For the first time in a while, he thought they had a chance to live through the hell that had engulfed them the past few hours. They made their way by sticking close to the small stands of trees that dotted the rolling countryside, moving from copse to copse, and using the natural breaks and bends of the rolling terrain.

Cannon fired from a nearby farmhouse situated at the crest of the hill to their right front. The farmhouse, almost two hundred yards distant, was a brick, stone and timbered affair topped with a red roof. The owner, a Dutch farmer and his family, had abandoned the place early that morning at the first sight of British soldiers in the area. Now, a Royal Artillery gun crew fired on the small detachments of American troops to their front, causing confusion and occasionally killing a man or two.

Creed halted suddenly, and turned to Gist. "With your permission, sir, I think we have some unfinished business to attend here."

Creed pointed toward the farm house just as the muzzle erupted in flame and smoke.

Gist, surprised at Creed's initiative, assented, "It would seem so."

Creed led his men toward the farmhouse at the double, a slow trot. The gun crew, attention fixed on the various groups of Americans fleeing the field, had neglected to post anyone to watch the back of the house. Creed's men closed the distance and rushed the crew from the rear. The blue jacketed gunners had been up all day and night and had manhandled the gun for miles through woods and brush. They were exhausted, so when surprised from the rear they broke and ran, but not before three of their number went down to musket fire. Their officer stood to fight but he was quickly overwhelmed and Creed ordered him taken prisoner.

From the hill, Creed could now see down the valley and across the small creek that ran southward into the river inlet. Behind the creek were the American lines.

He addressed the men. "If we stay as far to the north as the British will allow us we may be able to negotiate the creek rather than swim the inlet. We will take this British officer with us as he might have useful information. Sir, if you and Corporal Beall lead the men and take the prisoner, I will serve as rear guard with Private Beall. We shall spike the gun as well."

"Spike a gun?" Gist asked incredulously.

Artillery was a scarce military commodity in the Americas, so few of the militia or continentals would be skilled enough even to think of spiking a field piece, nonetheless to do it.

Creed suppressed a smile. "'I can do it. Private Beall will help. You and the others should head down toward the creek with our prisoner."

The men departed, prodding their captive along as they went. Creed set to work with a hammer and one of the gun's trail spikes, pounding at it until the spike had opened enough of a gap in the vent to prevent further use that day by the British. Jamming the fire vent would render the gun inoperable until it went back to a depot or armory and was re-tooled. It was a six-pound gun, relatively light and commonly used to support the infantry. Artillery poundage reflected the weight of the cannon ball: four and six-pound guns were for close support of infantry or cavalry. Nine-pound guns were the heavier field guns for artillery barrages in pitched battle. The larger eighteen and twenty-four-pound guns were used for sieges or coastal defense. The British used a mix of these weapons but only the smaller ones pushed forward with the initial column march by Clinton and Cornwallis.

When Creed finished, he and Beall began to work their way down the slope toward Gowanus Creek, which was between them and the safety of the American lines. Gist and the rest waited near a small stand of trees less than two hundred yards from the creek. Creed and Beall began to close the quarter mile distance to the men. Suddenly, a formation of twenty British light dragoons galloped down the hill from behind the brick house. Major Sandy Drummond led them, and they moved so quickly and were so fixed on getting to Gist and the detachment that they rushed past Creed and Beall.

"They want our prisoner back," Creed said in a steady, calm voice.

Gist and the detachment were surprised but not caught off guard. They were able to fire a volley just before the dragoons closed on them. Four troopers went down, their horses galloping wildly off, one with its rider dragging along by a boot caught in the stirrup, his limp body jerking and bouncing along the soggy ground.

Cavalry's success depends on infantry formations breaking when charged. Assuming that would be the outcome, the dragoons charged home. However, this was not a demoralized rabble but a small and determined group of warriors who held their ground and soon dragoon sabers were clashing against musket and bayonet. Gist suffered a minor shoulder wound from Drummond's saber slash when he attempted to stop Drummond from seizing their prisoner. Three other Marylanders went down to saber thrusts but their bayonets impaled two more dragoons who also fell mortally wounded.

After slashing Gist, Drummond pulled the young British artillery officer across his saddle. His horse was a large hunter, a bay, with the strength and stamina to carry two men.

"On me," called Drummond as he spurred his horse back toward the safety of the brick house. The dragoons rode right at Creed and Beall, who were now less than a hundred yards from the melee. To their fortune, the dragoons did not notice the two men crouching behind a tree stump. As they passed, Creed turned and pointed his Jaeger rifle at Drummond, now a good forty yards to his right. He aimed carefully but the jumper was moving quickly and weaving its way up the slope. He aimed for Drummond–taking care to avoid the artillery officer.

The round hit low, and stuck the side of Drummond's knee and deflected into the horse's flank. The spent round's velocity, broken by the impact on leather, flesh and bone, did little more to the horse than sting and bruise its ribs. However, the jumper stopped dead and with a shrill whine, reared upwards in pain and fear. The sudden stop sent Drummond and the artillery officer tumbling to the swampy ground, knocking Drummond unconscious. Beall and Creed were on them and once again took the hapless artilleryman prisoner, leaving Drummond for dead. The wounded horse limped off in pain as the dragoons turned back to the aid of their commander.

"Leave 'em be," yelled the dragoon sergeant, waving toward Creed and Beall. "Major Drummond needs our help."

While the dragoons spurred to Drummond's aid, Creed and Beall found the remnant of the detachment. They now numbered ten, including Gist. The Marylanders made their way to the creek, which was only twenty yards across and fordable. As they walked through the waist high water, a line of more than three hundred British infantry appeared on the ridge and fired an ineffective long-range volley at the Americans. Musket balls plunged into the muck along the near bank. A few went wild and careened into the water where they sunk. Safely across, some of the Marylanders jeered at the British, who stood in frustration as their quarry had gotten away.

Chapter 6

American Defense Works, Long Island, August 27th, 1776

From a hill just behind the American lines, the American commander-in-chief, Lieutenant General George Washington, watched with awe and horror. He heard the yells of fighting men and the sound of cannon and musket. He saw the Maryland Line stand fast and hold off the British. Washington turned to one of his aides, Lieutenant Abner Scovel.

"That I would have the honor to lead such brave men," Washington said. "It seems at least some of our men can stand and face the British. Would that we had more such men as these...more continentals..."

Scovel nodded. "Indeed sir. The Continental Line is the army's backbone."

Washington nodded. "Abner, I had excellent regiments from the Connecticut, Pennsylvania, and Massachusetts Line deployed from New York to reinforce this position. None fought with the near savage gallantry of those regiments from Maryland and Delaware. But even such gallantry may not suffice."

"It provides an example for the rest of the army to follow, sir." Scovel replied.

Washington slapped his riding crop against his boot. "Abner, in less than two hours of combat, we may have lost more than one thousand of our boys. And now just one final push by Howe could crush this army against the East River."

Washington's comments stunned Scovel. "Why, if that happens, sir, the war for our freedom and independence would end almost before it had begun."

"Rid your mind of such talk." Washington directed the comment at himself more than his aide.

"Find out the name of the daring officer who faced those dragoons and recovered the British prisoner," Washington commanded. "And ask Colonel Fitzgerald to question the prisoner. I must know Howe's intentions. Will he push on against now? Or is this all a ruse of some sort? The answer may well determine the course of this campaign...and perhaps the war."

Scovel threw up a hasty salute and set off to find Fitzgerald, Washington's intelligence advisor. Thus far, the general intentions of the British were easy enough to determine. They would use their command of the sea to maneuver forces along the Atlantic coast. Clearly, their major area of success would always come where there were adequate harbors and sea lanes. When they withdrew from Boston under rebel pressure, Washington wisely moved his base of operations to New York City in anticipation of the British moving there. Acquiring detailed tactical information was an altogether different matter. Colonel Robert

Fitzgerald was an intellectual although not dynamic officer who accepted the position because most of his peers sought field command or the more prestigious posts in the army such as adjutant general, quartermaster and the like.

Fitzgerald sat near the Brooklyn landing and gazed at the map laid out on an empty salt pork barrel that served as a makeshift desk. The colonel seemed to be talking to himself. Scovel sometimes wondered if he were daft.

"His Excellency sends his regards, Colonel," said Scovel, saluting perfunctorily. Scovel did not think very highly of staff work, especially intelligence work. He had long hoped to command Washington's Guard but was stymied by politics.

Fitzgerald did not respond immediately, absorbed as he was with the map. He finally looked up, and peered over his spectacles. "A good intelligence officer needs two things to be successful, Scovel: knowledge of his enemy's intentions and a good map. Of these, the latter is the more important as in things martial the earth often shapes our intentions. Unfortunately, I have neither. This old Dutch map is out of date and generally inaccurate."

Scovel ignored the remark and went right to the point. "Sir, a detachment of the Maryland Continental Line brought us back an enemy officer. General Washington is most anxious as to the British intentions and requests you personally question the prisoner."

Fitzgerald smiled wryly, "Well, one could assume they intend to defeat our army and take New York as their base of operations. The real question is whether he plans to end us here on Long Island, or execute another maneuver by sea and strand us here while he takes New York from under us."

"Indeed," replied the aide, "The initiative seems to be his. He has surprised us and now our options are few. General Washington prefers to stand and fight right here on Long Island. But it is necessary to discern British intentions as others are already urging other courses of action."

Fitzgerald eyed Scovel with the disdain a schoolmaster would have for a first year Latin student with plenty of energy and ambition but no inkling of the hard work ahead. Scovel was twenty-five, of average height and build, but had an understated energy that caused him to move about like a wolfhound.

"So it is, so it is," replied Fitzgerald. "This had been a very difficult thing to do. I have made some contacts with various local Whig factions as you know, primarily in Brooklyn, and over near Bedford. But it is quite difficult to communicate with them discreetly and the information they provide is often nothing more than vague rumor and innuendo. Or worse sir, disinformation aimed at personal or political vendetta."

The aide declined to proffer his own opinion of the value of local spies. Instead, Scovel fingered his saber tassel, openly bored with the conversation.

Fitzgerald continued. "However, one must play with the cards one is dealt. One local Whig leader has already contacted me. He provided us this map, sorry as it is, and has agreed to provide reports on things he feels might be of use. I have met him but have deliberately not asked his name, for the sake of security. There are British sympathizers about too. Many families remain divided in their loyalties, as are neighbors and friends. Then there are those undecided Americans. They just want to live their comfortable lives. They like the idea of freedom, liberty, and independence, but they also like the comfort and security the King provides them."

Now it was Fitzgerald's turn to evince boredom. He stood up abruptly and gathered the map from the make shift table. "Where can I find the prisoner?"

"The Maryland Line is reconstituting at Fort Greene. I suppose you shall find him there. Time is of the essence, sir."

Fitzgerald nodded and mounted his horse, folding the map into a brown saddlebag. With elbows and knees moving clumsily, he cantered down the road toward the town of Brooklyn and Fort Greene. Having no permanent staff, Fitzgerald questioned most prisoners himself. He pieced other intelligence together from the snippets of information he gleaned from Washington's staff and regimental commanders—when and if they bothered to report.

Fitzgerald's attitude stemmed from frustrations over the lack of resources for his intelligence efforts and the perceived lack of appreciation of it by all but Washington. There were times he wished he were back in the schoolhouse teaching Latin and Theology. He did not miss his family much. His wife died years ago bearing a son who died at child birth. His daughter had married a minister back in 1775 and not contacted him since they left to establish his church out near the Ohio. Still, he was devoted to the cause and its commander in chief, and had become intrigued with the challenge of being intelligence advisor to a man of Washington's character, prescience and nobility.

The Americans' fortified line along the western rim of Long Island was weak. It stretched several miles, from Wallabout Bay in the northeast to Gowanus Bay to the southwest. Gowanus Bay narrowed into a channel surrounded by salt marshes on either side and was easily defended. To the northeast, Wallabout Bay emptied into salt marshes along the coast as well, thus keeping the American flanks relatively secure. A rudimentary line of entrenchments anchored by three modest redoubts defended the open and rolling farmland between. Redoubts were field fortifications constructed of earthen berms, normally configured in triangle shapes to allow enfilading fire on attacking troops. The berms were often reinforced with logs, and when possible, stone, brick or masonry. In this case, they were earthen, reinforced randomly with cut logs and loose stone found nearby.

The Maryland Continental Line had little time to regroup after escaping the British assault earlier that day. From an original strength of almost a thousand that left Maryland, the entire regiment now consisted of just over a hundred men. Of the detachment of two hundred and fifty Continentals who fought alongside Major Mordecai Gist, only Gist himself and Creed's band of nine had escaped.

∞∞

Creed received orders to report to General Israel Putnam, acting commander of the defenses, with his prisoner. Jonathan Beall served as escort.

Putnam's command post was a small tent on the outskirts of Brooklyn. The older general smiled when Creed reported in. He had little to smile about that day, but word of Creed's exploit had spread through the army.

Putnam grabbed Creed's hand. "Damned glad you made it back Lieutenant Creed. That was some fine work you did—bringing your men back from certain death—and with a prisoner!"

Creed nodded but his face showed no joy. "Sir, most of my company is dead, dying or on their way to British prison ships. I do not consider that a good day's work."

Putnam nodded. "Nevertheless Creed, bringing anyone out alive against those odds is credible work. I now need you to see what you can learn from this prisoner, and quickly."

Creed glanced over to where Jonathan Beall held the officer. They had tied the prisoner's hands behind his back. He looked sullen and resigned.

Creed spoke. "Sir, neither Private Beall nor I have eaten since very early this morning. Could I trouble you to send us something, and I wager our prisoner has not eaten either. People talk more freely when their bellies are full, if you understand my line of thought, sir."

Putnam nodded at Creed and smiled again. "True enough, young man. See to him and I shall see what I can find."

Creed approached the British officer, who was sitting in the shade of a large maple tree guarded by a very weary looking Beall. He wore the blue tunic typical of an artillery officer. Creed soon learned that the officer, a Lieutenant James Simmons, was from Ireland and had served in the Royal Field Artillery for six years. When the food arrived, Creed went out of his way to offer Simmons a portion equal to his own. Boiled beans and bacon, cold, stale bread, and a pint of rum, it was a soldier's feast. Creed poured a few fingers for Beall, who watched with interest as the two officers talked.

Creed assured Simmons he wanted no military "secrets" and talked about Ireland at first—both agreed that they sorely missed the emerald island. Simmons was from Dublin, of Anglo-Irish ancestry—Norman soldiers who arrived during the time of Henry II and Strong bow. He had studied mathematics for a year but grew bored and sought a commission. His mathematics studies made him a natural for either engineers or artillery. Wanting action, he chose the latter. Simmons was vehement in his antipathy toward this American rebellion, although he also understood; having made the long voyage over, that these colonies, so far from Britain, needed a measure of autonomy. Creed readily agreed and assured Simmons that was mostly what this fight was about, the recent declaration of independence being merely a tactic to pressure the King.

Although Simmons resisted direct questions, he did opine that the British planned to defeat the rebels on Long Island before they crossed over to New York. He assured Creed that with more than thirty thousand troops, including artillery, German mercenaries, Scots Highlanders, and some of Britain's finest infantry regiments; smashing the rebellion was simply a matter of time. And he assured Creed that time was running out for the rebels since some of Britain's finest generals: Howe, Cornwallis, and Clinton, were leading the effort to crush the rebellion.

In all, they had a very amicable conversation. As they finished the last two fingers of rum Creed commented, "I shall be sad to see such a fine officer as yourself spend the rest of the war a prisoner. Perhaps we can exchange you. We'll likely send you to Boston and eventually you will stay in a prison, probably somewhere in northern Massachusetts..."

Simmons' face reddened, "Why, that's pure poppycock. Your rebellion will be crushed before I could arrive there. Within hours, General Howe will take these ridiculous works of yours, drive you all into the river, and seize New York without a fight. We have several batteries of field guns, cavalry enough and plenty of infantry: Highland infantry, Hessian mercenaries and many fine British regiments. We have ample supplies of food, powder, and shot. Moreover, we have a martial spirit that will crush your rebel notions of independence. Your colonies in rebellion will quickly sue for peace."

Creed replied, "Or not...remember this, our own Ireland has never submitted to British rule, and it never will. Time is on the side of those who would be free. So let me recount. We now know the names of your senior leaders, and that they are predisposed to attack us here on these works before taking New York. You have provided the type and disposition of your forces, and your general scheme of maneuver. Now, is there anything you would rather not tell me?"

Creed smiled sarcastically and motioned to Beall. "Private Beall, please take our good Lieutenant Simmons back to the Brooklyn Ferry for a short voyage to New York. I must report on all this to..."

Simmons exploded in rage. "You think you have useful information? You have enough to know it is time to despair, run like the cowards you are or pray before meeting your maker!"

Shortly after Beall had led him off, Colonel Fitzgerald arrived, determined to put the upstart officer in his place. Dispensing with the amenities or even military courtesy, he stood over Creed with a boot placed on the log where Simmons was just sitting. "I understand that you are Lieutenant Creed and that you have a British prisoner ready for me to question."

Creed stood up and saluted, then stood at ease. This stern and gawky looking old man reminded him of one of the monsignors he had known in Ireland. "Well, yes and no sir. I am your very Lieutenant Jeremiah Creed and I did have a prisoner here but he is being taken back to the ferry for disposition by..."

Fitzgerald snapped. "On whose authority? I was directed by General Washington to personally question him."

Creed, replied calmly, "Well sir, if you act quickly enough you still can. Or you may hear my report as I think I have most of the information you are seeking."

"Go on," said Fitzgerald brusquely.

Creed went on to relate all he had learned from his prisoner. Fitzgerald listened attentively, impressed by the speed with which Creed had interrogated the prisoner, and the quality of the information.

"How did you get him to talk so quickly?"

"Quite simple, sir. I had a meal with him and gleaned all through our conversation. His braggadocio was enough to provide what we wanted."

"Well done," said Fitzgerald tersely. "I must report all this to General Washington. I suggest you return to your command. Where can I find you if I have further questions?"

"My company was destroyed this morning while serving under Lord Stirling, who is by now either in the hands of the British or God. All that remains is a squad and Major Mordecai Gist."

Fitzgerald hesitated a second. "I see, yes. A most unfortunate affair. Very well then. Report back to Major Gist, I am sure he can make good use of you in the coming hours."

ಬಿಂಕ

Washington's dilemma grew with each hour as he pondered the situation with his aide, Lieutenant Scovel. Reports from the regiments flowed in sporadically at best. The British had moved into a cordon that paralleled his lines and the American defenses were nowhere near ready. Howe merely had to push a little at him to destroy his divided and outnumbered force. Perhaps this was still all a feint. Were the British aiming to take New York in a *coup de main* and cut him and half his army off on Long Island?

"Has Colonel Fitzgerald interrogated the British prisoner?" Washington asked. His voice was irritable and his mind drifted. He was tired, and knew a stack of tendentious correspondence from various congressmen awaited his attention as well. The politics of the war oppressed him more than the overwhelming resources of the enemy. Each congressman had an agenda, and so many important decisions such as resourcing; selection of officers and even strategy required their approval.

"He is doing so even as we speak," Scovel answered.

Washington set out to walk among the wounded and disheveled men still working their way back into American lines. There were hundreds of them. Washington tried to say something to encourage morale although his presence was enough to bolster their spirits, at least temporarily. He knew what they needed was rest and food. And there was little enough of that to go around.

Appointed Commander-in-Chief by acclamation, George Washington was considered the one man who transcended the numerous factional grievances among the colonies, and so in some ways he represented all of their hopes. His dignified bearing and natural ease among men of all stripes provided the measured leadership the new army and new nation needed. By driving the British from Boston, and then beating them to New York, Washington demonstrated a martial prowess that his modest achievements during the French and Indian War did not portend. While the Continental Congress with all of its squabbles and machinations represented the best and worst in man's instincts, Washington's dignified character represented only the best.

Washington's eyes welled up as he watched his beaten and downtrodden soldiers. "Have the chief surgeon attend the most seriously injured and evacuate them to New York. Those who can still fight must be given warm food and sent back to their units. We will need every man when General Howe comes at us, and that could be soon. I am going back to inspect the lines but I want to be told immediately if we learn anything from the prisoner."

ഇരുഗ

Creed's men finished perhaps the most satisfying meal they had ever tasted: fresh sausage and eggs obtained by the brigade commissary, compliments of one of the many abandoned local farms in the area. Although there was a vocal Whig minority, most of western Long Island was generally Loyalist. The original Dutch inhabitants had grown prosperous under British rule.

The men were finishing a hard-earned second mug of hot coffee. Beall gulped down the last dregs of his mug and pondered the past few days' events. He had learned much from his first taste of combat. Lieutenant Creed had taught them all well, he thought. The men performed with valor and efficiency against the best the enemy could field. He thought it sad that so few survived, but all had done their duty—especially poor Jorns. Beall found Creed a different kind of man than he was used to in western Maryland. Honest and trustworthy but with a more cavalier style, and flair for the right word but also for the right action. Despite the hardships ahead, Simon Beall now had confidence: in the cause; in the men; in his leader; and in himself.

When he saw most had finished eating, he spoke. "Listen up, boys. We've been through a lot in two days. More action ahead, too. The lobsters won't wait long to attack and they have the men and the cannons to smash us. But we'll give a good accounting and kill as many of them as we can. There are many grieving families in Maryland who need revenge—and we are the boys to get it for them. We've seen a lot since leaving Frederick. I just...hope...enough of the company makes it back so can rejoin the regiment. With Lieutenant Creed in command."

They murmured their assent. Most of the men from the Light Company, Maryland Continental Line were from the area around Frederick, Maryland. Lying at the foot of the Catoctin Mountain range, Frederick was a small but growing farming town in Maryland's central panhandle. An area of small yeoman farms rather than large plantations; it was the part of Maryland that prized freedom, not chattel slavery. Moreover, it was the gateway to the western frontier. Trappers, tradesmen, and shopkeepers settled there, building the beginning of the new nation's east—west commerce. The region's settlers hailed from Scotland, England, Ireland, and Germany but also included some French who had come down from Canada to trade in fur pelts, and a smattering of Flemish and Dutch.

It was frontier America at its best. The people reveled in their freedom and independence. They were self reliant and self-sufficient. Most of the able-bodied men, and many women, could hunt and fish. They were adept at the musket and tomahawk. Even the town people hunted and trapped on a regular basis. The state had recruited the line companies from the plantation and maritime areas around Baltimore and Annapolis, but the Light Company of Maryland's First Continental Line Regiment came from the frontier.

The Bealls were a long established clan in Maryland. The cousins were second-generation settlers in the Catoctin region. Both had fathers and uncles who had fought there when the Indians from Ohio, Upper New York, and Canada launched their depredations during the French War some twenty years previously.

Simon Beall was an accomplished blacksmith. Aged twenty-six, he was skilled at his craft and wise beyond his years. He was literate both in the Bible and in many of the political tracts that circulated in the area. He worked his father's blacksmith shop and for all intents ran it. He had a good head for business, too. He engaged with the post dispatch serving the area and contracted for the Beall blacksmiths to service the wagons and horses that carried the post trade from Frederick to Baltimore and Annapolis. It brought in a steady flow of money, ensuring the business would prosper. Simon had joined the Continental Line out of pure patriotism. He understood, from his reading of numerous pamphlets by Thomas Paine and others, that it was the right of the Americans to be free from royal interference. Subservience to a king was nothing more than a form of slavery. Americans, and all men, had the inherent right to freedom and self-determination. He thought through this each day as he sweated and toiled in hammering out metal products over a hot fire.

Jonathan Beall, twenty–two, worked as a laborer on his family's farm. The second of two boys, he knew that he would never own the farm but he enjoyed the work and was good at it. He joined the Continental Line to serve his country, but also to make his break from working a farm that ultimately would belong to his older brother, Nathaniel. He hoped to save enough of his soldier's wages to purchase his own piece of land farther west where it was cheaper and easier to come by.

Both Beall cousins stood just about five foot eight inches, but had broad shoulders, thick trunks, and muscular forearms that evinced the hard physical labor of their lives. They were also both very skilled woodsmen, spending their free time traveling the western Alleghany Mountains in search of game or pelts as the season allowed. Now they were making their mark as soldiers and patriots, giving up a very comfortable life and a promising future in defense of such intangibles as "liberty" and the "rights of man."

Throughout the colonies, most areas were divided over what course they should take in dealing with the king. Frederick was no exception, the majority of the Bealls' family and friends going for liberty and independence from the crown. The men who volunteered to serve the cause had little idea that they would be thrust so soon into the center of the action. Moreover, they certainly had no idea that it would be so brutal, so frightening, or so uncomfortable. The boys from Maryland thought they joined an essentially local rebellion while in fact they had volunteered themselves into what was the beginning of a global conflict that would change the world forever.

Chapter 7

Brooklyn, August 28th, 1776

George Washington dipped the nib of his pen into the ink well and hurriedly scrawled his signature across a series of orders. Colonel Fitzgerald's intelligence report disturbed him and, based on that, he called a council of war to determine whether to stand and fight or retreat to New York. To hedge his bets, he had ordered that both military and civilian craft be ready should he decide to withdraw.

Washington wiped the excess ink from his long fingers, placed the stack of orders in a worn leather pouch, and handed it to an aide. "Ask the Quartermaster to ensure that each regiment distributes what food they have left and feed their men. There will be little opportunity to eat during the next two days."

Washington then looked over to Fitzgerald. "Fortunate that they have not attacked us already. Howe's caution is interesting, to say the least. He has inexplicably provided us time to take pause and prepare for the worst. Could this be a subterfuge?"

Fitzgerald was nibbling on an over-ripe peach. The sweet juice refreshed the palate but soon its sticky sweetness made the oppressive August heat seem even worse. He was a clumsy eater and, noticing that some of the pulp and juice had dribbled onto his tunic, he wiped his mouth with the edge of his sleeve.

"Based on what Creed learned from the prisoner, the British appear to be preparing for a major siege and then an assault on our works," Fitzgerald replied. "Howe is cautious, but confident. He may even be wagering that we will bring more men here from New York, not to launch a surprise attack there so much as to capture more of us here. He sees us as trapped.... I am afraid he may well be right."

Washington frowned. He was in fact very worried about the situation. He recognized that he had divided his army in the face of the enemy among and had done so twice. And he made other poor decisions that had caused their current dilemma. But he feigned a confidence that would serve him, regardless of the turn of events.

"Well, let us hope he proves overconfident and continues to give us time."

"But time for what?" Fitzgerald asked. Both men shook their heads in consternation.

The duty sergeant had rolled up the white canvas flaps of the command post tent in the hope of a breeze providing some comfort, but the stagnant air enveloped everything. Off to the southwest they could hear the occasional pop of a musket firing. Fitzgerald could see men, carts, and carriages moving back and forth to the earthworks. Washington had insisted that they constantly improve the defenses. Soldiers not at their posts were turning spades and swinging picks to add thickness to the slopes of the entrenchments, which they reinforced with stone and wood, or deepened the trenches between the forts that made up the American lines.

Washington now had many decisions to make. He needed to appoint new commanders and reorganize some units, many now at a fraction of what they had mustered that morning. Washington knew well that by any reckoning his situation was grave. The British had his army in a trap and he needed to decide on a way out.

೮೦೦೮

Jeremiah Creed woke early that morning from a fitful sleep with a nagging headache. Stress and fatigue wore on him, but he shrugged them off. The Light Company, all eight of them, were sleeping at the regiment's encampment north of Fort Greene. Creed's men were due to muster at five, have breakfast, and then receive their next assignment.

Creed nudged his noncommissioned officer. "Corporal Beall, at daylight you will need to awaken the men to eat and make ready."

Beall sat up, and was alert and ready. "Yes sir."

Creed said. "Looks like rain today so make sure they take so whatever cover they have."

"And where are you off to, Lieutenant?"

"To see Major Gist. Many from the regiment have straggled in over the lines. He is reorganizing the companies, filling some out and combining others. I hope to make sure we are not merged into a line unit."

"Would they really do that?" Beall asked incredulously.

In the three months that he had served under Creed, he had become a believer in the light infantry and in what they could accomplish. Beall had assumed duties as Company Sergeant after Sergeant Hudson came down with fever during the march north from Maryland. Beall took to it naturally. He was a Patriot volunteer, but he was beginning to enjoy the military life, especially the specialized work of the light infantry.

Creed stared at him with intensity. "When times are complicated, men often seek simple solutions. The simple disposition for the Light Company is to use its remaining soldiers as replacements for other weakened units. I will try to avoid that, and get us reinforced to at least a half strength company."

Creed's face showed he was not very confident of success.

Beall shook his head in disbelief. "That's officer business. Gives me a headache, but good luck, sir."

It was still dark, with a faint glimmer of light to the east. Creed figured he had an hour to sun up. At headquarters, he discovered Gist already up and drinking coffee. Gist offered him a cup. Creed preferred tea but gladly accepted the coffee and piece of Gist's stale biscuit.

Creed took a bite of biscuit and grimaced at its rock-hard texture. "Sir, I am here to discuss the future of the Light Company."

Gist took another swallow and nodded. "We are restructuring the remnants of the regiment, at least until replacements arrive..."

Creed interrupted, "I think it inadvisable to break up my command and..."

Gist cut him off. "What in Hades gave you the idea that we would do any such thing? You shall remain the Light Company, First Maryland Continental Line, but unfortunately at the strength you have."

Creed fought to hide is delight. "That is certainly more acceptable than the alternative I had envisaged. Thank-you, sir."

Gist looked at Creed ruefully. "I am giving you eight more privates from head-quarters. They are inexperienced, but good, solid men. Only wish I could give you more."

Creed felt great relief he felt that his command would stay intact. "These will do nicely, sir. I assume such men as these new men are handpicked? "

Gist smiled wryly. "On the contrary. These men were selected at random to serve in the regimental headquarters. You must integrate them into your company as best you can. It is all I could do for you, Jeremiah. These are hard times for the regiment. Colonel Smallwood is distraught from missing our first battle. Now he hardly has a regiment left to command."

"I appreciate the replacements, sir. I'll do my utmost to make proper light infantry of them," Creed replied.

ஐௐ

Dawn broke with a bright red streak on the horizon. Then the sky slowly dark-ened and by mid-morning had become overcast, with a light breeze beginning to stir. Creed assembled the old and new members of his Light Company. As with so many armies, these new men had been randomly plucked from the fighting units to perform administrative functions such as clerks, orderlies, sentries, or couriers. But they were neither happy nor proud to have missed the big fight.

Creed spoke with confidence. "Major Gist has placed you under my com-mand, so as far as I am concerned you are now members of the Light Company.

Corporal Beall here is our acting Company Sergeant. Treat all his commands as if they were my own. I have asked Corporal Beall to walk you through some of the basics of light infantry tactics. You will not be experts, of course, but we hope you can adapt quickly as our survival, and yours, depends on it."

Simon Beall stepped forward, "I will inspect all of you new boys at noon. I will also inspect the old members as well."

He grinned at the men, who groaned at his words. "I want your leather brushed, muskets cleaned and oiled, bayonets sharpened, and water bottles filled. I will also inspect your flints, ball, and powder. Each man should have at least twenty rounds and dry powder. Finally, you will be clean-shaven and have your hair tied back in a tight queue, no powder. Any questions?"

No one spoke. Beall appeared formidable and competent. That put them at ease.

Beall nodded. "Very well then, you are dismissed."

Creed himself went back to roll up his lined canvass mantle. It performed triple duty as overcoat, blanket and rain coat. With the weather changing he thought he might need it. He then washed, shaved and inspected his own kit. Creed was traveling light: his French-made pistols and sabers were with his horse back in New York. He cleaned the Jaeger rifle taken from the unfortunate Hessian and sharpened its sword-bayonet. He examined the sword carefully. The straight blade was more than double the length of the typical seventeen-inch musket bayonet and had the feel of a short saber in the hand, yet it extended the thrusting reach of the shorter hunting rifle to almost that of the typical musket with bayonet. The rifle had plenty of cloth patches but he was down to a handful of rounds. Fortunately, it had a bullet mold built into the stock so he was able to take some of his musket balls from his haversack, melt them down, and in half an hour he had recast thirty rounds. He hoped that he would need no more to get through the next few days. By the time he was done, a very light rain had begun to fall and the wind picked up a bit.

Major Gist appeared unexpectedly.

Creed stood up and saluted. "Sir, the new men are preparing their arms and equipment for an inspection at noon."

Gist pursed his lips. "That is all very well, Jeremiah. However, I am here on a different matter. It seems that you have been summoned to a meeting with General Washington."

Creed pointed a thumb at his own chest in surprise. "I, sir? Are you certain?"

Gist nodded. "Yes, a courier from headquarters just informed me. You must proceed immediately. I am to join you, it seems."

಄ಐ

Gist and Creed spoke little as they walked the mile back to Brooklyn and army headquarters. They observed the hubbub of frantic military activity all around them, each wondering why they had been summoned. Soon they could see the gabled Dutch houses in the town less than a mile off.

At length, Creed turned and asked Gist the question that gnawed at him. "Sir, do you suppose we are summoned to a court-martial?"

Gist looked astonished. "Court martial? For what? Fighting our way through the British army? I should think not."

Creed cocked his head and pondered Gist's reply. "Perhaps so, but we did leave Lord Stirling and the others at a critical time. If that is the case, I will take full responsibility. I all but forced you to come with us."

The road into Brooklyn was narrow and already spongy with mud from the rain. Creed and Gist had to make their way through small groups of soldiers trudging along the road in both directions. Many heading back toward the ferry were wounded or sick. There seemed to be so many wounded.

The previous day's combat was the most violent and bloody that the North American continent had ever seen. Despite the setback, it seemed as if the army had accepted hardship and setback, even defeat—as the price of freedom. Most of Creed's company had disappeared in the maelstrom. He might never learn their fate. Moreover, Gist lost more than half the regiment in the space of a few hours, yet was walking with him to this war council almost as though it were a stroll in the park. What kind of people were these Americans, Creed asked himself?

A company of Pennsylvanians marched past them toward the front. They moved on stoically despite the previous day's disaster. He wondered if he could measure up. He wanted to think he could. After all, was he not now one of them? The previous day's slaughter changed everything for him. Before the fighting at the passes, Jeremiah Creed was an Irishman, living in America, but today he was an American who had left Ireland. He now knew the difference and the thought of it suddenly filled him with a sense of well being, and of responsibility. He was born and bred Irish, everyone is born and bred to something—but he had willed himself an American.

Brooklyn was really just a small farm village, painted in bright colors with neat shutters and a mix of thatched and wood-shingled roofs. General Washington's command tent was in a small orchard near the Old Dutch Church. The church's tall white steeple dominated the town with its simple cross sitting at the top. To Creed, it seemed nothing like the impressive churches and cathedrals he had seen in Europe. The French churches were especially different from these simple places of worship. Yet he found the simplicity of the American churches refreshing and in their own way, inspiring. A sense of power and awe suddenly overcame him. He realized now that he stood in the center of great events, both for his new country, and indeed the world. He said a silent prayer before the church and then followed Gist into the headquarters tent. Creed now knew that this summons was not about punishment, rather, something daunting and important was about to be thrust on him.

Chapter 8

Washington's Headquarters, Brooklyn, August 28th, 1776

The rainfall increased as they drew closer to Brooklyn. Still, it pelted them lightly and felt refreshing after the previous day's oppressive heat and humidity. Washington's command post pulsed with activity as his orderlies and aides busied themselves trying to organize the gaggle of field-grade officers and generals gathered to discuss the way ahead. Creed was astounded to be part of all this. As a light company commander, he was at the lower end of the military chain—at the tip of the spear. His role, as a cog in the machinery of war, was to lead small groups of men in the face of the enemy. Now he could observe how senior officers made the big decisions that sent men to death or glory.

One of Washington's aides, Captain Charles Pickering, ensured each officer sat at his appointed place—either at the table, or seated on a box or carton placed around the tent. Some, such as Creed, had to stand, making it easier to see the map which Fitzgerald had spread across the table in front of Washington.

Fitzgerald was already talking to the group seated round the table. "The British are situated just opposite our positions, perhaps a half mile away," the colonel said. "The wind and tides have kept the British fleet out of the East River. This has stalled their attempt to envelop us from the sea, at least for a while. I am not sure how long this will last but fortune favors us for now."

"When do you anticipate they will attack?" Washington asked. His calm voice and demeanor cloaked the crisis he faced.

"That, sir, is yet unclear, perhaps when the weather breaks, perhaps while it intensifies."

"So you tell me...nothing." Washington stated in a controlled but suddenly more agitated voice.

"Precisely," replied Fitzgerald, not reacting to the commander-in-chief's emotion. "My point being for the next thirty-six hours the advantage is his. He expects us to stand fast in our works, leaving the initiative to him. Our best course of action is to exploit that notion."

"In what way?" Washington asked, this time in a calmer voice.

"I leave that discussion and the decision to you and your field commanders, sir. The intelligence officer who taints his information with suggestions of actions and counter actions is no longer an impartial intelligence officer, but a second rate operations officer."

"True enough," Washington answered with a nod. He looked slowly and deliberately into the faces around him, "Does anyone have thoughts on this?"

Many did. They went around the tent, several times. There was a heated debate but the group, though divided in opinion, wanted to make a stand right there in Brooklyn. Creed was most interested in Mordecai Gist's thoughts; the regiment still had fight in it. Creed thought for sure he would recommend the army make a stand now. However, Gist kept silent.

A stout colonel from a Pennsylvania regiment spoke in a low and deliberate voice. The wind was picking up a bit and the tent flaps were snapping in a slow cadence as he spoke. "Yesterday, my regiment took part in the bloodiest day this continent has ever seen. We stood firm against some of the finest professionals in the world, surrounded and outnumbered tenfold. Half my command is now gone with many dead or dying. However, many of the enemy are also gone—we inflicted casualties upon them and I hazard they know now that free men fighting for their country as well as their liberty are equal to them in a fair fight. Our defenses here are prudent and our flanks are secure. If he besieges us, we might wear him down. If he assaults us, we will bloody him as never before. We could tie him up for the rest of the summer, giving us time to reinforce and fortify New York and the main land."

He cleared his throat for he was visibly shaking. He took a sip of wine from the small glass that had been served to each officer seated around the table.

Another colonel, this time from a Massachusetts regiment, spoke up. "Yet the British have much at stake here, too. Do they risk all in a quick victory or defeat... or grind us down?"

An officer from New York spoke. "They have freedom of movement through a powerful navy, freedom of action through a professional and disciplined army, and the resources of a global empire from which to sustain pressure on us. I dare say they will attack us, but not until they have every gun in its place and the weather favors naval action to our rear. If we win a victory against the British army to our front, we risk defeat from the British navy to our rear. From such a defeat there would be no recourse but annihilation or surrender."

Creed looked at Washington's face for some sign of how he was taking all this, but his visage was impassive.

General Israel Putnam now spoke, "Gentlemen, I have thought long and hard upon the nature of this enterprise. Whether it is for our rights as Englishmen we fight, or the creation of a free nation, our best hope of unity and survival is the Continental Army and its leader, General Washington. The men follow him; officers respect him; and it the Congress heeds him. The survival of this army and its commander means the enterprise continues. Destroy either, and the nation is doomed, and the rights of free men will be set back a hundred years. For those reasons, I reluctantly vote to vacate our position and prepare defenses in New York. If need be, we can repair to other defensible terrain so we can continue to fight and pray that Providence and the will of the people will triumph over a despotic king and his mercenaries."

A barrage of murmurs erupted. Creed, and most others in the tent were astonished at the candor and complexity of thought Putnam had displayed. He essentially and succinctly summed up a strategic vision that few could have entertained.

General Washington hushed the assembly just as succinctly. "I need more information and more time to decide. Another council of war shall meet tomorrow. Meanwhile, prepare your units for any eventuality. General Howe surprised us once; he may endeavor to do so again."

�

Through tent the flaps, Creed noticed a stone-faced private from Washington's personal guard. The harsh-looking young man stood sentry in front of the tent with his well-oiled musket held at parade rest. As Creed was exiting through the flap with Gist, Fitzgerald grasped his forearm and signaled him to remain, but Gist to leave. After the tent cleared, Washington motioned to Pickering and Scovel, who secured the flaps and left.

Washington poured each of them the last of his flagon of wine. "Lieutenant Creed, I want to personally thank you for your gallant efforts at Gowanus."

Creed blushed uncomfortably.

Washington raised his glass and nodded his head in salutation. "I am as yet unsure what action to take."

Creed startled and for a moment, the idea of court-martial returned.

Washington continued. "So I am compelled to call on your services once again, Mister Creed."

Creed nodded nonchalantly but he was in fact stunned and confused. "The Maryland Line is at your disposal, sir. I am sure Colonel Smallwood and Major Gist eagerly await your instructions."

"The efforts of you men from Maryland are noteworthy, Lieutenant. But what remains of your regiment will not go into the line, at least not all of it just now."

Washington looked at Colonel Fitzgerald, then at Creed. Creed became more surprised and confused.

"It is not what you suspect," said Fitzgerald, with an amused look.

Washington smiled. The sober-minded general had a dry sense of humor despite the adversity he faced day in and day out. "I need a strong and tested unit to cover the ferry during the movement across, should that be our course. Chaos and panic often accompany such actions, particularly at night and most particularly in the face of the enemy. Already individual soldiers and small groups of men are deserting the line to make their way back to New York. Solid and confident troops acting as both provosts and reserves will provide some sanction against such exigencies."

"I am sure the First Maryland is honored to have your trust and confidence, sir."

Fitzgerald broke in. "There is one minor detail. We, uhumh, I, would like to borrow your Light Company to be exact."

"Borrow? I do not understand, sir." Creed replied.

"To perform a special mission—a hazardous mission. Critical to the success of this most risky enterprise. Lieutenant Creed, you are just the man for this special operation."

Fitzgerald tried to seem apologetic but he was not very successful.

Creed's faced reddened and it was not from the wine. "I entered this war to lead men in battle, sir. As part of a fine regiment. I have neither the skill nor the interest for detached action. My place is with my regiment."

Washington interjected. "All well and good, but it must be done. Your Light Company is detached from the First Maryland Continental Line, effective immediately. You, Lieutenant Creed, will receive no written orders. My aides are even now informing Major Gist of this—detaching your command and requesting his complete cooperation with your mission. And remember, this must be kept strictly confidential."

Creed's brow furled in consternation, but he accepted his duty. "I understand sir. Strictly confidential."

Washington's face softened. "We'll return your company to the Maryland Line soon enough. We just need you now."

Fitzgerald turned again to the map of the New York area. It showed roughly where the American entrenchments ran from Wallabout Bay to the Gowanus. Diamond shaped markings indicated each of the forts anchoring the line. Opposite the entrenchments were several oblongs, each with a question mark next to it. These indicated suspected British positions. Each oblong had a name alongside it: Grant, Von Heister, and Clinton.

"Each of these enemy formations is now in possession of some artillery, we believe." Fitzgerald used the plural term "we" while he, in fact, was the "we." Fitzgerald's intelligence consisted mostly of reports from line units, based on observations from sentries or the occasional patrol. He also consulted with General Washington, who considered somewhat of an authority on intelligence,

mapping, and reconnaissance based on his experience as a surveyor and his military experience on the frontier during the war with France and the Indians.

Fitzgerald continued, "We are as yet unsure whether General Howe will
attempt a coup de main, a quick thrust against some point in our lines, or an all
out assault along our entire line. Or whether he will invest our positions with
parallel trenches and blast us with artillery until we surrender. If he is attempting
the former, we need to know how quickly we may expect an assault, as an assault
while the army attempts to cross the river would lead to complete disaster. It
could lead to its total destruction. "

"And if it is the latter, sir?" Creed asked.

"If it is the latter, then the question is how quickly he can invest us, as well
as the location of his artillery batteries. Your mission, Lieutenant Creed, is two-
fold. Make diversionary probes against the British in such a way as to convince
them we are defending these lines indefinitely; and take the measure of British
dispositions."

Fitzgerald looked at Washington, then back at Creed. "We must know if an
assault on our lines is imminent."

Washington nodded, "The British may try something totally unexpected such
as a movement by sea to take New York while our forces are divided. Any information you can discover to confirm or refute this possibility would also be critical to our next actions."

They spent another thirty minutes going over details such as where he should
depart from and return to, the signals to use, and of course, the passwords to get
through the American lines. This was most critical as many operations failed
because of the confusion facing the sentries, guards, and pickets. The password
for that evening was already with the field commanders: "Liberty."

On his way back to his unit Creed he began to think of various courses of
action he should now take. He knew this would be risky work for men who had
already risked much.

಼ೞ

Jonathan Beall was finishing a short letter to his parents back in Maryland.
The family was unusually literate for a frontier family and all the Bealls were
keen readers and writers. The page was smeared as the low quality ink he used
was splotched by the rain that worked its way through his make-shift shelter. He
thought of quitting, but it had been several weeks since he posted his last letter.
He wanted to ensure that they knew both cousins were alive and still fighting.

Beall was known around Frederick for his quiet, forthright manner. He was
seen as was a sympathetic and trustworthy young man with an inquisitive mind
and mild demeanor. He joined the cause to strike a blow for his country and to

do his duty. Like most of the others, Beall never thought that the war would take him so far from home, not for so long. Now he stoically bore the hardships, made bearable by the presence of his cousin and so many familiar faces from home, men who had joined for similar reasons.

Brooklyn
28 August 1776

...And so a terrible battle was fought, perhaps lost, but the men from Maryland fought bravely and gave the British a licking as well. I hope never again to partake in such slaughter as I have witnessed but I assure you that if I do I will look after my cousin and do my duty to my country. I can promise no further. God bless both of you. Pray for us here in New York and pray for our just and glorious cause.

Your loving and obedient son,
Jonathan

Beall placed the nib and the ink container into his breast pocket and folded the paper neatly, placing it into the same pocket. He hoped to post it when they arrived back in New York.

Just as he finished, his cousin Simon called the company together. "Lieutenant Creed is back with new orders for us. Each of you is to prepare your weapons and twenty rounds. If this infernal rain continues, we might not even require that. Fill your water bottles. Sharpen and oil your bayonets. Each man will draw four biscuits; that must last through tomorrow. I will inspect each of you and your kit before we leave."

The men went to work. The rain had picked up but they were able to find a large makeshift lean-to that another unit had abandoned. That kept most of the rain from drenching everything.

Creed refused to have an orderly; he checked his own gear. He checked his ammunition and powder. He dried off his bayonet sword, rubbed it with oil and placed it in its scabbard. He then worked through the plan again. The company, now totaling sixteen, would pass through the lines of a Connecticut regiment near Fort Greene where its Adjutant, a Lieutenant Tallmadge, would escort them through. They would patrol along the British lines, executing probes at three locations. The first objective was the road junction just south of Fort Box, the southern most American fort. The second objective was east of Fort Putnam, on the other side of the defenses, more than a mile distant. The final objective was the intersection of the Jamaica and Flatbush Roads. Fort Greene would be their reentry point. At each objective, they would observe British activity and make a quick probe on the British pickets in order to convince them that the Americans were there to stay. Creed reckoned each phase would take about two hours, six hours in all. He would depart at nine-thirty at night. He hoped the wind, rain and clouds would make it dark enough for them to close on the British without being observed. Otherwise the mission was doomed.

He gave Simon Beall final instructions, "Once the men have prepared their arms and have eaten give them some rest, for it will be a long night."

Beall replied. "Should you not rest too, sir?"

Creed shook his head. "No time. I am going forward to the lines to arrange our passage. The passing through lines at night is the most dangerous endeavor in warfare."

Chapter 9

British Headquarters, Long Island, August 28th 1776

General William Howe had already dashed off his first report of the battle. It would soon be making its way across the Atlantic in a frigate. Howe thought it essential to ensure his account of things was the first to reach London, as he knew well that he had many detractors, not the least of whom were his subordinate generals. His men had fought brilliantly, as he knew they would. Fortunately, for him, the rebels had not. Yes, there was some fierce resistance for a while but mostly it was butcher's work. He would need to ensure that his officers maintained better control of the men. Scores of wounded and surrendering rebels had been beaten and bayoneted to death. According to reports, the Hessians did most of the bayoneting. The German troops had a special bloodlust, but the Scots did their share as well.

Still, it was a pretty good day's work, a feint against their front, capped off by a brilliant flank march to cut off the entire force from their base. Major Drummond of the dragoons had found a spy willing to show him a way around the rebels. Howe planned to mark him for special recognition. In Howe's estimation, this would to go down as one of the greatest maneuvers in military history at least since Wolfe scaled the Heights of Abraham and humbugged that most unfortunate Frenchman Montcalm.

Howe held a brief meeting with his commanders and took reports on their accomplishments and losses. The estimates were perhaps 400 rebels killed and almost 1500 wounded, compared with British losses of fewer than four hundred. Most of the British casualties came in the desperate and failed attempt by those Maryland troops to break through Cornwallis' men. Howe opined that even a wounded animal, when cornered, can suddenly strike out desperately and cause grave injury. For that reason, he decided over the objections of his subordinates to be very deliberate in his next moves. He would wait out the weather, move his fleet to the East River, and enfilade the Americans on the Brooklyn Heights from the rear. In the meantime, he would begin to invest the American lines with siege works, maneuvering his guns into forward prepared positions. Then the rebels would catch hellfire from two sides, the Royal Navy's broadsides and the Royal Field Artillery's precision fire. Mr. Washington would soon surrender to him with negligible British casualties. Why, they would beg to become his prisoners! He chuckled to himself and poured a large goblet of claret.

৪০৩

Lieutenant Benjamin Tallmadge greeted Creed politely and then read the short note signed by Washington.

To officers concerned,

"Lieutenant Jeremiah Creed is acting on my personal orders. All who read this are to cooperate fully with him and render such assistance as may be required for the success of his mission."

Signed,
G. Washington

Like Creed, Tallmadge was in his early twenties. He stood a bit shorter than Creed and had a medium build, with wispy chestnut hair and kind, dark, intelligent eyes. Little more than a month earlier, he had been a Yale graduate serving as a schoolmaster in Wethersfield, Connecticut, but now he was Adjutant of the First Connecticut Continental Line regiment under the command of Colonel John Chester.

Tallmadge spoke politely. "Lieutenant Creed, your mission must be of great importance. I wish I could go with you, as I have extensive knowledge of the terrain before our lines. I made a point to reconnoiter on horseback for more than a mile in each direction and before the British arrived as far as the Flatbush crossroads. So let us spend a few minutes and perhaps I can sketch you a modest map of the area."

Creed thanked him and for the next twenty minutes, Tallmadge sketched from memory a map showing the basic terrain features: larger hills, wooded areas, creeks, and farms. He also marked where he suspected from his personal observation the British lines to be. Tallmadge, as with most of the American officers, had no prior military training; most of his decisions and actions comprised nothing more than good common sense. Creed added his own thoughts as well. The key was to mark the terrain near the exact spot in the American lines where he and his men would return. Tallmadge volunteered to meet them at that spot one hour before dawn. He would have a small lantern lit and would cover it with his cloak and uncover it every ten minutes for no more than fifteen seconds. This would guide them back to American lines.

When they finished, Creed folded the precious map and placed in his vest pocket. "I shall return here in four hours with the company. Once it is dark enough, we will advance through your lines. You have been a tremendous help, Lieutenant Tallmadge."

"The honor and the pleasure are all mine, Mister Creed. Word of your men's gallantry yesterday has spread throughout the camp. It is a privilege to serve with men as brave and daring as you bold Marylanders. Yesterday was a grim day of work for this army but none had grimmer work than you."

Suddenly, the enormity of what he and the Marylanders had faced over the past twelve hours hit Creed. He was so busy doing the immediate things needed to survive the awfulness of the fight that he hardly reflected on the magnitude of their loss. The promise he made when they first mustered in Frederick had become a sham in the course of a half day of combat. The fact that he led them with cool professionalism, brought as many through as any man could, and inflicted casualties on the enemy, offered little compensation. He almost came to tears, but fought them with the wipe of a dirty sleeve across his brow.

"Yes, our men fought well under trying circumstances. Nevertheless, they did so not because of me but because of their discipline and commitment to the cause. The determination of a few good men is what brings success, not political slogans and platitudes. I fear I did not fully live up to their trust."

Tallmadge's face darkened. "Any ambivalence I felt toward our cause was erased by the savagery displayed by our enemies. Stragglers reported the whole-sale slaughter of men attempting to surrender, even the wounded. You are right Creed; determination is the key to our success. We must remain undaunted and never give up this fight. To do so would betray the fallen, and honor the butchers. However, the Cause must have leaders to succeed. From what I have heard, you demonstrated the kind of leadership we need. I hope that when the time comes that I show one measure of your leadership."

Creed flushed at the compliment. "Thank you for the kind words, sir."

He saluted with a slight forward bend at the hips and departed.

When Creed arrived at the company, his men were sleeping under the primitive lean-to, made from tree bark and scraps of wood, which they had commandeered. They had also made a small one for Creed using his haversack and blanket. Exhausted, he threw himself into it and soon fell asleep.

৪০০৪

A soft rapping on the frame of the makeshift shelter awakened Creed. One of his new men, Private Elias Parker, stood over him. Parker was a dark, burly man of twenty-seven. Over six feet tall, he was a, a full inch taller than Creed, with broad shoulders and powerful arms. Parker claimed to be one-quarter Indian, although he never mentioned the name of his tribe. In the few months since he came to America, Creed had had minimal contact with the indigenous population. Few Indians remained near Frederick but the settlers there still spoke in both awe and revulsion of them because of the savage fighting during the French and Indian War.

Parker smiled broadly. "Sir, it is after seven. The company is up, and ready. We are having a last mug of coffee and hard biscuit. Please have some."

Parker owned a fishing boat in Annapolis, although he was raised in St Mary's, a town further down Maryland's eastern shore that once served as the colony's capital. As with most men of the sea, he did not waste words, preferring his conversations direct and succinct. Parker had a canny sense of things and the experiences, and hardships that he endured as sailor and fisherman made him resourceful and courageous.

He had joined the Continental Army out of a quiet, unspoken patriotism, and a need to show that a man had a responsibility to defend freedom. Several months earlier, emotion-racked, he turned his boat over to his partner and kissed his wife and daughter good-bye. His hopes for a speedy return to them were soon dashed. Now time seemed to stand still.

Creed smiled gratefully and rubbed his eyes, "You are a kind and wise bene-factor, Private Parker. Normally I prefer tea to coffee but anything hot before a fight, eh?"

Sleep had enabled Creed to shake the morose mood that affected him after his conversation with Tallmadge. He gulped downed his biscuit and coffee,–he was a notoriously fast eater, a bad habit he had since youth, but then again a good habit in times of combat. He reckoned he should have the company at the lines in an hour. After that, it was just a matter of waiting for darkness to shroud the battlefield.

‎⁩⁫

Mud covered everything. A light rain, sometimes only a fine mist, sprayed down on the weary men; it had sprayed constantly for several hours. By now the Americans' modest defense works were rain soaked. Their trenches became canals and the earthen berms a morass.

Creed signaled to Tallmadge and motioned the patrol forward of the trenches. His original few wore the light infantry hunting frocks. However, his new men wore the dark blue continental surcoat, typical dress of the line companies from whence they came. Speed and stealth were critical. He wanted them as unen-cumbered as possible. They left water bottles, overcoats, and blankets behind, carrying only musket and bayonet, plus a knife or tomahawk.

Creed and Jonathan Beall carried the German hunting rifle and sword-bayo-net. Weapons were loaded and firing hammers locked and covered with pieces of oilcloth to keep the powder dry. They had fixed bayonets–they would use cold steel first. Creed ordered that nobody fire without his approval. To assist their departure, Tallmadge had a passage cleared through an abatis—a tangle of tree trunks and sharpened limbs—blocking the trail. The clouds, rain and mist had indeed darkened the sky and reduced visibility to about twenty yards. That would provide just enough darkness to obscure them from British sentries, or so Creed hoped.

They made their way forward, moving slowly in a diagonal to the right. Creed kept the men in single file to facilitate control and direction. The British lines were a mile away but their pickets likely half that distance. To his dismay, they spotted the first British picket just three hundred yards from the American lines. The British lines were closer than he thought.

Creed whispered to Simon Beall, directly behind him in the formation. "Have your men set up to the right. I shall move into the brush with the other file and probe deeper. We must determine where the British lines begin and if possible, what those men are doing this far forward."

Beall asked. "Could this be the advance guard of another attack?"

Creed replied. "I hope not. We have experienced one too many such surprises already."

The corporal nodded and moved his men into the woods. He had come to trust his officer implicitly.

As they moved into the brush, the inexperience of the new men soon became evident. They struggled through the wet branches and kicked up stray roots and stones. Creed feared this would alert the British so he halted a moment to take stock of the situation. Despite the wind and rain he could hear the British pickets. At first, he suspected a trap. Then he realized that the British, thinking that it was over for the rebels, had grown careless. Perhaps careless enough to give his patrol the advantage.

His file moved on again, quietly. Jonathan Beall took up the rear. Privates Smith and Johnson were from the Light Company as well but the other four men were not. One of them was Parker, who stayed just behind Creed. The Marylanders had successfully made their way around the British but something did not seem right to Creed. There were six British, and they were busy walking and marking something that was indistinguishable in the darkness.

Creed signaled to Parker and the two moved forward in a low crouch, just under the lowest branches of the trees. When they got within thirty yards, they dropped to their knees and high-crawled through the thick grass. The brush was wet and the ground was soggy, making the going difficult. A wet branch snapped back and hit Parker's face. For a moment he wondered why he joined the rebellion's land forces instead of the navy, but he soon shrugged off his doubts and focused on the mission. No matter how he got himself in with this small band of men and their hopeless mission, he was determined to be part of it.

They found a vantage point in a small stand of trees twenty yards out, where they could make out the uniforms of the men.

Creed was stunned at what he saw. "My God, they are not pickets but Royal Engineers!

Parker whispered. "How can you tell?"

"Blue uniforms, not red. And see what they are about. Marking the area—surveying. Two are officers, the others sergeants. "

Parker shook his head. As a seaman, he knew the jargon of sailors, but army talk was strange and new to him. They could hear the British voices, mostly cursing at the wind and rain. One was busy trying to keep a lantern lit and had it covered with a cloak to screen the flickering light from any would-be observers. Creed took a few minutes to compose his thoughts and decide what to do next. The situation had changed. Something unusual was afoot.

Creed whispered, "Let's see if your eyes work as well in darkness as they say. Go back and tell Jonathan Beall to bring up his file. Then find Corporal Beall and return here with his file."

Parker wiped the water from his hat brim. "Aye, sir."

Minutes later, Creed huddled the group to plan the next move, the rain and wind muffling his voice as they stood around him in an apple orchard. The surreal scent of the trees added a strange backdrop to this impromptu conversation in the face of the enemy.

"Lads, a bit more than 100 yards from here there is a group of engineers surveying the area around the trail."

Then he pointed toward the other side of the orchard. "I am guessing that they have some sort of survey plan on them. I aim to attack them and take that plan. This has no small risk, but I am going to stake this mission on it. "

The men looked at each other. They wondered what this meant, not for the mission, but for their ultimate survival. Creed saw their angst but was determined to proceed.

Simon Beall also saw the men's unease and spoke. "Just tell us what you need sir. The boys are itching to get at the bastards."

The truth was that most were not. However, Beall's bravado steeled them just enough.

Creed smiled. "I thought no less. We will rush the engineers from two sides. No firing unless they fire first. No prisoners either—there is never quarter for sappers or engineers. However, we must dispatch them quickly...quietly. They must have a map, perhaps a schematic or something that will prove useful to our leaders. Corporal Beall, your squad will cross the orchard and move into striking position. I shall take the other squad and circle around the British. Private Beall will stay well to the back of our line and provide security in case there is a returning party of British. I shall approach them as if we are a relief party coming from the British lines and hope get into bayonet range before they discover the trick."

Creed's men were stunned. It was a bold plan, almost unthinkable. The old members of the Light Company nodded. They already had a taste of this officer's boldness, but the others had not. Only hours ago most of them were clerks and orderlies. Now they faced death among the British under most trying conditions. Creed's men were quickly discovering that warfare has little to do with the field of battle, and much to do with those things that take place before and after battle. However, they had no time to dwell on it.

The group moved out quickly and silently with the rain muffling the sound of their boots slogging through mud or their bodies snapping twigs and breaking tree branches. Soon, they were all in position.

Creed summoned two of his new men who wore continental blue. "Let me switch coats with one of you lads—in the dark, your blue continentals will give me the appearance of a British engineer. I will do all the talking. Be sure you stay right behind me. In this darkness we just need to confuse them for a few seconds before we strike."

Parker and Creed exchanged jackets. They both had their hats placed squarely on their heads, British style, rather than the jauntier slouch of American headgear.

Creed smiled suddenly and whispered with a perfect British accent, "Alright lads—it is time to take the stage..."

If any of the men saw the humor in it they did not show it. They moved forward resolutely, weapons on their shoulders as if they were in a route march. The rain pelted the mud puddles as they walked forward. With the wind picking up, the British survey party did not notice them until they were almost five yards distant.

At that point, one of the engineers looked up at them and spoke. "Bit too soon to be bringing work crews up here, ain't it? Eager to get yerselves bleedin' soaked?"

In his excellent British accent, Creed replied, "Sorry to be such trouble to you, mate, but the colonel suggests that you get things here moving more quickly. We do not have all night, you know."

Creed saw Simon Beall and his men approaching from behind the British, whose attention had now turned exclusively to Creed. The Americans struck before the engineers realized this was no work crew. Creed stepped up to the first engineer, a broad shouldered sergeant, and snapped his rifle's butt into his jaw, sending him crashing into a pool of cold mud.

One of the sergeants cursed. "What the bloody hell do you...they're rebels!"

The other engineers now rushed at Creed, who stepped aside as Parker and the others lowered their muskets and charged the engineers head-on with fixed bayonets. Simon Beall's men closed from behind and in less than a minute the unfortunate engineers lay dead or dying in the deep puddles of mud. It was a slaughter, but Creed's men were desperate and determined. The British had bayoneted many Americans in the previous day's fighting and this was, in part, pay back.

A search of their pockets yielded only personal items. Frustrated, Creed ordered his men to search the area. The dark, rain and wind, made it a daunting task. They worked their way around the rocks and bushes as the weather whipped at them from all sides.

Finally, Parker called out. "Sir, take a look at this!"

Parker found that that the engineers' lantern was sitting on a crate that contained a hard leather valise with two straps and buckles. Creed opened it. To his delight, there were several maps of the area, engineering charts, and plans. After a cursory review, he placed them back in the valise and slung it over his shoulder.

The contents of the valise had changed the plans for the night's events. From a quick glance at the documents, he saw that the British were preparing siege works. That meant there would be no immediate assault, only a deliberate bombardment and investment. Creed knew he had to get the valise back to the American lines right away.

Creed spoke crisply. "Our plans have changed, lads. We have the information His Excellency needs. Now we must get it to him as expeditiously as possible. Let us depart before 'the colonel' really does send a work crew."

Creed smiled but his men found no humor in the night's work. They retraced their way, focused on speed, not stealth and snapping through branches, high grass and bush. Jonathan Beall led, followed by Parker. Creed walked with Simon Beall. As they moved along, Creed reconsidered his plans. He decided to continue on to the next objective and confirm the extent of the British advance. However, he would send Simon Beall back to Tallmadge with the valise, for he knew Fitzgerald needed to see its contents as quickly as possible. And by proceeding to the next objective he might draw any British attention away from Beall. A good plan but there was one small complication.....

ᏸᎧᏣ

Shots rang out from the direction of the American defense works a quarter mile to their front. Creed rushed forward through the dark rainy woods and reached a large open field broken by the occasional stand of crab apple trees. He knelt behind one where Simon Beall soon joined him.

Creed grabbed Beall's shoulder. "A British patrol, straight across this field - not much more than a hundred yards away."

Beall looked at him. "Has the British attack begun?"

Creed smiled. "No, the British rarely attack at night and never in the rain. They are attempting to draw fire from our lads manning the defenses. Listen."

Individual pop-pops pierced the windy night air and flashes from a score of muskets cut the darkness. Teams of redcoats had fanned out along a quarter mile of the front and were now sniping at the Americans.

Beall nodded. "I see, sir. What should we do?"

Creed replied. "We will move forward carefully in two files and go right at them with the bayonet—the lads are becoming quite good at it."

He grinned. This time Simon Beall grinned back. Despite the desperate situation, Creed's wry humor was building confidence in Beall and the other men.

They moved out at a fast walk. The rain had tapered to an occasional drizzle and the wind now blew in light gusts. It was completely dark. They could only hope that stray rounds from the American lines would not catch any of them. When they reached the place where the British troops should have been, the British had gone.

After a while, the firing from the American lines ceased. Creed signaled Simon Beall over. "They were indeed probing. Likely they are quite a ways from here by now."

Beall seemed disappointed. "Should we not pursue them, we are light infantry and..."

Creed raised his hand. "Not this time. Tis only a quarter mile to our return point. Take the three men from your squad. Go quietly until you get within range of our lines. Then make as much noise as you can—you must clearly show them that you are not another British probe!"

"Beggin' your pardon Lieutenant, but how in damnation do we do that?" Simon Beall rarely raised his voice or swore, but he was clearly worried.

Creed smiled. "Why, you sing! Sing Yankee Doodle! Sing it as loudly as you have ever sung. Sing as if your life depends on it, for it may well."

Simon Beall nodded grimly. "Very well, sir. Sing we shall..."

Creed grabbed his shoulder in reassurance. "I know you can do this, Corporal. The army's fate is in your hands. But take great care. Crossing the lines is a most dangerous proposition, especially at night."

Simon Beall looked at his cousin. "Stay safe, Jonathan. And take care of our lieutenant."

Jonathan choked and lamely nodded. "Good luck, Simon."

The sturdy corporal removed his hunting jacket and affixed it to the end of his musket in the fashion of a flag. He swung the valise over his shoulder. He motioned to Privates Clyde, Fryer, and Gilbert to follow. "Let's go boys. Just follow me."

They four moved off into the darkness. Creed formed what remained of the company in two groups. He led one, Jonathan Beall the other.

Creed un-slung his hunting rifle from his shoulder and he and the others proceeded down the trail that led back to the next objective, the Flatbush- Jamaica road intersection. Creed's easy confidence in the midst of all the confusion of the dark and inclement weather captivated the men. He had won their trust, but all knew the risk they were taking.

Storm clouds moved rapidly across the night sky and now a light but steady rain came down again. The foliage thickened just enough to keep them at a walk. The trail was narrow, winding, and uneven, and heavy wet tree branches blocked the way. The trees were mostly secondary growth. Over the years, the Dutch farmers harvested them for firewood. The new growth was thick, making each step forward, or backward, an event in itself. After what seemed hours, they came to a narrow creek running through a gully in front of them. Creed reckoned it ran northwards, either toward Wallabout Bay or directly to the great Long Island Sound. Although it was a small creek, the rain of the past few days had engorged it to almost a yard deep and almost three yards wide. Its loud rushing, together with the wind and rain, muffled all but the sharpest sounds.

Suddenly, Creed halted and grabbed Jonathan Beall's shoulder. He strained his eyes against the darkness, trying to gain a visual. Beall saw nothing.

"The British lines are just over there. With this poor visibility, their pickets could be as close as fifty yards apart. If we stumble into one the game may well be over. However, with this wind and rain, we may just slip by...."

Creed removed the sword-bayonet from its scabbard and slung his short Jaeger rifle across his back. He gripped the sword in his right hand and looked intently at Beall with his piercing dark eyes.

"This will make for quicker and quieter work if we happen to stumble upon one. I will cross first and toss this guide rope back to you. Have the men hold it so they don't get swept away. Cover our crossing, and then follow."

Creed crossed and then signaled the men forward. He guided the small band into the creek. The cold water quickly seeped into their shoes and leggings, chilling their legs and making them feel heavy. Beall soon followed, and covered the rear of the file. Creed's ways were starting to affect the men. Their leader's example, the need to fail neither him nor their comrades, now motivated them to great exertion.

They pushed through the brush, but stayed near the trail so as to spot any oncoming British first. They were within musket shot of thousands of enemy now but they had one advantage; the enemy was yet unaware of their presence.

The ground began to rise slowly until it formed a flat ridgeline that ran north to south. After a quarter mile, they reached the summit. Creed moved his men off the trail and out of sight. He and Beall made their way to the ridgeline and lay flat to avoid silhouetting themselves against the sky. They shivered from the raw cold but there was nothing to do but ignore it. To the east Creed could see points of light flickering through the rain and mist. For a split second, he thought the stars had fallen or that he had become disoriented by the darkness.

Then he realized what they were. "Look there. Enemy campfires. Less than a half mile off, I should say."

"What next Lieutenant?" Beall was fearful of the answer even as he asked the question.

"Well, that depends, lad. I now think that the lads on our works were not firing on a probe, but at another engineering party seeking a site for siege works and batteries."

"Should we not report this to headquarters? Simon should have already delivered the valise." Beall hoped for a quick trip back. Although a brave and stoic man, he did plan to survive this war if he could.

Creed nodded. "Perhaps..." He thought for a second. "But no, we must first find a way to slow their bloody schedule down a bit. General Washington needs time to take action. The British artillery park must be somewhere east of those campfires. Artillery needs powder—we shall do our best to divest them of it. Get the lads up. We are moving down there."

Chapter 10

Simon Beall moved his men through the woods and thick underbrush at a deliberate pace, stopping frequently to get his bearings. Darkness and windswept rain made their going treacherous, and frequently one of them would stumble over a root or a stone under the brush and grass. The rain now blew nearly horizontal, stinging their eyes as they walked. Beall thought he could make out the outline of their starting point along the defenses.

Beall was intent on carrying out Creed's orders. He knew that the valise with the British papers could save the army. Not long ago, he was a simple farrier, a blacksmith, on the edge of a small but prosperous British colony. Now, he led frightened but determined men under the most trying conditions with the fate of the new country at stake. Beall tried to stay focused on what he needed to do, one task at a time. He learned from the experience of managing the blacksmith shop in Frederick that it was the best way to weather hardships. His eyes welled up with tears as he thought about home, his parents, his sister, and his friends. He thanked God that he had no wife or sweetheart to worry about. Things were hard enough.

When Beall was a youth he had loved a girl, Joanna Schultz, daughter of a local baker. With her blonde haired, large frame, blue-eyes, and buxom shape, Joanna seemed the perfect match for a future blacksmith. He danced with her at town social events. They walked together many times and talked incessantly about their dreams and desires in life. He felt that there was a strong bond between them. It seemed stronger each time they were together. Despite their growing affection, or because of it, when she turned seventeen her father suddenly married her off. Her new husband was a baker in Annapolis—a German baker. Beall determined then never to fall in love again. Perhaps that was why he felt little remorse during the fight against the Hessians.

Beall now pondered how to get through the American lines. If they were too secretive they could be mistaken as a British patrol and come under fire. If they made too much noise, a British patrol might ambush them, or the Americans on the defense works might fire at them in the confusion. He realized now that Creed was not joking when he told them to sing "Yankee Doodle" as they neared the American lines.

The last half mile back seemed an eternity. Visibility was poor, less than fifty yards, in some patches even worse. They picked up a narrow trail that worked its way through the woods and brush, hoping that it would lead them west. The trail finally led to a flat open area with waist high bushes and patches of wild marsh grasses. There Beall saw what looked like a low wall to his front left. They were fifty yards from the American works! He could make out the defenses–they looked different from where they started under the watchful eye of Tallmadge.

"We missed the return point, boys. Damn it to hell!" he said softly.

"Should we go back and find Lieutenant Creed?" Gilbert asked.

"No time, Private Gilbert. We are going in right here," he replied flatly. Beall led the men cautiously toward the lines. His mind raced wildly as he tried to decide on their next move. Identify themselves to the defenders? Sneak across like thieves? It was a decision he would never have to make.

Musket shots suddenly rang out in a staccato volley that rolled along the American lines breaking the through the wind and rain. Beall went down instantly. The valise dropped from his shoulder into a rain puddle, sinking in muddy water as black as ink. Gilbert, shot through the eye, was dead before he hit the ground. Fryer, struck in the chest, had a musket ball punch a hole into him the size of a fig. Both lay dead in a pool of blood and muck. The third in the file, Clyde, dropped his musket and ran toward the American lines screaming and waving his arms to show that he was friendly. The soldiers on duty were anxious that a night attack was underway and feared this was a British trick.

The young lieutenant in charge grabbed a loaded musket from a dumb-founded private. The officer took careful aim, and, when Clyde was no more than five yards distant from the base of the works, fired a shot that shattered his throat and severed his spinal cord.

"Damned musket rose on me! I aimed for his heart." He looked sheepishly at the stunned soldier, who before that night had never seen a man die violently. The officer returned the musket as nonchalantly as if he were on a duck hunt.

ဆာလ

Creed and Jonathan Beall crouched under a stand of bushes only fifty yards from the British campfires. The rest of the men waited twenty-five yards away in a small glade to their rear. Creed and Beall saw an array of what appeared to be wagons covered by shrouds.

Beall asked. "What are they sir? Supply wagons?"

"No Jonathan, guns. British field artillery. Enough to pound our army to hell." Creed replied.

They were in fact, eight large-caliber guns with large brass barrels and heavy wooden carriages and wheels that reached chest high. The guns fired twelve pound iron balls. The anchor of the field artillery, a twelve-pound gun could fire more than 900 yards with accuracy and devastate formed troops or defenses at 600.

The British had covered the guns with blackened canvass tenting, to keep them dry and hide them from prying eyes. There were no gunners in sight, most of them fast asleep in the tents. No sentries either, the rain and wind deemed no doubt the best guardian they had. However, it showed a bit of arrogance for them to think the rebels would not dare so far in bad weather.

"I am going into their camp; send Parker to come with me. You remain in charge here. If I do not return within thirty minutes, take the men back to our lines." Creed said.

Beall nodded and fetched Parker, who had better sense for this kind work. He moved naturally in the dark, and seemed to see more clearly than the rest of them. Creed put him in the lead and the two made their way very carefully around the edge of the British camp. They saw no sentries. The British tents were scattered, not in neat rows. They all faced southwest, away from the prevailing wind and driving rain.

Creed pointed towards the guns. "We are going in. The wind and rain make it difficult for the British huddled under their dry tents to hear or see us."

They moved forward at a crouch. Creed held his hunting sword out at the ready. He had reloaded his rifle, the bullet tamped down and wadded tight. An oilcloth cover protected the hammer and touchhole from the rain. They slowly made their way to the British guns. Each move increased their risk of discovery and they knew it. Parker, who had weathered dangers on many a dark and stormy night at sea, had never felt so afraid. He thought he saw a sentry move in the darkness ahead of them but as they drew closer he realized the bushes had made a coward of him. He swallowed and put his fears away.

"Are we looking for anything in particular, Lieutenant?" Parker whispered.

"I believe the British man-handled these guns here," Creed whispered back. "In any case, the narrow roads and the terrain are very difficult. That plus this rain makes it unlikely that they brought the caissons with them."

"Caissons?" Parker asked. "What are they?"

"Heavy wagons, designed to carry munitions for the guns. Without them, each gun is limited to perhaps a dozen shot and like amount of gunpowder. If we can find the powder, we can blow it. That might delay their ability to blast our defenses. Set them back by a few days, with luck. Where to find them is the problem..." Creed's voice trailed off suddenly and he cocked his head to signal his intent to move again.

Suddenly, a torch light flared and quickly extinguished. An enemy patrol had moved out into the wood line not forty yards distant. Creed waited until they were long gone.

They moved around the guns, but found no sign of caissons. Pools of mud covered the area and the thick brown liquid that seeped into their shoes and socks made a sucking sound with each step so loud that they feared discovery. But nobody heard them.

They peered under the canvas covering the large field pieces. Next to each gun lay two boxes of cannon shot. One contained eight iron cannon balls, the other, six bags of grape shot. Each bag of grape shot contained sixty musket balls. The artillerists of the day used the larger round shot to break down defense works or to shatter formations of troops at long range. Grape shot turned the cannon into a large shotgun firing a swath of lead balls that could devastate infantry. Nevertheless, both types needed powder.

Parker's powerful grip suddenly clamped Creed's shoulder and turned him back toward the east. Almost since he could walk Parker spent most of his time on various types of fishing boats—his eyes were accustomed to seeing things under all kinds of conditions: fog, storms, darkness, rain, snow, and even hail. Failing to do so could result in lost time, a missed rendezvous or a collision against rocks, sunken vessels or another ship.

Parker whispered, "Sir, I see something back there...about thirty yards distant and hidden behind those trees."

It was a tent. Though they could barely see it, it looked different from the others. The only canvas showing was the peak, so it rose out of the ground like a four-cornered cone, barely distinguishable from the trees and bushes to the east.

Creed's eyes lit up. "Good work. That must be the powder tent. It is common knowledge that they separate it from the others for safety and dig down a few feet to contain the blast in the event of an accidental explosion. God bless them, for they have made our work all the easier."

Just then, a strong gust of wind sent the canvas pyramid bucking, loosening some of the pegs holding the tent to the ground and sending them dangling and bouncing haphazardly in the wind. The occasional peg slapped the side of the tent making an annoying clacking sound that even the rain and wind could not muffle. Two men emerged from under the canvas to tighten the pegs down as Creed and Parker knelt on one knee and watched from behind a large oak tree. Satisfied that things were secure again, the two Britons quickly made their way back into the tent to seek its protection from the inclement night.

Creed frowned. "This complicates things."

Silently, Parker drew a wicked looking blade from its leather sheath. The knife was actually a multi-purpose tool. He used it on board ship, a simple bone handle reinforced with brass with a twelve-inch long blade. The blade had a razor sharp edge that curved to a very sharp point. The upper blade, serrated like a saw, could perform work on the lines, cut through netting, wood or hemp, or gut, scale and filet even the largest fish.

Creed's eyes widened. The thought of butchering two men while they sat helplessly sheltering from the elements...even his battle hardened nerves would not allow it. These Americans are made of something else after all, he thought. Parker was willing to do the dirty work that Creed could never bring himself to order. However, when they reached the powder tent, Parker surprised Creed and with a quick flash of the upper blade brought down one side of the tent. Creed instantly realized what Parker intended and sheathing his sword, he un-slung his rifle.

"Bloody hell!" one of the gunners cursed. "Not again. This time the whole bleeding side is gone. Come on Jimmie, it'll take the both of us to fix it."

Even in the wind and rain Creed recognized a lowland Scots accent. As the two men eased out of the tent, Parker and Creed greeted them with their rifle butts. Both men caved to the ground without a sound. They dragged the hapless guards into the wood line and lay them behind boulders. They paused a moment, chests heaving from exertion, breadth steaming in the cold night drizzle.

When they returned to the powder tent Creed explained his plan. "We will pour a line of the gunpowder and use strips of the canvas tenting to act as the "tunnel" to protect the powder from the rain. I will then light the powder and blow the whole lot. In the confusion, we will gather the rest of the company and make our retreat. Do you understand?"

Parker nodded. In about ten minutes, all was set. Creed retrieved a final piece of canvas from the tent and under its cover struck his flint. Nothing would light. Despite their best efforts, the kindling and leaves were too wet. The powder was already dampened beyond use, he was foiled by the same raw elements that provided him the cover and darkness to get this far.

Parker's impatience was obvious. "It won't light, Lieutenant. Nothing could light in this soaking rain."

Creed nodded. "Let's try something else."

He returned to the powder tent in the hope that the British would be careless enough to leave a lantern or other nearby combustible materials. Then he noticed a crude wooden chest lay in the center of the storage tent, but it contained neither powder nor combustibles. The chest contained several tools—including a large axe and a chisel.

He signaled Parker over, grinning like a boy who found the cookie jar. "If we cannot blow the powder, we will let the Good Lord's rainfall soak it for us after we break open the powder boxes with the Britons' own tools."

Inside ten minutes, they had cracked open all the boxes. Creed and Parker then went to work cutting open the powder bags contained in each. When they had finished, they exited the shelter, cut the guy ropes holding it up, and exposed the lot to the driving rain. They scattered the powder, ensuring that the endless soaking would soon render it useless.

"Our work is done here." Creed spoke with more hope than conviction. "If the rain does its work the British guns at this position will be silenced until they can move the caissons up. This weather may render the roads just muddy enough to delay their supply efforts."

ဆာလ

The two made their way back to Beall and the rest of the men. "Alright, lads, time to make our way back. Keep your oilskin covers over the hammerlocks and flints. We must move through the British lines. Fix your bayonets, please."

They headed back through the darkness, rain and wind, moving quickly, not worrying about noise or discipline. Creed hoped that speed would trump stealth, and get his men back safely. He was wrong.

"Who goes there?" cried a British sentry. He was close, too close for comfort. Perhaps twenty paces to their front. The way back was blocked. How did they miss him on the way in? Perhaps there had been a change of the guard as they slipped by. Or perhaps he had fallen asleep earlier and was now awake. It did not matter. Creed had to act decisively.

"At them with the bayonet, lads!" Creed called out loudly, wanting the sentry to react.

He did, but his shot made a muffled "woof." A bad round, thanks to the weather. Creed's men rushed the sentry, whose companion emerged from the darkness. The second sentry fired as Creed closed, with his men right behind him, two abreast. This sentry's powder was dry. The shot rang out with a sharp crack, alerting the camp. Fortunately for Creed, the shot went high—though barely, punching a hole neatly through Creed's hat.

The sentry lunged at Creed, who parried the redcoat's bayonet, stepped inside his reach, and slammed him in the chest with the hilt of his sword. As he did, a bayonet pierced the luckless sentry through the left armpit, killing him instantly. Parker drew his bloodied blade from the sentry's body. The sentry collapsed lifeless into the mud-soaked earth. Beall and another private dispatched the first sentry with their bayonets. It was quick work. Then they heard cries of the more soldiers stirring in the camp.

Creed said, "Tis in our best interest to depart now, lads. Parker, take the lead if you please."

Parker took the lead followed by the men in single file. Beall covered their rear. The loamy mud slowed their pace. Each step they took required considerable effort and rendered an annoying suck-sucking. Behind them to the east, they heard cries from the relief party and a ragged volley of shots. Fortunately, only a few of the British weapons could fire in the rain, and those made a low popping sound barely audible in the wind.

Parker kept his head low and his eyes primed for trouble ahead. A sense of pride overcame him. Creed chose him to enter the British camp and now to lead the way back. His first mission had filled him with fear of failure. He now had the confidence Creed tried hard to instill in all of them.

ℰℭ

Tallmadge was awakened shortly after two in the morning to receive word that the next regiment over, a Pennsylvania unit, had fired on a British patrol probing close to the lines. Could Creed and his patrol have been misdirected and returned early? Worried, he rode out to check. When he arrived at the front lines, he found the company commander, a short pudgy captain of thirty, attempting to sleep in a leaky tent. The captain, now cranky as well as wet, only reluctantly rose from his cot to meet Tallmadge.

Tallmadge informed him that he had sent a patrol out that night, and feared it might have been them returning that drew the American fire. Although skeptical, the captain agreed to allow Tallmadge through the lines. "I am quite certain those were the British, Lieutenant Tallmadge. We had several sightings of British patrols earlier in the night. My men have a keen sense for these things."

Tallmadge smiled politely. "I am sure that they do, sir. And it is too early for our men to be returning, but it would assuage me greatly if I could verify this, with your permission of course."

The captain looked thoughtfully for a second, wondering if he should let this stranger into his command. Anxious to get back to sleep, he grunted his agreement. "Very well, but be careful. There may be redcoats about. Sergeant Stout, please escort...Lieutenant...Tallmadge...through our lines and help him look for his lost patrol."

Tallmadge accompanied the sergeant and four weary, wet, and annoyed privates over the chest high works and makeshift barricade. Morale in the army, particularly the militia units, was low, and the weather only worsened it. The militiamen were in the last few weeks of their enlistment and hoping to get home safely to their farms and villages. The British attack had now put them at risk of not getting home as planned.

Tallmadge's stomach sank when they found the place where the "British" patrol was sighted. Even in the dark and without a torch he could see they were, as he had feared, the Marylanders. He examined the first two; they lay side by side in a heap with puddles of blood mixed with water forming a small lake around them.

"Over here Lieutenant, poor bastard was shot clean through the throat." Sergeant Stout practically choked the words out and had to hold his belly hard to keep from vomiting. The damage was horrific. The musket round made a hole the size of a small walnut in the front of the man's throat but the head was all but severed in the back. The soldier was without a weapon—probably attempting to surrender to his own compatriots in desperation. Shot dead by friendly fire. Well, in darkness, such things could and too often did happen.

One of the militia privates signaled Tallmadge over to a fourth body. Simon Beall moved slightly when Tallmadge examined him. He was alive and barely conscious. In the dark, the musket round went high and had grazed his skull, giving him a bloody scrape and a mild concussion. Another lead ball had torn through his left forearm; his large hand still grasped his tricornered hat.

Tallmadge muttered. "This was the patrol's sergeant. We must try to save him, poor fellow."

Tallmadge's throat went dry as anxiety surged through him. He had never been in combat and these were the first casualties of war that he had ever encountered. "Go back to your unit and fetch a couple of blankets. We need to get this man back to the surgeons at once. As for the others...find a chaplain and some shovels."

Despite his youth, the soldiers reacted instantly to Tallmadge's demeanor and apparent self confidence. Within minutes, they had another party out with blankets and a shelter-half, a canvas sheet that two soldiers looped together to form a small tent meant for two that barely fit one. The men laid Beall between two blankets and wrapped the canvas shelter over him to keep as much wind and rain off him as possible. Tallmadge took the liberty of checking his pockets for valuables. He found a few coins and some writing materials. Suddenly, Beall's eyes flittered open. He spoke to Tallmadge in a low, halting voice.

"Lieutenant...sent us to deliver a package...important British papers. To... General Washington..."

Beall suddenly closed his eyes and passed out. Tallmadge could barely contain his excitement at the news but nodded calmly as they carried Beall off to the regimental surgeon.

Tallmadge decided to examine the area for signs of other members of Creed's patrol and to find the "package" with important British papers. His mind raced with excitement: what kind of package, and where was it? He paced in a semi circle starting seventy-five yards back from the farthest body. After what seemed an eternity but was less than twenty minutes, the burial party returned.

Tallmadge realized that rummaging in the dark, wet woods was futile. However, he turned one last time to retrace the final twenty-five yards Beall and his men had walked. The earth was so waterlogged and muddy that pools of dark ooze had formed around the immediate site where each man fell. He checked each spot one last time, more from desperation than any logical hope of finding something. As he stepped where Beall had fallen, his heavy black riding boot caught something in a shallow puddle.

Tallmadge stumbled and fell to his knees, soaking his britches in the mud and cold water. "God damn it!" he cried aloud in frustration and anger. Tallmadge, a schoolmaster and the son of a minister, was a man of strong religious beliefs having studied scripture as well as the classics at Yale. He almost never swore and generally maintained a serene composure when others sank to despair or emotion. Nevertheless, the events of the past two days and that awful night had gotten to him.

Tallmadge stood up, but lost his balance again as his boot heel caught on something lying at the bottom of the puddle. It felt odd as it moved slightly with the pressure of his boot heel. He unsheathed his infantry saber and poked at the bottom of the muddy pool. It felt unusual—the thin blade pierced something—neither wood nor stone. He reached down for the object. Tallmadge's heart skipped a beat as he pulled the something heavy and wet out of the mud, the package—was a leather valise. He sheathed his saber and moved at a brisk walk back toward the lines. Whatever British papers the valise contained had to get to the commander-in-chief. The planned rendezvous with Creed was not long off, so he had little time to waste.

Chapter 11

Creed signaled his men in. They were standing in a small clearing surrounded by light woods. Less than 100 yards ahead was the creek they had crossed earlier—the British front lines. They had about an hour or so until dawn, not that dawn would bring much daylight. The cloud cover would paint the sky a dark inky gray that would not brighten till well into morning. The rain had slowed once again to a light intermittent drizzle and the wind had abated.

"Alright, lads, we are almost done with this awful night." None of his men reacted to his comment. They were too exhausted, wet, and cold. Their fear, however, was gone. The hardships they had just endured had taken them beyond their fears. They were veterans now.

"We will return in single file," Creed said. "Private Parker will lead the first section, followed by Private Beall and his file. I shall take up the rear. If we encounter a sentry, move quickly to the right. Then I'll take the lead. Our goal now is simple: to cross the creek and return alive. Any questions?"

A private named Clemens, a store clerk back home in Frederick, asked. "What if one of us is wounded, do we stop to help him?"

"We shall certainly try," Creed said. "But we must return at all costs."

He knew that any unit's effectiveness had nothing to do with flags and slogans and everything to do with confidence and trust. This included the confidence that if wounded, they would not be left on the field of battle. Nevertheless, Creed's mission had to succeed at any cost. Men and mission, the combat leader's two imperatives, often conflicted.

The Marylanders advanced through woods now enshrouded in mist. There was no pre-dawn twilight; the weather gave them that advantage. Parker reached the clearing first, his section in single file behind him. They saw no sign of the British. A small walking path ran above the creek and bordered the edge of the woods. Parker signaled halt. Unsure what to do, he moved his section into a line along the trail. Just as he did, a British patrol rounded the bend to Parker's right. Parker decided to challenge them. His years on the sea made him nothing if not decisive.

"Who goes there?" Parker's voice boomed loud and confident.

"Servants of the King," was the reply.

Not a British accent, noted Parker. "What servants be ye?" Parker tried to affect a British accent—tidewater Marylanders and Virginians spoke a subtle version so the distinction blurred just enough.

"King's Militia, Second Company, here to guard the lines back to the Flatbush Road. We were told that there was a gap here to prepare..."

The Loyalist officer suddenly realized that this was no British unit. He shouted out nervously to his men, "Those are rebels before us, men! Present—fire!"

The Loyalist platoon fired a very ragged volley that tore into the woods like hot sleet. Because of the wet weather, little more than half of the muskets fired but four of the shots struck home. Two of the Marylanders died instantly from head shots that sent them sprawling backwards into the wet brush. Two more were wounded, one of them mortally, and began screaming in pain and fear.

Parker yelled, "At them, boys!"

The survivors charged from the woods onto the trail and moved straight at the Loyalist officer leading the column. Parker parried the officer's weak saber thrust and bayoneted him in one swift movement. Private Potter appeared at his side and quickly dispatched a Loyalist militiaman before turning his attention on a second. Although wounded, Private Jones was also on the trail and in heated combat with a Loyalist sergeant. Jones ignored the burning pain from his wrist as he slashed and parried at his opposite number. His focus was on killing and surviving.

When he heard Parker's cries, Creed immediately moved right to cover his flank. Jonathan Beall followed with the remaining men and charged the rear of the Loyalist column. The Loyalists panicked and ran back down the trail, leaving their weapons behind.

Creed stood breathing heavily as Parker reported. "We got eight of them, sir."

"How many of our lads?" Asked Creed.

"Three dead, one wounded...Henson. Badly I'm afraid," said Beall.

Shouts and noise could be heard in the darkness. Creed said, "Sounds like more company, lads. We need to go. Carry Henson and let's be off."

Two men carried Private Henson, who oozed blood from a hole in his groin. Creed knew Henson could not survive but he resolved not to leave him to the mercies of the enemy. Loyalists were especially uncompromising and brutal in seeking to prove their loyalty to the crown, often through the most atrocious acts of treachery or brutality to their fellow Americans. Creed, like most Patriots, conveniently ignored the fact that the rebels often reciprocated.

Creed plunged into the creek, wading through the rain-engorged waters. He fought against the fast moving current and finally made his way to the other side. He then turned and helped each of his men move out of the cold, muddy water. As the last staggered up the soggy bank, he was down to nine men.

The 27th Royal Inniskillens, a British regiment recruited in Ireland, had rushed a company to relieve the beleaguered Flatlands Militia. They formed a skirmish line on the trail along the creek.

The company commander, an experienced captain, gave the order, "Proceed at skirmish pace and drive the rebels back to their lines."

The company sergeant bellowed out commands up and down the line that now covered a front of almost seventy yards across the dark, rugged terrain.

Creed turned and saw the British silhouettes. "If you have any dry powder, load now."

Despite the rain and the creek, his men had done a good job keeping their powder dry. "Fire on the British as they come out of the creek. Then move toward the rendezvous point."

Minutes later their scattered shots ripped across the British line sending redcoats plunging into the wet bushes for cover.

"Pull back, now. On me!" Creed cried.

His men needed no further encouragement. They marched off quickly, Beall staying back to cover their escape. The men had taken turns carrying Henson and now fatigue had begun to set in. More firing erupted from deep in the woods. The lobster-backs were on Beall's heels. Why would the British come this far past their own lines? Then it occurred to him. The gap in the British lines was not an oversight. The British had pushed forces forward to cover the engineering and construction parties preparing the siege works. The entire area might be swarming with enemy units moving forward. Despite all their valiant efforts and exertions, Creed and his men might already be cut off.

ಬಂಛ

Tallmadge had finished a note to Fitzgerald. The contents of the valise clearly revealed British preparations to invest the American positions. Tallmadge realized this meant that the British were not planning an immediate assault. Investing even the makeshift American defenses would take days at the least, perhaps longer. So Washington had some time. The question Washington faced was–time for what?

Tallmadge had called for his most reliable noncommissioned officer. "Sergeant Rutledge, take my horse. Ride to General Washington's headquarters in Brooklyn. Find a colonel named Fitzgerald and get this note and valise to him. Entrust them to no one else."

Rutledge saluted and sped off–the small sorrel spraying mud behind her as she cantered down the rain soaked road. Tallmadge folded his hands together and silently prayed the commander-in-chief would receive the message before dawn. He also prayed that Creed's party would return by then.

ಬಂಛ

Dawn broke at last, revealing a dreary canopy of steel gray clouds covering the sky from horizon to horizon. Creed and his men continued to struggle with Henson, but had slowed to barely a walking pace. Suddenly, Henson went into convulsions. The trauma of his wound and the constant bouncing over the shoulders of his comrades had finally taken its toll. They never did quite stop his bleeding and his face had turned from the ashen gray of shock to the deathly white that presaged the worst. Creed halted the patrol to examine the wounded soldier himself. He felt a very faint pulse, and putting his ear to Henson's chest, heard shallow breathing. Creed realized the man did not have much longer to live.

Creed's voice trembled as he spoke. "I need a volunteer to remain with Henson. Once we get back to our lines, I shall return with more men and a stretcher. To continue carrying Henson this way puts us all at risk. The shock of traveling is killing him."

Beall suddenly appeared from their rear. "Sir, I spotted more Britishers both north and south of us."

Creed did not tell the men he feared they were surrounded. "Very well. Everyone re-load. We shall move out two abreast. Any volunteers to stay with Henson?"

"No need sir," said Parker. "Henson is dead, poor man."

Creed cocked his head and stared probingly at Parker, "Take his personal effects then. No time to give him a proper burial. We move out two abreast, behind me."

They heard shouts from the British skirmish line to the east, now only a few hundred yards distant. Unencumbered by a wounded comrade, the Marylanders now moved quickly. They now had enough light to see the American lines, barely a quarter mile off. The terrain had opened up into rolling farm fields mixed with small apple and peach orchards. They moved southwest in the hope they would reach the rendezvous point. Then came the deep 'pop, pop, popping' of musket shots to the south.

"The British seem determined to shake hands with us," Creed said. "We'll forgo the rendezvous point and head west instead. Under these circumstances I believe Lieutenant Tallmadge will understand."

"I can stay and hold them off a while longer, sir." Beall offered.

Parker cast an annoyed look at Beall. "Only if I can join you. I shall stay with Jonathan, sir."

Creed replied. "No, lads. We shall all return together, as a unit, or die in the attempt."

More musket fire suddenly erupted from behind them. Creed feared they might not out-run the British skirmish line after all. "Quickly now, lads! This is now as much a race as a fight."

The Marylanders began a slow trot across the farmlands toward the west. Fortunately, the British fire came from almost two hundred yards away. They had wasted their powder. Just then, a third unit arrived to complicate their escape. Now the elite grenadier company of the Inniskillens was closing fast in a determined effort to block their escape. Fifty men in column of fours, moving quicker than skirmishers, spread across rolling terrain. Creed and his men had to move fast or face annihilation by these ferocious soldiers. The American lines lay less than a quarter mile distant, but at sixty yards off the grenadiers already had them in musket range. The enemy column crested a slight rise, and then went fifty yards down the slope and out of sight.

Creed decided on a bold gambit and called the men in on him. "Seems I was wrong, lads. We must yet fight our way back. Form a volley line here, double load and take a knee. When the British crest the hill, aim at their knees. Two volleys, then move on me. Most of their fire should pass over our heads."

The men's spirits improved. They had been through much, but running was worse than fighting. Several began to smile.

"This is more like it," said Private Jones. Potter nodded. Without a word, Jones adjusted the makeshift bandage on his wrist and slowly reloaded.

The grenadiers marched over the crest, intent on destroying the rebel unit to their front. In the gray morning their fixed bayonets lacked the normal gleam that usually sent fear through the hearts of even the stoutest defenders. The grenadiers moved forward with confidence that their power and momentum would carry them right through the rebel pack and their work would soon be finished.

Creed gave a crisp command, "Present...Fire!"

Eight weapons unleashed a small but lethal volley that mowed down the first row of grenadiers like a scythe cutting through wheat. Then Creed and Beall fired their rifles with deadly effect; taking down at two more grenadiers and disrupting the Irishmen's attempt to return fire. With cool discipline, the Marylanders rapidly reloaded muskets and a second volley tore a small gap in the column.

"On me!" Creed yelled.

As one, the Marylanders moved at a run toward their lines. They raced up the opposite slope and reached a point about a hundred yards from what looked like the American positions. Creed could see blue-jacketed militiamen running to and fro, confused by the action to their front.

The Marylanders halted to recover their breath. A few stood wheezing from a mix of exhaustion and nerves. Most realized this was likely their last chance to stop the British.

Creed spoke. "No time to rest, lads. Load double shot and kneel."

They each calmly reloaded. Once more they took a knee and presented their firelocks at the mass of red closing on them. This time, a young Irish subaltern led the attack with his straight infantry sword held high.

Creed aimed his rifle at the subaltern. "Steady, lads. Let them get close now... Present...fire!"

As one, the Marylanders fired a horrific blast that shot flame and smoke in all directions. Creed squeezed the trigger of his Jaeger rifle and drilled the subaltern between the eyes. The young man staggered forward two more steps and then collapsed with his blade tumbling harmlessly into the muddy soil. Four of the lead grenadiers screamed shrilly and clutched themselves frantically before they too fell to the sodden ground.

The surviving grenadiers broke and ran in panic as two angry sergeants tried to rally them with curses and threats that only Creed could comprehend: the man spoke Irish. Beall, who had not yet fired his rifle, took careful aim. The range was almost one hundred yards, but the gray morning light enough for him to chance a long shot. Beall hesitated, and then thought of Henson. The shot shattered the spine of one of the unlucky sergeants just as the last of the grenadiers disappeared over the crest.

"Follow me now, lads," Creed ordered. The Marylanders formed up and moved straight toward the American lines. This time, an American officer at the works was ready for them. The soldiers standing morning guard in that sector of the line had watched the last engagement. Elated at seeing a British unit run before American soldiers, they stood and waived tricornered hats and beavers in series of huzzahs. After the American defeat at the passes, this small victory provided a welcome tonic.

A corpulent officer with a double chin greeted Creed with a crisp salute. "Captain Richard James, in command of Second Company, First Connecticut Continental Line."

"Lieutenant Jeremiah Creed, Light Company, Maryland Continental Line." Creed returned the salute.

James grinned broadly. "Handy work, Lieutenant Creed. We received word from Colonel Chester to watch for you. He was concerned when you missed your assigned meeting with Lieutenant Tallmadge. I am delighted that my company was your consolation prize. Your little skirmish will inspire my men and raise their morale. Lord knows, they have as of late had little reason to cheer."

James provided a guide to escort them back along the lines to Tallmadge's location. Tallmadge had suspected the musket fire had something to do with Creed and was waiting for him. They conferred inside the Tallmadge's small, leaky tent with a couple of boxes serving as table and chairs. Tallmadge took careful notes of the entire night's affair as Creed explained them over a tin of stale but pleasantly hot black coffee. It was not until Creed finished his report that Tallmadge told him of the terrible fate of Simon Beall and his other men. Creed stared lugubriously into his cup as he listened.

When Tallmadge finished, Creed looked up. "I should have known. The darkness, rain and wind. Our lads along the entrenchments inexperienced and fearful of a British attack. I had not given my "Yankee Doodle" order lightly. God's will, I suppose."

Tallmadge looked at Creed with sympathy. "God's will indeed, Lieutenant Creed. However, the Lord works in strange ways. We can take some comfort that Corporal Beall survived. And of course, the information has gotten to the commander-in-chief."

Creed nodded glumly. "That is true...although I left too many of our lads for the British to bury."

Tallmadge. "Yes, but you brought the remainder back safely...and it appears the British have more of their own to bury. This war is about keeping that count in our favor, and I daresay you have done your part this night."

Creed nodded back. "True, but somehow not much comfort..."

Chapter 12

British Headquarters, Jamaica, Long Island

General Howe had not bothered to consult with his subordinates. He had a firm sense of what he was about as an officer and as a member of the elite in a society built around privilege and class. Certainly, he allowed his subordinates to express their opinions and that they assuredly did, almost to a fault. Howe knew that his decisions were widely disdained by his lieutenants and by the majority of the officers in the army.

"What of our plans to invest the rebel works, Sam?" Howe asked as he finished another dispatch back to "Horse Guards," the nickname for British Army Headquarters. Howe wiped the dark ink from the pen nib and placed it almost ceremoniously in its container beside the ink well. Brigadier Samuel Cleveland was commander of Howe's artillery park. He was a meticulous and thoughtful man. Unlike his commander and so many others around him, he had risen up through the ranks, first as an engineer and later as an artillery officer.

Cleveland's dismay showed on his face. "The weather has slowed our progress quite a bit, Milord. Furthermore, the Americans conducted a series of raids last night–and seemed to have made off with the plans and drawings for Lieutenant Pickard's Battery. This should not pose a major problem, though. More critical to our immediate situation is the powder for Captain Twist's Battery. Another group of American raiders struck the forward logistics point and exposed all the gunpowder to the elements. Useless it is. Now with all this rain, it will be at least twelve hours before resupply is possible. The terrain is impassable, even on the roads, and will remain so until we get some relief from the weather."

Howe's dark face brightened a bit, but he composed himself quickly and feigned disappointment. He was looking for reasons to delay attacking and he wanted time to invest and bombard the American positions.

With a "Tsk," Howe spoke. "That is a shame. Well, no point initiating action until we have established proper forward works, and have sufficient munitions to commence bombardment from all three batteries."

"We still have one good battery we can put in action. "Cleveland replied.

"You mean Brill's?" Howe asked.

"Yes Milord. We could commence with Brill's Battery only, pin down the rebels, and give them something to think about." Cleveland suggested this coyly, knowing that his commander-in-chief would not take the bait.

"No. We will commence an all-out bombardment only when we have proper siege works and all the batteries are in place and supplied. Besides, a few days to stew in his own juices will do Mister Washington well."

The British command in America and the government in London refused to recognize George Washington's rank as a General. They addressed earlier missives to negotiate with the rebel forces to "Mister George Washington, Esquire," greatly annoying the proud Virginian. It was a deliberate insult to him, and to the American cause.

Cleveland's face flushed and his scowling demeanor showed his obvious frustration with his cautious commander.

Howe smiled patronizingly. "You will see, Sam. Time is on the side of His Majesty's forces. We should use it to our advantage."

Cleveland tried to maintain his calm but failed. "Milord, many of us fail to see any advantage in delaying the inevitable. The rebels are physically and morally crushed, a large-scale assault will result in their surrender or their slaughter. A bombardment might give Washington and those rogues time to find alternative solutions to their dilemma."

"Nonsense, there are no other solutions but to wait out the inevitable. My brother Richard assures me that our Navy will soon cut off their escape across the river. I stand firmly of the opinion that they will submit, after a proper bombardment. Do what you can to expedite our forward works and getting your battery re-supplied. Leave the strategic decisions to me, Sam."

Howe glanced over at Generals Clinton and Cornwallis who stood silently through the whole dialogue. They had tried to convince their commander to take more aggressive action, although they would not let on in front of Cleveland, a commoner who should never have risen to flag rank.

"This will all work out in good time gentlemen", Howe went on. "Trust in me. Victory is ours."

ഇവ

Brooklyn, Long Island, August 29th, 1776

When he finished his report and discussion on the night's events, Creed stood up, donned his weather-worn hat, and forced a smile.

"Enough self-pity for me. What is done is done. There is much yet to do. I am bringing the company back to the village. They need to dry out and rest. After what they have been through it is the least that I can do for them."

Tallmadge nodded, "Brooklyn is mostly an armed camp, but there are some homes there that have opened themselves up to the army. I am sure you could get permission from Major Gist."

"Aye, that I could, but there is no time. I need a request from your regimental commander, seeing as how they assigned us to your command for the duration of the mission. It is a technicality for sure, but what are technicalities for if not to be used to good effect?" Creed smiled as he said it.

"Very well, we will settle with your major at a later time," said Tallmadge. As the Adjutant, he was effectively in day-to-day charge of regimental activities and personnel. He had the authority to sign for the commander in such matters so he hastily wrote out an order, signed it, and handed it to Creed.

"Remember, until so ordered by the commander-in-chief you are attached to my regiment—if anyone questions this..."

"I know what to tell them. Thank you, Lieutenant Tallmadge."

"I think we may now address one another on more familiar terms, please call me Benjamin," said Tallmadge.

"Benjamin it is then, and I am your man, Jeremiah." Creed replied with a grin.

Tallmadge took hold of Creed's shoulder in a parting gesture and the two young officers shook hands.

Creed rounded up what remained of the Light Company. The thought of more marching drew groans, until they realized that Creed's intent was to find a home so they could dry out and sleep under a roof. They reached Brooklyn before ten that morning. Creed was by now familiar with the streets that made up the largest village on Long Island. He went straight to headquarters where Washington's aide, Abner Scovel, read Tallmadge's note and granted Creed the rare privilege of billeting his men with civilians. By eleven o'clock, the remaining soldiers of the Light Company, Maryland Continental Line were occupying a clean and dry barn on the small property of Jan Braaf Esq., prominent Dutch lawyer and merchant.

Jan Braaf was a willing and gracious host to Creed and his men. "You may rest and change in my room, Lieutenant, your men may use the barn—it has plenty of good dry hay. Marta will make pig's knuckles and sauerkraut—with some black bread. And we have some beer, though not much. The past few weeks have been disruptive."

"Indeed they have, sir. And we are beholding to your hospitality." Creed smiled and shook Braaf's beefy hand.

In short time, the men had settled in and stripped out of their wet clothes, which they hung out to dry as best they could in the barn. The Braafs provided some spare dry blankets which the men had to share; they did so gladly and easily as it was often the custom for travelers to double up when sleeping, a matter of practicality even in prosperous colonial America. They would sleep through until around three at which time Marta Braaf would serve them a hot meal. Food could wait. They were sleep-deprived and near the end of their ability to think clearly.

 හැ

Jeremiah Creed was not so lucky. At eleven thirty, Scovel awakened him. The commander-in-chief wanted Creed to attend another war council at army head-quarters, which had moved to a large stone house near the ferry landing.

Creed sat in the back of the large room. The generals, along with Fitzgerald, sat at a rough-hewn pine table with the commander-in-chief. Standing and sitting around the room were the rest of the colonels, the commanders of every regiment on Long Island. Creed learned several things during the ensuing discussions: Washington had appointed General Thomas Mifflin commander of the remains of Sullivan's brigade. The First Maryland Continental Line would soon return to New York. Creed realized this did not affect him. His unit remained attached to the Connecticut Regiment. An unctuous major in a pristine uniform presented a tedious and gloomy report on troop staffing and the supply of the forces now on Long Island.

After the administrative and logistical discussions, Washington asked Fitzgerald to address the assembled officers. Fitzgerald rose to his feet and stretched his lanky frame, posturing like a schoolmaster on the first day of class.

"I shall attempt to keep this brief, gentlemen. So far, the weather has cooperated with us. The seas, rain, and wind have kept the British fleet out of the East River, so our connection back to New York remains, for now, unimpeded. Furthermore, information gathered by Lieutenant Jeremiah Creed seems to confirm my expectations."

Several line officers in the tent murmured disapprovingly among themselves. They had little use for this "Intelligence Advisor." Many of them held the very idea of intelligence in contempt, considering it a dishonorable practice, a form of the black arts used by French Jesuits and other papist deceivers.

Fitzgerald thrust his left hand into his waistcoat pocket and removed an old timepiece. He glanced at it, for effect, not the time. He then took his right hand, pushed his wispy white hair back, and thrust his jaw upwards like a Roman senator making a speech on the state of the Republic.

"General Howe will procrastinate by building siege works to invest our positions. We now have evidence that shows most demonstrably a British plan to construct such works. These will take time. We also have information from scouts led by Lieutenant Jeremiah Creed that the British engineering efforts are already underway. However, I am pleased to report that his men were able to reduce the number of the King's Royal Engineers by a few."

The last comment was met by laughter and guffaws from many of the officers. Although Creed's mission was secret, word of his exploit spread like wild fire through the beleaguered army. Even the strictest secret is subject to the whims of its holders.

Fitzgerald raised his voice, "And he was able to sabotage most of their powder stores. This will delay General Howe's ambitious plans. But make no mistake; he soon will have batteries capable of reducing our defenses. If the British fleet can get the tide and wind to cooperate, he may yet be able to destroy the army decisively and end the war right here on Long Island."

There was nothing but sullen silence from the assembled officers.

Rising with his large stately frame towering over the group, General Washington spoke.

"Thank you Colonel Fitzgerald. Gentlemen, we had suspected as much, but now we have incontrovertible proof of General Howe's intentions. Unless some-one can refute this information and present cogent arguments to the contrary, I plan to evacuate Long Island and focus our defense on New York. With our forces reunited there, we can make our stand. It pains me to give up this fair part of America but I am afraid this island has become a trap. I have sent for Colonel John Glover and his regiment. His Gloucester sailors will commence moving the Army at dark. God willing, I expect all our forces to be across the East River by dawn. What say you?"

There was great murmuring, pro and con, throughout the tent. Disagreement was rife among the officers. They argued over the state of the army, the position in which they now found themselves, and the appropriate course of action to take against the British, but on one thing all agreed: General Washington was the lodestone of the Continental Army and the Glorious Cause and his decision was final. After several minutes, Washington raised his hand and silence settled on the group.

"Gentlemen, since there are no objectors, we now have our decision; let us put it into action with some deliberate planning. The Continental Army will depart this night. To speed the effort, local craft will augment our own transport fleet. We shall move each regiment, in order, from the front lines to the ferry. Each regiment shall take up the space remaining, so the last regiment must cover the entire front. As much equipment and as many provisions as possible should be moved back as well. Most importantly, if we are to convince the British we are still in the lines, and to conceal our moving off the island, we must main-tain strict secrecy. I hope the surprise of this movement will give us respite, allow us to reunite our forces, and negate the advantage of the British Navy. Even then, we have long and arduous work ahead of us. Now gentlemen, are there any questions?"

A short, pugnacious looking colonel stood up. "Sir, Dan Hitchcock, Eleventh Rhode Island Line. What will become of the citizens of Long Island should the British take their frustration out on them? Is it not our duty to stand here and now, thus showing our resolve to fight and defeat the soldiers of the King, as well as protect our people? Is it not cowardice to retreat at such a late time?"

The assembled officers grew as silent as the cemetery at the Old Dutch Church–many felt the same way.

Another colonel chimed in. "Why are we rebelling if not to fight? How could we, in all good faith, abandon our fellow citizens here to the ravages of the British?"

A third wearing New York regimentals stood up and waved his hands. "Already we have word of many rapes and seductions of the women on Staten Island, and that place a strong Loyalist bastion. Are we cowards to leave these people to face the redcoats on their own?"

Washington's face reddened, but he otherwise maintained a calm air as he firmly replied. "This is not about cowardice, or about manhood, or even protecting the innocent. It is about maintaining the army at all costs, for the army is the lifeblood of this cause, the cause of freedom and liberty. If I must abandon a half-score of cities to survive and win, I shall. If I have to bite my tongue while innocent Americans suffer indignities at the hands of ruthless mercenaries, I shall. If I have to bear calumnies and insults for perceived cowardice and incompetence, I shall. And I will suffer all of this for one thing, our new nation and our liberty. So now I charge each officer and man to do his duty. Please return to your commands and prepare them. Detailed march orders will be forthcoming. Meanwhile, great vigilance must be maintained. Colonel Fitzgerald and Lieutenant Creed, please remain behind. May God be with all of you, gentlemen."

Washington's short but passionate speech had changed these men. The entire group rose in acclamation with loud huzzahs and cheers. Creed flushed with the emotion of the moment and forgot his fatigue. He forgot the losses of his command over the past few days. For the first time, he realized the truly unique situation that his adopted land faced and he felt fortunate to be part of such a worthy enterprise. In Ireland, he often dreamed and sometimes even talked of freedom, but here men were doing something to achieve it!

As the tent emptied, Abner Scovel offered Creed a seat across from Fitzgerald and General Washington. Scovel summoned an orderly, who soon returned with cold chicken and potatoes and poured them a modest red wine. Washington bade them all to eat and Creed did so ravenously. When they finished, the orderly brought in a tray of roasted apples covered in cream. Creed finished his in short order and was on his second glass of wine when Fitzgerald began to speak. Washington and Scovel quietly finished their meal as he spoke.

"Lieutenant Creed, your actions in the past few days have been remarkable and have possibly provided this army with its ever-so-slight chance of survival."

Creed stared at Scovel, then Washington, then back to Fitzgerald. All three looked expressionless at him. This was disconcerting, especially after the rousing talk given by the commander-in-chief to his assembled commanders.

Fitzgerald continued. "If the weather holds in our favor, if the tides push the British fleet back into the New York harbor, if we can fool the British Army sitting half a mile in front of us, if we can deceive their spies for a few hours, if we can organize enough boats, if we can move thousands of men quietly and in darkness, and if we can act in a matter of hours—our chances of success are still less than fifty-fifty. We shall need the blessings of a Divine Providence, and the efforts of many extraordinary men to succeed. In the scheme of military affairs, this is a high risk endeavor."

Creed knew he was right. Initially, his experience and intuition had warned him so. However, the power of General Washington's words, and his own naïve, romantic, Irish hopes had made him believe they would prevail. The orderly came by with a refill.

"I am afraid you are right, sir," was his reply. "But what has any of this to do with me and my men, few as they now happen to be?"

General Washington looked at him sympathetically and then spoke, "You recently displayed talents that are needed by the army, Mister Creed."

Washington glanced at Fitzgerald, who nodded.

"But I have a place with the Maryland Line, at least I had. Now I am with the Connecticut Line, or so I had supposed." Creed said. His stomach was churning and his legs felt weak. Although his command was down to a handful of men, it was still his command. Although he had backed into this war and the Maryland Line, he was now fully committed to both.

Fitzgerald shook his head. "Jeremiah, His Excellency has need of your talents. And yes, Major Gist has already been informed, as has Colonel Smallwood."

Creed was startled. He had not had a chance to speak to Major Gist. "But what can I do alone? I want to command an infantry unit—in the Maryland Line."

Washington interrupted him. "For now, your unit remains attached to the First Connecticut Continental Line. First Connecticut will anchor the deployment back. That is, it will remain on the line until most of the others have departed. They will surely have need for an experienced unit that can operate on independent missions if needed. And I dare say there will be a need."

Creed hung his head in submission. "I serve at Your Excellency's pleasure." Creed could not think of anything else to say. A good soldier followed orders, even those he did not accept.

Fitzgerald spoke in a hushed tone. "It is critical that we intercept any spies or deserters who might cross over the lines during the next twenty-four hours. We have strictly controlled knowledge of our plans and intentions. Written orders will state that the commander-in-chief has decided to accelerate our current defenses and bring reinforcements from New York. Commanders will announce these plans to their subordinates where it is expected that word of it will leak out."

Washington joined in. "Additionally, John Glover's boats arriving this afternoon will be fully loaded with equipment, indicating reinforcement of our position here."

Fitzgerald nodded. "His Excellency hopes this ruse will provide us time. Then, just before twilight, Scovel and Pickering will provide each regimental commander with his actual instructions. These new instructions will countermand the original plan. The strictest secrecy is of course necessary throughout the latter part of this operation."

Washington rapped his large knuckles on the table. "You, Jeremiah, will deliver the First Connecticut our actual plan of withdrawal. If the British in any way gain knowledge of this enterprise we are doomed. Security is our first priority."

Creed smiled cunningly, "And the second is..."

Fitzgerald smiled back, "Luck me boy, plain luck. For this to succeed we will need some of your Irish luck to boot!"

"Ahh, so that's why I am here, sir." Creed laughed. "To bring some Irish luck to these Connecticut Yankees."

Washington smiled approvingly. He liked Creed's honesty, pluck and humor. He addressed the group in a low voice. "Yes, we need your luck. Now it is time to move on to other business gentlemen. Lieutenant Creed, although you are now under the command of Colonel Chester, he will be informed that you may receive special orders from me." He glanced at Fitzgerald and Scovel. "These will be communicated to you by either Lieutenant Scovel or Colonel Fitzgerald."

Washington then retrieved a folded and sealed sheet of parchment from the table. "Give this order to Colonel Chester but ask him to burn it after he is done reading."

Chapter 13

Creed did not return to the Braaf household until well past three. His men, with the exception of Jonathan Beall, had eaten and were now sleeping. Beall had offered to help with kitchen cleanup. He wanted to be around civilians and knew this was probably as close to a home as he would see for quite some time. More importantly, it enabled him to be around the females, specifically Krista Braaf. She had already talked with him a quite bit during their short stay. She spoke shyly, and softly, often modestly keeping her eyes down. Their small talk turned to the army and the war. These were not just the first soldiers she had ever seen. Since she spent her entire life within a few miles of the village, these were the first non-Brooklyners she had ever met.

"How does it feel to be so far from home, Private Beall?" she asked demurely. "I could not imagine being away from mama and papa for days, never mind for weeks and months. And such a long journey, walking day in and day out."

He blushed, knowing that she was impressed that he was a soldier, and a Patriot. "It is an awful thing to be away from home, Miss Braaf, but also exciting," he replied. "Often, too exciting, in truth. Now, with my cousin Simon wounded, it will be all the harder. We joined the regiment together and I worry for him."

"And I worry for my brother as well," she quickly interjected.

Beall was a local boy, fighting homesickness as well as the British. "At least your brother Jan is fighting near home. I sometimes wonder what all this has to do with Maryland. Lieutenant Creed says that after the British are done up north they are coming south sure enough. I believe I'd rather fight them there."

"Well, if it is any comfort we are glad you are here helping our cause," Krista said. She smiled and her dark blue eyes widened, causing a burning in the pit of his stomach.

The back door suddenly opened. Creed had returned from headquarters. He went straight to the kitchen searching for more food, and began hurriedly finishing some of the pig's knuckles left over from dinner. He had walked in on their conversation.

"Pay no mind to me, you two. I will eat the rest of these lovely things on the porch and then catch some sleep. But Jonathan, please make sure the men are up and ready by five. Have them clean and oil their weapons and arrange their gear."

"Are we going somewhere, Lieutenant?" Beall asked while keeping his eyes fixed intently on the young lady.

"In a manner of speaking, we already have. We already have." He grinned mischievously and left tipping his hat to Miss Braaf.

"You will be leaving us then? So very soon?" Her disappointment was obvious. Beall took her hand awkwardly. "I am just a soldier anyway..."

Krista abruptly hugged him in an embrace that conveyed her suddenly awakened passion for this weary and homesick private, who had at once become her love and her hero. Beall shivered with surprise. He had almost no experience with women outside of his family. However, he composed himself and gently, then intensely, returned her embrace. The two held on to each other tightly for several minutes. Neither speaking but both savoring a moment they knew might never repeat itself. Then Beall released her and softly stroked her chin. She rested her head on his chest for a while.

At five, Creed checked on his men. He found them inside the barn, preparing their equipment. Some sat on piles of hay. Others sat up in the loft, their muddy feet dangling just above Creed's head. It was dark and dreary. The rain continued and had increased to a heavy drizzle. The wind had picked up too. The men began to stand up when he entered the barn, not just from military discipline but because he genuinely commanded their respect.

Creed signaled them to remain sitting. He stood looking at the men with his feet apart, hands on hips. "Lads, I can tell you that we remain detached from our regiment and will continue to serve under Colonel John Chester of the First Connecticut. The Maryland Line, happily for them, was sent back to New York to rest and refit. You must stand by until we receive further orders. This may be the only rest we get for some time, so use it wisely."

He glanced at Beall who turned away, his thoughts on Krista. "Our gracious hostess, *Mevrouw* Braaf, will bring supper at seven. I hope to return by then. It will just be buttered bread and black coffee but she assures me the Dutch make the finest coffee in the world. Seeing as I have only been as far as France, I could not tell if she was jesting."

৮০গ৪

Tallmadge was surprised when Creed arrived at First Connecticut regimental headquarters and asked to speak to Colonel Chester privately. The two sat at a small table in a somewhat spacious leather tent.

"So we have the honors, it seems." Chester said hoarsely. Chester turned the written orders over and under, as if there were some hidden message on the reverse side. The candle that flickered on his desk provided only a modicum of light by which to read. He rubbed his bleary eyes as he paused to think. He realized all too well that the "honor" portended grave danger to his men.

The colonel squinted at Creed. "Your company's attachment makes this whole affair all the more intriguing, Mister Creed. Not much of a reinforcement, if you do not mind my saying so. And you are, how is it, 'to stand by for special orders from army headquarters,' as well? Makes it difficult to plan your role if I cannot be assured of your presence..."

Rain drops pelted the tent making the pause seem an eternity. Creed was in an awkward position and he knew it. "Sir, I have no more knowledge of what headquarters has in mind than you do. My men want to be with their regiment, but they are content to do their duty. We are far from home but we are determined to serve as best we can."

Chester, taken back, cleared his throat and replied. "Of course Mister Creed, you are correct. My comments were in no way meant to impugn you or your unit. Lieutenant Tallmadge has said nothing but grand things about the gallantry and resourcefulness of your entire band. Speaking of Tallmadge," he went on, "we must inform him in of this. He is my right arm, and if the regiment is to move at night along a several-mile front, he will be the key to our successful execution of the mission."

Creed hesitated a moment, then nodded. "My orders were to tell only you sir, but as commander *in loco,* I defer to your good judgment."

Creed smiled to himself. He was glad of the decision. He liked and trusted Tallmadge. When Tallmadge entered the tent, he looked annoyed at being cut out of the conversation.

"I see your discomfort at our private conversation, Benjamin, but I think we can now let you in on our secret." Chester said with an impish grin. "

Tallmadge nodded impassively, but after he read the orders, he sucked in his cheeks. "Oh my, this shall be a risky enterprise. Move the entire army off the line, cross more than a mile of treacherous waters in a summer rain storm, in the face of the most powerful army and navy ever assembled on this continent."

Creed winked, "Oh yes, and without the British knowing. I believe that General Washington hopes to have us all back in New York in time for morning tea."

Tallmadge was not amused but Chester chuckled. He was beginning to like the brash man with the strange accent.

Chester addressed them both. "So gentlemen, it seems we have our work cut out for us. We currently defend a front of two hundred yards, a nice enough challenge for the boys. This plan calls for us to extend our right flank each half hour until the regiments to our right have cleared to the rear, then we cover the entire front of more than two miles. And, we are to appear to be the entire army. Under the best of conditions this is a near impossible task, but in this wind and rain?"

Tallmadge replied, "We can do it, sir. The critical part will be security. We should inform the company commanders only just before the first movement takes place. We shall do so face to face, no written instructions. The men will be told that the army is moving off the line to prepare a counterstrike against the British."

Chester nodded and then pointed at Creed. "Mister Creed, your first order under my command is to move your unit here to regimental headquarters. We shall try to find some spare raincoats or cloaks, those hunting jerseys are grand in the bush, but do not protect much from the elements. It will also make you appear normal members of the regiment and help deflect suspicion."

Chester took the orders from Tallmadge, and held them over the flickering candle. The paper lit and flamed, sending swirls of smoke towards the peak of the tent. The pungent smell somehow bothered Creed. He saluted, and left the two to their final planning the pivotal role for what would be in one of the most daunting operations in military history.

Creed returned to the Braaf house after the meeting. He saw Mistress Braaf looking at him from the kitchen window. He looked back, and then quickly turned his attention to the issue at hand. The men were in the barn awaiting his return. "Private Beall, gather the men and prepare to depart."

Creed entered the Braaf home and gathered his belongings. He shook Braaf's hand and kissed the hand of his wife, who blushed. Braaf took no notice.

Krista Braaf curtsied and asked in a trembling voice, "When will you return, Lieutenant?"

Creed wanted to tell her the truth, having seen the way she and Jonathan Beall had taken to each other. "Oh, soon I suppose, Miss. We have some night duties, routine for a light company such as ours." He winked at them. "Most likely by dawn."

The gentle tone of his voice reassured her. Krista rushed off.

"Did I upset her?" Creed asked.

"No, I suspect she wants to steal a few moments with young Jonathan."

"I noticed an attraction between them. Well, he is an honorable lad."

Marta nodded. "I think so, too. Now, we will have a good Dutch breakfast for you when you return tomorrow morning." Creed looked her in the eye and she met his with an intense stare. Uncomfortable with the way she returned his look, and her husband's obvious presence, he thanked her and then hurried out.

Braaf looked out the window and watched his daughter talking with Beall as the men gathered their equipment. They were taking all of their gear. Braaf suspected that they had no plan to return, but said nothing to his wife. His role in the local Whig movement taught him well how to contain knowledge of things, for the protection of the cause and the individuals serving it.

***

Beall and Krista sat alone under a small gazebo in the garden. They listened to the raindrops pelt the gazebo roof and watched the droplets stream endlessly around them in a curtain of water. In that sense, nature gave them privacy while fate denied them time. Beall whispered. "I shall write to you, Miss Braaf."

She looked up. "I would like that...but...I do not write very well. There is so little chance here. I have never had anyone write to me. Besides, if the English come, how will our letters arrive?"

Both realized then the strong likelihood the British would come and separate them for God knew how long.

"I shall find some way to get mine to you. On the other hand, yours will likely never reach me in the field. But you may write to my ma, in Frederick. She can hold them."

"No, I shall hold them here. That way, you must return to me and read each letter..."

Their eyes met in a joyful smile. They kissed tenderly, then warmly. Then, without a word, Beall left her to join his comrades. He felt sick in his heart just thinking that he might not see her for some time.

***

Not long after the Marylanders departed, a visitor arrived at the Braaf home. It was Cornelius Foch, there to summon Braaf to a meeting of the local Whig faction. At thirty-eight, Foch, had a face worn and weathered from years at sea. He had the thin but strong build typical of so many seamen, dark hair flecked with grey, and piercing gray eyes that folded downward almost into slits. Most unusual for these days in Brooklyn, he was a transplant from the Netherlands, not a home grown Knickerbocker, the colloquial term for the descendents of the original Dutch settlers in New Amsterdam. Though taken by the British and renamed more than a century earlier, New York still had a very large Dutch population and many of its largest landholders were of Dutch descent.

Foch owned one of the numerous ferry companies that operated between Long Island and New York, and was surprisingly quite well off. The populace on western Long Island tended to be Loyalist so the Whig faction here operated discreetly, if not clandestinely. Moreover, Foch had a secret he shared with nobody. With the arrival of the American army on Long Island, he had planned to seek out their intelligence officer, a Colonel Fitzgerald, and offer to provide him information on the movements of the British and the activities of Loyalist organizations and sympathizers. Wisely, Foch thought it best to keep his plan from everyone, even his closest associates. The fact was Foch's ferry business and other shipping interests reaped only modest profits. He made most of his wealth through smuggling. The recent troubles between the colonies and Britain only increased his profits from that quarter.

He paid four of his best workers and seamen to do "special errands" for him. They made deliveries of various items, usually by night and mostly by sea. They ranged up and down the coast of Long Island, New York and as far as Westchester. These men did not know nor want to know the details of these jobs; they just naturally assumed they were involved in some of Foch's shadier business deals. Many locals correctly suspected Foch engaged in smuggling and occasionally piracy. Foch paid his men a very handsome sum for the risks they took. It seemed to Foch these times made many Americans risk-takers.

Marta walked in as Foch and Braaf were discussing the evening meeting. Although she was aware of her husband's political activities, Mistress Braaf was ambivalent about the politics of the day. Foch eyed her discreetly as she poured him a mug of coffee. He always thought her among the most attractive women in Brooklyn. No small compliment indeed, as the Dutch women from these parts were a stunning lot with radiant skin, narrow waists, and bright eyes. She turned her head away quickly but they had met each other's gaze for a second. It disturbed her that she was attracted to him. She was attracted mostly to his eyes, but also his sense of command, his confidence. She heard the rumors of his activities but she ignored them although at a certain level that added to his attraction as well. She did not like politics but she liked mystery and men of action.

Her husband Jan was talking and seemed not to notice the exchange of looks. Marta was not sure what business her husband had with him this night. Foch came to the house once, sometimes twice a week. Occasionally her husband was off on his boat, *Golden Hen*, which Foch docked to the north of the Brooklyn Ferry. In addition to the *Golden Hen*, Foch's ferry company included half a dozen smaller craft. They were mostly coastal utility craft, similar to whalers, with crews of four to eight oarsmen and a coxswain. Each could ferry up to twenty people, several cattle or a ton of cargo. Marta lowered her eyes from Foch's intense gaze and quickly excused herself to leave the men to their talk.

Foch spoke in a low voice after she left. "We must be very careful tonight, Jan. Something is afoot. General Washington is sending an officer to meet with us in the church. We must make sure none of the Tories learn of our meeting."

Braaf spoke excitedly. "Of course, I suspected as much. The young men who stayed here today have departed, and they took all their things. That means they are on the move. The question is, which way?"

Foch's eyes narrowed, "Interesting news, indeed. Well, the Continentals must need our help. About twenty of us will be there. We must go."

Braaf went into the bedroom to get his raincoat. He kissed Marta on the cheek and asked her not to wait up for him, ordering her and Krista to stay in the house until he returned.

"And when that pleasant lieutenant and his men return?" she asked.

"There is little chance of that happening, Marta." He departed in a rush. As he left, she looked pensively through her neat white lace curtains, watching as the two men heading down the lane toward the church. Unconsciously, most of her attention was on Foch.

The Whig faction met quietly in the old church, a wooden framed building with a stucco white exterior and a maple trimmed interior. It sat almost eighty worshipers comfortably, although larger numbers could gather there if they all stood. The Whigs had moved most of the sturdy pine chairs to the side, and sat in a semi-circle bantering back and forth.

Each had arrived discreetly, ensuring their movement had not been spotted by Tories. They discussed the events of the past few days but soon digressed into a flurry of political statements. Exasperated, Foch led the discussion back toward things they could do to support the rebel forces.

"*Mijnheern*, we simply have not done enough to help the army."

"But Cornelius, we have given them supplies, food and shelter, what more can we do?" A skeptical burgher asked.

"Help with the defense works would be a useful beginning." Foch snapped.

"Many of us have assisted in that..."

"For a price, eh?" Foch asked sarcastically.

"Well, we must still make our living. Most have us have families to care for, Cornelius Foch. And we cannot simply board ships and leave our homes as you can."

Braaf stood up, "Dare not attack Cornelius Foch, *Mijnheern*. He is loyal...he is... our leader." He turned to Foch. "But maybe they have a point Cornelius. It is not unpatriotic to be ambivalent."

A tall man, the local butcher, spoke. "The British will take their revenge on us Whigs whose politics crossed the line to actively support the rebel army. I am afraid."

Braaf was of the same opinion. The proximity of this mighty British host made him feel the necessity of toning down of their actions. But he decided to say no more and silently vote with the majority.

At nine o'clock, the back door to the church was flung open and Lieutenant Abner Scovel entered the meeting room. The group stood up, mutely staring at the young officer. Scovel removed his tricornered hat and gestured with his right hand. "Please sit down, gentlemen. Thank you for receiving me at this late hour, but I think you understand that the circumstances we face call for unusual measures. I am Lieutenant Abner Scovel, aide-de-camp to the commander-in-chief, who personally asked me to address you. We are preparing military activity against the British and shall act this night. There will be movement of our soldiers in various directions; many will deploy to assault the British."

This was a lie. He knew that these men would see through it soon enough, but he hoped that by time they did a spy or line crosser would make his way to the British. However, if the British saw through the ruse it would be too late to mount an assault. It was all part of Washington's gamble.

As Washington had put it, "If we do not actually deceive the British, let us to confuse and delay them.

"What exactly is going on, *Mijnheer?*" Foch spoke for the group.

"Well, yes, several things, as a matter of fact. First, we ask that you men to be most vigilant and alert for potential spies. Our actions must take place in the utmost secrecy. Second, there will be some modest redeployment of forces to New York. However, this is merely a subterfuge, as His Excellency, General Washington has ordered reinforcements over for a decisive battle against the British."

"What is it you require of us?" Foch asked.

"We will require much from you gentlemen. To begin with, we need use of any watercraft you have, starting at ten this evening. Also, if you have farm hands or dockworkers who could assist with loading and unloading supply craft, that would be of great assistance. His Excellency asks for as many men as you can muster at the Brooklyn ferry landing at ten o'clock." Scovel hoped he hadn't said too much.

"Will there be compensation for this?" One of the men asked. Scovel looked startled. "His Excellency is counting on your patriotism and love of country. He is counting on the loyalty and support of all true patriots in Brooklyn."

Braaf stood up, his large frame towering over the young officer. "Lieutenant Scovel, if we engage to support this activity..." He looked at Foch with a disbelieving eye, "You must be well aware that we put ourselves at great risk. Providing food and other sustenance to an army is one thing but actively supporting forces in rebellion places our homes and lives in great jeopardy."

Scovel feigned sympathy, "Sir, I assure you that the British will have no knowledge of this enterprise, and that in any case our intent is to drive them from Long Island, making you all the more safe and furthering our cause."

Scovel did not relish telling another lie, but knew it was necessary to ensure success of the plan. Braaf, a reasonably good attorney, noted discomfort on Scovel's face. Was this demoralized and weakened army really going on the offensive or was this all a ruse that would needlessly put them all at risk? He dared not air his thoughts in public.

He whispered to Foch in Dutch. "Cornelius, he is not being completely truthful with us."

Foch's eyes widened for a split second and then he stood up and addressed the group. "I for one am in full support of this enterprise and my entire ferry fleet, small as it is, will be at *Mijnheer's* disposal at the appointed time. I encourage all of you to do likewise."

The group began to talk in a rumble of approbation. Pleased that his mission had succeeded, Scovel quietly slipped out of the church.

Chapter 14

The regiments received their final orders, the real orders, and prepared to move. These orders specified that each unit leave its large tents and other equipment to suggest that they were still in the entrenchments, but they would take all munitions and critical supplies down to the ferry. By midnight, more than a third of the regiments had departed their positions. As they did, the First Connecticut quietly expanded its front, moving always to the right, heading south from its position at the northernmost reaches near Wallabout Bay.

The first Continental regiment had departed the Brooklyn Ferry earlier that night. Rain and wind made the event even more hazardous than normal in the treacherous currents of the East River. In all, almost fifty patriotic Whigs risked everything that night in various support functions. Most served as stevedores, helping the quartermaster's men pack and load heavy equipment. Foch was busy barking orders to his boat captains. His *Red Hen* stayed at dock but his six other craft joined the scores of others that had come over with Glover's Gloucester Regiment, made up of seamen, whalers, fishermen, and the occasional privateer or smuggler. These hearty and determined men from Marble Head and other places along the Massachusetts coast worked feverishly at the oars and tillers moving men and cargo back to New York.

Braaf, reluctantly, was helping guide the regiments through Brooklyn and down to the ferry landing. It did not take him long to realize that this was, in fact, a withdrawal from Long Island. All the soldiers were coming back from the front and no one was going forward. He suddenly thought of his son Jan. Would he be leaving too?

He went to find Foch. "Cornelius, have any New York regiments moved through yet?"

Foch nodded, "I believe most have. Why?"

Braaf replied "Of course, I should have known Jan would depart with his regiment. This is most upsetting. I must...I must...go and compose myself, Cornelius." He choked with emotion.

"Yes, go and compose yourself, Jan. We cannot have you blubbering while the men are working so hard. Come back when you feel well."

Foch shrugged to himself. The fussy hen tired easily.

☜☞

Not many miles east of Brooklyn, in the village of Bedford, Major Sandy Drummond sat on a rickety old cot in the leaky British hospital tent to which his men had taken him. The rain and wind were picking up. It seemed the whole world was water logged. Much like England, he mused. Drummond nursed a brandy in the desperate hope of reducing the pain in his knee, damaged but not destroyed by the lucky shot of some damned rebel. The round had pierced his riding boot at the knee but his breeches had a large black buckle attached to the boot on the inside. The round struck the buckle and the impact cracked bone and caused major contusions, but did not enter his flesh. Instead, it deflected and hit his horse's flank, causing it to bolt, throwing Drummond unceremoniously onto the sodden mud of the Gowanus wetlands. The fall did more injury to the knee than the shot did. The surgeons told him that in a few days, he would be limping and in a few weeks, perhaps a month, he might be back to normal.

Drummond had no time to wait for nature's course. A message from his Loyalist contact in Brooklyn indicated that he had important information, and that they needed to meet at the eastern most point of the swamp at Wallabout Bay at two hours past midnight. Drummond had the surgeons slit open the upper part of his high riding boot to reduce pressure on the swollen knee. A day of rest and food, plus the brandy, had done him the world of good. Now with a make-shift crutch he would force himself through the pain to hobble and ride. They had put down his horse after it came up lame in the fracas, but the replacement, a local gelding named "Shoe," appeared to be a fine animal. His gear was mounted and his horse ready.

At the commencement of the British landing at Gravesend, Drummond, one of the first British officers ashore on Long Island, had found a volunteer informant from among the locals, a secret Loyalist. This informant provided him two men as guides along the back roads of Flatlands through the village of New Lots to Howard's Tavern. Once there, the tavern keeper and his son were "persuaded" to guide them farther along the Rockaway Trail to the unguarded passes on the rebel flank.

Drummond was among a small circle of officers who believed that the key to crushing this rebellion lay in using the local Loyalists to advantage. In his mind they held the solution to the whole affair. Drummond thought the Loyalists were as British as anyone in the army, perhaps more so. They were solid men who built a "new" Britain here on the shores of a vast continent. Drummond scrupulously supported the need to suppress rebellion but held views sympathetic to the Whigs in Parliament. They favored accommodation with the colonies to end the crisis, not confrontation. So Drummond, while a most relentless foe of the rebels, was a most accommodating friend to the Loyalists.

"Sergeant Digby, bring my horse, if you please." shouted Drummond. Digby was an old dragoon trooper. In his mid-forties, with graying hair and more than a few missing teeth, he had served in the regiment for almost twenty-five years.

Digby was loyal to his King, his regiment and his major, but nothing else. He rode well, handled pistol and saber well, and could see to the ordinary day-to-day things. He was not educated but had a devious, almost crafty sort of intelligence. Moreover, as with most of the professional soldiers of the 18th century, Digby had not a small avaricious streak.

"Aye, Major" replied Digby breathlessly, "I'll have Shoe to you in a minute, I will."

Digby had groomed and cleaned the new horse for the major. The horse was almost completely black, gray flecks on its muzzle and up and down its lower legs the only markings; it was not as tall as an Irish-bred horse but it seemed strong and agile. The previous owners provided the horse at quite a discount to the King. He chuckled when he thought about it. Digby thought it an ironic coincidence the former owners named the horse Shoe, given Drummond's injury.

After Digby and two troopers helped Drummond mount Shoe, they proceeded to Wilmet's farm about a mile north of Bedford. At the farm, they met two Loyalist guides whose task it was to take them to the rendezvous. Neither Loyalist revealed their names; it was better that way, Drummond thought. The same two men had guided him successfully around the American Army, so they had proven their reliability.

"Will this blasted weather ever change?" Drummond asked as they rode through the dark. He was just making small talk now. He already knew that they were not members of any of the numerous Tory factions on Long Island although they professed Loyalist sympathies. Perhaps it was better they were not Tories. This area did not lack for loyal subjects, Drummond thought, just good British organization and direction. Well, he might just be the one to provide it, if he could convince the colonels and generals of it. Shoe advanced slowly and carefully along the dark and muddy trail. So much the better, thought Drummond. His knee pained him enough. He could not imagine a trot or canter.

They arrived at the rendezvous a few minutes late. They saw no sign of anyone. "We were instructed to light a lantern if nobody was here yet," said one of the guides.

"What treachery is this? Expose ourselves in this way?" asked Drummond.

"We are not fools, sir. We have done this before. I will cover the back of the lantern with our cloaks so that the light is visible only from the bay. That is how our associate will meet us."

These Dutch colonial accents grated on Drummond who muttered half aloud, half to himself, "It is about time we met again...hopefully something important calls us here."

They lit the lantern. It flickered in the wind and rain but maintained a weak light just visible enough from the open water. Suddenly another light flickered off the coast—a boat!

It was only a small rowboat, not much more than a dinghy. The boat maneuvered with great difficulty toward the coast, as the wind and the tide kept pushing it westwards. By time it had beached and the meeting finally took place, they had fallen an hour behind schedule.

ଔଓ

Creed and his men had taken up positions at the northernmost redoubt of the American defenses, half way between Fort Putnam and the swamplands along the coast of the bay. They stood watch taking turns, two at a time. Word had come down that one of the regiments near Fort Putnam had spotted a possible line crosser. There was no way to patrol every inch of the American lines. Sentries frequently made mistakes in the darkness; the wind and rain made things even worse. The so-called line crosser could have been a deer, a civilian anxious to get back to his farm, or something nefarious.

Somehow, despite the confusion of the night, Tallmadge had obtained several spy glasses. He provided two to the Light Company. Creed had his men use them.

Just after two that morning, Parker scrambled down the creaking twelve-foot ladder tied to the parapet.

"Lieutenant, I see a lantern! "

Creed's heart skipped beat, "A lantern? Where? "

Parker replied, "Right off the coast, maybe 500 yards northwest of here, in the swamp."

Creed rubbed his chin "Could it be a navigation signal for smugglers?"

"No. Smugglers don't normally use lanterns. I believe it is a signal of some sort, sir."

Parker's sharp eyes, honed from years of standing watch on fishing craft in the Chesapeake, lent great credibility to his claim.

Creed looked over to Beall. "Report this to Mister Tallmadge. I will investigate myself. Parker, you and Private Gribble will come with me."

Gribble, an accountant before joining the Maryland Continental Line, was not an original member of the Light Company but had adapted quickly to the unorthodox methods they employed.

Creed, Parker and Gribble made their way north. It took them almost twenty minutes to reach the marsh flats along the coast. From there they proceeded east along the edge of the marsh. They could move faster now, as the area was desolate and surprisingly flat and open.

They finally reached the place where the lantern had glimmered. They saw a group of men not more than thirty yards distant, conversing over a lantern partially shrouded by a raincoat. There appeared to be at least six, too many to attack directly. Creed decided to flush them out. In the confusion of the night they might have a chance to capture one.

"Are your flints dry?" he asked his two companions. They nodded grimly, as they were now both experienced at fighting in wet weather

"Load buck and ball. We will fire a volley at the gaggle of them. Aim for the lantern. Then reload quickly. We may not hit them but they will break and run. Once they scatter, we will try to hunt them down. I certainly would enjoy the company of a prisoner on the walk back."

"Buck and ball might not leave us one worth taking, sir." Parker said.

Buck and ball was a close-quarters load favored by the Americans. A large caliber musket ball augmented by three or four buckshot combined for a devastating effect.

He grinned at them mischievously. "Pray then that the good Lord spares us one."

Parker was now used to his grim humor and chuckled softly.

"On my command now, just aim center of mass, let Lucifer do the rest. Steady... present...fire." A rain-muffled volley flashed and popped. Curses and groans pierced the night as two men fell to the ground: one of the men from the beached boat and the other one of the guides. Horses began to whinny and snort in terror.

Creed was not amused to hear the horses. "Cavalry! This changes things a bit, lads. Head back, on me. Quickly now!" Creed felt he might have taken on more than prudence would normally allow. They began a slow run to evacuate their ambush site. After thirty yards of zigzag running, they turned into the marsh itself, where they stopped to reload.

"Buck and ball again, sir?" Parker asked.

"Yes, but quickly."

Their chests heaved as each went through the motions of tearing cartridge, ramming ball and paper and priming flints. A wall of high cattail grass surrounded them. Like a grass fortress, it made them feel secure.

Creed's volley had sprayed the conspirators huddling around the shrouded lantern. One of the guides was lifted from his feet by the impact of ball and shot and flung towards the water's edge. Drummond hobbled to him but the unlucky soul lay staring up from the wet sand, his eyes already glazed in a death stare. Drummond cursed loudly and limped across the sand toward his horse. Digby held Shoe ready, and helped him mount. Drummond fumbled with the stirrup but finally got Shoe settled, and drawing his saber, set off with Digby and the other troopers to find their assailants.

The wounded boatman had a belly shot and was bent over in agony desperately trying to hold his entrails.

"I'm done for!" He moaned in pain. "Help me, please."

"He's right," said the leader. "We can't waste a moment on him. We must make way before they fire again."

They pushed the boat out into the lapping waves, and began frantically rowing into the darkness and safety of the Sound. They left their erstwhile comrade to his fate, to bleed slowly to death in the salt marshes of Long Island.

"Don't let those rebel ambushers get back alive!" Drummond yelled as they trotted towards the sound of the shots. In their haste to avenge the ambush, they rode right past the tall marsh grass where Creed and his two companions hid, reloading their firelocks.

The dragoons rode slowly along the treacherous ground, poking into the salt marsh reeds in search of their prey. Seeing nothing in the dark bushes, Drummond and his men turned back and formed a line. They proceed slowly with sabers drawn and pointed low to run through any bushwhacker in reach. The dragoons, who jabbed the bush with their sabers, just missed seeing Creed's party as they emerged from the marsh. They were twenty yards away. Creed and his men lowered their weapons and aimed.

"Fire!" Creed ordered. The volley rang out over the marshes. A single round hit one of the dragoons, and his horse galloped off in fright. The other horses bolted too. Shoe had never experienced combat and it took Drummond, experienced horseman though he was, some time to regain control of his new mount. By the time he did, his men had scattered.

He called in exasperation. "Digby! Sergeant Digby, form on me! Sergeant Digby!"

Drummond could hear the muffled cries of his troopers and the snorting of their horses off to the west. Drummond reached down to his damaged knee, which now throbbed painfully. He loosened the buckles and gently rubbed it. Then he pulled a small flask from his saddlebag and took a long swig. The brandy helped dull the pain, and it warmed him against the chill of the rain and wind.

A few minutes later Digby came up with the two troopers.

"Are you alright, sir? The lads and I and can hunt down these buggers." Digby's tone was almost patronizing.

Drummond masked his anger with bravado. "Never mind that, Sergeant. We must return to headquarters and report our interesting news to General Howe—work more important than filleting a couple of rebels."

୫୬ଓ୪

General Washington sat pensively on his horse watching as each unit embarked from the Brooklyn ferry. It was nearly daylight. Most of the regiments had already safely returned to New York. In all, his men had performed superbly under the most trying conditions. Morale was good, although nerves were on edge as each man realized that if the British discovered their precarious position it would bring disaster. When the weather cleared the British Navy would make its presence known, of that he was sure.

However, the evening was not without its challenges. Confusion in orders had caused an entire regiment to pull out of the line prematurely, leaving a dangerous gap and creating the potential for a panic, courting disaster and ruin. Washington himself had to intervene to get the regiment back in it rightful place and wait its turn to depart.

An hour before dawn, Fitzgerald was packing up his makeshift office, in preparation for his departure to Manhattan. He had sequestered himself in a small leather tent to take reports and develop a more comprehensive listing of what forces opposed them: his estimate had the British at more than twenty thousand, just two thirds of their actual number of thirty thousand.

Suddenly, he looked up from his figures and saw two men, locals, standing at the open tent flap.

"Colonel Fitzgerald?" asked the tall, portly man with the thinning light hair and lazy eyes.

"Do I know you?" Fitzgerald replied. The men looked familiar.

"Colonel, I am Jan Braaf and this is my colleague, Cornelius Foch. We are with the Brooklyn Whig faction. I must say that the army leaving puts all of us here at risk. Is there any hope for us that you will return?"

Realizing who they were, Fitzgerald laughed. "Of course there is, when Ireland is freed by England."

Braaf retorted brusquely. "I see no humor in this, Colonel. My son joined a militia company that has now been assigned to one of the New York regiments. His mother is anxious as to how long he might be gone."

Fitzgerald continued his sarcasm. "I suppose there are many such mothers as his. In any case it will be quite some time. Depends, you see, on the whereabouts of the British Navy, which as you know, is a bit larger than ours."

He looked back toward the East River that was now crowded with numerous small craft going to and from New York, "Come to think of it, do we have a navy?"

Foch responded, "Well, *Mijnheer*, you have the use of my boats. And after you have departed, you may count on me to help the cause. I own the *Red Hen* and several smaller craft. You may later have the need to receive reports on forces and activities here on Long Island. My men and I know every harbor and cove from here north to New Rochelle, and east to Syosset."

Fitzgerald's eyes brightened. He thought he saw the dawn sun starting to rise to the east and lighten things. "Well that is an interesting idea, sir. How do you propose we arrange for this?"

Foch had been working on his plan for some time. He provided Fitzgerald a well-made and accurate map that showed several points along the New York, Westchester, Connecticut, and Long Island coastlines. Each was marked with a three or four digit number and a letter.

"I will have a boat at each location on the day of the month marked. We shall rendezvous then."

"How do I know which day?" Fitzgerald knew, but asked anyway.

"The first two numbers show the month, the last two the day. So, '0101' would be the first of January. The letter *a* means morning tide, *b* evening tide. A red flag hoisted means British or Loyalists nearby; cancel the meeting. A white flag means all clear."

Foch had done his homework, but he had engaged in smuggling, as all successful merchants did, to make a profit. Secret rendezvous were routine for him.

Fitzgerald's eyes narrowed as he took the measure of this obvious opportunist, making such a bold and risky proposal right here in the middle of a thousand fighting men during a most dangerous military operation.

"How can I trust you...be sure that you will not turn to the British first chance?"

"By relying on your instincts Colonel. In the end, there is no other measure of trust."

Fitzgerald eyed him closely. He looked like a pirate, certainly a smuggler; the perfect type to enlist in such an enterprise.

"Very well sir, but we shall need some way to verify each other's people. Face to face, that is. I suggest something simple: my agent will say 'Did you once sail on the *Eagle*?' Yours will reply, 'No, I sailed on the *Talon*'." Naval terminology seemed appropriate to Fitzgerald under the circumstances.

Foch recognized the irony and grinned, "Very well Colonel. I will not disappoint you. I saw the bravery of your men these past few days. I have concluded that to defeat the British we will need more such brave men. We need daring and cunning men, both in uniform and out."

"So true, Mr. Foch. Now tell me, what is your real motivation? I can tell from your accent that you were not born in the colonies. Why volunteer to take this risk? It goes beyond patriotism to spy. Is it gold you are seeking? The Congress has authorized no monies for such activity, so anything we pay comes from His Excellency's own funds. And I can assure you, sir, those are not robust."

"I have my reasons, Colonel. I support the Cause, which is one reason why I came to America. I also have a score to settle with these English. Moreover, there may be a time that I will need some special, ah...'concessions.'"

"Concessions, is it? Revenge, is it? The 'Cause', is it? Ah, I can see that you are a complex man *Mijnheer* Foch. By the way, we should not use names or titles in any correspondence. For surety's sake, anyone corresponding for me will be called 'Mister Smythe' and you or anyone representing you will be 'Mister Jons'. Do you understand?"

Foch responded solemnly, "Perfectly...Mister Smythe...your agent? Mister Jons...mine? However in such things I represent myself. Safer that way. Don't you think?'"

Fitzgerald nodded with intensity. "All the better. Therefore, is it agreed—you work for me and for our Cause?"

Foch looked down, then into Fitzgerald's eyes. "Why, yes...that is why I am here...the Cause...I agree."

Fitzgerald wrinkled his brow and pushed his glasses to the bridge of his nose, "If the army is driven from New York, a certain agent of mine, a Mister Smythe will need your services to send me information from the enemy's bosom, so to speak. This will be dangerous business. Do you understand...'Mister Jons'?"

Foch frowned, then grinned, nodding ever so slightly, "Perfectly...'Mr. Smythe'."

Taking his measure of the man, Fitzgerald twisted his head at an angle, "Now, I bid you good day and good luck. We both still have much work to accomplish."

Foch turned and walked off with Braaf on his heels.

Braaf was completely stunned by the turn of events. What madness was this? He just witnessed the formation of a conspiracy between the defeated rebel forces and his friend, a conspiracy against the British who would likely soon occupy Brooklyn. Political support for the American cause, as a Whig, was one thing. But conspiring to spy on the King's forces was quite another.

"Cornelius, what possible reason could you have for such a rash offer?" Jan Braaf finally managed to stammer out.

"I meant what I told him, Jan. I was not born here but I am a true Patriot. If the British come and stay, the war will no longer be one merely one of muskets and bayonets, but of brains and stealth. That is my forte, and it is yours too. I shall need your help."

Braaf stomped his foot like a petulant child, "I cannot! I will not be involved..."

Foch turned suddenly and grasped his friend's massive shoulder. "You are already involved! I need the support of a man like you for this to work. Political action alone is not enough. If the English come, and most importantly stay, our Tory friends and other Loyalists will force us to go underground."

Braaf did not answer. He knew that at least for now had no choice but to support his friend and colleague. He paused a second..." Very well Cornelius. But we must keep my family out of this at all costs."

"Of course we will." Foch replied softly, almost to himself. Then his thoughts turned to Marta. He wondered how she ever could have married such a fussy old hen. He thought, perhaps he would name a future ship after him, *The Old Hen*, to match the *Red Hen*. He laughed to himself.

Chapter 15

Tallmadge was waiting for Creed when he returned to the lines. "What happened out there, Jeremiah? We heard the musket fire."

"'Twas our fire you heard, Benjamin. I think we got couple of them."

"Couple of what?" Tallmadge pressed. "Are the British so bold as to advance on our flank along the marsh?"

"No, at least not yet," Creed replied. "There was a boat. I believe we interrupted some mischief. Whoever was on that boat was meeting British dragoons. Tis likely that whoever led the British around our unsecured pass at Jamaica had new information to pass on to the redcoats. I would wager those dragoons now know the army is returning to New York. The British might yet have time to overwhelm the remaining forces, including this fine Connecticut regiment of yours."

Tallmadge grimaced. "It is your regiment now as well, Jeremiah, but your point is well taken. We must get word back to General Washington and inform Colonel Chester immediately. As the rear guard, we will surely take the brunt of a sudden British assault on the lines. My place is here, with the regiment. You must go back to the ferry landing at once and inform His Excellency."

Creed nodded and turned to Beall. "Make sure the lads have dry powder and enough ball and flint. If my fears prove correct, we may yet face more action before we depart this island."

ଚ୍ଚେ

Drummond pushed himself hard. When his small force reached Wilmet's Farm, they eased their horses into a slow trot so to make the final leg south to British headquarters. Dawn would soon break and God only knew how far along the rebel retreat had already progressed. He reckoned that a swift movement by just a small British force might yet enable them to rout the rebels and capture their ringleader, Mister Washington. That might just end this independence madness. After half an hour's ride, they passed through the pickets surrounding British headquarters.

Drummond went first to Cornwallis' tent. He announced himself to an orderly who did not hide his displeasure at having to come out into the rain and awaken the general. After what seemed a long fifteen minutes, the orderly opened the canvas flap and led Drummond into the tent. Cornwallis was up and had another orderly helping him with his boots.

"So Sandy, what vital information do you bring us on this fine morning?" Cornwallis asked in a tone both cordial and sarcastic.

The orderly poured both officers a glass of claret. Drummond gladly took the glass of the dry red wine, a favorite among the British officers at all meals and all hours.

"Well sir, I met with our 'friends.' God knows finding them was difficult enough."

"Did your friends have any information of interest?" Cornwallis asked.

Drummond nodded. "It seems...that Mister Washington started sending his troops back to New York last night. There are also rumors of reinforcements coming back over from New York. I say the rumors are a ruse to confuse spies—spies like our friends. They are evacuating under our noses using the darkness and weather as cover."

Cornwallis cocked his head. "Yes. It makes sense. We thrashed them and now they have no stomach to stay and fight again. I must call a meeting with General Howe immediately. The trick will be to convince our most coy commander; ever the betrothed, never the bride."

They both laughed. The comment was a direct reference to Howe's caution, but also an indirect reference to his American mistress, Mrs. Elizabeth Loring, whose Loyalist husband Joshua traded her pliant body and her affections for a lucrative position as the head of the Commissariat for Prisons.

"How is that leg of yours?" Cornwallis suddenly realized that Drummond had a crutch and was showing some bit of discomfort.

"Tolerable sir, thank you. I am afraid that it will have to hurt for now and heal in good time. I cannot afford to go to surgery and then rest it for God knows how long."

He grimaced, thinking that a surgeon would only render it worse and then he would be out of action for weeks, if not longer. None of that for Sandy Drummond, he thought. The war would end soon enough and he wanted his share of glory.

"Well Sandy, your dedication and service are commendable. I shall see that the appropriate people at Horse Guards know of it. Meanwhile, prepare your squadron. I'll have six companies of grenadiers from Thorne and a battery section from Sam Cleveland to support your assault on these damned rebels—once our good commander gives the order."

"Your trust in me is not misplaced sir." Drummond saluted and with some bit of difficulty made his departure into the dwindling morning rain.

꙼꙼꙼

At dawn, Creed arrived at what remained of General Washington's headquarters. The sun was straining to burn through the last of the clouds, as the previous day's rain dwindled to a final cascade of misty droplets. Heavy fog now blanketed the entire area. It permeated everything, nature's curtain call signaling a change in weather. Creed was soaked, caked in mud and in the throes of the familiar soldier's battle with fatigue.

When he arrived at the old church, the American camp was gone. He followed a regiment of New York militia marching quietly, almost despondently, through the early morning fog toward the Brooklyn ferry. Creed guessed that Washington must have moved his camp there so he followed the column. He soon found General Washington astride his horse, watching the last few regiments work their way to the ferry landing. His entire staff, including Fitzgerald, had already crossed over to New York. Visibility was now less than ten yards in most places, so Creed was fortunate to find the commander-in-chief and his one remaining aide-de-camp, Alexander Scammel.

"Well, my dear Lieutenant Creed. You look like an Irish terrier that picked on a cranky badger." Washington smiled; his tone was affectionate and his words meant as a compliment, not a rebuke.

Creed grinned. "Sir, it is very hard to do morning ablutions in all this fog. Feels like home, it does. However, I have you important news...a good probability exists that a spy in our midst transmitted your true intentions to the British."

Washington glared. "What makes you think such a thing, Jeremiah?"

"I interrupted a secret rendezvous between British dragoons and some men off Wallabout Bay, but I am afraid that I was too late to thwart their perfidy. The dragoons rushed off, although we left at least one in the swamp with Maryland lead in him. Still, we must assume the British were alerted and will act with haste to exploit the news."

Washington frowned and turned to Scammel. "Ride at once to General Mifflin and instruct him to accelerate movement of his division from the lines. This time we can afford no confusion here."

Washington looked at Creed. "Earlier this morning, Mifflin precipitously moved some of his forces from the trenches, causing a potentially fatal gap in our lines. Fortunately, Scammel here corrected the situation and sent the men back to close the gap. "

Creed replied. "Our Irish luck holds then, sir."

Washington smiled knowingly. "Jeremiah, tell Chester to maintain his position. He must hold until Mifflin's men have boarded. We can only pray the fog hangs long enough to finish the night's good work."

Washington reached down from his horse and grabbed Creed's hand, almost as if to draw strength from the younger man. "And Jeremiah, impart on him the urgency of the situation. His actions and yours are critical to the safety of the army. Godspeed to all of you."

And a good night's work it was. Thanks to the hard work of the troops, civilian volunteers, and contract teamsters, they had saved most of the artillery. These stalwart men dragged and manhandled heavy guns through mud and windswept rain. At the ferry, they carefully hoisted each piece onto the oddly-assorted craft for transport across the treacherous East River, which bubbled like a cauldron of boiling oil.

Creed passed through the village of Brooklyn on the way back, and he decided to stop by the Braaf house to thank them for their kindness and generosity their brief stay.

As Creed approached the house, he saw a light and shadows moving in the kitchen. Someone was already up. He rapped his knuckled softly on the shutters. They opened and Marta Braaf greeted him with a warm smile. He had not really noticed before how really beautiful she was. Perhaps the morning light and the heavy mists provided a romantic setting that had been missing before. Although ten years her junior he found her very attractive. Perhaps the tensions of three days' combat had overcome him.

Marta Braaf spoke in her sultry voice. "What a welcome surprise to see you, Lieutenant Creed...and at this hour. We did not expect your return."

Creed suddenly felt embarrassed—he had no idea why he stopped by this house in the midst of battle.

He forced a smile. "Just passing by, *Mervrouw*, when I realized I had not said a proper farewell, nor thanked you for your hospitality to the lads."

Marta lowered her eyes. "It was my pleasure.... I mean our pleasure, to serve you. And it seems I must do so again. Please come in and rest a bit."

"Rest would be a fine thing right now but I must be off to the lines."

She smiled. "Then come have some coffee. It is fresh."

The aroma hit him suddenly and he could not refuse. He was exhausted and wet and knew that some coffee would revive him. He entered the kitchen, trying unsuccessfully to prevent his boots from soiling the cleanly buffed wooden floor.

She moved about with swaying hips and spoke while she fixed his drink. "My husband has been out all night, on what business I can only imagine. I expected him home by now. So I thought I should have coffee and bread ready."

Marta turned and smiled gently. She handed Creed a steaming mug and proceeded to slice freshly baked bread and some cheese.

"There are many locals helping the army this night, perhaps he is with them." Creed explained. He felt uncomfortable discussing the army's departure but surely, she knew there was activity all around. She sat next to him and slyly slid her chair against his.

"I think so." She said. "Yet I worry so much. This war frightens me, especially with my son now a part of it. My husband is involved in Whig politics. If the British arrive I fear what will become of us. He is gone often and without notice, leaving us, leaving me alone."

She lowered her head, then raised it and looked at him in a way he had not expected from her. Slowly, she slipped a small, plump hand over his wrist, softly stroking his black curly hairs.

Creed ignored it. "Do not worry. Your husband is a good man and a clever man. He will know what to do. As for the British, they will not stay here long."

Marta said. "Can you stay...a little longer, Lieutenant Creed?"

He knew he had stayed too long already but he wanted to reassure her without hinting at something else. "No m'am, I must go. Orders require me at the front and I have tarried too long already."

He downed the bread and cheese and took some extra food she handed him wrapped in blue and white linen cloth. He placed it in his jacket. She put her arms around him in a motherly way, kissed him on the cheek, and then held him in a warm embrace that was anything but motherly. Creed was stunned and did not know what to do. She smelled good and the embrace brought him feelings he had not felt in a long while...then he thought of Emily back in New York.

He stepped away politely. "You are too kind, m'am. Thank you...again...for everything."

"Thank-you Lieutenant, for easing my loneliness, even for a brief moment. Please stay safe."

He gently took her hand and softly kissed it, then left.

When Creed reached the end of the street, he heard the sound of footsteps from behind him. In the thick fog he could not see who it was. He gripped the hilt of his sword-bayonet and stepped behind a nearby maple tree. The footsteps trailed off, then suddenly someone was moving through the fog in front of him— Krista Braaf. She wore only her morning coat and slippers, and her golden hair was in tangles. Breathless, she nearly ran through Creed who had to grasp her shoulders to steady her.

"Oh, Lieutenant Creed, I am so glad I was able to catch you before you..."

Creed cut her off. "Miss, I must be going. I have urgent business to attend."

"I know. Please do me the favor of delivering these letters. One is to Jonathan, I mean Private Beall. The other is to my brother, Jan."

"Surely I have no way of knowing where he or his unit is."

Krista threw herself into his arms and began to sob. "But you are my only hope. Neither may return to Brooklyn for months."

Creed softened. "Very well, miss. I will take the letters. And I will see what I can do. But now, you must listen to me. Head right home and stay there. There might well be bad business this day. Keep your mother there too. You must promise."

She looked at him with teary eyes. "Yes. I promise."

Creed took her hands in his, and gently bowed his head in farewell. He then began to double time back toward the trenches. He had indeed tarried long enough. The fog might soon lift and the British begin their assault.

Creed found Chester and passed on Washington's orders. The Connecticut men were anxious to leave. When Creed arrived at the redoubt and the remnant of his company, he provided his men the bread and cheese but he kept Krista's letter from Jonathan Beall. Now was not the time to distract a young man's mind when it needed to concentrate on the job at hand. For that reason, his mild infatuation with *Marta* Braaf and her affectionate ways were even more vexing. Creed had affairs of the heart in his past. He considered himself somewhat worldly about such things, but now his dedication was to a Cause and his heart belonged to a young woman who shared that dedication. Creed determined to focus on the mission, and to get his men safely back from the hell that was Long Island...and to see Emily once again.

"How goes it here?" Creed asked Beall.

"Tolerable, thus far, sir. Are we going to leave now?" Beall asked wistfully. He had mixed feelings about leaving Long Island and his voice showed it.

"I hope so. Keep two men on watch. I must see Mister Tallmadge."

It was half eight now and the fog still lay thick across the entire western end of Long Island. The sun was trying to break through, but miraculously for the Americans, the gray pall continued. Creed met with Tallmadge who informed him that the Light Company would deploy to defend the Flatbush Road just north of Fort Greene and provide security for the regiment's retreat. Tallmadge had attached a file of seven of his best men, making the Light Company, the last unit scheduled to leave Long Island, little more than a dozen strong.

ॐ

The Stanley House, New York

Emily returned home at dawn. Nancy had spent most of the night worrying over her mistress' whereabouts and met her at the back door with a suspicious stare.

"Where have you been, Miss Em? I have been worried no end. It is dangerous for a young woman out alone at night...or were you alone?"

Emily flushed beet red but ignored the implication of an assignation—a romantic tryst. "Nancy, you know me better than that. I do appreciate your concern, but I was totally safe. I had hundreds of our fine young soldiers to protect me."

Nancy smiled knowingly. "Sorry Miss Em. You know how I am. And I know how soldiers are with beautiful young women."

Emily blushed again. "Then you must know how I am with soldiers.... After dinner at Lady Dunning's, I began to head home. However, word spread through the city that the army was returning from Long Island. I found a cooperative and patriotic merchant who opened his store. I purchased some food and other comfort items which I carried down to Murray's Wharf. The wounded came across first, so of course I rendered what help I could."

Nancy furrowed her brow. "So the doctor's daughter plays doctor too? How bad was it?"

"Quite bad...no, Nancy, it was awful!" Emily put her face in her hands to hide the tears welling up.

She composed herself and continued. "Many of the young men were carried straight to the surgical hospital over near the North River; a long, bumpy ride for men whose limbs and bodies had been torn and pierced by metal objects. I mostly helped with compresses and tightening tourniquets. Carried pails of water. I think the worst of it was the cries of those facing the knife. And the aroma of putrefying flesh was overwhelming. It was horrible. But necessary...the poor young men..."

Nancy said. "You best get some sleep, Miss Em. I'll take care of breakfast for the guests and wake you at noon."

Emily sighed, and then smiled. "You are such a dear, Nancy. Thank you. But wake me by eleven. I am afraid I will have much to do today."

ಬಚಿ

Lord Howe's Headquarters, Bedford, Long Island, August 30th, 1776

"So, you see Milord, we must act immediately, otherwise the rebels will have humbugged us, by God!" Cornwallis slapped his right glove into his left palm for emphasis. Clinton, Howe, the Hessian Von Heister, and Grant all attended this dawn meeting as well.

Howe smiled patronizingly, "My dear fellow, we have these rebels where we want them because I have proceeded with deliberation, not haste. The people who provided you this information have their own interests. I am sure of that."

Cornwallis replied. "Sandy Drummond assures me that his informant is loyal to the King and provided this information at the cost of at least two of his associates, not to mention one of our dragoons. Need I remind you that they led us to the pass that brought us before these lines so handily? An immediate and all-out attack is in order, I assure you we shall sweep what rebels remain into the sea. More importantly, we might yet bag Mister Washington and end this rebellion. Many, if not most of these Americans are loyal to the crown. A strong British presence is all that is needed to encourage them to come out openly."

"On that we both agree, dear Cornwallis. This tragedy of a rebellion must not veer any more out of control than it already has. That is why we must proceed with patience and deliberation. A pell-mell attack could jeopardize everything. Even the smallest check of our forces could provide the rebels the aid and comfort they need to continue. Once this fog clears, I will make a determination as to our next course of action—either formal investment of their works or assault. We shall meet again at ten this morning."

Cornwallis raised a hand in protest. "But by then it may be too late! I already have a flying column prepared to go in. This campaign, this war, could be over in hours."

He was getting vexed. Not at Howe, whose position and caution he understood all too well, but at the others. None of them supported him vocally, even though they had each told him separately that they agreed with him and disdained Howe's caution. Ironically, the politics of the British high command was one of Washington's most important assets, and he was not even aware of it.

Drummond had assembled his entire squadron of dragoons. Just shy of a hundred men, they made a splendid and imposing sight in their red tunics and brass helmets. Their dragoon muskets loaded, sabers drawn as if on parade, they were formed in a column four abreast and almost twenty deep. This was the largest body of cavalry to deploy in North America. Behind them, in dense columns, were the grenadier companies and a short battery of two six-pound guns pulled by horses. Cornwallis had ordered them to be prepared to charge the rebel works on his command. They were to drive deep into the American lines and proceed up the Flatbush Road to the Brooklyn Heights. Their objective was the ferry and God willing, the American headquarters and commanding general, Mister Washington, along with it. Yet it was well past dawn and there was yet no word from their esteemed commander-in-chief.

"Blast this fog to hell!" muttered Drummond to Colonel Thorne. The dragoons and grenadiers, as well as the guns, were under the overall command of Thorne but Drummond would lead the charge. Colonel Roger Thorne was himself a bold and audacious officer, yet even he had to reel Drummond in at times. They had a mutual respect born of many years service together as well as personal ties. Thorne served as a young subaltern under Drummond's father. He was at once Drummond's mentor, and in a small way, rival for the affection of the men. Thorne's command was a composite battalion of grenadiers of six companies from several regiments, a division of two light companies, Drummond's squadron of the 17th Light Dragoons and a battery of four six-pound cannon. The British organized the infantry into divisions of two companies for tactical employment. Each division was under the provisional command of a major or senior captain.

"Patience Sandy, patience. Your time will come. Trust me." Thorne was a bit patronizing in tone but in the heat of things Drummond hardly noticed. Like a hound anxious for the hunt, Thorne thought to himself. Dangerous at once to the quarry and the hunter, if not controlled.

Drummond exploded, "The time is now! I can sense that they are in disarray, if not in full retreat. It may be too late once the fog lifts."

He did not tell Thorne of the meeting with his Loyalist contacts and their report of a possible withdrawal. He reserved that knowledge to himself, Lord Cornwallis and Howe.

"I shall not release you until we have such authority. You know that Lord Cornwallis is as eager as you or I to advance on these rebels, but General Howe is still in command. However, I am sure that the order will come soon enough."

Normally, Drummond was extremely calm and judicious in his handling of such affairs, but his bloodlust was up. Whether it was to avenge his damaged leg or the loss of a good dragoon earlier in the morning, it was high time to finish the business.

Chapter 16

At last, the word came. Chester finally received orders to move back from the defense works and assemble at the Brooklyn ferry for the return to New York. Tallmadge mounted his horse and made his way back with the last company. The fog still hung low, but it was obvious that the morning sun was rising and visibility would soon return to normal. Tallmadge was torn about leaving. He had joined the army in part to avenge the death of a dear friend at British hands and wanted very much to meet them in combat. However, his analytic mind gave him insight that few young officers had: by retiring to New York now, the army avoided certain destruction.

Chester was with the lead company. The colonel sensed that his men had mixed feelings as they departed. With the rain and wind gone, many of them hoped the British would throw themselves on the American lines and be broken as they had in Boston the previous year. Unfortunately, Brooklyn would prove no repeat of Breed's Hill. The Connecticut men believed strongly in the cause and in the ideals of the Declaration of Independence recently signed by Congress. They hoped the war would end with a victorious final battle before the heights of Brooklyn. These hopes now evaporated as slowly but as steadily as the morning mist through which they trudged. And as they slogged through the endless mud puddles, it slowly dawned on them that this was not the end but the beginning of many such painful, tedious, and ignominious movements. Fatigue, hunger, boredom, and terror would provide a painful brew that many of them would drink over the next few years.

The regiment snaked its way along the Flatbush Road through the war-torn village of Brooklyn. In the morning stillness, the town was particularly quiet, almost eerie. Its stolid burghers, who had toiled through the night in rain and wind to help the rebels, had now repaired to their homes to hide the valuables from the anticipated depredations of a British army in triumph. The Old Dutch church, dark and empty that morning; stood like a silent monument in defiance of the enemy. Many a passing soldier wondered if the building would be standing much longer.

ဆာ

Cornelius Foch was in his cabin on board his flagship, *Red Hen*. He had just hidden the note of payment he received from Washington's Quartermaster General—script payment for a job well done. It was worthless now. However, if fortune turned favorable for the rebels, the note might have value. It might enable him to bargain his way out of a bad situation, so he carefully hid it inside an old mahogany clock that sat on his captain's chest.

Foch was nothing if not a deal maker. He began his lucrative career as a Ship's Master by chicanery. Ten years earlier, he had been an able bodied seaman on a British merchant ship that plied its trade between the English coastal ports and Rotterdam. It was good work and it enabled him to learn English fluently. However, the Ship's Master was a vicious sea dog who beat the men when he was drunk, which he was most of the time. They profited little from their efforts and risked much as he occasionally engaged in smuggling. Foch and the crew were fine with that, except all the risk was theirs and all the profits his.

The final straw came when the Master decided to enter the slave trade. It was to be a "one-time" event: sail to west coast of Africa and pick up a load of slaves for a pittance worth of British and Dutch goods, sail to the Indies or Carolinas and return with a load of rum, molasses and other goods in demand on the Continent. The idea of this incensed most of the crew. These cynical, whoring, drink-besotted men considered trafficking in human chattel an abomination. To them, even piracy had more honor. Foch was able to win over enough of the crew to gamble on a mutiny. Therefore, it passed that when they were at sea heading toward Africa, they got the Master and his closest officers drunk, hogtied them, and put them to sea in a skiff. Foch and the crew headed directly to America, without slaves, to begin anew. While underway, Foch had the ship's name changed from *Sturgeon* to *Red Hen*.

The Master survived and returned to England but for some reason British maritime law never did catch up with Foch, although an admiralty court had indicted him as a pirate and mutineer. A little gold in just the right hands went a long way. Initially based in the Leeward Islands of the Caribbean, Foch arrived in New York because of a loose partnership he had with the Gaults, a family of shrewd Flemish Jews who had interests in banking, trading and smuggling stretching from Antwerp to the Antilles and then New York. Now this rebellion posed both a challenge and an opportunity that he planned to exploit.

At dawn, Braaf knocked on his cabin door and stuck his head in. "I am leaving now, Cornelius. Are you sure you will not come home to have breakfast with us? I will make sure Marta prepares something special."

Foch shook his head. "*Bedankt*, Jan, but no. I have much work to do to secure traces of the Whig faction from prying eyes. The Tories will surely identify us as the Whig leaders during the British occupation of our town. I do not want to leave any evidence that might make their efforts any easier than it already is."

The idea of spending some time at the Braaf house intrigued him. Marta Braaf was a remarkable beauty. Any time he could spend in her presence was a thrill.

He had tasted the charms of so many of the doxies of New York, as well as in Rotterdam in his youth, but her earthy and gracious beauty intoxicated him beyond his wildest imaginings. And in some inexplicable way, he felt that she had feelings for him too. Every now and then, he thought he caught a subtle glance his way. Perhaps it was his imagination. Worldly as he was, he just was not sure.

"If you change your mind..."

Foch cut him off. "I won't. I must cover our tracks as best as I can. We are both at risk, as are the others."

"How do you..."

"Do not ask any more, Jan. Go home to your family. They need you as much as does the Cause."

౭ఎ౧ఆ

Tallmadge did not give Creed a specific time for the Light Company to return to the ferry. He left it to Creed's good judgment. Creed had, after all, more experience than he. When the First Connecticut was gone, Creed decided he only had enough men to defend the approach from the Flatbush Road. Since it was the major artery leading into the village, the British were most likely to advance along it. He placed five pairs of Continentals on each side of the road, ten yards apart. Parker and Beall formed the center pair. Creed wanted his two best men to anchor the line and be the last to drop back.

"So Elias, I will get to see what sort of soldier you are at last." Beall teased Parker as they stood at their new post. The two had begun to bond the shared experience of combat.

"I am a sailor by trade, a soldier by stupidity. What excuse do you have for being here?" Parker answered flatly. He looked up and down the line. He could barely make out the pair on either flank. That was good. The fog was still hanging low and visibility was poor. Nevertheless, he knew it would not be long before the sun finally did its work and burned it off. Parker immediately regretted his rebuff to Beall. The Maryland farm boy had become like a younger brother in the short time they had served together.

His whisper broke through the fog. "Jonathan. Sorry for the remark. If I could have chosen anyone to fight alongside me against the lobsters in this God-forsaken place, it is you."

Beall returned the sentiment. "And I you, Elias. With Simon hurt, you are my best friend in the unit."

"Even though I am not an original member of the Light Company?" Parker asked.

"All the more so, Elias, all the more so", said Beall. Beall thought about Simon. His gruff, sometimes overbearing cousin had a heart of butter and was the most decent, forthright person he knew, except now maybe Elias. Jonathan's parents and grandparents had fought the Indians to keep their homes in western Maryland and now he was standing shoulder to shoulder with one and pledged to give his very life for him.

Before he deployed the men, Creed had addressed them. The newcomers looked very anxious, but not nervous. He thought it the calm of the innocent. "Check powder, double ball please. Second round will be single ball. Then we shall retreat by pairs, first the wings, then the center pairs. On my command, of course. Each pair will drop back twenty yards from the one before it. We shall fire individual, two-man volleys as we move back. If they charge or come with cavalry stand back to back. If we are overwhelmed, try to make your way back to the ferry, stay in pairs if possible."

Creed knew that a determined charge would sound their death knell. He had to get them back before that happened. Retreat was at his discretion, and as a Roman Catholic he did not favor suicide. These men were too good, too dedicated to die needlessly. It was now a question of timing, and as Colonel Fitzgerald would view it, luck. The morning fog still enveloped the trench works as well as most of western Long Island. He just needed his luck to hold out and the fog to linger a bit longer. Creed smiled to himself and wondered if he still had his rosary. A gift from his mother, he always carried it with him although he too rarely used it for its intended purpose. He fumbled through his pockets and sure enough, found it. For the first time in a very long time, he prayed.

ಬಂಞ

The First Connecticut began loading into boats for the ride across the East River and the safety of New York. General Washington had already made the trip. A few stragglers still lingered at the ferry. Many of those were deserters or malingerers who had raided the local establishments and were now too drunk to go. A single company of the Pennsylvania Line, rough looking men from the west, guarded the ferry approach. Soon they would be gone as well, the last to cross.

Tallmadge was directing the troops onto the boats at the ferry launch. The boat crews were tired from a night of constant toil against the wind, rain, and tide. They had struggled heroically against time and the elements to accomplish a near miracle in annals of military history. The retrograde of an army under adverse conditions in the face of a vastly superior force was an impressive feat.

"I expect you shall ride back with the last company, Benjamin." Chester was preparing to embark with his staff.

"Yes sir. Just two more companies left. I shall depart with the last. I was actually hoping that Mister Creed would be back by now but I suspect he is waiting until the last possible moment. So far the fog is holding in our favor, thank God."

Chester nodded. "Indeed. But I suspect the British shall not be too far behind us. We might yet see some action."

"One would hope. The boys are spoiling for a taste of combat." Tallmadge winced as he said it.

"Indeed," replied Chester distractedly. Both men were looking toward the bluffs overlooking the ferry in a last attempt to ascertain whether Creed was falling back. Even the bold Pennsylvanians were starting their way down to the water and safety.

Chester boarded his craft clumsily as it rocked and wallowed in the river's choppy water. Tallmadge saluted him, and then waved. He watched the boat drift deeper into the fog and disappear from view. The smell of the salt air invigorated Tallmadge. The river was tidal, and the water was brackish, being only a few miles from the open sea. He paced nervously, glancing back and forth from the river toward the bluffs and the village beyond, anticipating the fog lifting, the return of Creed's company and the arrival of the British. Tallmadge spotted a small open fire where the boat crews were warming themselves in the early morning chill. He pulled his meerschaum pipe from his vest and tapped in a piece of dark tobacco. He grabbed a bit of straw and lit it in the fire of a nearby lantern, then used it to light the pipe. Fine morning for a smoke, he thought. When the final company loaded off, he tamped out his pipe and hopped aboard a boat with some of his men. Unfortunately, he was going to have to leave his horse to the British, as there was not room for it on any of the remaining boats. Tallmadge tethered the horse to a post along the wharf. He stroked its muzzle for a while and then took a carrot from his saddlebag. While the animal chomped on the unexpected treat, he sadly left it to its fate.

The longboat shoved off abruptly and Tallmadge almost lost his balance as the boat shifted and rolled across the East River. The crew rowed sluggishly; exhausted from the long night's work battling the tide and wind. Each boat had logged several trips that night and despite the fact that most were tough veteran sailors, whalers and fishermen, they were past the point of exhaustion. The fog still lay heavy across the water, so visibility remained poor.

As his boat headed back toward New York, Tallmadge gazed up at the heights of Brooklyn and thought back on the carnage of the last several days. He had lost friends and relatives in the fighting. The fate of so many of them was still unclear. He would later learn of the bayoneting of prisoners and the mistreatment of many others. For now, a pall of helplessness, regret and fatigue gripped him.

ஐௐ

Braaf returned home just before dawn. Marta gave him a gentle hug, but quickly pulled away. She fetched him coffee while Krista brought him bread and smoked sausage. While he ate, they told him of Creed's impromptu visit. He did not find it unusual. He was aware that soldiers often gravitated toward food, drink, and beautiful women. Braaf said very little, nodding and grunting in reply to them, and when he finished he went straight to bed. While he slept, the two women sat by the kitchen fire and talked.

"Mama, will there be fighting here?" Krista asked.

Marta answered, more out of hope than conviction. "No, Krista, I do not think so. There are so few soldiers left. I think the English will come but there will be no destruction or bloodshed. We will be safe."

Krista asked. "Will we be forced to let them...these English...into our home?"

"Perhaps," replied Marta without emotion.

Krista's eyes widened. I would not like that. I would not feel...comfortable with strange men around."

Marta looked at her and realized that her girl was now a beautiful young woman. "Yes, it would be very uncomfortable but we had those men from Maryland here and it was no bother. We were fine. More than fine..."

"Yes, mama but they were Americans and.... Private Beall was so kind and easy to talk to..."

"And handsome, no?" Marta laughed knowing her daughter had taken to the young man.

Krista blushed and then smiled, "Well, yes, handsome too." She lowered her eyes demurely.

"Well, their young officer was handsome too, I suppose." Marta replied saucily.

"Mama!" Krista smiled widely.

Marta gave her a nudge and put her fingers to her lips, "I may be an *Oud Mevrouw*, but I still have eyes."

They both giggled. The two sometimes behaved like sisters rather than mother and daughter. And indeed, Krista noted the way her mother looked at other men. At least certain other men like Cornelius Foch and that nice Lieutenant Creed. Foch bothered her. She loved her father and Foch was his closest confidante, but there was something in his eyes...

Chapter 17

Sandy Drummond rode alongside the column inspecting his men. They sat their mounts impassively, each focusing on the battle so long anticipated. He checked flints, belting, queues, and the edges of their curved sabers. It was already past dawn but remarkably, the fog still covered the entire front, hiding the American positions behind a gray cloak and severely limiting visibility. Drummond wanted to attack in the fog. If it cleared before he could launch his assault the rebels would unhorse many of his fine cavalry before they could close with them.

There was yet no word from either Cornwallis or Howe. Even Colonel Thorne had grown frustrated and returned to headquarters in the hope of spurring a decision from Howe. Drummond halted at the head of the column, and gazed in the direction of the defenses. The fog was now lifting, if ever so slightly. He had little time to waste.

Drummond decided on a subterfuge to break the gridlock. He dismounted from his horse and, taking paper, pen, and ink from his saddlebag, scrawled a note to Cornwallis:

Augst, 30th, 1776

My Lord,

The rebel lines are strangely quiet and the fog appears to be shifting. The present lack of Visibility advantages us. Therefore I am going to lead a Reconnce in force with the Trps at hand. Should these actions precipitate an Engagemnt, I shall send word to you immediately. I will attempt to take their Works with a "coup de main." That should be the signal for a general advance. These actions are taken to preclude a Rebel counteraction or withdrawal from the Island before we can dstroy them in detail.

Responsibility for this move is mine alone.

I remain as Ever,
Your most humble and obedient Servant,
J. Drummond
Major, 17th Light Dragoons

Drummond provided the note to a lieutenant from the lead grenadier company, not a mounted dragoon. It would be almost an hour walk back to the camp along the water logged and winding road. Such a trip would normally take less than fifteen minutes for a horseman. He chuckled at the ploy, and then grimaced at the risk. However, Sandy Drummond did not come to America to avoid risk.

"Colonel Thorne has not returned from his meeting with General Cornwallis. I shall not wait much longer for these gentlemen to make up their minds. Go to headquarters. Present this letter to Colonel Thorne. He will know what to do. If you cannot find the colonel, take it directly to Lord Cornwallis."

The young officer frowned. He suspected what Drummond planned and did not want to miss the action while serving on this errand. However, he saluted and made off in a vain attempt at "at the double." Drummond smiled as he watched the officer plodding through the ankle deep mud. He was confident that it would slow him down and buy them time, time for decisive action.

"Sergeant Digby, please ask Captain Cheatham to see me."

A few minutes later Captain Robin Cheatham arrived at the head of the column. He was Drummond's second in command of the dragoons, a good officer, and experienced. Cheatham was an older captain, in his late thirties. He was a little shorter than average; just about five foot four, and thin. He had a beak-like nose, and kept his thin strands of graying brown hair tied back in a loose queue, giving him the appearance of an impoverished country minister.

"Sir!" Cheatham presented himself formally and saluted, even though the two were on a fist name basis.

"Robbie, I need you to take six troopers forward to within spitting distance of the rebel lines. Try to ascertain their disposition. I have reason to believe that they have humbugged us, staged an evening departure back to New York. If that is so, we may yet be able to catch some of them in the act of fleeing. Try to ride along the front for a bit, and see what you can in this damned fog."

Cheatham nervously rubbed his neck. "Could that be possible, Sandy? The weather and visibility last night were some of the worst we have had yet in this cursed place. Such a movement would be difficult enough even in good weather. Our rebel friends could not have possibly risked such a bold move..."

Drummond slapped his right fist into his left palm and his face turned red. "Good God, man, do I have vacillation above me and below me? This army came here to fight the rebels, not discuss them!"

Cheatham's eyes widened at the outburst. Drummond was a friend and had no cause to snap at him like that.

"Should I engage if challenged?" Cheatham asked icily.

"Of course, but get word back to me right away and the whole column shall come to your relief. I am looking for some morning sport. Find it for me, Robbie!"

Unduly chastised, an annoyed Cheatham saluted and cantered off.

ᔆᗡᏟᎡ

The sense of hearing sharpens in poor visibility, especially fog and mist. So it was with Creed's men. They heard the sound of horses' hooves clumping through the mud. They were very close, perhaps as close as fifteen yards from the American positions. Soon they could hear saddles creak and buckles and spurs jingle. In the fog-enshrouded stillness, it seemed like the clanging of church bells. Creed's men stood frozen as the noises drifted across the Flatbush Road and then trailed off as the horsemen continued south.

The dragoons reached the vicinity of Creed's southernmost pair, two Connecticut men. Suddenly the fog broke, raising visibility to more than one hundred yards.

The lead dragoon spoke. "There's the lines, Corporal. Don't look like much, does it?"

The scouting party turned and approached the seemingly deserted works almost to the trench line.

"Let me try a little reconnaissance by fire, eh?" said the corporal. "See if we can't flush out the rebels."

He un-slung his light musket, which was shorter in length and range than the infantry's musket. He cocked back the hammer; and aimed at the top of the muddy earthen berms. The shot broke the silence with a sharp crack that reverberated across the field. The other dragoons watched curiously as the lead ball slammed harmlessly into the berm with a soft thud. It had, however, the desired effect.

In nervous reaction, one of the Connecticut men stood up over the berm and returned fire. At less than ten yards, the shot easily hit the lead dragoon, toppling his lifeless body from his horse into the mud. An alert trooper grabbed his horse's reins before it could bolt, while the others returned fire with their short dragoon muskets, hitting one of the Connecticut men. He collapsed backwards clutching his head as blood streamed over his eyes, blinding him. His partner, hands shaking, returned fire on the dragoons. His shot went high.

The British began to reload from the saddle but before they could, another pair of Americans opened fire at them from the right. A second dragoon took a musket ball in the arm, shattering it so it hung limp. He screamed in pain, then cursed soundly and turned his mount about. Another dragoon's horse collapsed from under him, sending the rider plunging into the soft wet earth.

Cheatham rode up waving his pistol. "Get that man on a horse and pull back! "

Two more shots zinged past Cheatham. The Americans had gotten a bead on him. Cheatham waved his pistol towards the direction of the column. "Pull back now. We cannot match them."

The patrol rode back out of sight and range. Cursing, Cheatham yanked his horse about and cantered after his men. He'd had enough of Sandy's Drummond's madness.

At the sound of the first shot, Creed ran down the line to check on his men. He saw one of them face up in a mud puddle, face caked in blood. He was young, no more than seventeen, and on the stocky side. The dragoon's shot had drilled him through the forehead.

Creed, seeing the man's partner on the verge of collapse, placed a comforting hand on his shoulder. "Your pal's gone, but he did his duty. Now we must do ours—for his sake."

Tears rolled from the young man's eyes but he nodded. Creed went on. "Just remember the drill, and stay calm. Remember, the lobsters are nervous as we are."

Creed moved up and down the skirmish line trying to bolster each pair of men.

One of the Connecticut men said, "The fog is lifting sir, shouldn't we head back?"

"Soon lad, soon...we must hold on just a bit a little longer." Creed replied.

Cheatham led the dragoons back to Drummond. They had a trooper killed and were minus one horse.

"What happened, Robbie?" asked Drummond.

"Sandy, the rebels seem to be holding those lines quite aggressively." Cheatham replied.

"How many rebels did you count?" asked Drummond skeptically.

"Well actual men, I believe I saw a total of twenty," Cheatham lied. He knew where this was leading. Drummond did not care what the actual number was. He has already made up his mind to attack.

"And you think a score of men along a front of at least one hundred yards is normal? How many were there north of the road? South of the road?"

"We found them only on the south end." Cheatham answered. "I think we panicked one of them."

"Panicked them? We shall soon find out. Move the squadron to the north of the road. I will send the grenadiers forward in column after a short battery fire. The two light infantry companies will hasten to the ferry landing. We may yet bag a straggler or two. The squadron will round up the retreating rebels. Just remember, we are not bloody Highlanders or Germans, I want no butchery here. Many of the locals are friendly to the crown and I want to keep it that way."

୫୦୧୫

Tallmadge's boat hit the quay with a rough thump. He raced along the docks to make sure the companies arrived in good order. Then he glanced across the East River. He saw the fog beginning to lift and thought about Creed and his men. They were risking all for the cause and for the lives of their brothers in arms. He felt it unfair that these bravest of men had little hope of survival and escape. Suddenly a thought came to him.

Approaching Chester with a determined look he said, "Colonel, I am returning to Brooklyn."

"What? Nonsense—what in blazes for, Benjamin?"

"I believe in my haste I left a copy of our regiment's roster and other important papers. And my horse is there. I have time to retrieve them if I go right now."

Chester eyed him. He knew what his Adjutant was thinking. Besides being a brilliant young man, Tallmadge had remarkable sense of honor and compassion.

Chester looked at the ground and then glanced across the water. The fog was clearing quickly now. "Very well Benjamin, retrieve your horse and the papers, but take a squad with you."

Within minutes, Tallmadge had eight volunteers, all good Connecticut men from New Haven, skilled and experienced at rowing small craft around the coast of the Long Island Sound. They would row themselves to save space on the boat so he would have room for his horse, perhaps even Creed and his brave men. Half way across the river, they saw the fog start lifting quickly now, increasing visibility to slightly more than 100 yards. The passage seemed eerie as their boat moved in and out of the fading mist. Suddenly, they heard sporadic cannon fire to the west.

Tallmadge said. "The British are ranging our abandoned lines."

As they drew closer to the heights of Brooklyn and the ferry, he could hear the faint pop of musket fire working its way back through the fog.

Tallmadge turned to a corporal pulling frantically at his oar. "The British assault is coming at last. The great charade is up."

The corporal replied. "Then we should turn back, sir?"

Tallmadge stared at the bluffs just ahead. "No. Pull harder. We must try to help those brave men."

୫୦୧୫

They could but faintly make out the silhouettes of the advancing British.

Beall whispered to Parker. "Elias, in the fog, they look like an army of ghosts."

Parker mumbled his reply. "Wish they were. Also wish this fog would make up its mind. Either hide us or give us a clear shot at them."

Although lifting, the fog was still very much a factor, remaining concentrated in dense clouds along the creek and in the low farm fields. However, visibility was already 100 yards or more in many places.

Beall shivered. "The dragoons are moving to our flanks. Look Elias, infantry moving up!"

Parker replied. "Looks like a flock of bishops to me. Are they sending chaplains to pray for our surrender?"

Beall knew better. "Them's grenadiers, Jonathan. Biggest and meanest of all the lobsters. They are serious, this time."

Wearing their distinctive headgear, much like a smaller version of a bishop's miter, the grenadiers deployed from the road and stood shoulder-to-shoulder in a long red line. As the morning sunlight began to break through the clouds, bayonets, sabers, and halberds glistened impressively before them.

The Americans watched the British formation with such intensity that they failed to notice the two small cannon being set up on a small hill less than 200 yards to their left front. Thick patches of fog still hung across their front and screened the British gun crews as they positioned and lay in their guns. Now, the fog thinned out, revealing the guns' silhouettes to the defenders.

Beall pointed at them. "Looks like a pair of big mountain lions poised to strike us."

Parker shook his head impatiently. "Let them roar, then. This waiting is tiresome."

The first rounds that roared from the battery sailed wide and far over their heads.

They heard Creed's voice call out, "Steady now, lads. Just trying to frighten us, is all."

However, Creed knew the gunners would soon adjust fire and blast them from their positions.

The scarlet-coated grenadiers moved forward at a slow march; drummers beating the rhythm meant to keep the pace, inspire the men, and strike fear into the enemy. It was successful at all three. They marched in companies sixteen abreast and two ranks deep. With the light infantry on their left, and the dragoons on their right, this force comprised the elite of the world's finest professional army coming right at them.

Standing on the parapet, Creed watched the attack unfold. He knew that it was now over for them there, but if he could lead his men back to the ferry before the British closed with them, he might still get them to New York. After all, he thought, he had just prayed for a miracle.

The grenadiers reached within eighty paces of the breastworks.

Creed called out to the men. "We shall fire as I have instructed: two volleys then fall back. Concentrate on their center. Aim waist high."

The head of the British column reached to within sixty paces from the breast-works—killing range.

"...Present...Fire!" Creed yelled.

Eight grenadiers tumbled to the ground, their screams and plunging bodies slowing the pace just enough. The defenders frantically reloaded and fired their second volley into the head of the column. Five more grenadiers in the front ranks fell, their flailing bodies and muskets tripping the men behind and sending them tumbling in all directions. The column maintained a steady advance up the road toward the breastworks. Creed's men had begun to move back as planned, flank pairs, then the center pairs. The center pairs took time to re-load and fire independently into the head of the column, downing a few more grenadiers and slowing it just enough. Finally, the last pair turned about and headed toward Brooklyn.

Creed remained at the parapet, the last American to defend the fortifications on Long Island. He raised his hunting rifle and sought a suitable target. The fading fog was drifting across the front of the advancing formations. The light infantry and grenadiers had almost reached the defense works. A few scrambled over trenches and under abatis. He swiveled his rifle at a large grenadier sergeant exhorting the men forward and twirling a halberd above his head with berserker-like fury. Creed's shot drilled him in the head and sent his halberd spinning harmlessly into the wet grass.

Creed ran down the road toward Brooklyn, where he found two of his teams: Parker and Beall, as well as two other men from Frederick. Musket and cheers erupted as the British breached the defenses at last.

Creed spoke between breaths. "Some of the other lads...firing...at the British... on the run. Head back toward the village...find a suitable place to make another stand."

Beall replied loading his musket as he spoke. "Sir, shouldn't we go directly to the landing? The ferrymen will be waiting. Further delay now puts them at risk."

"No. We must slow down the British one last time...then we shall make our way there..." Creed felt guilty, for he knew the next stand would be their last. The men all nodded. Their trust in Creed was unquestioning.

They moved at a slow trot toward Brooklyn until they came upon some barns and woodsheds at the outskirts of the village, where they stopped and took cover.

Suddenly to their front, a company of British grenadiers charged up the road. Creed and his men fired with deliberate aim and three grenadiers fell, clutching themselves as they tumbled into the mud. Creed and his men ran off into the fog.

The cannon fire increased; the British had now brought up more guns and pounded the trench works north and south of Brooklyn, sending plumes of mud and bits of wood flying in every direction.

ഇൗരു

From his vantage point, Sandy Drummond sat astride Shoe as he watched his mighty phalanx plunge into the American defenses.

He waived his saber. "Grenadiers forward!"

Drummond knew whatever rebels remained had taken to their heels. They needed to move quickly if they hoped to bag any prisoners. He needed something to show for his transgression against Howe's orders.

"Grenadiers, to the village!" he shouted, "Light infantry, to the ferry! "

He spurred Shoe along and watched his dragoons fan out in search of stragglers. The light infantry and moved south toward the ferry. Brooklyn was about to fall into British hands, joining the rest of Long Island in an occupation that would last almost seven years.

ഇൗരു

Tallmadge's squad tied up the longboat just as the British overran the defense works. Thorne had moved up more artillery, and stray shot began to hit the road near the ferry. The rain had turned the ground soft and mushy and rounds sunk harmlessly into the mud.

"No sign of Mister Creed, sir." Said one of the men.

Tallmadge nodded. " Load muskets and take positions at the ferry. I must find my horse."

The patient sorrel was right where he left it. She looked at him with a face that displayed a confidence in him that few people ever had. After some hesitation as to his next move, he mounted, and rode up over the bluffs into Brooklyn.

Tallmadge rode into a town that seemed as empty as a New England graveyard. The flotsam and debris of the rebel army was now the only evidence of its once formidable presence. The few inhabitants who remained were behind battened shutters waiting for the inevitable arrival of the British. With vestiges of the morning mist and fog swirling in patches, Brooklyn seemed surreal, almost haunted. Word of the ravages suffered by the female population in Staten Island had reached Brooklyn. Yet Staten Island was Tory, what would become of the village that had housed the rebel army?

Tallmadge heard the sound of feet slopping through the mud. To his surprise, a pair of the Connecticut men he'd detailed to Creed emerged from the haze.

Tallmadge's voice trembled. "Where is the rest of the detachment? Where is Mister Creed?"

A thin youth from Redding replied. "Last seen 'em back on the parapet sir, busy shooting at the lobsters. Dragoons and infantry stormed the breastworks north and south and..."

Shots rang out. They looked up as a trio of grenadiers turned the corner of a building.

Tallmadge spoke. "Make your way back to the ferry. Some of the boys are waiting there with a boat. Tell them I shall be but fifteen minutes. If I do not return, they are to depart without me."

They hesitated, not wanting to leave the officer or the others.

"Go now!" Tallmadge shouted.

They took off at a run, leaving Brooklyn to Tallmadge, Creed...and the British.

Tallmadge wanted to even the score with the British. The slaughter of so many of his compatriots, friends and relatives had gotten the better of him Moreover, he felt that he owed Creed a chance of surviving this hazardous mission. He spurred his horse straight into the band of grenadiers.

As he swept down on them, Tallmadge used the weight of his horse to bowl them over, cutting and stabbing wildly all the time. Not long ago he was a civilian, a man of letters, not of action.... Expertise with edged weapons was not something one learned at Yale. Still, he struck surely, and two grenadiers fell under his blade and a third was crushed under his horse's hooves. Tallmadge felt a rush of doubt, fear, hate, and excitement all at once. He had killed his first men and although he had not enjoyed it–he experienced a sense of accomplishment that a classics teacher could never attain. He had done his duty, but still was not satisfied. He thirsted for more action and a chance to avenge his lost comrades.

Tallmadge spurred the sorrel up the Flatbush Road. Suddenly, he heard shots and shouts to his left. Turning, he saw two of the Marylanders go down under the blows and slashes of another group of grenadiers. Drawing his heavy pistol from the saddle holster, he charged once again. He closed on the group, now locked in fierce combat, shooting the first grenadier in his way. The ball pierced the man's neck and sent him down choking on his own blood. Tallmadge smashed the skull of a second grenadier with the empty pistol and sliced off the arm of a third with his blade.

He wheeled his horse and charged the remaining grenadiers who broke and ran for the safety of a nearby building. The grenadiers began loading, intent on dispatching the mad rebel horseman. As they did, Tallmadge reached down, pulled the surviving Marylander up behind him, and spurred back down the road toward the ferry. The grenadiers fired, but their volley missed Tallmadge as he galloped out of range and out of sight.

"Where is Lieutenant Creed?" Tallmadge asked the wounded man as he helped him into the arms of his men waiting by the ferry.

"Not sure sir." He gasped. He had three bayonet wounds oozing blood. None appeared fatal but the worst was yet to come if they could not get him to a doctor soon.

"Lieutenant Creed ordered us to fall back in pairs, once we discharged our volleys. If he did not make it back by now he likely is dead or captured."

"How many British are there?" Tallmadge asked.

"I would reckon we were attacked by at least a thousand infantry, dragoons, and artillery. They are right behind us."

Tallmadge reloaded his pistol while the men moved his horse and the wounded soldier onto the boat. By then the fog had cleared completely, much to Tallmadge's dismay. His eyes scanned the field that sloped down from heights above the ferry. Rocks and shrubs lined the crest. A few large chestnut trees dotted the skyline as well. It occurred to him that he should have left a man to stand watch up there as they loaded the boat. Once the British had the heights they could fire at the boat and threaten their safe passage back across to New York. He dared not tarry in the hope of helping Creed or any of the brave men that stood the ramparts with him. Tallmadge thought to himself that, sadly, bravery was often ill rewarded.

As Tallmadge feared, a band of British dragoons suddenly appeared on the heights. They dismounted and began skirmish fire at the Connecticut men. The first few rounds fired high over their heads and scattered widely. If they could just shove off, they would be out of range in minutes. The tide was coming in, however; the journey back would be much more difficult.

Tallmadge regretted leaving Creed to his fate. He scanned the ferry and the heights for one last sign of Creed's band. A shot pinged off the bow of the boat, and the ricochet nearly hit him.

Tallmadge gave the final command. "Shove off, Mister Farley: have the men pull hard! We must get out of range...

The wounded Marylander stammered. "I'm glad to be leaving Long Island, sir, but not Mister Creed."

Tallmadge nodded grimly. He took hold of his horse's bridle, steadying her with his familiar voice. The boat rocked and began to move sluggishly across the river.

A company of British Light Infantry swarmed now the docks. Musket fire erupted from the dockside but the rounds fell short. Tallmadge could not resist the urge to remove his hat and wave it at the frustrated British on shore. Somehow, he took solace in their frustration. Although his friend's fate seemed grim, the Continental Army had escaped destruction and, after all, he had retrieved his horse.

⁎⁎⁎

As Creed, Beall and Parker ran through the Brooklyn streets, just enough mist remained to mask them from their pursuers. They moved past tightly-shuttered houses set in neat rows, each on its half-acre plot. Flowers bloomed in gardens and from the gaily-painted boxes hanging from windows and porches. Inside, the frightened burghers huddled for solace against the sounds of soldiers running, shouting, and shooting in hot pursuit of Creed and his men. Suddenly, Creed heard the dull plopping of hooves as they pounded along the rain-soaked ground.

Creed and his men jumped a picket fence and hid behind a well in the front garden of a slate gray house. They hunched down, with bayonets at ready, keeping a low silhouette as the dragoons passed by. The horsemen, hell bent to make it to the ferry landing, paid scarce attention to their flanks. Creed and his men once more moved from house to house until they passed the Old Dutch Church. They saw a company of grenadiers running up the road. Now the village came alive with musket shots and anxious shouts and curses. Creed knew they had run out of time. Brooklyn was awash in redcoats.

"I do not know about you lads, but I could use some rest." Creed said in a very earnest tone. They looked at him in disbelief. Then, he grinned, "Follow me."

Creed made his way up the street until he came to the Braaf home at the edge of the town. With an ease that hid his fatigue, he jumped over the locked gate and headed to the barn. The barn had no stalls. They saw two small brown cows tied in the corner, and a few stacks of hay piled in the middle. The loft was accessible by a tall wooden ladder. Creed scrambled up, with his men close behind. They threw themselves prone onto the loft floor, exhausted.

Creed talked in a hushed tone, "Check your flints, quietly load, and remove your bayonets. If they storm up here, the blades will be handier unencumbered by five feet of musket."

Parker grunted between deep breaths. "Greater danger...is if they try to burn us out. Rather be shot..."

Beall gasped, "Shot...more likely we'll be hanged. Isn't that right, sir? The British hang men found behind their lines."

Creed gazed out at the street through a gap in the planks. "Only if you are in civilian attire...or in a British uniform. 'Twould be better if we are not discovered at all."

"Sir, what is the plan for escape?" Parker asked. "We are surrounded by red coats and their numbers will only increase."

Creed replied. "Tis likely the numbers will increase, but that might be to our advantage. The longer we remain here undiscovered, the likelier they are to think we are dead or gone. Patience is our best weapon.

Parker's eyes narrowed and he chuckled sarcastically. "Patience? Our survival depends on patience, sir?

Creed grinned. "Yes, patience...and luck too. Prayer might help as well. While we wait, I myself will pray. Do you lads pray? If you don't, now would be a good time to learn."

They stared at him but did not reply.

"Very well then...we shall rely on luck."

"Now, I will stand first watch," Creed said, motioning to the corner of the loft, "In three hours, one of you will relieve me. Get some rest while we wait this out. God knows we shall need it."

Chapter 18

Drummond rode slowly through the village, his eyes searching left and right for a sign of rebels, although he was confident none remained. Brooklyn stood uncannily quiet after the rebels fled. The residents remained behind closed shutters and doors. The morning fog had burned off and now was little more than a slight haze that promised a warm afternoon. He felt elated and was in high spirits despite the throbbing pain in his knee. His plan had worked almost perfectly. Had he waited for orders from the generals he might still be sitting in Bedford nursing his bad leg. He overran the American defenses in minutes and even bagged a few rebels in the melee. Regrettably, only one was captured alive.

Colonel Thorne rode up at eleven. "Damn fine work, Sandy. Despite your charade, Lord Cornwallis is pleased with your action. And despite all his hesitancy, so is General Howe. He sent you a letter. Your connections do impress."

Thorne laughed, but Drummond took the letter without replying.

With Thorne's arrival to take command, Drummond moved the dragoons to an apple orchard located just west of Brooklyn, north of the ferry road. Here they could set up camp, rest, and refit. More importantly, they could come and go unobserved.

By the afternoon, the weather had cleared and the hot summer sun began to dry out the sodden land. Drummond sat in his tent dining on chicken and Madeira wine. There were certainly amenities to seizing one of the most prosperous towns in America. He summoned Sergeant Digby for a private discussion.

Drummond offered a surprised Digby a seat and some food. "Well, Sergeant, that was a nice bit of work this morning. Not a grand battle, but certainly a cleanly executed operation. Often times, that is all the better."

"Indeed sir, always more important to see the enemy on the run than to slug it out with them. At least, that's the soldier's perspective."

Drummond carved a leg and wing and placed them on Digby's plate, taking care to keep the breast for himself. Bread and cheese completed the fare, and some apples freshly obtained from that very orchard.

"I need you to do some work for me this evening, another job that requires your unique combination of discretion and cunning." Drummond smiled and as he spoke, handed Digby a sealed envelope.

"At six sharp, you shall be at the location contained in this note. You shall meet a man described therein. He in turn will give you a sealed envelope. Meant for my eyes only. There will be future meetings.... I need your complete dedication and discretion in all of these matters.

Drummond handed him a second envelope. "Open this and look inside. Then return it to me."

Digby took the envelope and clumsily ripped it open. His eyes widened in surprise to discover several crisp notes totaling an amount that exceeded six month's pay.

Drummond looked intently at the stunned Digby. "Select from the squadron two troopers you can trust. No louts, no laggards, and no Irish. I want good solid Britons who are very loyal to the King, to General Howe, and most importantly, loyal to me. From now on, the three of you will perform special duties for me. "

Digby nodded, but could not get the crisp notes out of his head. "If you don't mind my askin', sir...what is the purpose of the money?"

"Operational money, which I will keep it under lock and key until needed. I failed to mention that, you will receive double pay while in my special service, paid at the end of such service as assurance of your attention, loyalty and discretion. Obviously, any lapse in judgment or security will result in forfeiture of this pay and court martial. Do you understand all that I have said?"

"Yes sir.... I do." Digby swallowed hard while wondering just what he was getting himself into. Nevertheless, he saw the potential benefits: exemption from regimental duties and a large bonus, just for following "special" orders.

Drummond raised his glass in one hand and held one of the apples in the other. "Well then, Digby, I propose a toast to our future endeavors. We shall call our little enterprise Golden Apple, which is also the name for a spy I have amongst the rebels. We shall refer to him as such in all dialogue and correspondence."

"Well then, sir.... To Golden Apple! "Answered Digby with his glass raised.

ဆာ

Washington's Headquarters, New York, August 30th, 1776

"What will their next move be?" General Washington asked.

Fitzgerald looked at Scovel, then back at his commander-in-chief. "That depends on a few things, not the least of which is the weather. Howe needs the weather to cooperate so that the Royal Navy can ferry them in numbers sufficient to sustain an offensive."

"Well the weather is now starting to clear. Assuming it continues to clear, how soon might he make his move?" Washington asked anxiously. He had moved his headquarters on New York Island from Bowling Green to a place just north of the City of New York, and spent every waking hour working frantically to prepare his defense of the island and the city.

Washington's emotion bothered Fitzgerald. Normally dignified and staid, the stress of the campaign had clearly proved taxing on the commander-in-chief.

Fitzgerald tried to calm him without giving him a false sense of security. "My opinion is that Howe will delay a few days, as seems to be his nature. If almost anyone else were in command, the attack would come today, tomorrow latest. I think that we have a week at least. Exactly when and where he comes depends on the weather and tides, and he could land at one or more locations."

"Therefore, we shall need to maintain troops near all of them." Washington replied.

Washington seemed distracted. He had just finished a letter to Congress outlining the events of the past several days. The tension, which had overwhelmed him more than he would admit, affected the staff. When finished, Washington's letter highlighted the discipline and courage of the Continentals, reiterated the imminent departure of some of the militia units, and ended with the need for more recruits and more supplies. Unhappily for Washington, these were to become common themes in his correspondence with Congress throughout the war.

He handed the letter to Scovel, then stood and stretched his large frame. "After dinner I shall ride out and inspect our progress on the defense works. Colonel Fitzgerald, do whatever you can to determine the British plans. We have relied all too long on bad weather and luck. Now we need information."

Fitzgerald removed his spectacles and a smile crossed his face, "I should like both sir, but as you know, luck trumps everything."

Washington threw his head back in laughter, something he had done infrequently in the past few weeks. The commander-in-chief buckled on his sash and saber and donned his leather riding gloves. Before he departed, he grasped his intelligence advisor by the forearm and looked him in the eye.

"You have done much to help this army survive, Colonel Fitzgerald, and for that I am thankful. Unfortunately, your work is only beginning." Then, with a modest bow, Washington departed.

ഇൽ ഗ

During several undisturbed hours in the loft, Creed and his men took turns watching for the British. They could hear the symphony of an army on the move: feet tramping; men laughing; sergeants swearing; drums beating; fifes piping; horses snorting; and wagons creaking. Earlier they heard soldiers enter the Braaf's garden and house, but surprisingly, none entered the barn.

Beall grew nervous. "Sir, our presence here places all the Braafs in grave danger."

Creed nodded. "Aye, but they are the only locals we can trust implicitly. *Mijnheer* Braaf is the local faction leader. He would never give us up. Besides, my first duty is to get you two back alive...so ye can wreak more havoc on the lobsters."

Parker spoke in a soft voice. "I think the lieutenant is right. They can claim, in truth, that we stole in and they had no knowledge of us...."

Creed knew that would not protect the Braafs but said nothing.

The light now entering the gaps in the barn's roof indicated noon. The midday sun heated the barn and intensified the smell of cow dung and straw. The barn door opened and Krista Braaf entered carrying two buckets and a stool. Creed noticed Beall watching her every move with rapt attention. In the midst of war and surrounded by the British, Beall's feelings for the Dutch maiden remained intense. Then, on an impulse he would never himself understand, Creed decided to act.

"*Mademoiselle.*" Creed called gently in his French accent. "*Mademoiselle.*"

Krista looked up toward the loft. Her blue eyes widened in shock.

"*Mijnheer!*" she yelped.

Creed held his fingers to his lips. She reflexively covered her own mouth, blushing with embarrassment at responding so loudly. Beall reached for her as she struggled to the top of the ladder. Their eyes met and for a second they said nothing. Then she embraced Beall with fervor, before letting go and lowering her eyes.

"*Mijn Gott*, we thought you were all dead or gone. The British have chased all the Continental soldiers back to New York." She talked in hushed tones now, realizing the danger they all were in.

Creed spoke to her with a warm smile, "Surely you did not think we would leave Long Island without providing you a chance to say farewell to Private Beall, did you?"

She blushed again.

Creed smiled gently. "We need to wait here until dark and then make our way to the ferry and try to steal a boat. With only twenty thousand British soldiers between here and the ferry, it should prove quite easy. But in the meantime, we would be grateful if you could obtain some food for us...discreetly."

He squeezed her small hand in a brotherly gesture.

"Yes, Lieutenant, of course. You all must be quite hungry. I am so glad you are all safe." She cast her eyes briefly at Beall.

Krista climbed down the ladder and made her way to the larder to find some food. But she trembled, as she knew that they were all in grave danger. She needed to be very careful as all of their lives were now at risk. Her thoughts turned to Beall and she shuddered anxiously, she cared for him in a way that seemed both surprising in its ardor but also quite natural. Krista found a loaf of bread and a small piece of smoked ham. There were some apples in the larder as well as cheese. She gathered them quietly into a canvas sack; then realized that they would need to drink as well. She went to the wine cellar and found a small bottle of homemade apple wine. It was sour to her, but she knew that soldiers liked such drink. A short time later, she was back in the loft with the modest fare.

"We are greatly obliged, *Mademoiselle.*" Creed said as she took the items from the sack.

"If you give me your water flasks I will fill them at the well." Krista bravely offered.

"Only if you promise to be extremely cautious, young lady. Keep them in the sack in case someone observes you."

"Of course *Mijn....*"

"Please, call me Lieutenant Creed. We are in America, not the Netherlands." Creed interjected with a grin.

"Of course, Lieutenant. But then you must all call me Miss, not *mademoiselle.*" She answered, blushing. She looked over at Beall and closed her eyes demurely.

A little after two, Marta Braaf called Krista and Jan to dinner. It was a modest beef soup but lush with fresh vegetables and a few small pieces of beef. Krista thought that what remained she might bring to the barn that night. Warm food would be good for the young men.

"Papa, how long will the English be here?" Krista asked. She hoped that per-haps they would soon leave and her band of soldiers would be able to depart safely.

"That is difficult to say, but I think they will stay a long time, at least some of them. A British sergeant had come by earlier that day to canvass our house. They were assessing who lived in the village and how many bedrooms were available. The need to quarter soldiers is a sign of a long occupation."

Braaf thought to himself that his Whig faction would have difficulty meeting. Perhaps it was time to give in to the inevitable and stop such activities, at least so long as the British controlled the area. He had a pragmatic side. He saw Krista's eyes look downward in dismay.

He tried to soothe her. "Perhaps Congress would yet make some accommoda-tion with the King and end all this madness. I will talk with Cornelius about all this very soon. He will know."

Braaf thought to himself that Cornelius would accept the reality of their situ-ation and make some accommodation. In any case, protecting his family was Braaf's main concern.

৪৩৫৪

Twilight brought Krista back to the barn with a tureen full of the leftover soup. She managed to find a nice piece of bread too. Her mother produced an unending supply of baked goods; it was her way of staying busy, Krista thought.

The men enjoyed the warm meal. Most of the army had been on meager rations, or even no rations. As soldiers, they understood that one never knew when the next real meal would come their way.

Krista wanted to spend some time talking privately with Jonathan but there was no opportunity. She wondered if he had read her note. If he had, he showed no sign of it. Well, she did not have any experience with men so surmised he had read it but did not understand it. Her feelings for him were complex. She was attracted to him and thought him the nicest man she had known. Despite being a soldier, he seemed kind and gentle. Still, he was a soldier, and worse, came from a strange land, this place called Maryland. Yet her heart raced when she recalled their last embrace. She would do anything for just one more.

Beall looked at her with a fervor he never before experienced. Every sense seemed out of control. He wanted to get away to keep her safe. He wanted to grab her to his bosom and never let go. He wanted to shout to the world and damn the British. But he just sat still and took in her beauty.

"Krista, we must discuss our plans for this evening, it would be better and safer for you if you did not know of them." Creed winked at her in a friendly manner.

"*Ja*, I must go down and milk the cows again, it is time anyway. When you have spoken, knock on the loft rail and I will come fetch the soup pot, and bring you up some fresh milk." She smiled and looked up at Beall whose gaze fixed on her in rapture.

As she swept down the ladder, the toss of her light hair caught Creed's attention. He shot a glance at Jonathan, who was looking lost. Creed suddenly realized that he still had Krista's note in his pocket. In the action of the past few days, he had forgotten to give it to him. There was no point in giving it to him right now. Beall needed to keep his head clear for the time being.

"Just exactly what is the plan for this evening, Lieutenant?" Parker asked, looking askance at Jonathan.

"What do you propose we do?" Creed surprised Parker and Beall with the question. Surely their officer was not asking for their opinion.

"The British must be preparing their next move. By now they have occupied the ferry and everything around it." Parker opined.

"Very good, Private Parker, so what does that tell us?" Creed answered with the emphasis of a schoolmaster. Educated by a series of tutors, as well at a religious school in Ireland, Creed once dreamed of being a schoolmaster.

"Head in the opposite direction?" Beall added to the discussion.

Creed said. "Very good! But where? And how?"

"They will have patrols and pickets from the Gowanus to Wallabout." Parker opined.

Creed nodded. "Well then, obviously we will have to move east, then north toward the coast, and we need to get to a boat."

Parker replied "If we could make it to the ferry area undiscovered, we might have a chance to commandeer one."

Creed looked at Parker. "Ah, the direct approach. Bold and quick. Very well, your seamanly skills will get us past the Royal Navy."

Parker nodded mutely, "The British will have searched the ferry area high and low, also the village. Most of their patrols will be looking in the outer reaches north, south and east of here."

Creed was proud of his little exercise in the Socratic method. He felt strongly that leaders should train the next group of leaders. He knew that for this revolution to succeed, for this nation to succeed, it needed leaders at all levels.

The door to the barn abruptly flew open and three British soldiers entered. Surprised by the sound, Krista stopped her work and spun about. Most of the barn in was now in shadows but she recognized one of them. He had come to the house earlier in the day to search it. She supposed, wrongly, that they had returned to check the barn.

"Well, well, what have we here? Our pretty little Dutch missy, busy with her cows and all."

The soldier was very tall with the ruddy complexion so common to men with red hair. She could tell from his uniform that he was the leader, but unaccustomed to military attire, she was unsure of his rank. She smelled alcohol. The men had been drinking. Her father had beer or wine but rarely hard liquor so she had no way of knowing that it was rum.

"*Mijnheer*, papa is in the house if you must speak to him." Krista tried to say it matter-of-factly. She was racked with terror, not for herself but for the three brave men in the loft. Her chest heaved uncontrollably and her eyes lowered, but this only inflamed the worst instincts in the men.

"It's not your papa whose attention we want, Missy, it is you. Now, is she not as lovely as I promised, lads?"

One of the others laughed in agreement. "Yes indeed. The women of Brooklyn make those of Tottenville pale in comparison, and God knows we had our fill of them!"

The other, a small slender man, seemed unsure. They stacked their muskets on one of the barn's wooden uprights, and moved toward her slowly. Her hand gripped the milk bucket handle tightly. It would make a fine weapon and at least one of them would pay a price for this. Her mind raced. Should she fight them and cause a disturbance sure to bring more soldiers? Or succumb to them meekly, in the hope that they would leave the barn when they had their way with her, thus saving the men hiding above. She decided to succumb, but first would try to talk them out of it.

"Surely you gentlemen know that your general has ordered that civilians, especially women, were not to be harmed?" She dared not look up at the loft for fear of giving the men away but she thought she heard the faintest of movement.

"Orders are meant to be ignored by the likes of us, missy, besides after a hard fought battle they always overlook these things." The leader's voice grew huskier as his lust began to rise. He knew that the army punished only a handful of such transgressions on Staten Island, despite numerous charges and courts-martial. He stepped up to her now and began slowly caressing her face, tracing his hand along her firm, rounded cheek bones, then over her lips and chin and along the nape of her neck.

"Please...do not." She implored in a firm but failing voice. A cold numbness was coursing through her body and she began to shiver uncontrollably. She closed her eyes in resignation and dropped the bucket as the leader tore open the top of her cotton farm dress and ran his large course hands on her plump, shapely breasts.

"You will all be lashed for this!" She emphasized the "all," hoping the reluctant young soldier would waiver and talk the others out of it.

"The time for small talk is over, missy." The big man picked her up and slowly walked her toward a small pile of hay in a dark corner of the barn. The other two followed, anxious to watch the show and then partake of things themselves. By now, even the young soldier had given in to his baser instincts.

It took all Creed's strength to prevent Beall from leaping down from the loft when the soldiers first accosted Krista. He grabbed him by the neck, looked sternly into his eyes, and covered his lips with his right forefinger indicating silence. Creed then pointed at his Jaeger sword-bayonet, indicating they were to use no firearms. As Krista tried to engage her attackers in dialogue, Creed was able to whisper some quick instructions to Beall and Parker.

As the lust-enraged soldiers dragged Krista to the barn's corner, the Marylanders made their move. In the meantime, Krista had decided that she was not going to make this easy for them after all. She began to push, punch, and scratch wildly. The leader of the group tore the front of her dress all the way open, fully exposing her breasts. The two other soldiers then pinned her down on the hay while the leader mounted her.

Parker's seaman skills enabled him to silently and swiftly shimmy down one of the wooden uprights, not much different from climbing down the mast of a tall ship. Creed and Beall used the ladder, but the three soldiers, now preoccupied and struggling with Krista, did not notice them.

The young soldier died first; Parker's fishing knife slashed his carotid artery killing him instantly in a sudden spurt of blood. The second soldier let go of Krista, pulled his bayonet from the scabbard, and stabbed at Parker. From the darkness, Creed struck at him like a cobra and ran the sword-bayonet into his throat. The soldier's eyes widened and blood dripped from his mouth as he too dropped to the floor—dead before he hit the ground. The leader of the group was so far into the thrall of his lust that he scarcely realized what was happening. Still thrusting at Krista, he turned just as Beall grabbed him by the shoulders. Parker drove the hilt of his massive knife into his face, breaking teeth and bone. The soldier tried to break free from Beall's grip but Beall rammed his clenched right fist into his belly, slamming his solar plexus. Stunned and drained of air, he collapsed to the ground in a spasm of pain. Before he could regain his breath, Beall's boot was on his throat. He looked up and his eyes widened in a final moment of terror as Beall ran his sword-bayonet into the soldier's mouth and out through the back of his skull. It took Creed and his men less than fifteen seconds to send three of His Majesty's finest to hell.

Beall dropped his sword and ran to comfort Krista, who lay on the pile of hay in a ball and cried. He held her gently and tenderly kissed her head. "It is over now, Krista, we have sated their lust. There are no British soldiers to harm you now."

She said nothing for a few minutes until her sobs subsided and she began to compose herself.

Creed gave them a few minutes alone and then came over to them. He smiled gently. "Are you alright, Miss Krista?" She nodded and clutched Beall tightly.

Creed went on in a soft, calming voice, "You are a very brave girl. You refrained from screaming to save us from discovery, and put yourself in harm's way by doing so. You not only saved us, but you gave us a way past the British. We need to get you into the house to your mama, as we still have some work to do here."

Chapter 19

Fitzgerald was not a happy man. The loss of Creed and his men vexed him. Although he now had an espionage relationship with "Mister Jons," he knew that biweekly communication in a fast-moving situation would not be enough to quench the commander-in-chief's thirst for information. Washington wanted more intelligence and had summoned him and Scovel to discuss the matter. The single Continental standing guard presented arms as Fitzgerald and Scovel entered the building that served as Washington's headquarters. Large but unpretentious, the house belonged to a prominent Tory who had left to seek refuge behind British lines. Made of white clapboard, it had a small center hall with two large parlors on the main floor and four bedrooms on the second. Washington occupied one room and his aides and staff officers occupied the others.

"His Excellency is most anxious to determine Howe's next move," Scovel warned him as they walked in together. Scovel had barely slept in the past three days and Fitzgerald could see the effect. The young officer looked haggard. The entire army suffered from the stress of recent events and lack of rest. Fitzgerald himself worked tirelessly but intelligently, ensuring that he slept at least four hours in a twenty-four hour period. Fatigue affected the brain even more insidiously than the body and as an intelligence officer, he relied more on the former.

As soon as they entered the room, Washington posed the question: "Colonel Fitzgerald—I need to know what the British are planning...when and where the British will attack."

"Well, we know what, but knowing where and when is the challenge," Fitzgerald replied. "To accomplish that, I need to expand our ability to gather information. I do have an agent on Long Island but our arrangement calls for infrequent meetings, not particularly helpful given our current circumstances. Creed was to have provided us a more responsive intelligence-gathering capability. However, as he is now missing on Long Island, we must find another such person. What does your Excellency say to young Benjamin Tallmadge?"

Washington grimaced and shook his head ever so slightly. "He has a good reputation, but his actions at the ferry proved a bit free-wheeling."

Scovel spoke. "Yes sir, but he returned with at least one of Creed's men and provided our last report on the British activities in Brooklyn. He has a fine mind, and is courageous—somewhat resourceful I would say."

Fitzgerald agreed, "Yes, he and Creed are very similar types, types we shall need to use extensively if your Excellency is to have the information you need to defeat the British."

Washington nodded. "I suspect you are both correct. We will not defeat the British through force of arms alone. This is not Europe, where all is decided on one grand battle, siege, or campaign. This is a clash of will more than a clash of arms. We need the political will to continue the Cause, and to suffer the adversity we will surely continue to face. I am afraid the past few days are a harbinger of things to come. To survive, we will need the backing of the people and the support of the Congress. Patience, and information, that is to say intelligence, will be the keys to frustrating the British and bringing them to terms."

Fitzgerald said, "And some good Irish luck would not hurt things either."

All three laughed, Washington for only the second time in several days. He found this need for "luck" humorous...so long as his luck held.

He quickly turned serious. "I do not want to risk the displeasure of Colonel Chester. He commands a fine regiment, and would not be sanguine about releasing his adjutant in the midst of hostilities. As much as we could make use of young Tallmadge, we cannot do so right now. However, I propose we expand our efforts by the use of suitable volunteers from Thomas Knowlton's ranger battalion. See him as soon as possible, Fitzgerald. Perhaps he can identify, let us say, a few good men that we could detach for special activities. I must have more information on the British."

Washington went on. "The situation is turning grave. Desertions drain the army by the hour. I have deployed our remaining forces in three divisions." He pointed to the map. "One is in the city of New York. Another defends the midsection of the island and the third watches the north."

Washington had all three divisions constantly building up the defenses. But the strenuous work had taken its toll on the soldiers' strength and morale.

"I plan to meet the British with stiff resistance this time. We shall use the excellent north-south roads to rush reinforcements to execute a counter stroke wherever the British land."

"The British have already begun harassing bombardments from the heights of Brooklyn and from ships traveling up and down the East and North rivers," Fitzgerald replied, "but this does not necessarily provide any clue as to where they will attack."

"What is the most likely enemy course of action?" Scovel asked.

"Most likely, they will simply strike the southern end of the city, right across from the heights. It is the shortest distance and they could then bombard our southern works from both shore and naval batteries." Fitzgerald opined.

"Yes, I am sure you are correct," interjected Washington. "If they strike too far north, we could move to directly to New Jersey."

Fitzgerald nodded. "The tides work against a northern thrust. Kingsbridge is safe."

Footsteps sounded on the floorboards outside the door and Charles Pickering burst into the room, breathing heavily and obviously excited.

"I have important news, sir!" He exclaimed.

Fitzgerald and Washington turned and faced him, Fitzgerald peering petulantly through his spectacles. He did not like interruptions when he had the ear and the attention of the commander-in-chief.

Washington remained calm and asked flippantly, "Have the British agreed to surrender?"

Nobody laughed. Pickering's face flushed. "No sir, Lieutenant Jeremiah Creed is alive! He arrived on the island not thirty minutes past and is even now on his way to headquarters!"

ဆာ ငာ

Braaf sat at the kitchen table trying to explain the impact of the British occupation with Marta. The increasingly discomfited world of the Braafs was completely shattered when Creed and Beall brought Krista into the house. They had no idea the men had hid in their barn. Marta fought the urge to cry but maintained her outward composure and took Krista straight to her bedroom. She then called for Jan to bring warm water and soap. His hands trembled and his mind raced as he waited for the water to heat. This was now serious business. Three dead soldiers on their property would most likely bring a death sentence to all of them. What should he do? He could turn the men in, but they had saved his daughter. Should they flee? Where could they go that the British might not some day be? Fleeing would be admitting to murder. Eventually someone would come looking for the men, so there was not much time.

A few minutes later, Creed reentered the room dressed in the uniform of one of the British soldiers. The uniform was a bit ill fitting and had some bloodstains but overall he had all the look of a member of the Royal Army. With a grim smile he proclaimed, "Corporal Creed, late of Light Company, First Maryland Continental Line, now Second Company, His Majesty's 28th Regiment of Foot, at your service!"

A man who could find humor in the midst of so much horror amazed Braaf. "You have ice water in your blood," Braaf muttered.

"I beg your pardon?" Creed asked.

"*Mijn God!* What madness is this now, Lieutenant Creed?" Braaf said.

"The lads are now dressing those beasts in our fine Continental uniforms, I am sad to say. However, it is our best solution. We will simply bury them in an orchard or field far enough away from here. No one will question the burial of three rebel casualties. From there, we shall disappear into the chaos of this occupation. You must wash away the blood in the barn, use lye, and then cover the area with straw and dung."

Braaf shook his head ruefully, "You are mad! How will you cross the river?"

Creed was a little surprised by Braaf's resistance. "Not mad, merely desperate. As for crossing; I shall resolve that when we reach the water."

Creed helped Braaf carry the cauldron of warm water to Marta who, once recovered from the shock of seeing him in a red coat, thanked him with a hug that was at once warmly grateful and somehow sensual. He smelled the aroma of her clean soap and cooking spice and felt her breasts pushing against his side.

"I know this was not your fault, Lieutenant." She whispered breathily. "Thank-you for saving my Krista. Now, take care of yourself. "

She kissed him once on the cheek. Jan was seeing to Krista and paid no notice. Creed, although he liked her smell and touch, pushed back just a little. Without saying a word, he bowed, kissed her hand, and departed.

A half-hour later, they were in a farm field a quarter mile from the Braafs. With a score of homes and farms between them, nobody could connect the burial to the family, even if the British found the bodies later. They dug a shallow grave, three feet deep, and tossed the bodies in.

"I need one of you lads to jump down there and tamp them down tightly," Creed said.

Beall and Parker looked at each other in disbelief.

Parker drawled, "Very well, I will do it. Jonathan seems ill at ease with gore and offal."

Beall stiffened. "I have skinned many animals and wallowed in their gore and offal, as you say, but I will defer to you on this opportunity, Elias."

Parker grunted and jumped in. They heard the cracking of lifeless bones and the indescribable sound of strange gasses exploding from the corpses' innards. In a few jumps, he had pressed the lifeless forms deep into the muddy soil.

"Throw the canvas over them and cover up this small window to hell." Creed said bitterly.

They tamped the soil and grasses back over the grave until barely noticeable. Then they returned the cart and tools to the Braaf barn, and drew their weapons out of hiding. Creed and Beall slung their Jaeger rifles and sword-bayonets over their shoulders like war trophies and held the British Brown Bess muskets at slope arms. Parker did the same with his Maryland issue musket.

"If anyone asks, the non- English weapons are trophies of war—the bounty of any honest British soldier," Creed advised.

Before they departed the farmyard, Jan Braaf met them at the ga
gentlemen. You know that I am a senior member of the Whig fac
Brooklyn. Our leader is my friend and colleague, Cornelius Foch. I
you to him. He is a ferry operator and seaman and he owns several boats. When
I explain what happened he will help you to cross the river."

Creed was polite but to the point. "Sir, that is most kind of you but your place
is here with Marta, that is, with *Mevrouw* Braaf, and Miss Krista. We cannot
allow you to risk your family any longer for our sakes. And the fewer who learn
of tonight's events, the better."

"Nevertheless, I insist. Krista is asleep in bed with Marta. We have several
hours before dawn. If we are challenged you can say you caught me breaking the
curfew imposed today. I shall return after dawn and, God willing, you will be
gone by then."

Creed could not dissuade Braaf, whom he knew to normally be a cautious and
prudent man. Creed allowed that Braaf was a Patriot and this was a war. He must
take some risks. The British had already damaged his family.

"Ah, you must have some Irish in ye," Creed replied with a wink. "Very well
sir, show the way."

Brooklyn appeared quiet when they departed, but up ahead the full strength
of the British Army was evident. Tents of all kinds lined the road and filled fields
and orchards. As the road closed in on the ferry, several taverns and boarding
houses were still full of revelers, mostly officers and senior sergeants, and more
than a few devious privates. There were the usual doxies plying their trade as well
and some could be seen departing with customers of various ranks. As Creed and
his men neared the heights, they saw a pair of sentries posted ahead. The British
were already laying heavy guns to bombard New York and once again, engineers,
gunners and a few unfortunate infantrymen were working as if it were mid-day.

They were about a half mile from Foch's *Red Hen*, the small brig Foch lived
on and used as his office and flag ship. A large coaching house, called "*Gouden
Adelaar*," dominated the cross roads just before the heights. Made of brick, stone,
and timber, it was as large as many similar European establishments Creed had
visited. Raucous noise and laughter came from within.

"We should avoid the roads and go north overland for say a half-mile or so,"
Creed announced unexpectedly. "There will be few patrols or sentries there.
Once beyond the British lines, we can turn west and make way toward the coast."

"You know your way around our land, Lieutenant Creed?" Braaf commented
rather than asked.

"Some. I have been through here before, during the movement from New
York. I have had to develop a good eye for the land since I came to this country.

There are so few roads and almost no maps."

He smiled faintly. "Now, I propose that you three go on without me. I will meet you at the *Red Hen*, later."

"*Mijn Gott*, you are not coming with us?" Braaf was aghast. Parker and Beall looked at each other knowingly. By now, they always expected the unexpected from their officer. They were actually proud of it.

"No, I shall meet you there just before dawn. That will give you time to convince your colleague to risk his life and property to help a couple of unfortunate rebels. We can leave with the morning wind and tide."

"But...where are you going? What are you doing?" Braaf asked in a low voice. He grew suspicious. Would this man turn them all over to the English?

"*Mijnheer*, earlier I told you that there are some things people are better off not knowing. This is one such occasion."

Creed handed his Jaeger rifle and bayonet to Beall, and strutted toward the entrance to the "*Gouden Adelaar*" with his Brown Bess slung over his shoulder. He jingled the good British coin he had taken from the dead soldiers, delighted to have a chance to spend some of it in the name of the new United States.

⁝⁞

Braaf, Beall, and Parker made it to the *Red Hen* in under an hour. The night was dark, but calm. A forty foot long, two-masted brig sat gently on the water, a small watch lamp the only light. Braaf called out softly from the pier. Beall and Parker did not understand him as he spoke in the Dutch dialect peculiar to America. Kip, the watchman, recognized him and roused his master. Foch was quite surprised to see his friend at such an hour, during the British occupation and curfew, and with a pair of redcoats. His sleep-shrouded mind raced to assess what could be happening. Were the British here to arrest them as rebel spies? Anxiously, Foch bounded down the small wooden gangway to the pier.

Eying the two redcoats with suspicion, Foch addressed his friend in their Dutch dialect, "Jan, what is the meaning of this, what do these English want from us?"

"Do not be disturbed by the uniforms, Cornelius, these men are Continentals. Stranded in Brooklyn...during the British attack. We must help them to cross to New York. There is also one more coming later."

"Jan, if I cross to New York without permission from the English I risk hanging. Surely you know that."

Foch spoke with emphasis but dispassionately. In fact, he sailed many times without permission, and over his lifetime was guilty of a number of things that also put him at risk of hanging.

"Cornelius, we both know that you have risked more than this in the past! As Whigs we risked the wrath of the Tories. Perhaps it is time for us political Whigs to take action like Patriots!" Braaf spoke with emotion and passion that surprised even him. Only hours ago he had decided that his Whig leanings should be toned down to ride out the British occupation. He just desperately wanted these men gone and would say or do anything to make that happen.

Braaf's tone surprised Foch as well. This was not the Jan Braaf he knew–the fussy old hen. Something had changed him, but Foch decided not to pursue the issue. It could wait until later.

Foch hesitated, and then switched back to English, "How soon will the third get here? It will be dawn in a few hours and I must get back by then or I risk the British cannons."

"Within the hour. We should prepare the *Red Hen* now so we can be off as soon as he arrives." Braaf was lying; he did not want to risk Foch losing heart.

Foch raised both hands in a gesture meant to wave off the idea. "I will not risk the *Red Hen*. They may take one of the smaller craft, less noticeable too. Let us have a brandy, and then you three will help Kip prepare the boat."

In the meanwhile, Foch had other business to prepare.

Chapter 20

Jeremiah Creed entered the *Gouden Adelaar* looking like any one of a score of British soldiers in the establishment. He had done his best to cover the bloodstains on his uniform by rubbing red clay over them. To the casual observer, he looked like a soldier who had been involved in digging trenches or performing other "fatigue" duties assigned to lowly infantrymen. Like the others, he was without his weapon, which he was obliged to leave outside the entrance. Creed went right to the taproom, which was full of patrons, even at this late hour. Most were soldiers and officers, each on different sides of the room, all in animated discussion. There were also more than a half dozen "working women," plying their trade of encouraging men to purchase drink, and in some instances, a bit more.

The barman gratefully took the coin he plunked down, then brought him the ale and mutton that he ordered. A hardworking soldier, in his case a corporal, would start the night with food and drink. After a sip and several bites of the food, Creed began to chat with those around him.

"So how long do we expect to be on this forsaken dung heap of an island?" Creed asked one of the more sober looking sergeants standing at the counter.

"A good question," the man replied sourly. "If Billy Howe had half the balls of a grenadier, we would be gone already. These damn rebels would have been ours for the taking if we had continued with an immediate attack. Now we have to fight our way over to New York."

The disgust in his voice was obvious. Creed played into it.

"They say Billy's balls are saved for his Betsy."

"Aye, he is a randy one, that's for sure." The corporal laughed.

Just so, morale in my regiment is likewise low, I tell you," Creed said.

"Could not be lower than we Inniskillens," the corporal countered. "Why, we chased a band of these running rabbits right to their defenses and then halted after just a few casualties. Imagine, running from bleeding rebels!"

Creed restrained from smiling, but it was good to know these lobster-backs had felt the sting of his Light Company. "So we surely must be launching an attack tomorrow? Our good general must surely know how we feel."

"Not the likes of Billy Howe. We hear that he is establishing batteries at several points along the coast. He wants to pound the rebels and confuse them before he attacks...if he attacks."

Creed pushed back from the bar in feigned indignation. "Surely he will attack, the question is where and when, right?"

"Well, yes, I suppose that is true. We hear the Navy will be in action tomorrow. Perhaps when they are done we will finish our work."

"More likely when randy Billy is done with his Betsy!" Creed replied.

The corporal guffawed and raised his tankard. "Drink up laddie. Here's to randy Billy, the longer he stays randy, the longer the campaign!"

Creed moved on and engaged several others in the room. He was not surprised at the confidence they expressed in their abilities. Nevertheless, none of them seemed to know where the attack would be and when the attack would come. One of the establishment's most sought-after women had eyed Creed as he entered the tavern and immediately marked him a possible customer. From experience, she knew it was best to let him unwind with food, drink, and soldier talk before she made her move. Now he was ready for her advances. As she moved through the crowd of soldiers, she caught Creed's interest. The two maintained eye contact as she sauntered boldly up to him and placed a well-manicured hand on his arm. Creed thought her the most interesting looking young woman in the room.

"Well *Mijnheer*, you seem to have been working very hard today. Such dirt and mud..." She found Creed very attractive; one of the benefits of her line of work was the occasional presentable customer, but this soldier nearly swept her off her feet.

"Well Madam, His Majesty requires a day's work for a day's wage, something to keep us out of trouble while waiting to be killed." He smiled mischievously; his square chin and dark eyes distracted her somewhat. For his part, he found her quite fetching, medium height, shapely and with fine light-olive skin set against dark hair and slightly oval eyes. Perhaps some East Indies Dutch blood, he thought, or French or Spanish. It was hard to tell, especially in the evening light.

"I am not the 'Madam' here, that would be 'Fat Rosie'." She pointed to an extremely short; porcine looking woman with dark hair, poorly powdered, wearing an expensive dress with cheap looking jewelry.

Creed laughed, "Fat Rosie?"

The young woman began to stroke Creed's arm. "I am afraid so, although why requires no explanation. She was born in Scotland but came to Long Island when she was just twelve. She runs the women here, former mistress of the owner, Coos Dederick. Coos spends most of his time in New York, where he owns several establishments, although they say this one in Brooklyn is his best."

"Well it certainly has the best looking women.... So what do you do here, darlin'?" He started to flirt.

"Provide hospitality in any way possible, for the right price." She stuck the tip of her tongue out and grabbed his arm tightly. "In your case I might be persuaded to strike a bargain."

Creed found her very intriguing. "I should like to know your name first."

"Call me Griet, which is short for Margriet. Now let me show you the quieter part of the house..."

ଚଠଓଔ

Creed was putting his boots back on. Griet kicked the covers off the bed and eyed him carefully. For a fleeting moment, she thought she noticed a pensive, almost sorrowful look about him. She knew the look well. His heart, if not his mind and body, belonged to another woman. Still, he had exhausted her with a passion that surprised and thrilled her. Most of these soldiers were brutes and quick to the mark. He actually seemed to care about her. Therefore, his haste was somehow disturbing.

She flitted her lashes at him. "You seem in a hurry *Mijnheer*. Are you returning to your ale so soon? "

"Well Griet, there is a war and I must return to my unit."

Creed fought the guilt he felt even as he struggled to maintain his composure and focus on the mission. Over the years he had romanced many women and bedded many a doxie. But since visiting the Stanley House, he felt something in him had changed. This night's work had been purely business. He patted her gently on the rump.

"What unit is that?" She asked.

"28th Regiment of Foot. I say darlin', are you a rebel spy?"

"No, just interested in who I sleep with," she replied. "I never did get your name, by the way."

"Just call me Sam." Creed eyed her carefully. She had compelling features, smoldering dark eyes, ample bosom, and lustrous dark hair, not your ordinary doxie.

"Well Sam, you will have a long way to go to find your regiment. The 28th have moved northeast of here. How did you get left behind?"

She noticed the clay stains on his uniform. In odd places she thought. Was he a deserter, she wondered? The English would pay her well if he were.

"Well, I was with a work party digging graves for dead rebels, there were many, and they were starting to stink. The surgeon thought it might be a health problem with all the rain, although I do not see how. Do you know precisely where they went?"

"To a place called Draaken's Neck, five miles from here. You will have a long walk, Sam."

Creed had finished buttoning his tunic. "How did you learn all of this, I should think there are better conversations you could have with your visitors."

She laughed mischievously, "My last visitor was a young officer, younger than you. He was smitten with me. Are you smitten with me, Sam? Of course not... oh well, he liked very much to talk about his job. I believe he said he was an 'Adjutant,' I believe that was the word, for a General Clinton. Yes, he named several regiments and the 28th was certainly one of them. I believe he was in that regiment. *Ja*, I am sure he was. He is down stairs still."

She was a remarkably astute and intelligent woman, Creed never failed to marvel how so many intelligent and beautiful women unfortunate circumstances forced into this trade. "Could you point him out to me? He might be able to provide a pass to get me back; otherwise I might face the lash when I return."

She rose from the bed, the sheet falling to the floor, and kissed him softly on the shoulder. "I would not want to see that strong back broken by the lash."

Creed waited in the dark of the coaching house stable. He convinced a stable hand loitering nearby to go in and tell the young adjutant that a corporal of the 28th was waiting with important information from General Clinton. He hoped to elicit more information from the officer. His bluff had to work if he was to make the rendezvous at the *Red Hen* in time.

A young lieutenant entered the barn. He appeared not more than eighteen, even in the dim lamplight. Bought his commission without spending time as ensign, Creed supposed.

"Sir, Corporal Samuel Williams, Second Company. I was busy with a work detail and missed the departure. I was hoping, if it would not be too much trouble, sir, that I could get a pass from ye so as to get back without having to face any charges."

"I am not fooled by your story, Williams. You have dawdled here for the drink and whores, you scoundrel. Fifty lashes would be too good for you." The young officer slurred his words so Creed played to his condition.

"Well sir, I did partake of some refreshment, vertical and horizontal if you excuse the expression. Now sir, I must get back to the regiment. Could I trouble you for a pass and directions to the place they call Draaken's Neck? "

The drunken adjutant hiccupped and then grinned. "Very well. I suppose the quicker you return the quicker you shall receive your just desserts. The Second Brigade is preparing to assault the rebels"

Creed feigned humility. "Why there, sir? Brooklyn is closer to New York."

The officer hiccupped again, and then rolled his eyes. "Because, you sod, we can get more ships there and it is hidden from prying eyes across the river."

"All four regiments?" Creed led him with a bluff, as he had no idea how many regiments the Brigade had.

"No, it is reinforced now to eight regiments—that is eight battalions, including the grenadiers and artillery. And some dragoons. Your sergeants can explain it all."

"Yes sir." Creed replied. "But could you direct me there? I have no sense of direction, being from the city and all."

"Then listen as carefully," he hiccupped, "as your drink-besotted brain will allow, for I shall not repeat myself. Now, here is how you get there..."

೮ఎంఆ

The officer's inebriated condition, combined with his lack of map reading skills and abysmal sense of direction proved somewhat unhelpful. Nevertheless, Creed reckoned from the man's rambling that Draaken's Neck was a peninsula approximately three miles north of Brooklyn, near a village called Bushwick, a farming village with a small harbor. Creed doubled back and headed to the area north of the Brooklyn ferry, where the *Red Hen* had its berth. It was now an hour until dawn. The sky had cleared, and visibility improved. They might still get off the island alive, if Braaf could deliver a boat.

Creed walked along a small trail that split from the main road to the ferry. Griet had told him it would help him make better time. Apparently she paid occasionally made "house calls" to the crew of Foch's little fleet. Braaf had not taken the trail for fear of running into British patrols but Creed had to take the risk, time was now essential. He arrived at the *Red Hen* just before daylight. Without a word, he clambered aboard the brig, where Beall greeted him at the top of the gangway with a mug of tea.

Creed looked around and frowned. "The ship is not rigged for sail, why not?"

Beall replied. "Sir, Captain Foch will not risk sailing it as the British will notice it is gone. Instead, we will take a longboat with four of his men. With all of us pulling oars we will make better time than a brig, and there will be less chance of a British vessel or sentry spotting us."

He downed the tea. It tasted bitter, just what he needed to wash the taste of the doxie from his mouth. "Fair enough. Where are Braaf and Foch? "

Beall pointed toward the stern, the rear of the ship. "In the captain's cabin, sir."

Creed entered the cabin without knocking. It was a small room, not much larger than a closet, really. It had no windows and only the dim light from a small tallow lantern. With little ventilation other than the gaps between the planks, it reeked of body odor and tobacco.

"*Mijnheer* Creed, so nice of you to return from your nightly romp. Did you have success?" Braaf was impatient in his question.

Creed replied. "No *Mijnheer*. I did not. I apologize for the delay I have caused. I have put you at enough risk today. We must be off."

Braaf introduced Foch who greeted Creed coolly, but in a businesslike manner. "Your men have risked much for our cause. Helping you return to the army is the least we can do."

The words sounded good but his tone showed ambivalence. Creed found Foch's look and demeanor devious. Why was he risking this?

Then Creed noticed a map lying out on the cabin's small desk. It would help immensely if he could visualize the route he needed to take, and perhaps even the location of the Draaken's Neck. "*Mijnheer* Foch, do you mind if I check the direction we are to take using your map? Seeing it on a map would be very helpful. "

The Dutchman paused a moment to reflect. "Of course, you are right. We mariners always prefer accurate maps and charts over dead reckoning and memory."

Foch turned to the map and pointed to several landmarks. "We are here, just north of the Brooklyn ferry. That barren island marks the one-third point across the river. The water moves erratically all around it so you will be on your guard and need to avoid rocks. Once past the island you are in the open channel. At this time, the tide will be favorable but it will be almost daylight. There might be British ships on watch in the harbor. So head west by south west when you clear the island and make straight across to New York. With luck you, will be across with thirty minutes of hard rowing."

Creed scanned the map, intently memorizing points and assessing distance. He scanned along the Long Island coast from Brooklyn and past Wallabout Bay, about three miles he estimated. There, near the village of Bushwick, he saw a small peninsula jutting west and then curving north, like a curved dagger, or a dragon's neck! Draaken's Neck was about one mile directly across from another inlet on the New York side marked Kips *Baii*–Kips Bay. This confirmed his suspicions; the British must be planning a move on the middle of the island, near Kips Bay, not the city!

A few moments later, one of the crewmembers knocked on the cabin door. "Time, *Mijnheer*."

Creed shook Foch's hand, then Braaf's. "I hope Miss Krista feels better; she is a very brave girl. Please pass my compliments to *Mevrouw* Braaf as well."

"Captain Foch, could I possibly borrow this chart? It will help immensely. As the senior person on this boat, I shall be in command and will return it to your senior mate when we disembark."

Creed's demeanor and earnestness completely disarmed Foch, who even under the best of circumstances would not release such a valuable item to anyone, much less a strange soldier that he had just met.

Foch rubbed his stubbled chin. "This is not possible. I have only a few of these, they are expensive and difficult to obtain."

Creed broke into a sympathetic smile. "I assure you that it will be returned unblemished—we all must take risks for the Cause, sir."

Braaf looked at Foch, who was rarely nonplussed. Surprisingly, the young Patriot's charm beguiled the cynical and crafty seaman. Foch stared intently at Creed. "We already risk the gallows by assisting you gentlemen...behind British lines...in British uniform. If captured, you will be hanged immediately as spies. And we would surely follow you to the gallows."

Creed peered back at him intently, but with a more subtle charm, "I am well aware of the risks we all are taking for the Cause. But as a leader of the Whig faction here in Brooklyn, I hoped you might be especially supportive. You have done so much for us. We just need this one additional favor."

Foch nodded. "Very well, but you must hand it over to Coby, my senior mate, once you are on shore."

Creed bowed his head and smiled. He then carefully folded the map into his tunic. Without further discussion, he walked through the hatch and followed the waiting seaman over the side of the *Red Hen* and onto the waiting longboat. A rugged looking man with a weathered face sat at the helm—Coby, Foch's senior mate. These men did not use family names readily. Creed reckoned many of them were involved in smuggling and other nefarious activities to supplement their income.

Creed immediately grabbed an oar; then he and the others moved the sleek craft out into the river. Nobody spoke. Creed sat up front to watch for British ships and keep them stayed on the right course. He did not notice the lantern glowing off in the marshes no more than half mile away. The same lantern his men saw the night of their encounter with the dragoons.

Chapter 21

Parker's leg muscles cramped as he tried to maintain his balance on the narrow board that served as a bench. He sat on the mid-starboard seat of the whaler. Fortunately, Parker was used to all sorts of boats and handled himself adroitly despite the discomfort. He relished the chance to get out onto the water once more. Behind him sat Beall, who had never been on a boat such as this and showed it. Until coming to New York, Beall had never been on open water and now fought nerves and a queasy stomach.

Beall whispered, "Elias, I do believe I will be sick."

Parker replied with a mild jibe. "If you can stand the gore and offal you can surely stand the gentle rocking of a boat at sea."

Beall replied, "Not the same. Ooh, my. "

"Just turn your head over the side when the time comes. Meanwhile, focus on the man before you and keep pulling. You'll soon forget your landsmen's belly."

Creed spoke. "Enough chatter, lads. Concentrate on the oars as these men do."

Four rough-looking mariners from Foch's fleet completed the crew. They were experienced, hard-looking sailors who spoke little, were harsh in manner, and weathered in appearance. They pulled the long oars in unison; the creaking of the oarlocks and the quick dip of the oar paddles into the cold water were the only sounds. Fortunately, the waters were relatively calm and the tides and winds favored them, so they made good progress despite some slippage as their boat approached the barren island in the swirling waters.

After a while Jonathan whispered, "I am feeling better now. Thanks for the advice, Elias."

Parker looked back and scowled. "Next time, you stomp on the offal. Now just keep on rowing."

The red glow of dawn on the eastern horizon promised a pleasant day. Behind them, the village of Brooklyn was beginning to stir fitfully as it began its third day of British occupation. The taverns had closed after a busy night. In the various camps that now stretched from Gravesend to Bushwick, the British Army began its morning routine of stand-to, victuals, and the day's orders.

In New York, Washington already had his troops up and digging the ubiquitous trenches and ramparts intended to stop the British. As he had explained to his officers, he had organized the Continental Army into three divisions: they were deployed to lower New York, the central part of the island, and covering Haarlem and the King's Bridge. The latter's mission was to guard against a thrust to the rear that would cut the army off from the mainland. The British had humbugged him once with a successful flanking thrust, made all the easier by his inattention to his exposed flank. Washington had determined that he would not make that mistake twice.

&)C&

Beall asked. "Elias, how much longer will this take? My wrists are sore...and my posterior."

Parker replied. "A mountain man like you should prove stronger..."

When Parker turned back to speak to Beall, his sharp eyes noticed the faint glow of a lantern a mile back and just north of where the *Red Hen* lay at anchor. It looked oddly familiar but he did not know why.

Creed's voice turned his attention back to the west. "Ships...about four hundred yards to the front."

They could see a line of sailing ships, mostly transports, moving up the river. The winds were causing them to tack very sharply east–heading their direction.

Creed called back to Coby at the stern. "Steer south by south west, Coby. We need to maintain enough distance from them to avoid their top watch. It is yet dark enough that they might miss us."

The previous week's storms, some of the worst in memory, had blown numerous trees into the waterways surrounding Manhattan. Normally a danger to small craft, in this situation they provided the little party's potential salvation. Creed was hoping that in the early morning darkness, the British watchmen would not distinguish them from the floating debris.

The wind suddenly grew stronger and shifted direction, increasing the flotilla's speed and angle of approach. Creed saw its vanguard, a schooner with a pair of small brigs: armed war ships each with a twelve-gun compliment. The center had six transports of various sizes while the rear comprised two small frigates, warships of twenty-four guns each. Creed was alarmed, but felt that if their boat kept its pace, they might just slip by the British undetected.

The crew rowed frantically, pushing the bow of the longboat through the numerous waves that pounded the bow when they entered the channel. Their progress slowed to a crawl, and the British flotilla drew closer, now less than 100 yards off their starboard bow. Soon they would be passing at point blank range, the Americans heading down river, the British up river.

Creed spoke in a low, but audible voice, "Lock oars lads. Sit low and keep quiet. Coby, stay down so but maintain our current heading if you can. We must appear as drift wood to them, or we will soon become drift wood indeed!"

Reluctantly, Coby did as Creed ordered. He did not like these strangers and was not happy that the boss had ordered him to make a journey that had so much risk and so little reward. Coby and the others had no political leanings, being cynical and worldly sailors caught in the crossfire of the rebellion. Their main interests were money, drink, and women, although not necessarily in that order. Coby intended to dump the Continentals on the New York shore and head straight back, avoiding both British and American scrutiny. Moreover, he had to bring back the map. Master Foch made that clear. Coby, as with the other mariners, feared Foch, the stern taskmaster. However, Foch paid well enough that few willingly left his employ. Besides, they knew that if they tried to leave there could be retribution, as they had all been party to numerous hanging offenses.

Creed kept his eye along the gunwale to ensure that the crew did not silhouette themselves. They drifted south with the current. The British ships continued their upstream course. The convoy took less than twenty minutes to pass them by but it seemed like twenty hours to Creed and the crew. When the convoy cleared, they were within fifty yards of the last ship, a small frigate with twenty-two guns.

Creed sensed the men's impatience, "Keep quiet...just a wee bit longer, lads. Once we drift another fifty yards down river, you can row like we had the devil behind us."

To their misfortune the sun suddenly rose above the horizon, bathing the entire river in a dim golden light.

Creed knew they had to act quickly. "Oars out, and pull hard lads. Maintain course, Coby."

The men resumed their task with vigor and precision. Then shots were fired from the direction of the flotilla.

"Chase boat!" Cried Coby, his smuggler's instincts now manifest.

There were two, actually. The British had indeed sighted the suspicious "flotsam" and launched a pair of longboats loaded with armed sailors and a few Royal Marines. They were 100 yards to the starboard rear and moving to close the gap. Needing no command from Creed, the men began to row desperately, their muscles pulling taught and burning with each stroke.

Coby decided to change their heading. He knew from years of experience on the river that their best chance to escape lay in a direct run to New York. Without saying a word to Creed, he pushed the tiller one quarter and the boat turned starboard heading west and directly for Manhattan. They crossed the bow of the British chase boats at 100 yards distance. They needed to make the half-mile run to New York and safety.

After the initial flurry of shots, the British had also put their men to work rowing, hoping to get within musket range or even seize the runaway boat. The next few minutes were crucial. The British had more men rowing; swifter craft, and strong, determined oarsmen. Before long, they closed the gap to fifty yards.

The New York shoreline was a still more than a quarter mile distant. Creed and his men knew there was little chance of outrunning their pursuers.

Creed decided to change the odds by disrupting their pursuers' tempo. "Try to hold her steady, lads. I'm going to stand..."

The crew thought he had gone mad, but Beall and Parker both smiled.

"He's up to something, Jonathan," Parker said under his breath.

Beall nodded, saying between grunting breaths, "Something that is...probably not good...for the British."

Creed removed his Jaeger rifle from its oilcloth cover. He stood, balancing himself on the balls of his feet as the boat yawed and pitched with the waves and tide. He aimed his rifle at the helmsman in the closest longboat. His mark was a large man half-standing at his position, a reasonably good target. With both boats careening through the waves, it was an unsteady shot but the distance was now only forty yards. The crack of the rifle over their heads was music to the ears of Creed's men. Clutching his shoulder, the helmsman fell back into the East River. The longboat slowed and began drifting to port. Creed immediately grabbed Beall's rifle and aimed at the helmsman of the second longboat, which had now overtaken its partner. Seeing what happened to his counterpart in the first boat, the other helmsman crouched low to present a less inviting target.

"I see this will be more difficult." Creed lowered the point of aim as far as he could down the center of the boat and squeezed off the shot. The ball caught one of the British sailors in the upper arm, bursting a massive, tattooed bicep and causing the man's oar to drop. The shot tore through the sailor's flesh, hitting the helmsman behind him just above the eye. He died instantly, sending the boat into a wild turn to the starboard and slowing it down. The Marines from both long-boats stood and returned a desperate fire. By then, Creed was back at his position, rowing along with the others. They had a small window of opportunity to gain distance from their pursuers. The British musket balls scattered wildly around the boat but one caught Coby in the back of the neck, shattering vertebrae and severing his spinal cord. His lifeless body lurched forward onto Beall, dousing him with blood, membrane and fluids.

Parker looked at Beall and saw the young farmer's disgust. "Gore and offal, hmm?"

Beall pushed Coby's body over the side and then courageously took the tiller, keeping them on course. His bravery and instant action saved them.

The Americans increased their stroke, draining the last dregs of their strength and stamina. The fire from the pursuing craft lessened to an occasional shot, now more harassment than danger. The New York shoreline loomed closer, just over one hundred yards away. Still, the pursuit boats were back on course and again closing the gap. Creed suddenly realized that the British might follow them to the shore and beyond. If there were no American troops in the immediate vicinity of their landing, they might still be in danger! He looked up and scanned the shoreline for signs of American defenders. All he saw was some small docks along the water and a few scattered buildings. Everything else was brush and small trees.

Suddenly, a puff of smoke appeared along the shoreline, followed by the boom of cannon. As luck had it, a gun section of two six-pounders from Captain Alexander Hamilton's New York battery was positioned in the tree line overlooking the shore. A cannon ball careened past Creed's boat and plunged into the water twenty yards short of the British. A second round landed just starboard of the first pursuit boat. The British turned back rather than risk annihilation from the shore battery. It was a fight they knew they could not win.

"Huzzah for Maryland, huzzah for America!" cried Creed.

Beall and Parker echoed the cry, but Foch's mariners kept silent and rowed for their lives. For them, this was just a job, one with great risk and no reward.

Creed waved his hat at the battery on shore, signaling that they were friendly. In a few minutes they were at the shoreline. Several New York militiamen rushed to the old wooden dock, and soon friendly hands began helping them back to shore and the army.

෴

After Creed and his crew departed, Foch offered Jan Braaf a bunk on the *Red Hen*, convincing him that it would be best if he got some sleep and waited a few hours before traveling back to his house. Braaf was exhausted, so he promptly took him up on the offer. As soon as Braaf turned in, Foch left to conduct "business." He returned just after ten that morning, to be met by a nervous crew.

"*Mijnheer* Foch, where have you been?" asked the senior mate on board.

Foch grew nervous, than angry. "You know better than to question my business. Why is the crew up so early?"

The mate replied contritely. "We heard firing across the river and saw the outline of a British flotilla."

Foch exploded in rage. "Damn them all—Americans, English—what do I care now? My boat, my map, and Coby might be lost. Well then, better they all sink than get caught. Back to your stations—now!"

The men scrambled to their posts. Foch thought to himself that the English had overwhelming force now. It was important to proceed with caution and plan for any eventuality.

Foch stood on the fore deck squinting across the water in the hope of seeing some sign of his boat. A bleary-eyed Braaf joined him, appearing more tired than when he turned in. Sparing the morning pleasantries, Foch continued to look out across the river, "I am not so sure our friends made it over safely. My men saw English ships and heard firing from across the water."

"Yes, it woke me, so I took a walk until my nerves calmed and then went back to sleep. I should go now, though, as Marta will be worried. I hope these damnable English leave soon. I cannot think of what happened, and worse, what might have happened to Krista. And next time could be Marta...."

"*Ja*, the English are *Duyvels*! Take care with them." Foch continued to squint across the river without looking at his friend.

₧₧

Braaf returned home at midday. The morning that he spent on the *Red Hen* was a fateful one at the Braaf house. At eight, a fist pounding on the front door awakened Marta. She tied her hair back and dressed hurriedly in a simple blue shift. She opened door to the longing stares of three British dragoons: Sergeant Digby and his two newly appointed companions.

His selection was curious, but it met his needs. One a frail, dark haired trooper named Peter Quaif, was resourceful but cagey. He was a sycophant who would serve the major and Digby loyally. Quaif would do whatever he was told, especially if there was extra income involved. He was amoral but if he was controlled that was a good thing. The other dragoon, Thomas Brent, was a strapping farm boy from Hampshire, loyal to the crown and the dragoons in that order. Brent was very religious but would do anything in the service of King and country. Although he obeyed orders without hesitation, Digby knew Brent could never intentionally commit an immoral act. However, Digby figured he could help Brent define the boundaries of morality to serve Major Drummond's purposes.

Digby addressed her in a surprisingly courteous voice, "Missus, we have orders to search your house and premises, if you please."

"Search our house, but why, sir?" Marta asked. She tried not to show her fear but she blushed deeply for a second, swallowed, and then regained her composure.

"Orders, ma'am, that is all I can say," replied Digby.

The dragoons spent the better part of an hour going through the house. There was no small amount of ogling both Marta and Krista. Soldiers would not be denied their "harmless" pleasures, especially soldiers who were part of an army of occupation. They finished the house and then went over to the barn. They spent a good half an hour going from the loft to the open area below.

Brent decided to go through the heap of straw and dung so fastidiously avoided by his Sergeant and his Quaif. Using a nearby pitchfork, he plunged the prongs into the straw and carefully turned it. He was about to stop, realizing that the effort was futile. He knew why they were searching there. Three British soldiers were missing. Some had reported hearing talk of visiting a "sweet young lass" seen earlier that day. A canvass of the town soon revealed that three the British soldiers were last sighted near the Braaf home and that the Braaf had an attractive daughter "of age." The idea that soldiers of the King would seek the favors of an honorable young woman disgusted Brent. He saw Krista when they had searched her room. She seemed sweet and innocent, but nervous as a young lamb. Now he knew why.

"Sergeant Digby, I believe I found something!" Brent's voice quivered as if he had discovered lost treasure. What he had found instead was more modest but of more immediate interest, a button. It was a brass button, from a military uniform embossed with the ubiquitous "GR" and a number "28."

"Ah, I think you have done it, me boyo!" Exclaimed Digby as he waved the button in his hand.

"This button was from one of them. We have proof that they were here."

"So does that mean we must arrest them, take them in?" Brent was distraught at the idea.

"Not yet, me boyo, not yet. We must report all this to the good major. He will know what to do. Not a word of this to any one until we report to him. However, we must wait until the Marster of the house returns. A chat with him might help shed some more light on all this."

They settled in until near midday when Jan Braaf returned. As Braaf entered the house, Marta rushed to him before any of the soldiers could get a word in. She spoke softly using their Dutch dialect. "Jan, these gentlemen have been search- ing the house all morning. They want to talk to you now. I overheard them...they have found a button. A British soldier's button...in our barn."

Despite the danger they faced, Marta was surprisingly composed. She spoke slowly and deliberately, emphasizing the words button and barn. Her eyes were wide open and her pert lips pursed tight. Braaf eyed the three dragoons ner- vously. Surely, he thought, they could not know what happened here.

"What exactly is the nature of your business, *Mijnheer?*" asked Braaf as he eyed Digby, instinctively disliking him.

"Begging your pardon sir, but we was ordered to search the house on the grounds that three of His Majesty's finest were seen coming here to visit your daughter. He eyed Krista's breasts lustfully, and then quickly averted his eyes.

"I do not like what you insinuate, Sergeant!" The normally phlegmatic Braaf suddenly felt rage surge through him like never before.

"I beg your pardon sir, and I certainly mean no disrespect at all, at all. It is just...that rumor in the camp named her, your Miss Krista that is, as the object of a nocturnal visit. That is all. So naturally, we came here to find out where they went. Now, were they here, sir?"

Digby eyed Braaf to gauge his reaction. However, Braaf showed no emotion. He decided to play into the story. Pure denial now would do them no good.

"*Ja*, they were here, but they left. I knew what they wanted and I threatened them."

"Threatened them, sir? How could the likes of you threaten three of His Majesty's soldiers?"

"I told them that one of two things would happen if they did not leave. I would report them to their commander who I am sure would have them face a court martial and possibly hang or..."

"Or what, sir?"

"Well, you see, as I am connected with the Whig faction here..."

Digby completed the sentence. "Meaning...they would not necessarily escape this island alive!"

Braaf regretted his indiscretion. He may have signed his death warrant and put his family at even more risk.

"You see sir, you communicated a threat to His Majesty's soldiers in the performance of their duties...begging your pardon sir but that is a grave offense."

"If their 'duties' include assaulting the virtue of a young maiden then so be it, Sergeant. I did what I had to do in defense of my daughter."

Digby knew that he did not have the complete truth from Braaf. The button they found indicated that a struggle occurred here. Nevertheless, he knew this middle-aged burgher could not have killed three strong infantrymen, even if they were drunk, which they most likely were. Digby tried to think things through. Had they deserted? Not likely, but not out of the question.

"Very well sir, but I must report all of this. We may return with more questions."

"As you see fit," answered Braaf, relieved they were going but sure that they would return.

৪০৩

Digby reported his findings to Drummond, who was not amused. "The message you retrieved for me this morning was from Golden Apple. It indicated that three men in British uniforms were making their way to New York in a longboat. Do you realize what this could mean?"

Digby's eyes widened, "My God sir, they are deserters after all."

"Perhaps, but I am not so sure. Perhaps the men were spies all along. Could there be more of them? Or, were these rebel soldiers, or even rebel spies, who made off in British uniform? Perhaps they accosted the girl. And if this is the case then where, pray tell, are His Majesty's missing soldiers?"

"I think I have a headache, sir." Digby was confused now. He realized he had a lot to learn in this business.

"Here, I will give you a note. Ride up to Utrecht and talk to the commander of these men. Get accurate descriptions of them. Then we will talk with our Dutch family again."

Chapter 22

Island of New York, September 4th, 1776

A corporal of the Washington's Life Guard ushered Creed into the general's headquarters, where the commander-in-chief himself greeted him. General Israel Putnam, Fitzgerald, and Scovel also attended.

Unable to contain his delight, Fitzgerald spoke first. "Well Mister Creed, none of us expected your return, certainly not any time soon," he said. "Tallmadge reported that your men held gallantly but that the inevitable surge of British force proved decisive and overwhelming."

Fitzgerald smiled the proud smile of a mentor satisfied that his pupil had succeeded beyond his wildest expectations. He then gave a puzzled look as he realized the man he spoke to wore the uniform of the British King. Realizing the cause for Fitzgerald's confusion, Creed smiled with a shrug. "His Majesty's Quartermaster did not clean our uniforms in time for our scheduled departure... so we borrowed these from a trio of obliging soldiers."

Creed then went on to relate all that had happened. Scovel took notes at key points, and Fitzgerald stopped him frequently to seek clarification on matters of importance. The sheer audacity of the men, Creed in particular, impressed them immensely. Creed told them of the British forces secreted at Draaken's Neck. He described the situation in Brooklyn, the encounter with the convoy, and his belief that British forces would land at Kips Bay. Creed presented Fitzgerald the map that he had cajoled from the reluctant Foch and used it to make his case clearer than words could. With Coby's death, he had conveniently neglected to hand the map over to the surviving mariners for Foch. The Continental Army could make better use of it, Creed reasoned, since it was more accurate than any map in Fitzgerald's paltry collection.

Creed provided very valuable information and filled in many gaps, in Fitzgerald's assessment, of British plans and activities.

Fitzgerald drew in his breath. "So...this is quite a bit to digest. I must admit, Mister Creed, you have cast doubt on my own assessment, which postulated an attack directly on the city or a gambit on King's Bridge to cut us off from Westchester. However, by landing at Kips Bay I suppose Howe intends to cut our forces in two while avoiding our strong defenses near the city."

Putnam remarked. "Moreover, he spares himself the hazards of the dangerous waters and tides near the Hell Gate. I have warned you of those treacherous waters, sir."

Washington now held Foch's map, his eyes carefully examining the features. Unique among the Americans, Washington had a keen sense of time, space, and terrain as factors of war. His exploits during the French and Indian War had helped him develop, hone, and utilize those skills. His flawed defense of Long Island was a tragic exception.

Washington shook his head emphatically as he glanced at Fitzgerald. "I am not yet fully convinced. I need more intelligence. Would that we had a spy in the enemy camp...."

Fitzgerald's eyes widened at the remark. Washington slapped the map back down on the small wooden desk and nodded at Putnam and Scovel. "Until then I shall concede this much, we must alert our forces near Kips Bay and generally along the central portion of the East River approaches. I shall increase the number of guns there as well. Nevertheless, we must still maintain significant forces to the north and the south. Wherever the British approach, we must order the division commanders to be prepared to move, either north or south, depending on the threat."

Scovel seemed skeptical. "Sir, there is really only the one major road from the city to Haarlem. To move so many men at once...we risk chaos." He braced himself for the expected rebuke.

Washington bit his lip and pondered the thought. "I am aware, Mister Scovel, but I am prepared to accept the risk and the responsibility. If somehow our estimate proves wrong I must have other options."

At this point Scovel suggested they dismiss Creed so he and his men could get some sleep, possibly bathe, and of course receive proper uniforms, certainly nothing in British scarlet. When Creed departed, the men continued debating the issue and Washington added detail to his instructions, which Scovel and Pickering would transmit to the subordinate commands. Putnam excused himself to attend to his own division.

After they had left, Fitzgerald and Washington talked alone, in hushed tones.

"Your point on intelligence is well taken, sir. I intended to bring this up later, but perhaps now is a good time. Before we left Brooklyn a gentleman approached me and offered his services, essentially as a spy."

Fitzgerald went on to explain the strange but timely encounter with Foch. "I used the name of our own Mr. Smythe and gave him Mr. Jons to use in secret correspondence."

"So you are...Mister Smythe and he is Mister Jons? Clever of you, Robert."

Fitzgerald grimaced. "Not exactly, sir. To Foch, I am Mister Smythe. But I have another operative, whom I recruited before we crossed over to Long Island. Here on this island. That operative is the real Mister Smythe."

Washington frowned. "I am afraid I do not understand. A spy, behind our lines?"

Fitzgerald swallowed hard. He had hoped to delay the discussion for as long as possible but realized the time had come.

"The day may well come, Your Excellency, that despite our Herculean efforts we must depart the Island of New York. The city occupies a strategic point that the British will likely maintain as their base for the duration. 'Mister Smythe' is a Patriot who can move in certain circles and report from within the bosom of the enemy. This is strictly a precautionary move on my part. Prudence mandates that I prepare for the eventuality despite my every wish to the contrary."

For a second, Washington's face reddened and his eyes bulged. Fitzgerald braced himself for the tirade he had long expected but hoped to postpone.

"As difficult a prospect as the thought of abandoning this post is, your fore-sight is commendable. I need men who can think of things that duty—and honor—preclude me. Tell me no more of 'Mister Smythe.' I merely need to know of his existence. But how will you communicate in the event we depart?"

Fitzgerald's body tingled with relief. "That is where 'Mister Jons'—that is, *Mijnheer* Foch and his boats come in. The British will be looking west and north should we depart—but pay less attention to the east. Long Island has so many Tories. For whatever motivated Foch to volunteer his services, I knew that I had to take the chance and accept his offer. The real 'Mister Smythe' will use 'Mister Jons' and his boats to pass information to us. However, if he is identified by the British, he will think his correspondence is with me."

Washington nodded. "And you will be safely ensconced with the army and out of British reach."

Fitzgerald smiled weakly. "One would hope."

Washington grimaced. "What do we do next?"

"I suggest that we send 'Mister Jons' a message to help confirm Creed's report. Conveniently, his mariners have not yet returned to Long Island, providing a convenient and timely way to arrange an unscheduled meeting."

"And 'Mister Smythe'?"

"I met with 'Mister Smythe' this morning. I equipped our agent with everything needed to provide us information—if we are forced from this position. A special cipher, locations provided by 'Mister Jons', and..."

"And what?"

"Why, your Excellency's thanks and esteem, of course. "'Mister Smythe' is a true Patriot. Not working for monetary remuneration. Still, your esteem is worth more than a thousand pounds sterling."

Suitably impressed, Washington approved the plan on the proviso that they use Creed as the intermediary and that Creed not be privy to the existence of 'Mister Smythe.' Creed would know only that 'Mister Smythe' was a cover name for Colonel Fitzgerald.

The next day, Fitzgerald summoned Creed back to a meeting at headquarters. Creed arrived clean-shaven, fed, and with a new blue Continental uniform covering his athletic frame.

"You look quite macaroni, Mister Creed. While you were resting, I sent young Scovel out to meet with your mariner friends. We released them to return to Foch, without the map, mind you."

Creed's surprise was evident.

"Do not look so puzzled. Foch is an agent of the Continental Army, reporting to me. We shall arrange a meeting with him...with you as His Excellency's representative. I do not need to stress the sensitivity of this assignment. It is of the utmost secrecy and no one can know of it. Have a glass of claret now and we can discuss the details of the enterprise."

Fitzgerald opened Foch's map, and called his attention to several pencil marks. These indicated departure points from New York, arrival points on Long Island, a meeting site just in from the shore, alternate sites and an emergency pick up point.

"A crew of handpicked men from Colonel Glover's Gloucester regiment will transport you by longboat from the point marked here as A to this point here marked AA, one mile north of the Brooklyn ferry. There, you will disembark and travel one-quarter mile inland, to the point right here, marked AAA. It is there that you will meet with a 'Mr. Jons'."

Creed rubbed his chin. "But how will I know that it is he? This...'Mr. Jons'..."

Fitzgerald cocked his head and smiled. "A fair enough question, my boy. You will exchange greetings to establish yourselves. Your challenge is, 'Did you once sail on the *Eagle?*' And the response is, 'No, I sailed on the *Talon.*' Do not engage in conversation beyond that. He should provide you with a packet or envelope. Simply retrieve it and move here to point Z, where you be met by the longboat. The longboat will transport you to point ZZ, which is right...here. Simple, eh?"

The complex plan dumbfounded Creed, and his face showed it. "Well, um, yes, extremely simple, sir. But I have a few questions, if you do not mind."

"Yes of course."

"What if we encounter British warships—on either leg?"

"Try to slip past them. If you cannot steer out of their view and try again. Mr. Jons will wait one hour, depart for two, and return for one half hour. On the return trip, you must avoid British ships at all hazards."

"And if we encounter British patrols on either passage, sir?"

"Do not allow yourself to become embroiled in a skirmish. Avoid them at all costs."

"And if the weather turns?"

"Always the wild card these days, it seems. You must push through despite the weather or conditions on the water. His Excellency is anxious for the results of this venture."

Fitzgerald wondered if he should reveal the identity of Mr. Jons but quickly disabused himself of the notion. Knowledge of the identities of both Mr. Smythe and Mr. Jons would remain with him and the commander-in chief.

Creed posed his final question, "Very well. When do we depart, sir?"

"The night of the 10th. That gives you some days to prepare. I suggest you study the map, meet with Glover's men, rehearse, and rest. In addition, Creed, it might be good for you fellows to seek out a chaplain as well. Perhaps even a Catholic priest, if you can find one handily enough."

Neither laughed at the weak attempt at dark humor. Both knew this mission, would prove Creed's most dangerous.

⅘⅙

Brooklyn, September 1776

Drummond arrived at the Braaf residence accompanied by Sergeant Digby and his two troopers. Digby pounded loudly on the door. When Jan Braaf opened it, the two dragoons grabbed him by the arms and dragged him into the barn. After they tied Braaf to one of the uprights, Brent and Quaif began another search.

Drummond put his face close to Braaf's. "*Mijnheer* Braaf, this button belonged to a soldier of His Majesty's 28th Regiment of Foot. We are searching the area, specifically your premises, for more evidence. I sense there was wrong-doing here on your part."

"I have no knowledge as to the fate of those men." Braaf protested.

Digby slapped him with a heavy leather riding-glove. "We expect no more from the likes of you, blasted rebel! You already admitted to chasing them off— now they were never here?"

Digby then twisted Braaf's arm back and Braaf cried out in pain. "I will snap it off if you do not tell us where."

Braaf was hysterical with pain and tears rolled down his cheeks. "They were here, but I do not know where they are."

He told the truth, as Creed had removed the bodies to an unknown gravesite. Digby twisted again, and Braaf turned himself back to minimize the tension and the pain. He began to slump causing his arm to pull from the socket. *"Ach...Mijn Gott..."* he screamed.

Drummond intervened. "Enough, Sergeant."

Digby eased up on Braaf's arm just before it snapped. Braaf slumped forward.

Drummond's tone was soothing but also ominous, *"Mijnheer* Braaf, we know that you are a member of the Whig faction—you admitted as much to my officers and there are plenty of loyal men in Brooklyn whose testimony against you we have already. Simply tell us where they are, and what happened to them."

Trooper Quaif called out, "Sir, I think I found something."

Drummond and Digby went over to the corner of the barn where Quaif had shoveled away another pile of straw and dung. The dirt floor had a dark carmine brown stain.

"Dried blood. Keep searching" said Drummond, who went back to Braaf and put his face close to his ear, speaking softly and firmly. "It appears there has been foul play here, sir. In the name of the King, I shall have to arrest you."

They searched another twenty minutes, but found nothing else. Still, the physical evidence was compelling: the button Krista had torn from one of her attackers and a stain of dried blood. Drummond mounted Shoe while Digby and his two men tied Braaf to the back of another horse.

As they left, Marta ran to the gate and grabbed at one of Drummond's stirrups. *"Mijnheer!* What is the meaning of this? Where are you taking my husband? He has done nothing wrong!"

She burst into tears. Braaf recovered enough from his pain and trauma to attempt to calm her fears. "I will be fine, Marta. This is just a big misunderstanding. I shall be home for supper."

Before Drummond could say anything Digby pulled her away; as he did, he let his hand stray not so subtly over some of her curves. "Now calm down, Missy. Yer man will be all right. He is in the King's custody now. Be good and maybe I will come back and comfort you later. You would like that, no?"

He stroked her cheek in mock affection and Marta pulled away from him and hurried into the house. Krista watched the scene from the gabled window above. She turned sick to her stomach with guilt as well as fear, thinking that somehow this was all her fault.

Digby shrugged, then mounted his horse and rode off behind Drummond. Braaf stumbled down the street, trailing behind Quaif's horse, both hands now securely tied with a rope tethered to Quaif's pommel. Several of the locals watched sullenly, some approvingly, as their hapless neighbor went to meet his fate.

ೋೋ

The next day, Braaf stood trial in front of General Clinton, whom Howe had appointed military Governor of Long Island. Clinton had been named commander of the next phase of the campaign, the assault on Washington's army in New York. However, Howe had received instructions from the Whigs in Parliament to try to parley with the Americans. This suited Howe as he strongly supported a policy of accommodation and reconciliation with the colonists. He preferred presiding over the good Americans with the beautiful Mrs. Loring as his consort, to waging war on the miscreant rebels. Howe arranged for a meeting between representatives of the crown and the rebels on Staten Island. As it turned out, the meeting would not bring about the reconciliation he and the parliamentary Whigs hoped to achieve. But it did buy Washington precious time.

After Drummond presented his evidence, Clinton found Braaf guilty of "felonious actions against His Majesty's forces in the field, resulting in their deaths." A catchall since there was no evidence that any crime occurred or whether there were actually forces wronged or injured. Clinton sentenced Braaf to hang, and had him remanded to the Brooklyn gaol, which the British had commandeered for their own purposes. His jailers however, were Tory Loyalists, not British soldiers. Clinton had wasted no time in contacting and organizing the numerous and now growing supporters of the King. A Brooklyn Home Guard Battalion had formed under the command of Stanislaus Kuyper, a trial lawyer who had opposed Braaf in numerous court cases and who had a strong hatred for Whigs. A platoon from this Home Guard Battalion guarded Braaf.

"Sentence will be carried out once it is approved by General Howe." Pronounced Clinton, who was glad to be done with this part of the affair. Clinton intended to make Braaf an example to dissuade rebels from any anti-British action and to bolster the morale of the Loyalists.

ೋೋ

Cornelius Foch arrived at the Braaf house just after ten that evening. Despite the late hour, Marta welcomed him with a surprisingly grateful smile. She and Krista had spent the last several hours crying and grieving. Word of Jan's fate had spread throughout Brooklyn and many town folk had already begun to shun them out of suspicion—or fear. Even Jan's closest and most ardent Whig associates steered clear of the house, assuming that the British had informants among the Tories who would report them. So they welcomed Cornelius Foch's friendly face. They desperately needed his support as they had lost almost all of their other friends.

"*Ach*, Cornelius, we did not expect to have you here. You must have heard that the British arrested Jan. They found a button from one of those awful British soldiers. Now we are being shunned by Jan's friends and enemies alike. It is awful."

"I know. I came as soon as I heard what happened to Jan. Everything will be fine. I am sure of that. Besides, you will always have a warm friend in Cornelius Foch."

He took Marta's hands in his and held them gently, but only for a moment. Marta's eyes began to tear. He pulled a crisp red handkerchief from his vest and slowly and deliberately wiped them. He then put the kerchief away and spoke in a firm and deliberate voice.

"I know this is difficult. But you must both be strong. No matter what happens or what they might do, do not tell the English anything more about what happened here. Moreover, trust none of your friends and neighbors. The English have spies among us. You must be cautious–for Jan's sake."

Marta had finally composed herself, finding his presence was very reassuring. They sat at the table in their neat kitchen. Krista busied herself brewing coffee. The aroma comforted them all.

"I feel so helpless, Cornelius; I just think that if I went and explained all of this to that English major he would understand."

"Hear me, Marta. The only thing that the English understand is that we are all enemies of the crown and murderers of His Majesty's soldiers. We could all hang. Now, I will do what I can to help Jan, but I can only do so if I know you will heed my words."

Foch spent another hour with the women, comforting them and ensuring that they would not do anything rash. It was near midnight when he left. He still had much business to attend.

Chapter 23

The "Holy" Ground, New York, September 1776

Major Aaron Burr fumbled as he put his boots on. The young woman lying on the bed shivered, and then shuddered a bit. The night with the young officer had provided quite a bit more excitement than she had expected. He was demanding and exact in his requirements. This officer was unique and she, as the "preferred" girl of Mrs. Dickinson's establishment, would know. She had entertained the most prominent of New York's businessmen, politicians, lawyers, and, sometimes, clergy.

Polly Fanning was nineteen, exceedingly tall–almost six feet–with very high cheekbones, hazelnut-colored eyes, dark hair, and gleaming white skin. She was slender, too. However, her bubbly personality and obvious love of life and men–especially older men–was her real attraction. Compared to most of her recent clients, Burr was young and vigorous, although he seemed mature beyond his twenty-five years. Nevertheless, there was a sinister air about him. She knew that he went down to the city on a pretext to visit her and that he was not at all averse to breaking rules, even military rules, if it was somehow to his advantage.

"So, will your army stand and fight this time?" she asked. "Most around here think you will be running from the redcoats like foxes before the hounds." She laughed at her own remark and tossed back her hair with a flick of her long, slender hand. Her sparkling eyes delighted Burr even as the words stung.

"I have no idea what we will do, my dear." Burr spoke the truth. General Washington went back and forth with the Continental Congress regarding whether he should defend New York, abandon it, or burn it. So far, they had reached no agreement.

Despite her questions, Burr reckoned that Polly was not a spy, just another New Yorker trying to ascertain her fate and the fate of her city.

"Well, if we leave perhaps I will take you with me!" was Burr's confident answer. His boots were on and now he put his gloves on slowly. He stood over Polly and gave her a lingering kiss as he caressed her under her nightgown with his soft kid gloves.

"I believe there will be more money to be made here when your army departs, dear Aaron."

She bit his lip mockingly. It visibly annoyed him. Burr slapped her harshly on her small, firm buttocks. Then, he roughly grabbed her chin.

"Listen my dear, New York is Tory now, but the day will come when it too will rejoice in America's freedom. Indeed, it will prosper from it."

She wanted to respond that hell would freeze over and that the King's men would soon have the rebels on the run and that everything would soon be back to normal. However, she refrained from fear of his reaction. She was a good judge of men. Although small in stature, she found Burr strong willed, and he had a vicious streak. Perhaps if there were enough such men the Patriots would win after all.

☯☪

The commander-in-chief had just finished reading yet another letter from the Continental Congress. It contained new guidance on what to do regarding the city—hinting at once at defending and abandoning the vital seaport—but not burning it. The recent parlay with General Howe was a ruse, a stall for time so Washington could build up his defenses, while preparing to evacuate the wounded and heavy equipment from the island, in the event they abandoned it. Although John Jay and his New York Whig faction were now working hard to root out the most active supporters of the King, New York was still a Tory stronghold. Since Washington's army had arrived in the city, the radical Whigs identified many Tories and brutalized them politically, mentally and even physically. However, if New York fell, the tables would turn once more.

Washington knew that if abandoned, New York would provide the British a solid base of operations which, coupled with their overwhelming maritime superiority, would afford them a strategic advantage. Without a powerful navy, Washington could never hope to retake it once lost. Destroying the city now would drive away many potential Tory supporters, make it harder to defend, and render it less hospitable for its occupiers. Moreover, it would send a message that the new nation was willing to use the any measures to survive, no matter how drastic. Washington felt generally confident in his defenses, but army morale was weak after the debacle on Long Island. Entire militia units were drifting away. The men who stayed were poorly supplied and equipped. However, many had shown that they would fight bravely when given the chance and properly led. If he could anticipate the British assault, he might just be able to lure them into another bloody encounter like Boston.

At mid-morning, Tench Tilghman knocked on the door of Washington's study and let in Brigadier General Nathaniel Greene. Greene, Washington's most able lieutenant had recovered from the virus that struck him down just before the British invasion on Long Island. He was a large man, portly but in a robust way, cutting a striking figure in his general officer's uniform. Washington could see that the fever had taken a toll on Greene. He was pale and much thinner than before. However, he was back with the army and now submitted a plan to burn the city and abandon it to the British. They went into heated discussion. At one time Washington had considered such action himself, but now he had firm guidance from Congress to spare the city, if he could.

Greene argued quite eloquently until Washington finally cut the Rhode Islander off with a wave of his hand. "I will take your ideas under advisement, Nathaniel, but I cannot support them at this juncture."

"Very well, sir," was the taciturn reply. Greene saluted, turned about, and exited the room, a bit too brusquely for Washington.

Greene went to find Fitzgerald. He hoped he could convince Washington's intelligence advisor to support him. A half hour later, he found Fitzgerald eating at a small relay house up the Post Road. Fitzgerald kept a desk in Washington's headquarters but spent most of his day in the field, gathering information from officers and soldiers. When Greene arrived Fitzgerald put down the piece of cold chicken he was eating and wiped his fingers and mouth. He poured a glass of Madeira.

"So, General Greene, I take it His Excellency does not support your plan?" Fitzgerald was smiling, as he knew that Washington, a very reasonable and collegial man, had occasions where he dug his heels in on issues just because he could.

"No, Colonel, and it troubles me no end. We must use harsh methods and make hard decisions if we are to triumph over superior British arms. We must prevent the army's destruction, for it now comprises the heart and soul of the nation...more so than that gaggle of politicos in Philadelphia."

"We live in a political world, General. Politics will ultimately decide our nation's fate. The army's role is to provide time to bring the British to reason."

Greene smiled and nodded, then helped himself to a piece of Fitzgerald's chicken. "In that sense we are both in agreement, Colonel. If the army is destroyed defending this island, the game is up. It must live to fight another day."

Fitzgerald replied. "His Excellency thinks that if he has the right intelligence he can position a defense to crush the British here."

Greene shook his large head. "You and I know that is a dream. Intelligence must posture us but not provide the sole basis for strategic decisions. Our strategy should provide that basis, regardless of the current intelligence on enemy movements. And our strategy should be to avoid decisive action and avoid entrapment here and destruction in detail, as almost happened last week."

Fitzgerald poured Greene a glass of wine. "You'll find this accompanies the chicken nicely. All good points, sir. It is a frustrating and thankless task to obtain good intelligence on the enemy. We must gain more knowledge of the enemy and use it to our advantage. We are under resourced in the espionage business, I am afraid."

Greene nodded emphatically, "You raise an interesting point, Colonel, one that I confess I had not previously considered. If His Excellency adopted my strategy, we would need even more intelligence, as the army would be in a cat and mouse game with the British. How many spies do you now have at your disposal?"

Fitzgerald looked incredulous. "Spies? Do you think all this is about spies, sir? I have no staff. We have no staff officers to work intelligence issues. We need so much more than...'spies'. Someone has to recruit them, meet with them, assess them, and make reports. Someone has to make judgments. Spies are only one part of the apparatus. And of course, we must deal with *their* spies, an even graver concern, I am afraid."

Fitzgerald, carried away with his own passion, suddenly recovered. His harangue stunned Greene, but now Greene realized the validity of his argument.

"Of course, you are correct, Colonel. This is complicated work. I should avoid simplistic comments."

Fitzgerald knew that now was the time to enlist another ally. "General Greene, if you support me with His Excellency so that I obtain help in these areas, I shall support your proposal to withdraw from the island."

Greene nodded his assent. He made a tough bargain but it was worth it. The army had to be evacuated and saved, thus saving the nation, and the cause.

80CB

The Stanley House, New York

Jeremiah Creed awoke at dawn to find his men up and eating. They had found a room back in the small boarding house run by the beautiful daughter of Doctor Reginald Stanley. Creed had not slept so long in weeks. It seemed that since he joined the Patriot cause many months ago his life had been a whirlwind, with little time for pause, reflection, and most of all, sleep. Of the three, sleep was the most important to a soldier. He once more shared quarters with his men. They had less than six days to rest, recover, and train for their new mission. Anxious to get the skullduggery over and rejoin the Maryland Line, he was beginning to suspect that it would be some time before that happened and he could return to command of an infantry company, even a line company. But to Creed, any line command was better than the war of shadows he had been abruptly thrust into, and from which there seemed no way out.

Ostensibly, they had returned to Doctor Stanley's boarding house because it was well situated for Creed's purposes; it was located in a hamlet near the intersection of the Bloemingdale Road and the Post Road on the northern fringes of the city. It afforded easy access to the both the North and the East rivers and to Colonel Fitzgerald, who was staying at a house a half mile up the Post

Road. Beall, however, suspected his officer had a more personal attachment to the establishment.

Parker and Beall were up before Creed and sat comfortably at the kitchen table enjoying breakfast.

Parker slurped at a ladle of oatmeal porridge. "What a wonderful place to stay after all of our troubles. And you say you were here before?"

Beall nodded. "In a camp just across the lane from here, by the orchard, although Lieutenant Creed was often seen visiting the house...and its lady."

Parker arched his eyebrows. "So, our officer has a personal side as well. I was beginning to wonder. God, I miss my family."

Beall felt guilty revealing Creed's secret. "Yes, I miss my ma and pa. And I miss Simon."

Creed entered the room, and took a seat at the table. He was freshly washed and shaven, refreshed and in good spirits, "So, lads, what is being served this morning? "

"Well, it is porridge, sir. Also some wonderful bread. And some fresh milk," Beall answered, with food in his mouth adding to his obvious enthusiasm for the humble but rewarding meal.

Creed pursed his lips, "Hmm, well I think I shall have some tea and perhaps some of the bread. I am not a porridge and milk person. I was served way too much of that as a lad back in Ireland. Is there any butter and jam to go with that bread?"

Creed's gregarious smile turned to awe when his order was taken, as Doctor Stanley's daughter herself was attending to the kitchen that morning. Creed's stomach churned and he tingled at the sight of her again. He thought that in all his travels and adventures he had never met a woman as beautiful, poised and intelligent.

"Tea, sir?" she asked, mostly rhetorically as she had heard his comment about the milk. As she poured his cup, she lowered her eyes in a gesture that was both modest and alluring. She had fine hands with long delicate fingers.

"Thank-you, um, miss." That was all he could stammer, before she turned with a swivel of her hips and left the room. Beall and Parker looked at each other, then downwards trying to stifle their laughter, but to no avail. The sight of their officer so smitten struck them as both amazing and amusing.

Creed cut himself a chunk of the bread and smeared it with butter. To get his mind off the beguiling young woman he turned his attention to the day's business.

"Well lads, we will meet with Colonel Glover and his Gloucester men this evening and do a full rehearsal for our mission. I thought it better we practice in the dark as it will be dark when we cross. The longboat we will use is armed with a small swivel cannon. In anticipation of any surprises I suggest each of us carry two muskets for the crossing. Once on shore, we shall each take one plus a pistol and a cutting weapon. I myself will have my German trophy. " He tapped at the long hunter's sword-bayonet he had acquired on Long Island.

Beall smiled, "I shall bring mine as well, sir, plus a tomahawk."

Most of the men of western Maryland were comfortable using the tomahawk for a variety of purposes. At seasonal and holiday gatherings there were various competitions where the men displayed its use: throwing, cutting, and chopping being the most common. Quite often, Beall won at all three of them.

Elias Parker looked up from the bowl of porridge he was devouring. "I shall also bring a tomahawk and my fishing knife."

"Well, make sure that your weapons are cleaned and oiled. And find some wrappings to protect them on the journey across. Meanwhile," he said, nodding at Beall, "I propose we find the hospital and check on your cousin and the others."

"Private Jorns never turned up in the surgery. He may be in a British hospital, poor soul." Beall injected.

"Let us hope.... More likely, they left him to die or some Hessian or Highlander butchered him. The rumor is that many of our men were killed outright while attempting to surrender." Parker's eyes narrowed in anger as he spoke.

Beall's face darkened. "Meant to demoralize us no doubt.'

Creed nodded. "Tis working, I'm afraid. There are many desertions in the army and few enough replacements coming in. What's worse, many of the officers are affected. His Excellency needs a victory over the British to reclaim our honor and boost morale."

Creed drained his tea and rose from the table. "Let's find our wounded comrades. It will do them and us all the world of good. Who knows when we shall see them after our next action?"

As the three left the boarding house, Creed caught a glimpse of Emily in the kitchen giving directions to Nancy. He forced himself only with great difficulty to focus on his men and the upcoming mission. He was still completely swept away by her beauty and dignified demeanor.

⁐◣

They made inquiries, and soon learned that the First Maryland's wounded were at a hospital in a field just outside the city, along the shore of the North River.

The hospital was in an old warehouse near the wharf. They knew they were near from the putrid smell that permeated the sticky morning air. The warehouse contained several hundred men; many wounded in combat but even more of them sick with a variety of ailments that followed the armies. The generally poor hygiene caused disease, especially typhus, to spread easily. The most innocuous wound could usually become infected. If not immediately cleaned or cauterized, sepsis could set in and result in a life threatening if not life ending situation. The hot and humid weather did nothing to ameliorate the situation.

An army surgeon greeted them at the door. He was relatively young and thin, and showed the fatigue of long hours and little sleep.

"Is our army sunk to sending officers to haul away the dead, now?" He remarked caustically when he saw Creed's rank.

Creed spoke with a crisp authority his men had not previously heard him use. "I did not come here to banter, doctor. My name is Creed, Lieutenant Jeremiah Creed, of the Maryland Line. I command the Light Company. At least one of my gallant men was wounded on Long Island and now is said to be here in your charnel house. I want to see him."

The surgeon cast his eyes down. "So many did not survive the trip back from Long Island...what is his name?"

Jonathan replied before Creed. "Beall, sir. Corporal Simon Beall. He's my cousin."

"I must check with the orderly. Wait here. Entry into the hospital is restricted. Very bad humors about. Losing more men to the bloody flux than British muskets."

Dysentery—the flux—was the most devastating enemy of armies, followed by typhus, measles and smallpox.

The surgeon returned with a shake of his head. "Nobody by that name here. Likely he's stacked like cordwood with the others awaiting burial. I'll check the burial list."

"No!" Cried Jonathan. "They said he had a graze to the scalp, nothing serious. Your clerks have made a mistake."

Creed nodded to the surgeon. "From the look of things here I fancy you make some mistakes. We shall look for him ourselves..."

"No, damn you. I already said the humors are about. You will infect the rest of your unit, spread it through the ranks, and we'll never be clear of your sick."

Creed could see days of stress had worn the man out. Most likely, he was a barber or dentist in civilian life, thrust into the medical profession by the strange protocols of the day. Certainly he was no graduate of Edinburgh medical college.

Creed replied. "This *is* our unit—and we are no longer part of the army—of a regular regiment. I'll have a look myself and humors be damned."

They pushed past the surgeon and entered the warehouse. It took a few moments to get used to the darkness but they knew they could never get used to the smell, nor the sounds. Men were strewn on the rough piles of straw that served as hospital beds. Rows of serpentine figures writhed in agony along the dirt floor. Cries, moans and screams assailed their ears while putrid flesh assailed their noses.

Parker spoke. "How can they treat men this way? Better I would die in battle than face this."

Creed replied. "Sad truth of it is...a soldier dead is less costly than a soldier sick or wounded."

They walked among the men. Some grabbed frantically at their ankles begging for water, begging for home, begging to die quickly. They saw a few hapless surgeons hovering over one figure. They were covered in blood. Even in the dark, Creed could see that it was fresh blood that clung to their smocks.

"What goes on here?" Creed asked.

An older looking surgeon replied. "This poor fellow took a musket ball to the head and one to the forearm during the fight on Long Island. He is fully recovered from the head scratch but the ball in his arm tore through flesh, tendon and bone. Now a grave infection has set in. We must amputate immediately to save his life. He is a big, burly sort and we need help holding him down. You lads look likely enough."

Creed asked, "Long Island? What is his name?"

The surgeon replied. "I don't know. He is a Corporal Simon, I believe, but no matter that, we must act quickly to prevent the infection spreading."

Creed grabbed the surgeon's coat. "Corporal? Simon? Corporal Simon? That would be Corporal Simon Beall!"

Creed pushed past the surgeons and sure enough, his Company Sergeant lay under a woolen blanket writhing in pain, his face ashen gray.

"Over here, lads!" Creed cried, barely heard over the din of the crying men.

"Oh my God, Simon!" Jonathan broke into tears.

Creed interrupted his lament. "Carry him to the table. Hurry boys, we have little time. The surgeon says he's done for unless they cut now."

Simon Beall's eyes opened and he recognized his commander. The other faces were only a blur. "That you, Lieutenant?"

He grimaced and moaned as three pair of strong arms lifted him.

"Tis me indeed, Simon. Jonathan is here too. We got off the damned island alive. Now we are going to help the surgeons make you well."

Beall startled, and then grew agitated. "Surgeons...make me...well? Whatever happens—don't let them butchers cut me...I need my arm! I am a soldier...I am a smith! I need my arm...."

Creed shook his head. "They must cut, or you shall surely die. Simon Beall with just one arm is better than most men with two. The company needs you back...and so does the army. We will stay by you."

Jonathan went numb and his head pounded. This was like some awful nightmare—much worse than battle. His cousin was also his dearest friend and companion. He knew Simon's innate pride would not tolerate living maimed and disfigured. "I am sure he'll be fine on his own, sir. Simon is strong...but he..."

Creed shook his head. "Not stronger than the poisonous humors that now coarse through his arm and will soon spread through his body."

The surgeon waited impatiently by the table as they lay Simon out. He sharpened his blades against each other like a town butcher.

Finally satisfied that they were prepared he nodded. "Give him a ladle from the rum jug. Then hold his arms and legs. The legs always cause the most trouble. The thrashing about. Got more than one black eye and swollen bollocks to prove it."

Parker, who remained silent through it all, grabbed Simon's legs and pinned them firmly down. Creed and Jonathan each held a shoulder. A surgeon's assistant held out the forearm and marked a line—just below the elbow joint. Jonathan turned away and wept. Simon lapped at the rum, and then threw his head back in defiance and turned away from the bad arm. An orderly stuck a leather strap between his teeth. Creed lowered his head and prayed a Hail Mary.

"Hold him steady now. It will be over in seconds, if I get the cut right. Otherwise he'll twist and I will have to hack through—very messy and the disease could spread anyway."

Creed nodded. "Think of home, Simon. Think of whisky. Think of women. Think of the lads who went down at the passes. Think of anything but this."

The surgeon quickly made an expert cut just below the elbow, slicing through flesh, muscle, tendon and finally bone. Simon screamed, thrashed out and tensed, but Creed and his men held him securely. Suddenly, he fell limp as dead a fish and passed out. The surgeon doused the bleeding limb with alcohol, then lit a torch and passed the flame along the tip in a primitive but effective cauterization that was capped off with the application of a tar like paste, followed by a bandage.

They carried him off to his hay where he lay quietly.

"He'll be out maybe twenty-four hours if he is lucky. By then we will really know what he is made of. From here on, it is mostly a matter of fortitude. Strong men come back quickly—the rest usually die within a few weeks."

Creed replied. "The country needs men like him. He is one of the strong ones—he'll return."

Chapter 24

Brooklyn, Long Island, September 9th, 1776

Drummond summoned Digby to his office. A summons from the major was not unusual, but this one had a particular urgency to it. Digby saluted and stood at attention. Drummond kept him that way, another unusual move. He held an apple in his hand and slowly bit into it. After chewing and swallowing the first bite, he spoke.

"Take a seat, Sergeant."

Digby sat down, puzzled by the strange procedure. He thought that he understood officers but this one was quite different. Nevertheless, he paid well.

"This is of the utmost secrecy," Drummond said. "We must meet Golden Apple tonight. You will accompany me along with Quaif and Brent. Under no circumstances can Golden Apple see you, nor you he, as the conditions of our agreement make me the only British officer who can know his identity.

Digby nodded. "Where are we going, sir?"

Drummond had a map spread out on the table and Digby could see a mark placed at the northeast shore of the peninsula that formed Wallabout Bay. "To an abandoned barn not far from here."

Digby cleared his throat. "Seems we been out that way before, sir."

"Yes, not too far from our last meeting, but this time, with Golden Apple, himself, not one of his hirelings. This is a meeting of significance. Do not tell your men where we are going or why. You will remain out of earshot unless I summon you. While we meet, your job is to provide security for us. Do you understand?"

"Perfectly, sir," Digby replied. "When do we ride?"

"At eleven. We rendezvous at midnight. An early arrival will allow your men to search the area for unwanted interlopers."

"That last time was a bit of an embarrassment if I do say so, sir."

"One that must not happen again, Sergeant."

When Digby left, Drummond removed his riding boots. His knee still throbbed from the impact of the bullet. He had lost some movement in the knee and even a slow ride caused discomfort. The surgeons had informed him that he might always have some pain, although perhaps not as great as it was at present, and would walk with a limp and ride with some difficulty. He took a spoonful of the medicine the surgeon had prescribed—something the man had found when posted to the Indies—and mixed it with tea and honey. It eased the pain and made him feel exhilarated, and was much more potent than rum or whisky.

S. W. O'Connell

By time they set out to meet Golden Apple the moon had already set. Drummond led the three dragoons at a fast pace. So fast, Digby feared one of the horses might stumble, as the night was black as ink and the terrain very uneven. After crossing several farm fields and orchards, they entered a light wooded area that bordered the high ground overlooking the bay.

When they finally reached the ridge above the bay Drummond suddenly halted Shoe and they dismounted. Brent held the horses while Drummond led Digby and Quaif to the crest. As they looked down into the darkness, they could just make out the shoreline fifty feet below stretching almost fifty yards out into the river. Just below them and some 100 yards to their right a lantern glimmered faintly.

"The all clear signal, that is Golden Apple," Drummond whispered to Digby. "Stand watch from here, and make sure there are no rebel spies about."

Digby nodded. Drummond unbuckled his scabbard and unsheathed his saber so he could make his way down the cliff more easily. He was gone from sight in a few moments. After a very long fifteen minutes, Drummond was back on the ridge. He was panting and grimacing from the effort but smiled tensely at Digby and gave a nod toward the horses, signaling their departure. Digby noticed the limp was all the worse for the climb and wondered why Drummond did not take one of them to assist him.

When they arrived back, Drummond dismissed the men. He had unfinished business to attend—in private. Once in his own quarters he lit two candles and then carefully opened the envelope left for him under the lantern. It contained a sketch map with several lines marking the American defenses along the coast. The map was not detailed, but it had enough clarity to help General Howe plan the expected attack against the rebels in New York. Drummond noted that the defenses seemed sparse with little artillery noted. It should be another day on parade, he thought to himself.

೫೦೬೩

The next day, Stanislaus Kuyper unlocked Braaf's cell door and let Major Sandy Drummond in. When the door closed, and Kuyper's footsteps faded down the hall, he grinned at Braaf, who eyed him with a fearful anticipation. Braaf's stay in the gaol at the hands of his former rival was not pleasant. Now this grinning major came to torment him, or worse.

Drummond addressed Braaf in a low but deliberate voice. "Well, things went quite perfectly—Golden Apple! Your man left the packet just where you said it would be. I must say, Braaf; His Majesty's forces owe their success in this campaign in great part to your efforts. First, informing us of the unguarded pass at Jamaica, then of the weakness in the Brooklyn defenses, and now this. This is valuable information. Perhaps I will receive recognition enough for promotion and more. And, should you play things out for me, there will be even more gold in it for you."

Braaf was not amused, "Things might have gone better if your stupid and lustful soldiers had stayed away from my home and my daughter."

"Plain bad luck. Not in the plan at all. Besides, our soldiers have deflowered many a fair maiden these past weeks, both willing and unwilling. Privileges of a conquering army, I am afraid. Well I guess your rebel friends did your work for you."

"Yes, fortunate that they were there. Krista was assaulted, but the worst was avoided at least. She would not have lived through their depravations. But why have you charged me with a crime you know I did not commit?"

"Well, because doing so enables us to advance our plan to the next stage," Drummond smiled slyly.

"What do you mean...the next stage?" Asked Braaf. He suddenly became suspicious of his erstwhile collaborator.

"Well you see, I decided to satisfy His Majesty's demand for justice and need for intelligence in one turn of the cards. You will escape from this gaol and make your way over to the rebel headquarters as an aggrieved man unjustly accused of murder. Once there, you will continue to provide us with information on the rebel forces, such as their numbers, morale, state of equipment and intentions. Oh yes, and try to determine if they have any spies in our midst, that will be worth a bonus."

Braaf sputtered his reply. "An interesting plan, Major, but I now have only two men working in Foch's firm, now that Coby has been killed."

Drummond replied. "Killed? How do you know? Well, no matter. Just an unfortunate and unanticipated consequence of this nefarious work, *Mijnheer* Braaf. Still, I am confident of the tight security that I have placed around our arrangement. I am the only person who knows your identity. My three men and three of our generals are the only people who know that I have a reliable spy code-named, Golden Apple. Since I have just 'met' with Golden Apple—nobody can connect you with the name. Even my own men."

Braaf's brow furrowed. "Meaning what, may I ask?"

"Locally, you will be known as a Patriot who has joined the rebel cause for revenge. Your daughter's unfortunate experience has proven a valuable accident. Her attackers are to be commended." Drummond smirked, infuriating Braaf.

"You are a swine!" Braaf burst out in a bellow that stunned both their ears.

Drummond smirked again, "Excellent. Your anger with me will be heard throughout the gaol. You will cooperate, of course, as these Home Guard ruffians would gladly have their worst with you, and more importantly, your family. And of course, your Patriot son would fare poorly once Mr. Washington learns that his father was the traitor who caused his destruction on Long Island."

Braaf's face flushed red. "Threaten my son as well? You are a sow! A filthy sow!"

Drummond ignored the insults and unfolded a map with coded markings of places where he would expect Braaf to leave packets. Braaf was surprised to see that the markings included not just the island of New York but also several in Westchester along the Sound as well as the North River valley. There were twelve in all.

"The instructions contained within the map must be safeguarded. Essentially, they give dates and times for meetings in the next three months. You will write your wife and daughter frequent letters that we will intercept and open as they go back and forth. Your letters should include the dates and times, as well as the selected meeting points when you have information for us. Use your imagination in getting it into context. You have a great intellect and are most resourceful. Meanwhile, we will continue to place gold in your account, and we will care for your family. I will see to it personally..."

Braaf cut him off, "Keep away from my family...and they must know nothing of this. They are innocent and would not be proud of a man who engages in this kind of work."

Drummond gave him a sympathetic look, "If you keep your letters discreet and your information valuable, when this rebellion is crushed you will be one of the wealthiest and most prominent men in the colonies. And a hero, you should likely be a hero after all of this."

Drummond chuckled at his own wit. Braaf, normally a very cautious man averse to risk, was devastated. He now knew that his trial and sentence were a mockery, a charade intended to take suspicion away from him. Spying for a British army that seemed poised to win anyway had been an easy although not casual decision that he pulled off expertly. However, to put oneself in the rebel camp as a spy was sheer madness. Drummond, his erstwhile friend, had played him perfectly; had trapped him. The British would hold his family hostage and force him to take any risks they demanded. The very idea of this plan made him sick. However, he had one trump card and he was certainly glad that he had not played it yet: Cornelius Foch.

Foch had approached the rebels to volunteer espionage services right under Braaf's nose. A big mistake, but proved that Foch considered him a most reliable Patriot and that he trusted him on a personal level. Yes, at a suitable time he might be able to use Foch's espionage to his advantage. When that time would be depended on many factors, most of them unknown at this point. Controlling his panic and despair, Braaf decided to cooperate with Drummond. Perhaps, once safe in New York, he could give up Foch in return for his gold, his family, and freedom from the stress of his spying. However, before all of that could unfold, he needed to make his "escape" to the rebel camp.

೫)೮ೱ

General Howe held an important meeting with his senior staff to decide on a course of action at last, with Clinton and Cornwallis once again its main executors.

Clinton spoke first. "The plan is complex, Milord. First, your brother Richard has agreed to launch diversionary moves by naval vessels up and down both the North and East Rivers. His warships will begin the attack with barrage fire at various defenses along the shore. This fire will be followed by a diversionary landing, mostly Royal Marines, on one of the islands off the northeastern corner of Manhattan."

Howe scratched his chin. "Why waste the time and effort?"

Cornwallis bristled; the diversion had been his idea. "Milord, this would indicate a movement toward King's Bridge or even Westchester. Washington would maneuver forces north to avoid being cut off from New England, weakening his center."

Clinton cut him off with a look. "Once these actions have been accomplished, the actual landing will take place just north of the city at an area called Kips Bay. Our brigade secretly stationed near Bushwick has only to sail directly across after the arrival of their supporting warships."

Howe nodded to the officers, "Despite my best efforts, gentlemen, it seems my attempt to obtain terms from the rebels has failed. So I am now compelled to act. I believe this plan is sound—but it relies heavily on the element of surprise...."

The specific points of attack were in great part determined by the information Sandy Drummond had provided to Clinton and Cornwallis. It enabled them to assure the reluctant Howe that now was the time, while they had visibility into Mr. Washington's dispositions. After discussing the plan in detail, the meeting adjourned. Generals Clinton and Cornwallis remained behind for discreet discussions with their commander. The subject was espionage.

A somewhat nervous Clinton opened the conversation, "Milord, Sandy Drummond informs me that he has prepared a scheme to place a spy among the Americans."

Howe startled. "Did I hear you correctly? A spy? Why...we are already receiving reports from the New York Tories, are we not?"

Clinton replied. "Yes, of course. The occasional Loyalist who steals across the water from time to time is of some assistance but their reports concern observations of the rebel army from without. We need intelligence from within. Moreover, we cannot always depend on the veracity and completeness of such irregular reports. If this resistance continues for any great period of time I for one would prefer inside reports from a spy rather than rely to the random reports of the Loyalists."

Howe thrust his hands behind his back and paced back and forth before the marble fireplace that dominated the great room that served as his headquarters. "An intriguing proposition, gentlemen. Still, this sort of skullduggery troubles me. I have never liked it. How sure are you of the loyalty of this spy? And who is it?"

Cornwallis spoke, "A Mr. Jan Braaf, a notable attorney and..."

"Braaf? Braaf? Was he not just sentenced to death by court martial? You want to use a convicted murderer of British soldiers to spy for us? What madness is this? This damnable war has cost us the approbation of many once loyal subjects of the King, has shed needless English and American blood, put some of our other colonies at risk, and now it has taken the sanity of my two best generals!"

The normally calm and affable Howe was more agitated than they had ever seen him. He pounded his right fist into his left palm.

Clinton quickly cut him off before he became apoplectic. "Milord, this murder trial was all a ruse to cover the plot. Rogue Americans killed those soldiers as they were in the process of deflowering Braaf's daughter. Ever resourceful, Sandy Drummond seized on this to charge Braaf with the crime and force him to cooperate further. He is now under death sentence so that his hatred toward us will allay rebel suspicions when he 'escapes' to the American lines. Meanwhile, his wife and daughter will be under the watchful eyes of His Majesty's forces and the Brooklyn Home Guard. It seems the commander of said unit loathes Braaf. It is a brilliant plan, I must say."

"Are all of these machinations really necessary? I find it somehow...unseemly." Howe's tone showed that he had already acceded to the scheme.

"Yes Milord, all that it now requires is for you to approve this death sentence." Cornwallis handed him the document, which Howe signed without reading.

Chapter 25

Island of New York, September 9th, 1776

George Washington threw his quill down in frustration. He had just finished a short note to Nathaniel Greene. In the several war councils at his headquarters many heated discussions took place among his senior officers, and now many were siding with Greene. Washington himself was close to Greene and held him in high esteem, often using him as his sounding board for military strategy.

Yet Washington found himself beginning to agree with Greene, as his latest correspondence from the Continental Congress displayed a remarkable indecisiveness. Congress was nothing if not indecisive. Its recent guidance to Washington was vague and conflicting, advising him at various times to defend the city, abandon it, and nearly everything in between. Many believed that if New York were lost to the British, it would afford the British a strategic position that only superior naval forces could get back. They correctly realized that the infant American navy, nor any other navy in the world, had the power to wrest it back.

Now, a dispatch from Philadelphia provided Congress' final guidance: Washington could defend or abandon New York at his discretion, but not torch it. The politics of a scorched earth strategy were fraught with consequences that Congress did not wish to address. This decision complicated things for Washington. He was sure the note to Greene would cause much consternation among his senior officers, but there was no turning back.

Washington turned to Scovel, hovering nearby. "Mister Scovel, please summon Colonel Fitzgerald, and then see that this letter gets to General Greene promptly." Washington said, handing Scovel the note.

"Right away, Your Excellency." Scovel saluted and departed.

Not long after, Fitzgerald arrived at Washington's command post, recently moved to the new defenses along the Haarlem Heights, a hilly and wooded area at the northern end of the island dominating the approaches to the King's Bridge and the upper North River. Washington had begun the process of strengthening the two forts on each side of the North River. Fort Washington, sitting along the western edge of Haarlem Heights, commanded the New York side. Directly across the river, Fort Lee, named after the army's second most senior officer, Charles Lee, protected the New Jersey side from atop the high cliffs known as "the palisades." Holding the two forts in tandem was critical if his army were to keep control the upper North River, maintain a foothold on New York Island and threaten the city should the British take it.

When Fitzgerald entered the room, Washington signaled for the rest of the staff to leave and pointed Fitzgerald to a straight back chair near his desk. "Is Mister Creed ready to depart on his mission? "

"Yes, tonight. He departs after dark and returns before dawn. His men and some volunteers from John Glover's Gloucester Regiment have been training for the past few days and Creed deems them ready. If the weather cooperates, there should not be a problem."

Washington folded his hands. "Let us hope it produces the desired result. So if you would, please review the plan with me."

ဢ‌ော

By seven that night, Creed, Beall, and Parker had finished wrapping and tightening their belting, weapons and equipment. Still without new hunting shirts, they wore standard blue Continental uniforms. Creed had the men blacken their belting and have their britches and stockings dyed a dove gray. Creed hoped darkening the white of the uniforms would make them less visible at night. They wore the standard-issue black tricorn hats but the only insignia was a green oak leaf pinned to the flap. In all, they looked better than most of the soldiers in the demoralized and poorly equipped rebel army.

Before they left, Creed made an excuse to speak with Emily, just in case they did not return. He reasoned that she would need guidance as to where to send their belongings. During the past few days spent in Dr. Stanley's boarding house, Creed had deepened his now more than casual acquaintance with Emily, finding ways to be with her whenever he could justify it. The chemistry between them had grown. She was taken with Creed's charm, exuberance and obvious intelligence; he infatuated by her diligence, beauty and natural grace.

When Creed entered the kitchen, he found Emily preparing the next morning's activity with the servants. She was very organized and ran her father's business quite efficiently during his absence. She planned meticulously, had a good head for numbers, and double-checked everything. She treated the servants with a politeness unusual in the mistress of a house. That perhaps impressed Creed more than anything did.

"Lieutenant Creed, this is unexpected. You are dressed...differently. Are you leaving?" There was obvious disappointment and concern on her face. She was alarmed. He was dressed for a field mission. He smiled to assuage her concern and then raised his eyes at the cook and wash girl. She politely asked the servants to go and they left the two alone.

He looked at her intensely, knowing he might never see her again and hoping to absorb her graceful features in his mind for eternity. "Leaving, no, I do not think so. We have duties to attend to this evening, that's all. The lads and I should be back by morning. However, we are temporarily detached from our regiment. That could mean we'll be posted somewhere else and not return for our belongings, few as they are. If we do not return I will find a way to contact you so that we can retrieve them."

Their eyes locked on each other. He could not tell her of the grave danger their "duties" posed and that they might not return because they could be killed or captured.

Although distraught, she was composed enough to see through him. "Jeremiah Creed, there is more to this, I know...but I will not inquire further."

He smiled again, and spoke reassuringly. "Seriously now, it is just night guard duty," he said. "Now that the lads are rested and recovered, we must do our bit. You know—vigilance against the forces of the King." His smile worked. She relaxed just enough and placed her soft hand on his hard wrist. Her gentle touch sent a feeling through him that he had not felt in a long time.

He removed the oak sprig from his hat and presented it like a knight gallant to a lady of the court. "Please hold this for me. I had no time to pick a rose."

Emily blushed. "I will treasure this more than any gem I own." She lifted her head and lightly touched his cheek. He took hold of her hand, pressed it for a moment over his heart, and then returned it to her, as gently as if it held a fresh egg. "Please stay safe, Jeremiah," she whispered. "Please stay safe."

He said nothing, afraid that if he said anything he would say too much, not of his mission, but of his feelings. Instead, he bowed his head and departed into the warm night air.

৪০০৪

Sergeant Ezekial Hazard just finished his last check of the nearly thirty-foot long whaling boat. The crew had greased and wrapped the oarlocks to muffle the sound of the oars. They had also removed the boat's small lateen sail and mast. There would likely be no time or room to tack on the dark river now likely crawling with British ships, smugglers and other rascals working the waters between New York and Long Island.

Creed and Hazard had checked the map and reckoned they could be at the landing point within less than an hour. The Gloucester men would pull the oars, while Hazard operated the tiller. Creed's men would stand watch. Elias Parker with his experienced eyes would be positioned at the bow, Beall mid-ship and Creed with Hazard. They carried nothing but their personal weapons, although the boat had a small one-pound swivel cannon forward of the mast. Hazard loaded it with grape shot and covered it with a fitted canvas tarp. The Gloucester men also had their short muskets and cutlasses, also wrapped in oilskins to keep them dry during the trip. If all went well they would not need to unwrap them. These experienced mariners ordinarily wore flat caps with a pancake rim, short dark blue wool coats, and traditional sailor's breeches. For this mission, they had exchanged their caps for black head kerchiefs. Security trumped tradition for Creed's small command.

"We are ready to depart when you give the order, Mister Creed." Hazard saluted as Creed approached in the dark, followed by Beall and Parker.

"Aye, aye, Captain!" Creed grinned and returned the salute in a mock sailor's voice. Over the past couple of days, they had worked closely on the plan and Creed had enjoyed working with Hazard and his men. Hazard was indeed a ship's officer in his real life, First Mate on a small whaler based out of Boston. Now he was a "soldier-sailor" in the Gloucester Regiment and captain of this small whaling boat that had been refitted to perform military missions in support of the Continental Army. Creed enjoyed calling him "Captain" and to his delight, it both flattered and annoyed the Sergeant.

Then Creed said dryly, "We can depart now. I'd like to arrive early and have a look around–to eliminate unpleasant surprises."

Hazard nodded and placed his men at their positions, six stalwart New Englanders on each side with the bold Marylanders spread from fore to aft in the middle. As the boat slipped out into the river, Creed looked out for signs of British ships.

During their final planning session for the mission, Creed and Fitzgerald had discussed the possibility of a British a trap or some sort of deception. Perhaps the British had co-opted Foch, a.k.a. Mr. Jons? He might have bargained to save his life in exchange for a luring the Americans back to face interrogation and death. And they could not rule out the distinct possibility that Foch was in the pay of the British all along.

But they had no time to assess the situation. Washington was desperate for more information. In any event, it was now too late for them to turn back. Creed and his men would have to take the risk. They all agreed that it was the right thing to do.

When they were all seated Creed could see from Beall's face that he wanted to ask something.

Creed whispered, "Is there something bothering you, Private Beall?"

Beall shrugged. "Just thinking of Simon–he should be here with us."

Creed nodded. "Aye. He would be an asset, even with one arm. They'll likely send him home though. If he survives the journey, he'll likely recover and perhaps someday join us again."

Beall changed the subject. "Do you think we will get back to the village by any chance?"

Creed startled. "What? Brooklyn? Thinking of young Krista, are you?"

In the darkness, Creed could not see him blush. "Yes sir. Until Simon got hurt, she was all I have thought of...except staying alive."

Creed thought of Emily and replied. "Keep those thoughts in your heart—but your comrades and your mission in your head. The rest will work itself out. If the Lord wills it."

Creed knew there was no chance of a meeting in Brooklyn but said no more. He now had his own affair of the heart to wrestle with; that was distraction enough.

They were midway across the river. The air had the strong salt smell of the sea, even this far up the river. The East River was really a tributary of the North River, as was the Haarlem River. The two waters intersected further north near the Hell Gate, the entrance to Long Island Sound. Creed could make out the shorelines of both New York and Long Island. The buildings in New York presented a spectacle of lamp-light along the southeastern tip of the island, then stretched north one half mile until it tapered off to the occasional glimmer from farms north of the city. Over on Long Island, the heights of Brooklyn to their front-starboard presented a more subtle display—occasional patches of light from buildings along the waterfront and the occasional house along the bluffs. The night air was surprisingly still. No sailing ships could move under those conditions but there was the chance they might encounter the odd whaler or longboat. Whether a Tory or a British patrol, pirate or smuggler—any or all could jeopardize the mission.

Chapter 26

The Brooklyn Gaol, Long Island, September 1776

Braaf heard the jailer's key turn the tumbler and unlock the cell door. He glanced at his timepiece. It was after nine o'clock. Unlike those in Europe, most jail cells in America were roomy, even airy, with barred windows providing both ambient light and occasionally a view to the outside world. Braaf's cell faced the courtyard but it still provided plenty of light. The cell door swung open and two members of the Brooklyn Home Guard put shackles on his wrists and led him out. No one told them why the British wanted the prisoner at such a late hour but they did not question the orders. Like most Tories, they assumed the British professionals knew what they were doing. Perhaps it was a late night interrogation. What did it matter? Braaf was a convicted man awaiting the King's justice.

The Brooklyn Home Guard was a newly-raised Loyalist militia unit whose members were zealous in their support of the crown. They pulled Braaf along as quickly as they could, intentionally jerking his chains so that he painfully banged into walls, door jambs, and other obstacles. They had fed him only scraps since his incarceration. To them, he was a Whig, a rebel, and a traitor, in addition to being a murderer of His Majesty's soldiers. They brought him to a nearby barn where Drummond's men waited for them. When Braaf's Home Guard escorts saw the barn, they were sure he was in for a difficult night. "Good for the bastard," they thought. Drummond, however, had other plans.

When the Tory escort left, Sergeant Digby unlocked the shackles from Braaf and offered him a tin of ale and a pig's knuckle. Braaf gratefully downed the brew and gnawed voraciously on the joint.

As he ate, Digby spoke to him in a condescending tone. "I apologize for being a bit overzealous with you, sir, and the missus. Was just doing me duty is all. You know...an act to ensure anyone watching would see that you was an enemy of the crown. All for show. You know that..."

Braaf made no comment. He knew the man was a sadist at heart and delighted in every pain and every indignity that he inflicted. When he had finished eating and the Brooklyn Home Guard was long gone, Digby motioned for Braaf to follow him.

"We have a horse for you out back, sir. Major Drummond sends his regrets for not being here in person but felt things would work better with just us. We must get you safely across before mid tide."

The gravity of what was going to take place had suddenly overwhelmed Braaf. He stopped as Quaif opened the side door of the barn. "Before I go, I must see my family."

"I am sorry sir, but my orders are to take you directly." Digby replied, politely but firmly.

Braaf knew what this meant, but desperate for a way out, he stalled. He grabbed onto the barn door in attempt to delay as much as possible, "Take me, take me where?"

His mind raced for a way out. Once mounted, should he bolt for freedom? To what end? These dragoons would out-ride him. If angered, they might punish him through his family. Dejected, he resigned himself to playing along, at least until he could come up with a course of action to escape his situation.

Digby smiled a pleasant but not particularly friendly smile. "We have a boat that will bring you across to New York, sir. Some Royal Navy and Marines will attend you. Nice chaps, or so I have been told. There will be new clothes for you and some gold to see you through. Once over, Major Drummond says your, er, 'friends' will take care of you. The major is always right, you know."

They arrived at a secluded place along the shoreline, just below the heights. The British boat had not yet arrived. Braaf's pulse quickened, he knew he had but little time to plot a way out. His mind raced feverishly for a solution to his dilemma. A naturally cautious and timid man, he simply could not countenance spying for the British behind American lines. The least mistake or indiscretion could result in the gallows—or a firing squad if he were lucky.

Braaf looked up the coast and saw that they were little more than a quarter mile from the quay where *Red Hen* lay at anchor. He thought back on his friend Cornelius and the arrangement he had made with the Americans. He fought the temptation to break free and make his way there. The British would never reveal that he had betrayed the Americans on Long Island. If they did, they risked losing support from other potential spies and informants. No, they would keep that secret. Moreover, Cornelius knew him only as his patriotic friend, falsely sentenced for murder. His family was hostage either way, but later he would give Cornelius up to the British in exchange for them.

Digby unlocked the shackles. They had re-shackled Braaf for the trip as part of the charade and as a precaution. Braaf rubbed his wrists. Digby removed some writing materials from his saddlebag.

"We have some time before the boat is due here, sir. I have paper for you. Major Drummond said you could write your family. Just a short personal note that we will deliver, that is all Major Drummond will allow. I warn you, sir: I must read it."

Braaf wrote a short note to Marta professing his love and devotion to her and Krista as well as his love for the cause of freedom and liberty. When Digby questioned his political affirmation, Braaf readily explained that if it fell into the wrong hands, that is, the Whigs, it would help minimize any suspicions of him and his family. Digby nodded, folding the stiff paper into an envelope.

Digby then handed him a small leather valise with a lock and key. "If this falls into the wrong hands your life and the lives of your family are in danger."

Digby's voice sent a wave of chills through Braaf. His mouth went dry and stomach turned. The valise contained special instructions for communication, meeting times and locations, and some rudimentary codes. It also contained a list of questions Drummond wanted answered—mostly about rebel morale and troop numbers.

Braaf knew that this was a very risky and dangerous enterprise, and he wanted no part of it. He tried to stall for time while he figured a way out. "May I have more ale, or some water? I am not feeling well."

Digby smirked, and then nodded to Quaif, who removed a water bottle from his saddlebag. Braaf took several sips and sat down on a fallen tree trunk. Tiny black flies whirled about his head, stinging his eyes. The warm night air and lack of wind made the coastline miserable. He stared off toward the north, thinking through his options again. There was a trail running half way up the bluffs that led to the *Red Hen*. If he could make a run for it, he might lose his pursuers in the dark and get there on his own. Suddenly, he heard a double click. Brent stood next to him with his dragoon pistol at the ready. He had a wry frown and looked at Braaf with great intensity.

"I am sorry sir. My job is to make sure that any second thoughts on your part are resolved in His Majesty's favor."

Braaf's voice choked. "I...I do not understand, and I resent the implication." He raised his voice as much as he dared.

Brent replied earnestly. "Any man who would betray his cause for monetary advantage needs special watching. You understand, sir."

Braaf realized then that he was, indeed what Brent implied. He, Jan Braaf, was a traitor.

Brent waived the pistol in the direction of *Red Hen*. "There is a boat there and you were friends with the owner, Mr. Foch is it? Leader of the Whig faction, ain't he? Well, a run to him will do you no good. I am faster than you, sir."

Braaf's heart sank. He was in Drummond's control. They always seemed one step ahead of him. At that very moment he at last knew that he had no choice but to go through with this mad English scheme. Imperceptibly, but as surely, his role changed from merely an opportunistic traitor to full-fledged British spy.

"I do not know what you mean. Cornelius Foch is politically a Whig, but he would not betray the King. As for me, and my need for the King's gold, why else would I risk my life? Why else do you risk yours so far from your home, your precious England?"

Braaf turned silent as Digby approached with the look of satisfaction one has when a job is complete. He had lit a small lantern and placed it on the dock.

"Very well now, sir. Your boat should be along shortly. When it pulls up to the slip, we will watch from here until you board. Say nothing to the sailors and marines. They will say nothing to you. As far as they are concerned, you are going to make some purchases in New York for Billy Howe's lovely Mrs. Loring, and will return on another boat. Privileges of the commander-in-chief, eh?" Digby laughed—the army reveled in the many jokes about their general's love life.

Then Digby handed him a ragged old cloak made of brown wool and a crumpled black hat that he pulled down to cover most of Braaf's face. "In the darkness this will hide your identity from the men on the boat. Many a drunken soldier has given away His Majesty's secrets in saloon and brothel, we would not want that."

Digby laughed at his own poor humor, as did Quaif, but Brent was mortified. Braaf said nothing.

"As soon as you are on board we will be off, so that we can sound the alarm about your 'escape.' I recommend you rest until then."

Brent eased the pistol hammer forward, but kept the weapon at the ready and pointed toward Braaf.

ಬಂಧ

Elias Parker saw the lantern light flickering low along the shore, no more than 300 yards off the port bow. It flickered for just a few seconds. That was all his keen eyes needed.

He faced back to Creed. "Sir, a signal light off the port bow. "

Creed asked calmly. "How far, Private Parker?"

Parker replied with equal calm. "Three hundred yards distant, sir, no more."

Creed nodded at the helmsman. "Turn one point to port."

The helmsman turned the rudder and the Gloucester oarsmen instinctively picked up the pace. They rowed expertly through the calm water so that the boat moved as if gliding on air. Within minutes, they pulled into a small wooden slip that lay in a cove a quarter-mile south of the *Red Hen*.

The signal lamp was covered but some of the light escaped the unsealed edges of the canvas. Creed's senses went into high gear. There was no mention of a lantern in his instructions and this lantern burned suspiciously like the one they had spotted in the marsh near Wallabout Bay several nights earlier.

He whispered softly to Beall and Parker. "Something is wrong. I do not think the lantern was meant for us. We may have once more disturbed someone else's meeting."

Instinctively, Beall and Parker drew their edged weapons—Beall his short hunting sword, Parker his fisherman's knife. From the shadows along the shore, a figure in a dark cloak emerged. Tall, he wore a floppy wide brimmed hat and carried a valise. In the darkness, they did not recognize Jan Braaf, nor he them. Digby sent him toward the quay, unaware that the approaching longboat was not British, but American.

Creed's mind raced as he assessed situation they faced. Was the lantern's presence a failure in communication and meant to be there all along? Had they had stumbled on a smuggling ring by some strange coincidence? Could these be the same British dragoons they had encountered the previous week, once again meeting an American spy? If so, why would this man approach the boat so readily?

The man in the cloak walked hesitantly towards the boat, and then looked back for a second. Finally, he clambered aboard the longboat, right behind Parker. Baffled and desperate, Creed decided to use the greeting provided by Fitzgerald. If the man responded then this was just a mix up. If he did not, well then he would have to make some quick decisions.

He fingered his sword hilt. "Did you once sail on the *Eagle?*"

The phrase stunned Braaf. He had heard it before. Foch and that American colonel, their spymaster, used it. His body froze in panic. In the terror and confusion which gripped him, he could not recall the reply. He looked to the shoreline. Digby and his three dragoons had already ridden off to announce his "escape."

Creed was flustered as well, and repeated the salutation, this time more intensely, "Did you once sail on the *Eagle?*

Braaf stammered a reply, "No...no. I sailed on..."

Creed stared at the vague figure before them. Braaf could sense Creed's suspicion rising. In his nervousness, and with the fear and the trauma of the past week, Braaf could not remember the counter sign. He realized this was the wrong boat. He tried to recall the brief but eventful meeting with that Colonel Fitzgerald. Yes, he remembered the name...it came to him suddenly.

Braaf blurted out the counter sign. "...I sailed on *The Talon.*"

Creed, exhaled in stark relief: the correct response! This had to be Mr. Jons... or his agent. Parker and Beall lowered their blades.

Creed whispered. "Very well. The lantern confused us. Not part of the plan, and drew us away from our destination by a quarter mile. No matter now. You may provide us your package so we can be off."

Braaf now recognized Creed's voice. He had to act quickly. What was the information they were they seeking? Surely, he had stumbled upon a communication with Cornelius. Braaf was a weak man with no sense for business, but he was a smart man who immediately realized the opportunity now before him. Cornelius must be attempting to send information to Fitzgerald. A couple of visits to the campsites and taverns would undoubtedly yield much; these English were cocky in their overwhelming power and their easy victories. Braaf at once decided to pass himself off as Cornelius' messenger. Once ensconced in New York he could seek help from among the many Tories and Loyalists. Moreover, he had Drummonds' gold to help smooth the way. Yes, the lawyer in him could talk his way out of the situation after all.

Braaf removed his hat and revealed himself. "Lieutenant Creed, I have information that can only be provided directly to Colonel Fitzgerald."

Creed and his companions were stunned. Braaf then told his tale, a combination of fact and fiction that he wove together masterfully. He told them of his arrest and conviction; the death sentence; interrogation and "escape." In his version, Braaf told them he fled and ran immediately to Cornelius who amended the meeting plans to expedite Braaf's escape to New York. It all flowed logically and Creed believed it. After all, Braaf was their benefactor and they had become close to him and his family during the short but eventful time in Brooklyn.

"What will become of your wife and daughter, sir?" Private Beall spoke with obvious worry. He rarely stopped thinking about Krista.

Braaf sighed both in earnest and for effect, "My only fear and regret is that the English or Tories might punish them for my escape, but Cornelius promised to keep watch on them. They are as safe with him as with me."

Although Braaf's statement was true, he had based it on conjecture. All that Cornelius would ever know is that his friend Jan had made a desperate escape. He knew that Cornelius had feelings for Marta that went beyond friendship and for that reason; he was sure enough that Foch would do his best to ensure their safety. He also knew that Drummond would also ensure nothing happened to his "hostages." Therefore, both British and American spies would protect them! The irony of it dawned on him and all of his fears and anxieties abated. He began to realize that his situation was suddenly shifting from that of powerless pawn to powerful manipulator. It was actually exhilarating.

෯෬

Cornelius Foch became very concerned. He had worked as aggressively as discretion would allow in the hope of learning British intentions. Through several days and nights of careful observation as well as painstaking elicitation at tavern and dockside, he knew that the forces now arrayed at Bushwick were to be the main attack force. He also knew that the attack could come very soon, most likely as an attempt to envelop Washington's defenses from the north. Just how far north he could not discern, but his observation of the comings and goings of British shipping led him to surmise that the British landing would likely take place at Kips Bay. He carefully stipulated all this in a letter for Fitzgerald, addressed to Mr. Smythe. However, despite two showings at the appointed meeting place, no one appeared. The next scheduled meeting was in a fortnight. He dared not advance the arrangement again. Foch was a pragmatist. He would only take so many risks in one week.

Frustrated, he returned to the *Red Hen*. It was a calm and warm night, so he decided to go on deck and have a smoke. He joined one of his able-bodied seamen, Eddie Riff, at the forecastle. He cut a piece of tobacco, tamped it into his Meerschaum pipe, and lit it. No sooner had he drawn the first puff than he heard the sound of muskets from out on the river.

Chapter 27

The Gloucestermen pulled hard at their oars. The sooner they were across the deceptively peaceful river, the better. All knew that the secret rendezvous had taken an unexpected turn. The boat cleared the small inlet and turned into the open river.

Parker first spotted the trouble ahead. "Longboat, dead on, sir!"

They all looked up and saw a British longboat coming right at them with a full complement of Royal Navy sailors at the oars and a Royal Marine party of eight in the thwarts. In the darkness, Creed could only distinguish their headgear silhouetted against the night sky and water. Unbeknownst to Creed, this British boat was to have transported Braaf to New York. Before Creed could give the command, Hazard steered hard a-port to pick up speed with the down-river current.

"Full speed, boys!" he called to his Gloucestermen. No urging was necessary. They were experienced seamen-soldiers who knew instinctively when there was trouble.

The crew of the British craft was also surprised to find another vessel in "their" waters. The Lieutenant of Royal Marines in command, James Greene, immediately realized he had a rebel boat before him and decided to give chase. In less than a minute, the British longboat came about in hot pursuit.

Hazard's quick action bought the Americans some time and distance. They had put almost 100 yards between themselves and the other boat. In the darkness, this was a safe distance. Shots from one moving vessel to another would be random and most would stray from their mark. Hazard maintained a bearing south along the river, less than a quarter mile north of the Brooklyn ferry, and a little more than a 100 yards off shore.

Greene did not have time to ponder the unexpected disruption of his mission. It had all been so secret. He had received orders to pick up and deliver a messenger to New York. His orders stressed secrecy and speed. Greene merely had to steer up the coast and head toward the lantern.

Greene muttered to the Marine sergeant. "The signal lantern is gone. Our passenger is likely now on that rebel boat. Prepare the lads for action, sergeant."

A bold assumption, but Greene did not make lieutenant by being cautious. At twenty-eight and promoted up from the ranks, Greene was a fast riser in the close knit Royal Marine Regiment where most of his peers were in their late thirties or older.

There was a slight haze drifting out in the middle of the river. Greene surmised that the rebels would take advantage of the river's current as long as possible. But eventually they would have to turn west and head to New York. A veteran of dozens of amphibious operations and six pitched naval engagements, Greene had no problem estimating the point at which the other boat would have to turn. He then set a diagonal course into the haze on a southwest heading, in the hope of intercepting them before they reached the New York side.

For a moment, Creed had taken his eyes from the longboat's dark silhouette to their aft. In that little time, their pursuers had disappeared. "The British boat is out of sight, Ezekial, we have lost her."

Hazard replied, "Are you sure?"

"Aye, Captain. I took my eyes off her for naught but a moment and she is now gone. Keep the tempo. She is out there somewhere."

Hazard nodded, "Once we pass the ferry landing we must turn west or we will enter the upper harbor and face choppier waters, uncooperative tides and the Royal Navy."

Creed replied lightly. "I defer to your judgment in such matters, Captain. Private Parker, anything before us?"

"No sir. The haze has thickened. I cannot see more than two hundred feet now."

The darkness and quiet made the final quarter mile south seem eerie. On either side of them, Creed knew that two great armies were preparing for their next clash. Creed also knew that to the north and south there were British warships and transports of all sizes whose activity could at any time disrupt the mission. They were racing against time and space, as well as a longboat full of Royal Marines. He mused at the predicament he had gotten into. After getting his men through the dangers on Long Island, Creed had now thrust them into a more perilous situation, once again on the water, at night. The irony brought a grim smile to his face.

"We should just about be on line with the city," Hazard announced. "I am going to turn starboard...now." He gently pushed the rudder and slowly turned the boat in a wide arc. He did it so skillfully that they scarcely realized they were now heading west instead of south. Only the change in speed with loss of the downstream current suggested it.

Hazard spoke to his men. "Pull harder now. We must maintain speed and fight the current or we'll float out into Upper New York Bay." The doughty mariner whispered to Creed. "Less than twenty minutes to landfall, if I have estimated correctly."

"I vouchsafe you have, Captain." Creed said with a nod.

Elias Parker's keen eyes were the first to make out the flickering lanterns of a British squadron anchored north of the Governor's Island. "Ships to the port, Lieutenant, maybe four hundred yards."

"Damn!" Creed cursed to himself. "How many?"

Parker narrowed his eyes. "At least six, possibly a frigate with a brig and some sloops o' war."

A British squadron lay in anchor off the Governor's Island. William Tryon, the Royal Governor of New York, had abandoned the city when the rebels took control and was "governing" his colony from a British ship. Using one of the brigs as his base, he had been arranging to return to the city when the British forces made their attack, thus changing his plans completely.

Creed replied softly, "Proceed on course gentlemen. Keep the oars as quiet as possible and remain silent."

They rowed on another five minutes when the faint but unmistakable sound of oars hitting water broke the quiet of the night. The splashing grew louder by the moment. It came from their starboard bow.

"Elias, Jonathan, take up your firelocks." Creed whispered to keep his voice from reaching the other boat. The two Marylanders drew their firearms from the wrappings, as Creed drew his. Suddenly the British longboat came into view, no more than forty yards distant. Greene's calculations had been spot on.

"Full speed, boys!" cried Hazard.

An unnecessary command since, once again, his men had instinctively increased their rowing tempo. This time it was to no avail. Lieutenant James Greene had estimated his approach perfectly. There was no way the Americans could escape. Greene and his men were between the Americans and the safety of New York. And they were closing fast.

Greene spoke calmly as they closed. "Very well, gentlemen. Our quarry has proven quite predictable. Now it is time to finish them. Marines, stand and present!"

The compliment of Royal Marines stood in the swift moving boat as easily as on a parade field.

Greene gave the command. "Steady now...fire!"

The volley echoed across the water. The muzzle flashes lit up the dark river for a brief moment. As fortune would have it, the movements of the two boats, their distance apart, and the darkness conspired to cause the volley to stray. Just two rounds struck the American boat catching the edge of the stern and sending splinters flying, but doing no apparent harm. The British ship closed on them, the Royal Marines reloading with a precision and speed that the Americans could never match.

Creed spoke with surprising calm, "They are firing a bit high. On my command, every man will get down as low as possible. We shall return fire immediately after their next volley."

The two boats were now twenty-five yards apart and on a collision course. Creed watched the Marines present their loaded muskets.

"Down!" He cried.

The second British volley rang out but this time hit home with better effect. The volley struck two of the Gloucester men on the starboard side. One screamed in agony as a musket ball broke through flesh and bone; his right arm hung shattered. The other slumped over–dead instantly from a ball that pierced his neck. The blood from his severed artery sprayed the prostrate Braaf with its sticky warmth. More would have fallen to the precise British fire had not Creed's precaution caused most of the rounds to clear just above the men's hunched backs.

Creed's next order was crisp and clear, "Stand and fire."

Creed and his two men stood and fired their weapons into the British, who stood upright while reloading. Their silhouette presented a large target that allowed each American round to count. They hit three Marines, all mortally. One fell overboard, the other two slumped back onto the rowing sailors, disrupting their rhythm for a few seconds. The British boat veered slightly off course. Creed knew, though, that the next volley from the British could undo them.

He turned to Hazard, "They are getting ready to fire again. Steer into them, Ezekial; they will not be expecting us to change course and attack. We shall take them or go down with them!"

Greene gave the command as soon as his marines had reloaded. "Present, fire!"

Hazard pushed the rudder to port, turning the boat starboard just as the third British volley rang out, causing it to miss completely. The men rowed at full speed toward their target. Surprised at the maneuver, the British slowed to attempt another volley before the impending collision. Hazard steered the boat directly at the oncoming British. The crew cringed in anticipation of the final, devastating volley and head to head collision that awaited them. But there was no final volley. At five yards, Creed fired the swivel gun straight into the oncoming boat. Eight two ounce balls ripped down the middle of the boat, tearing four marines and two sailors to bloody shreds. Screams and cries of the wounded and dying spread panic among those unscathed from the blast.

"You got the bastards good, Mister Creed! You got 'em good!" Hazard cried.

Parker found the small anchor located at the bow. He stood erect and tossed it at the British craft like a grappling hook. The two craft collided with a crunch. A Gloucesterman threw the other anchor onto the British craft as a second boarding grapple. The two boats were now lashed in a struggle from which only one could emerge the victor. Both sides knew it was knife-work now, kill or be killed. Men from both boats erupted in a cascade of shouts, curses and threats, punctuated by the horrific screams of the wounded Britons.

Creed was first over the gunwale followed by Beall and Parker. Two of the Gloucestermen joined them, cutlasses ready. Greene, seeing his bleeding and dying crew, knew well that their chances had dimmed but he determined to make a fight of it.

Greene and a wounded marine rushed forward to intercept Creed. Creed ran the wounded marine through the heart as he attempted to strike a downward blow. Pushing the Marine's slumping body toward Greene, Creed blocked his first thrust. He then spun the body aside, whipping his blade from the dead man's chest. Greene lunged at Creed a second time. The two blades clashed but Creed deftly and quickly turned into Greene, twisted his blade away, and struck it from his hand.

Creed wanted this madness ended. "Your craft is mine," he announced to the stunned Greene. "Surrender now and I shall spare your men."

Beall and Parker had squared off against two British sailors who came forward to help Greene. They dodged several vicious cutlass strokes before their blades brought the tars to their knees. The small boat clanked with the sound of metal on wood as the rest of the British, in shock and disarray from the savage attack, downed their weapons.

"I submit," answered Greene, breathing heavily from sheer exhaustion. He drew a white kerchief from his vest and waived it, then calmly used it to stop the bleeding from his left hand, from which a chestnut sized piece of flesh had been blown off by the grape shot.

৪০৫৪

A series of loud booms suddenly thundered across the harbor from both sides. Responding to the unexpected fire out on the river, an American artillery battery at the southeastern tip of New York began to fire wildly into the darkness. The British squadron anchored off the Governor's Island responded in kind, aiming blindly toward the sound of the musket and grape fire up river. The British fire was uncannily accurate and shot of various calibers soon began careening around them. Creed's surprise victory on the water would yet come to naught if even one shot hit home.

"Drop your oars and weapons over the side." Creed ordered his captives. The British hesitated.

"Do as he says." Greene said diffidently, his honor sufficiently upheld.

Stifling their anger and humiliation, the remaining British marines and sailors did as Greene commanded. The British oars, muskets, and sabers slid quietly into the waters now swirling from the changing tide. Grappled together, both craft were drifting down river and closer to the British ships below them.

Greene was a professional. He had lost this fight but he knew there would be more to come. In that sense, he had more acumen than the high command in both North America and London.

"I am Lieutenant James Greene, His Majesty's Royal Marines. To whom, have I surrendered?"

"Lieutenant Jeremiah Creed, First Maryland Continental Line, sir," was the calm, humble answer.

"I sir, am your prisoner." Greene handed his sword to the rebel with a slight bow at the waist.

Creed gestured toward the squadron that was continuing fire in their direction. "The tide will soon take you to the safety of your ships. You fought gallantly and almost bested us. However, I have no tactics with which to beat the entire Royal Navy so we must now take leave of you."

An eighteen-pound iron ball plunged into the water not more than twenty yards away. Another soon followed, splashing them with water. Both boats rocked from the resulting waves.

Creed wiped the wet from his brow. "We must get out of their line of fire or both our boats could be blown to splinters with the next salvo."

Creed saluted Greene and returned his sword. He then jumped back into the American boat, followed by Parker, Beall and the two the Gloucester sailors. Parker unsheathed his big fishing knife and cut both lines, separating the two ships.

Hazard soon had his men back at their oars and rowing toward New York. Shot from the British ships continued to disrupt the water around them. Greene and his men drifted down river with the tide, hoping that they would reach a British ship before a round careened into them or they drifted out into the lower harbor and the Atlantic. As the Americans approached New York, the fire from the British ships became scattered and eventually tapered off. However, those from the American battery to their front began to grow closer and more concentrated.

"It will be a shame if we are blown to bits by our own guns." Hazard said.

"I have seen the result of American militia artillery, Ezekial. I think we are better off in their sights than the sights of the Royal Navy. By Jesus, tis a good thing they cannot see us."

Creed chuckled, and then ducked as a shot sailed right over his head.

"Better if they did see us, Jeremiah—their poor gunnery would be our salvation," Hazard retorted with dry New England humor.

"Tis true indeed, true indeed," Creed chortled as the spray whipped around them.

Soon their boat was under the arc of the American fire and a few minutes later the battery ceased its futile exercise. Beall and Parker took to the oars in place of the two downed mariners.

Parker whispered to Beall. "Easy now, farm boy. You pull with a jerk. This is not tug-o-war in back woods Maryland. You'll sap your strength and lessen the thrust of the oar. Make a slow, even motion. Let your legs do most of the work."

Beall took the chiding in stride. "You took enough time to impart some of your waterman's knowledge, Elias."

"First chance I've had to tell you, farm boy. But better now than never, is that not so?"

Beall nodded. "It is. I'll try and return the favor some day."

It still took the tired band almost an hour to negotiate the swirling waters of the lower river. Hazard had steered a course northwest so they had to battle the downstream current as well. Their goal was the departure point. Creed did not want to explain things to curious sentries or annoying officers of the guard.

"Oars up!" Hazard announced, as if on regatta. As the boat slid quietly against the small wooden quay, Parker leapt from the forward port position and secured it.

Safely on land, Creed could finally turn his attention back to the intelligence mission. How and why was Jan Braaf in the middle of all this? He judged him a shy homebody, kindly even, and certainly no daring spy. His politics were Whig, but he was a man of the law and the ballot, not the cloak and dagger. Creed had pushed Braaf down after the first volley and down he stayed throughout the entire affair to include the return trip. Creed thought it better to leave him there until they were safely back. He lay quietly between the second and third pair of oarsmen.

As the boat hit the quay Creed tapped him gently. "Very well, *Mijnheer* Braaf, we are on the island of New York. It is not Brooklyn, but then again, what is?"

Creed's smile disappeared as he pulled Braaf up and saw the blood that soaked his brown cloak. Unknown to anyone, a stray musket ball had hit him during the firefight. Braaf's eyes were wide with fear and his breathing was measured and shallow.

"Man, you never said a word! Private Parker, attend here please, Mister Braaf has been shot."

Parker's time on the Chesapeake and other coastal waters led him to develop some uncanny skills in handling small injuries. Throughout the campaign, he had tended several broken bones, numerous lacerations and contusions, and the fevers. However, he had never treated a musket wound. He carefully pulled back the clothing and then cut the blood caked under garments away to reveal a neat puncture that entered Braaf's right side one inch below the rib cage. Parker knew the wound was serious. Only a surgeon could say whether the wound was mortal, but it was very grave nevertheless.

Parker shook his head. "The wound is very grave, sir. We must get him to a surgeon quickly."

A pair of Mariners helped Creed's men carry Braaf to the Stanley boarding house to await a surgeon. Finding one in the middle of the night was Hazard's task, as Creed set off to report to Fitzgerald. Creed looked forward to disturbing the colonel in the middle of the dark night to which he had consigned Creed and his men.

Chapter 28

Colonel Fitzgerald's Quarters, New York, September 11th, 1776

As Creed talked, Fitzgerald paced up and down the room, dressed only in his night robe and slippers. He and Creed went through several mugs of tea and Fitzgerald was on his second pipe. By the time Creed finished his report and answered Fitzgerald's many questions, the horizon was beginning to glow with a light coppery patina.

"Well, in the long run, a small naval victory against the Royal Marines is no consolation for the failure of the intelligence mission," Fitzgerald said. "Moreover, if poor Braaf now dies on us, we will have certainly failed. Our next scheduled meeting with Mr. Jons is not for another fortnight. The British will surely come before then."

Fitzgerald had taken to calling Cornelius Foch by his cover name, "Jons," even in private. On an island full of Tories and crawling with informants, a slip of the tongue overheard by the wrong party could bring disaster.

Creed said. "Well, sir, then it is now up to the surgeon, is it not? A butcher with a knife is all that stands between light and darkness."

Fitzgerald looked crossly at Creed, and then chuckled grimly at the thought.

"So it is, Lieutenant Creed," he replied. "Perhaps fortune will shine on us, and on poor Braaf. So much of this affair is based on luck, both good and bad."

Creed snapped. "As well as hard fighting by very brave men, some of whom died tonight. All because of this 'failed' intelligence mission of yours. God knows why they—or any of us—volunteered!"

Creed regretted his own impertinence as soon as the words were out. He realized he had crossed the line but the second mariner had bled to death during the trip back and he felt responsible.

Fitzgerald looked at Creed solemnly. "Of course my lad, you are correct. It seems intelligence work can be as dangerous as a pitched battle. Very well, I will report all of this to His Excellency. Now see to your men and Mister Braaf, and then get some sleep. Did you secure your horse and belongings?"

"Yes, sir. And thank-you for finding mounts for my men as well."

"Well, they shall need them. Report back at two this afternoon; we shall dine together with His Excellency and discuss all this again."

୫୦୯୫

Creed returned to the Stanley house at sunrise. He found Elias Parker and Emily Stanley assisting the acting surgeon, a Doctor William Thompkins. Thompkins was a local physician, not a military surgeon. That meant he had rarely treated a serious bullet wound. His main experience with violent trauma injuries was the occasional knife wound although he had once treated a bullet wound caused by a jealous husband gut-shooting his wife's lover.

"Lieutenant Creed, I have already heard so much about you from Miss Stanley. I am Doctor William Thompkins, a former colleague of her father."

Creed made a motion as if to shake hands but dropped it on seeking the state of the doctor's hands. "I am glad to hear that doctor. How bad is he?" Creed's look drifted to Emily, who blushed at his obvious distraction. Creed had a difficult time taking his eyes off her.

Thompkins cleared his voice loudly, regaining Creed's attention. "Difficult to say at this point, young man. I have done as much as I could, but could not remove the ball. It struck his hip and shattered itself as well as a few inches of bone. I fear a piece has deflected into his stomach and perhaps his loins. I stopped the external bleeding for now and I bandaged him with fresh linen but there has already been a great effusion of blood. We must keep him comfortable and as soon as he can take some liquid. Make sure he gets as much as he wants. Tea is good. Moreover, when the pain gets unbearable you can give him rum, as much as he can take. I shall be back tonight unless he turns worse. Call me in that event."

Creed nodded in reply and Thompkins departed into the early morning light. Creed looked at Braaf, now semi-conscious and moaning softly. His eyes, partially opened, looked cat-like to Creed.

"Private Parker, you and Private Beall must go and get some sleep. I shall stay with Miss Stanley awhile longer. I must meet with Colonel Fitzgerald after noon. Oh yes, and my sincere thanks to both of you for a job well done."

When Parker left, Creed took Emily's hands in his. Her hair was tied up in the loose bun she had hurriedly tied when the soldiers came back to the house. Strands were in disarray, her nightdress was stained with blood and other fluids from Braaf. Still, to him, she looked more magnificent than the finest French noblewoman dressed for a grand ball at Versailles.

"Miss Emily, thank-you so much for helping with *Mijnheer* Braaf. His family took good care of us when we were in Brooklyn. He seemed such a mousy fellow though. Hard to believe he was spying on the British. It takes a cold, purposeful mind to spy effectively. I never saw that in him."

"Mr. Creed, war makes people act passionately and even heroically when they ordinarily would not fathom doing so."

She blushed again after realizing her unintentional double-entendre. Creed smiled and kissed her hands softly. Their heads bumped gently and they both pulled back instinctively, then smiled.

Beall woke Creed shortly before noon. After a mug of hot coffee a bath was drawn for him and he was able to shave as well. His two men had already eaten and cleaned up; they did not favor baths as Creed did, preferring to wash with buckets of cold well water. After dressing, he checked in on Braaf. Emily was watching him. She was dressed in a light brown summer dress suitable for farm and garden work, but on her as attractive as a dress could be. Creed, always attracted to beautiful women, found his fascination with Miss Stanley uncanny. It was beyond any anything he had experienced.

He gently touched her elbow as he approached her and bowed slightly. "Good morning Miss Stanley. How is our patient doing?"

"Not well, I fear. He fell into a fitful sleep after you turned in and now burns with the fever."

Creed grimaced at the thought. Even the slightest wound turned mortal once infection and mortification set in. This did not bode well.

"Also, I went through his things after you went to sleep. I found this small valise. I did not open it, in case it was something important."

Creed smiled warmly. "Such a brilliant lass you are! Well, let us have a look at it."

The key was missing, probably lost in the actions of the night. Creed carefully pried it open with a jackknife. His eyes widened when he saw the contents, but he said nothing.

Emily could see in his eyes that there was something unusual about the contents. "Is it important?"

"No, not really," he lied.

The less she knew the better for her, he thought. She did not believe him, but said nothing. Creed closed the valise and took both of her hands in his. Their eyes met for a long moment and neither spoke. There was no need. Creed then released her hands, ever so slowly, picked up the valise and headed toward the door.

"I must depart for my appointment with the good colonel. We have much to discuss. As do you and I, when I return." He bowed his head and left.

ဆေC3

Creed arrived early for his appointment with Fitzgerald. They examined the contents of the valise, which contained what appeared to be instructions for meetings, plus what looked like a primitive code for use in some sort of secret correspondence. There were sketches with locations and times marked, mostly in lower Manhattan, the east coast of upper Manhattan, and a spot just north of New York in Westchester, called Frog's Neck. Finally, there were two envelopes, each with a letter of introduction. Each letter introduced the bearer to one of two names: a Mister Neeley and a Mister Van Ness. Both letters were generic introductions that could have supported any legitimate business or social enterprise but to Fitzgerald they clearly indicated espionage activity. The Neeley letter stated that Neeley should provide the bearer support for his enterprise and accommodate him wherever possible using his connections and friends. The Van Ness letter asked him to introduce the bearer to a prominent banker, unnamed, who would provide funds agreed to in a previous correspondence.

After carefully examining the contents of the valise, Fitzgerald wiped his forehead with a kerchief, and then impatiently wrapped his knuckles on the table as he tried to sort things out.

"If I were to dispatch a spy on a mission these are the sort of tools I would provide him. This portends a sophisticated plan for espionage."

"Is it possible the Whigs in Brooklyn have their own network established and he was trying to connect that with the Continental Army?" Creed asked.

"Not very likely since they could have, should have, brought it to my attention when he and Foch approached me at the Brooklyn ferry. If the British really sentenced Braaf to death and he escaped, how did he come by this? Moreover, these look too sophisticated for a political faction to be using. I suspect this is a British plot. Braaf and Foch may have been British agents. After all, their approach to me was rather sudden and, frankly, unaccountable. I should have suspected them from the beginning. "

"Yet both men were of the greatest help to us in Brooklyn. It does not make sense, sir."

"Makes perfect sense, my boy. When you involve yourself in these matters, true intentions are always opaque. The code of honor of a soldier plays no role when it comes to affairs such as this, Lieutenant Jeremiah Creed. That is something that you must learn soon enough."

Creed gave him a puzzled look. What did he mean by that remark? Would this delay his return to the Maryland Continental Line even further? He joined this great American enterprise to defend the cause of liberty and freedom in open battle, not through a series of perfidious exploits. The discussion ended abruptly when Beall brought word that Braaf was awake but feverish and asking to talk to Creed or Fitzgerald. It seemed dinner with the commander-in-chief would have to wait.

"Private, please make straight away to the commander-in-chief's residence and provide my apologies to His Excellency. Tell him Lieutenant Creed and I have important business to attend, with a friend of Mister Jons. He will understand."

Beall gave a salute and made his way toward army headquarters.

ഇഗ

Fitzgerald and Creed arrived at the Stanley boarding house to find Emily applying cold compresses to Braaf's head and trying to get some liquid into him. Parker had gone to fetch Doctor Thompkins.

Emily looked at Fitzgerald with eyes opened wide, as if to question his presence. Fitzgerald avoided her glance, but quickly turned his attention to Braaf.

"Tis alright Emily, he is a friend. My good friend, Colonel Fitzgerald."

She looked back at Creed and her eyes now filled with tears. "The fever is very bad and he slips in and out of delirium, but he is occasionally cogent. He asked for you, Lieutenant, which I thought normal, but when he asked for...for Colonel Fitzgerald...Private Beall thought that perhaps there was something significant that he wanted to say."

"He might indeed," said Fitzgerald crisply. "Now please allow us some time alone with him Miss...?"

"Stanley, Colonel, Emily Stanley," she replied. "Do not worry; I do not share my father's Tory leanings, I am just circumspect in who knows of my Whig sympathies." She smiled and her graceful look charmed even Fitzgerald.

"I can attest to that sir." Creed broke in, almost too eagerly, Fitzgerald noted.

"Thank you, Miss...Stanley." Fitzgerald gave her a nod and watched her as she left the room.

Fitzgerald examined Braaf. His head was hot and moist with fever. A yellow and white mucous, pus, and coagulated blood stained the bandages. The smell was beginning to become noticeable, a pungent odor of rot.

"Well, infection must have set in earlier today. It has progressed quite a bit. I would say this doctor did him no favors either. Those bandages do not look right. But we should have known this would happen, a splintering musket ball usually leads to infection and eventual death, even when the original wound is not mortal."

Braaf began to stir again. Creed applied a cold-water cloth to his head and face. After a few applications, Braaf opened his eyes. His breathing was shallow and he was deathly pale. He looked up and saw Creed and Fitzgerald sitting on a small bench that they had pulled up beside his bed.

"I shall not leave here alive...I am almost glad."

"Do not speak that way, *Mijnheer* Braaf," Creed answered. "We need you alive, as does your family. You should be able to leave this room in a few days time. Rest is all that you need."

Though Creed was sympathetic sounding enough, his mention of the family served to remind Braaf even death would not end his troubles. Braaf was a family man at heart from everything Creed knew about him. Better to coax things from him gently.

Fitzgerald began the questioning, "I assume that you were coming over to provide information about the British?"

"Ja...yes..." Braaf wheezed as he stammered out the words.

"And is that why Mister Foch asked to meet before the next scheduled rendezvous?"

"Yes, Cornelius, uh, he and I, spies for Colonel Fitzgerald and...No."

In his fevered state, Braaf did not recognize Fitzgerald. The voices swirled around him like faint echoes.

"We know that you were unjustly sentenced to death by the British. Do they really think you killed those soldiers? They must surely know that a man such as you could not and would not commit such a brutal act."

"I did not, that is...."

Braaf grimaced for a few seconds and then opened his eyes. Creed decided to try to force his story from him, before he slipped into a coma, perhaps for good.

"*Mijnheer* Braaf, I fear your fever may worsen. We must know the truth. For the sake of Marta and Krista, we need to know why you were at our rendezvous with *Mijnheer* Foch. You have my word that if anything happens to you I will do all that I can to help them, even during British occupation. And your son, Jan..."

Braaf startled at his son's name. Jan! In all of his machinations and rationalizations, his Jan's fate posed his biggest dilemma. While Jan valiantly if foolishly went off to join the Patriot cause, he himself had betrayed that cause to the British. He betrayed the Whig faction, his friend Cornelius and his family. The latter brought him a tremendous rush of guilt and contrition, even in his fever-wracked condition. In the end, he did it all for money, and the hope of putting himself on the winning side of the foolish rebellion.

"Jan...Marta...Krista...do not know, must never know!"

"Know what?" asked Creed, again wiping Braaf's forehead with a wet cloth.

"I work for an English officer, a major called Drummond. I gave him information about the Jamaica pass...I sent him guides...men employed by Cornelius but who did certain things for me..."

Fitzgerald was stunned. He wanted to jump in with many questions but decided to let Creed continue to engage the man.

"Who is this Major Drummond? Did he send you here?"

"Dragoon officer...an English swine! A bad leg, shot near Brooklyn. Very dangerous man...forced me to continue to work for him. I only wanted my money and to be left alone. I informed him of the pass at Jamaica.... Undefended.... Sent him guides. But I did not want to be a spy...I am not a spy...why...I am a Whig. Ask Cornelius, he can vouch for me."

Braaf spent the better part of the next half hour in a fitful fever, trying in his semi-delirium to explain how Drummond forced him into a staged "escape" so he could engage in espionage against the Americans. He fitfully explained how he rationalized a way to do both, and would have, until Creed unexpectedly arrived at his departure point. Braaf now felt ashamed, but also fearful for his family, which he had inadvertently made a pawn of both sides.

Fitzgerald now asked a question, "And what of your friend, Cornelius Foch?"

"Cut throat businessman...shrewd politician...smuggler.... But a good man...my friend...very loyal to...the American cause. I bribed his men. They did it for gold, but Cornelius does know."

Fitzgerald put his face very close to Braaf's and looked deeply into his eyes, "So, his offer to spy for me was not a British trick?"

"No...no...trick."

Fitzgerald grasped Braaf's shoulders, both to reassure him and to gauge his reaction, "Do the British know of our arrangement?"

"No..." He stopped and gasped, then coughed up blood. They feared he would die there and then. Creed propped his shoulders to help him breathe a little better.

"I did not tell Drummond...it was...my insurance."

"So they, Marta and Krista, do not know about Foch? Mister Smythe and Mister Jons?"

"No."

"And Jan? Is your son part of this?"

"No...God forgive..." was the last he said before slipping into a coma.

Fitzgerald had looked into Braaf's eyes in search of signs of deception. Despite the pain and fever, Braaf seemed truthful. Facing death, he needed to clear his conscience and come to terms with his perfidy. Even in this new so-called age of reason, most men still feared God and his laws. Fitzgerald took Creed aside and talked to him in a hushed voice. "Normally, I would turn him over to the Committee for Detecting and Defeating Conspiracies, but he will not live much longer—a few hours, days at the most. However, there may well be a way we can exploit this turn of events if we can keep his demise from the British and the prying eyes of Loyalists. I want you or one of your men to stay by his side until he is gone. Make note of everything he says."

"What is this Committee?" Creed asked.

"A new body established here in New York. John Jay is one of its organizers and leaders. They hope to identify spies and Tory sympathizers who are working

against our cause in New York. As you know, there are very many Tory sympathizers in the city and its environs. But so far, all the committee has accomplished
is the harassment of a handful of Tory sympathizers. They have also arrested a
few low level spies, certainly no fish as big as your friend here–a paid British
agent. Therefore, Mister Creed, you will have the honor of bringing him in. I
shall report all of this to the commander-in-chief when I return to headquarters."

Creed looked puzzled. "What should I do, sir?"

"Stay with Braaf. Dismiss the doctor from his services. The less he knows the
better. The British may attack at any time and chaos will ensue here, I assure you.
When that happens you must move Braaf, discreetly, out of harm's way. I will
send you word as to where to bring him–or his corpse. This man's perfidy cost
us Long Island and perhaps all of New York. We must now use him to achieve a
more long term advantage."

Creed replied. "To our advantage sir? How so?"

Fitzgerald spoke softly. "The discovery and identification of their spy must be
kept from the British. The British spymaster, this Major Drummond, must be
convinced that Braaf successfully arrived and is spying on us. Whether he lives or
dies, at this point, is immaterial."

This was a different kind of combat to Creed. It was not a battle, siege, or
bloody skirmish, but an equal part of the war and the rebellion. He sickened a
little at the thought of it.

Chapter 29

Kips Bay, New York, September 15th, 1776

The Yankee gun crew went lazily through its morning routine - gun drill. Because the army was low on ammunition the crews were forbidden to actually fire their guns. This took away any sense of urgency the exercise might once have had. Most doubted the British would land along the narrow half-moon sliver of beach called Kips Bay. Supplies of food, clothing, equipment, and, most of all, ammunition, were very low in the Continental Army. So was morale. Rumor was rampant among the men, and many officers, that the army would soon redeploy north to block a potential British attack there. In fact, the British seemed poised to strike anywhere, and soon. Almost everyone in the army felt that, despite their best efforts, the American defenses were inadequate to the task. The debacle on Long Island had begun a downward spiral of confidence that would be a long time halting.

The First Gunner practiced dead reckoning, the only reliable way of aiming at a target. He had ample targets, as numerous British warships and transports gathered less than a mile off shore. This had been the pattern for days. Vessels of various sizes sailed up and down the North and East rivers, posturing and reconnoitering the American defenses, such as they were.

All at once, the morning exercise turned real. The British warships began to fire at the shoreline defenses. The Royal Navy suffered no shortage of munitions and the barrage was fearsome, if not very effective. It did not matter. The effect on morale was tremendous. The gunner and his mates felt a growing fear as they tried in desperation to reply. Soon, however, scores of plunging iron balls sent huge piles of dirt and stone all around them, creating a foul dust that choked and blinded the defenders.

After returning fire with a few wasted rounds, the Yankee gunners' fears turned to panic. They had enough and abandoned their guns. Similar scenes happened along the entire line of the defenses covering the bay. Before long, the demoralized Americans saw a wave of longboats and flatboats arrayed for a landing, a landing that none of them had a mind to oppose. A few officers tried to stop the rout, the army's second in two weeks, but it was hopeless. To anyone watching the British land at Kips Bay, it appeared that this time the rout would end the war.

The sound of the cannon fire first alerted General Washington. Soon, reports came in from all three of his divisions: north, south, and center. Although the British attack was in the center, panic was already infecting the entire army. He had to move quickly if he were to avoid disaster and preserve his forces. He gave orders for the southernmost division, under General Israel Putnam, to withdraw northwards as rapidly as possible. Fortunately, Putnam's aide, native New Yorker Major Aaron Burr, was at army headquarters when the attack commenced. Washington sent Burr back to his commander with orders to withdraw as quickly as possible. More importantly, Burr's intimate knowledge of the city would enable him to guide the division northwards while avoiding the British. With only a few roads available this was to present a challenge—it was critical that Washington slow down the British before they cut off the American forces on the lower half of the island. To that end, Washington rode to the point of action to steady the defense by his personal presence.

When he reached the low-lying heights above Kips Bay, he witnessed a scene that rivaled the debacle on Long Island. His artillerymen had abandoned their positions after firing only a few desultory shots. Some had not even fired a single shot. Still worse, several regiments had fled with their officers making only half-hearted attempts to rally the men. To his front, he saw the remnants of one unit run past their officers, many without weapons, which they had dropped to expedite their flight.

With a series of curses rarely heard by his aides, Washington spurred his horse toward the unit.

"Hold your positions, damn you! Stand your ground. You are soldiers, not cowardly wretches! We must stop them here! Stand and fight for your country!"

A handful reacted to the commander-in-chief's display of courage and a small skirmish line formed on a hillock along the shallow sloping ridge. Suddenly, the heavy guns of the British war ships in the East River shifted their fire to sweep away the few remaining defenders. This would clear the way for the British infantry, who had formed lines and now advanced up the hill. As they drew near, Washington's small line broke and ran, leaving the commander-in-chief virtually alone to face the British. Anger bordering on insanity overcame him. Large eighteen-pound cannon balls sailed overhead and landed all around him, sending earth and stone splinters in all directions. Some sailed overhead to plunge the troops behind Washington into a blind terror. He reared back his grey charger but did not give up an inch. Men were flying past him as fast as their legs and arms could pump.

"Rally your men! Officers, rally your men! Stand and fight, damn you!"

The commander-in-chief rode among them imploring some, disparaging others, and he struck several blows with the flat of his saber as well. However, it was
all to no avail. A volley rang out from long range as a few voices from the British
ranks began to deride the Americans, whom they said were again racing away
like "the fox from the hounds."

"Look at those bleedin' rabbits run!" shouted one British grenadier.

"Ain't fair is it, we need some enjoyment, don't we?" retorted another. Some of
the officers even joined the taunting.

Washington turned his charger around to face the oncoming formation, now
slow-marching up the slope directly at him, bayonets gleaming in the daylight. In
minutes, he faced certain death or capture and the American cause would be all
but lost. More than anything else, his leadership provided the cornerstone of the
rebellion and the American struggle for freedom. He ignored the pleas of two of
the two aides desperately trying to get him back to safety. It was as though the
commander-in-chief, facing his second defeat in a fortnight, intended to fall on
the field of honor.

୫୦୯ଔ

As the British line closed to within musket distance of Washington, two shots
rang out. The leading British officer fell with a bullet tearing open his chest. An
unlucky soldier took a shot through the face, dying with his eyes crossed in shock.
Creed and Beall did not pause to reload their Jaeger rifles. Instead, they mounted
their horses and rode across the front of the British, whose rapid advance halted
with the downing of their lead officer. In the confusion, Lieutenant Abner Scovel
rode up to his commander-in-chief, grabbed the reins of his gray charger, and led
him back at a gallop toward the retreating Americans.

Creed and Beall started to follow the general's party but then halted at the
crest of the hill, dismounted, and hurriedly reloaded their rifles. The British were
already advancing up the slope, now at a quick time,—essentially a fast walk.
Their Jaeger rifles dropped two more attackers but this time the red line pushed
forward without hesitation.

Creed gave a sly grin, "Well, I believe we are done with our Yankee welcome,
let us return to the others."

Beall replied with a nod. They remounted and rode down the other side of the
hill and into a lightly wooded area to the west.

୫୦୯ଔ

The others were Emily and Parker, who were transporting a dying Jan Braaf
north along the Post Road, one of only two good roads from New York to the
north. The other road, the Bloemingdale Road, ran along the North River through

villages, farms, estates and woodlands until it reached the village of Bloemingdale where it intersected an east-west trail that connected it to the Post Road. The Post Road continued north to the King's Bridge where it crossed the narrowest part of the Haarlem River into Westchester. There it divided, with one branch leading northeast to Boston and the other up the North River Valley to Albany.

When the first barrage of the British naval guns woke them, Creed knew they had already waited too long with their prisoner. However, they had planned and packed for the event that they felt was imminent. They carefully covered Braaf with blankets and loaded him onto a small cart. He carefully stowed his luggage in the cart, but he removed his two matched dueling pistols and secured them across the pommel of his saddle. He girded on his French cavalry saber and selected one of his carbine muskets as well. These plus his Jaeger rifle and bayonet ensured he was prepared to fight his way through the British lines with his patient, now also his prisoner. Through the good offices of Fitzgerald, he was also able to obtain horses for his two comrades. Not the best mounts money could buy, but passable for their purposes. As it turned out, Beall proved an excellent rider, well versed and experienced in the care of horses. Unfortunately, Parker had much to learn and little time to do so, so he had the honor of riding in the cart with his horse tethered behind. Emily allowed them to borrow their draft horse, an old but still-powerful Percheron.

Creed led Finn out of the small stable behind the house and saw Emily climbing onto the cart herself. She wore a dove gray riding dress, white boots, and a plumed gray hat. He could not resist the urge to chide her, gently. "This is not a ride in the country, Miss Stanley. It would be better for all if you remain behind. It will be safer too. With your father's British leanings and Tory connections you will thrive under British occupation, I should think."

Creed said it only half jokingly as he took her hand and gently pulled her down and away from the cart. There was nothing but danger and near certain death where they were going. The idea of her being in harm's way made him more fearful than he would have ever thought.

Emily pulled her hand away and shook her delicate fist at him. "Father may be a Tory but I am not. I shall assist you with this wounded gentleman, and then I shall return with my cart. This is my war too, Jeremiah Creed! Why, if you can in just a few months go from being a simple Irish immigrant to a rebel fighter why then I can go from being a boarding house keeper to rebel myself."

Her eyes were bright and her creamy cheeks flushed with a passion he had not seen before. In his delight, he gave in to her at once. Besides, there was no time to argue and she knew the roads better than they did.

By the time they had loaded and prepared everything, both of the roads were crammed with troops and equipment fleeing north. Seeing chaos exceeding anything on Long Island, Creed decided to take the eastern branch, the Post Road. Although nearer to the British landing, there would be less traffic there and they could make better time. He led the cart and Beall took up the rear. They were not a mile along when Creed saw the British soldiers disembarking at Kips Bay. Fortunately, a trail intersected the road and meandered into the woods, over the ridgeline and then parallel to the Post Road.

He looked down at Emily and Parker. "Try to get the cart up this trail; it will not take the British long to cut the road here. My guess is that they will turn south or continue west to split the island in two. If you can get above that point and back onto the Post Road, you should be out of danger. Private Beall and I shall try to slow them down a bit."

"Where do we meet, sir?" asked Parker.

"Colonel Fitzgerald said that most of the army is withdrawing to a place called the Haarlem Heights. Try to find the Army's headquarters. We shall meet there."

Chapter 30

Creed and Beall turned west and cantered down the slope behind Washington's staff. The British began to run after them, but were too winded continue beyond the crest. A few of them fired at the escaping riders but their shots barely reached the dust swirls thrown up by the horses pounding hooves. A short time later, Creed saw the commander-in-chief and his party turn down a trail to the west where another body of militiamen had formed up in a desperate attempt to slow the British. It was mid-morning and already the heat of the day began to oppress both pursued and pursuer.

Creed halted under the shade of a stand of maple trees that ran along a boulder-strewn creek. They dismounted to water the horses while they sipped at their water flasks and then refilled them.

"Let's make our way over to the Post Road," Creed said. "There will likely be crowds of troops moving north so we shall ride parallel. They cannot be too far ahead of us. We should soon overtake them."

Beall wiped his brow with the back of his sleeve. "The heat is awful sir. Do you think Miss Emily will be able to make it to this Haarlem place?"

Creed nodded. "Aye, she is a strong lass. I am sure she can outpace the British."

They rode slowly, often dismounting their horses to lead them through ground that became increasingly wooded and hilly. The chaos of fleeing soldiers and civilians slowed their progress. They had to work their way through these mobs, from a few to several score or more, who jammed the road.

The army had lost much of its cohesion in its flight. Many of the men were barefoot and ill equipped. Some had discarded their muskets, favoring speed of travel over military necessity. The tramping of thousands of feet on the sun-dried dirt road stirred plumes of dust that lofted into the hot summer air. Creed and Beall had to mask themselves with handkerchiefs to breathe. They traveled past small farms and the occasional estate. To the south, they could hear the occasional musket and cannon fire.

Beall said. "Sounds like our men are making a stand, sir."

Creed shook his head. "No Jonathan, once an army's morale breaks, it no longer fights with purpose. You are hearing small packs of militia and continentals fighting off their British pursuers."

After an hour they stopped at a post house situated just off the road in a small hamlet called Yorkville.

Creed motioned towards the building. "Let's water the horses. See if we can find some grain for them as well. There will likely be little thought of transporting fodder up to Haarlem."

The livery boy, a medium-build black youth of sixteen named Thomas, managed to scrounge some feed for the horses. He offered Creed and Beall some mush as well as fresh apples. Each gratefully took a cup of the milky concoction and two apples.

Creed handed Thomas a copper but he waved it off. "If I can't join the army, least I can do to help fight them British."

Creed replied. "A grand sentiment, but the nation requires commerce, even in war time. So take the coin, lad."

Thomas nodded and tucked the copper in his pocket.

Creed asked. "Many of our troops come through here yet?"

Thomas replied with a grin. "Mister, you the only Yankees along the road to stop here. Rest of the soldiers just kept on goin' north. Where they headin' anyway? Better they kill them redcoats right here."

Creed took an instant liking to Thomas. Being new to America, Creed had had little contact with its African populace, free or slave.

"Are you from New York, lad?"

"I was born in Maryland, Calvert County to be exact. But mommy and daddy moved north after their master, Mister Peter Jeffries, freed them. He was a very religious Catholic man, Mister Jeffries. A good man...why we took his name. Freed all his slaves and hired back those who wanted work. Most stayed, but mommy and daddy feared staying in the south. Thought the north offered better opportunities for makin' money...and stayin' free."

Beall spoke. "Hard to believe anyone would leave Maryland. How did you arrive here?"

"Daddy was a stable hand on the Maryland plantation. He got work at this stable pretty easy. We serve the Post Road mail riders, coaches, and other travelers, mostly trade."

Creed looked about. "And your parents...?"

"Both dead, mister. The smallpox hit a few years back. "

Creed and Beall both lowered their heads.

"I am sorry," said Creed.

"That's alright, mister." Thomas handed them each a couple more apples.

"So, young fellow, did you see a cart with a pretty young woman and another soldier riding along? He would have a horse tethered to the back." Creed asked as he carved a chunk of apple and bit into it.

"No sir," answered Thomas. "I been out here all morning and seen nothing but rebel soldiers moving up the road."

"They were ahead of us down by the Kips Bay," Creed said, frowning. "We delayed to engage in a little sport with the British but surely we would have overtaken them by now, especially with all these men tramping up the road."

"Lot of side roads mister, maybe they decided to detour. Many have...cannot take the dust, you know. Maybe they headed west. Say, is she your wife?"

Thomas grinned, a wide becoming grin. Even though he was just sixteen he was wise to the ways of the world, it occurred to him that the pair might be detouring for a more bawdy reason, and Creed was perhaps a jealous husband in pursuit.

"No. Just a fine lady. She was helping us with a very sick man. The other fellow is one of my soldiers."

"Mister, I have been apprenticed as a post rider the past three years and ridden from the Bowery to Kingsbridge and even Westchester. And I know all the side roads, too. They could be anywhere by now."

"They were heading to a place called the Haarlem Heights. Is there a road that would be particularly favorable to that destination? Perhaps a local farmer advised them of a better route?"

"There is a narrow trail runs parallel to this road. 'Bout a quarter mile west. It connects again at McGowan's pass, a half mile north from here. Maybe they took that way to avoid the traffic and the dust. That is what I would do."

A large formation, more disciplined than the others, was just marching up the road past the stable. It was a Massachusetts unit, Continentals, surprisingly disciplined, and singing as they marched. Creed recognized the song, "Free America." Although a rebel song popular throughout the army, it was sung to the tune of "The British Grenadiers."

"Then take us there, Thomas." Creed said suddenly.

"What? I am no soldier, mister. I am no rebel. I am a stable boy, and a post rider, but that's all."

"Thomas, your ma and da were slaves once. We shall all be slaves if we do not defeat these British, so we must all be soldiers now. I appoint you an honorary Private in the Light Company, First Maryland Continental Line. Now get a horse and let us ride."

Creed's demeanor and sincerity struck a sympathetic chord with the young man. Without further word, Thomas ran to the wooden shack he called home, behind the stable, and gathered his few belongings. Some clothes, a blanket, and the family bible. Finally, he sat on the cot and donned his prize possession, a pair of black knee-length riding boots. He then put on a fine pair of silver-gilt spurs, once his father's fondest possession, and brandished an eight-foot leather lash that also once belonged to his father. Thomas could wield it with an expertise few could match. His father told him post riding was a job good for a few years, but moving horses was a lifetime profession. To that end, he practiced with the lash almost every day. With his uncanny eye, he could remove the buttons off a man's waistcoat before the man could close on him. In a few minutes, Thomas had saddled one of the horses in the stable. He figured the stable owner, a Tory, could do with one less horse.

∞∞

An hour later they were on the trail and almost at McGowan's pass. The trail was surprisingly empty; for some reason the Continental Army did not know of it. Although barely fit for a cart, it was wide enough for soldiers to march two abreast or horsemen in single file. There were fresh cart tracks on the path and bushes flattened along the shoulder.

Creed said. "Look there Jonathan, Miss Emily and Private Parker must have taken this route."

Beall said. "How can you be so sure?"

"Truth be told, I am not. But we can only pray tis them. Let's go up this trail, Thomas."

Thomas nodded and nudged his horse into a fast walk, nearly a trot. Tree branches whipped their faces and the occasional heavy limb nearly unhorsed them. Creed feared Finn might break an ankle on the broken ground.

Thomas suddenly halted. Creed and Beall did likewise.

He pointed to the right, "Mister, those *are* cart tracks...whoever they are, they turned off right here."

Sure enough, Creed saw the markings and the trampled grass and brush. But why would they do that? Then he saw why. There were other footprints on the ground, and more trampled grass as well.

"Lieutenant, I think I see something!" Beall exclaimed.

Beall dismounted and entered a thick patch of underbrush. "You had better see this, Lieutenant."

Creed dismounted and was beside Beall in a few strides. It was Braaf. The erstwhile spy lay dead, his corpse already puffing from gases and his eyes covered with a swarm of flies. Creed's stomach turned.

"Emily and Parker would not have dumped his corpse this way. Something must have happened to them. Check your weapons."

Creed mounted Finn and they resumed the search. They turned down the trail, chasing the spoor through a lightly wooded field, mostly fruit trees and the occasional maple or chestnut. Creed thought he heard noise up ahead, noise that was not a part of nature, the tramping of feet and the sound of a cartwheel moving slowly but steadily through the underbrush. Then they heard curses and ribald laughter.

Creed raised his hand and they halted. He checked the primer on his rifle, as did Beall. Then he checked his two saddle pistols, those fine weapons that he had taken with him from his farmstead in Maryland. Finally, he drew his saber, preferring it to the sword-bayonet when it came to mounted combat. He called Thomas closer and handed him one of his pistols.

"Could be Cowboys...or even Skinners...either way this could mean business, lads."

Over a dozen Cowboy bands ranged the roads looking for isolated American soldiers straggling to get north before the British forces cut the island in half. Worse than pirates, they were marauding killers who used the chaos of the rebellion for monetary gain and the pleasure of it. They always seemed to linger on the fringes of both armies, inflicting their depredations on the weak, always running from organized bodies of men. There were similar groups of Patriot marauders, known as Skinners. Cowboys and Skinners waged a parallel war with each other and against just about anyone they could rationalize as Whig or Tory, Patriot or Loyalist, as the case might be. This parallel war led to much savagery and retribution from both sides.

"Thomas, you stay close behind me," Creed continued. "If one of them accosts you, ride up to your target, aim at its center, and squeeze the trigger. Then ride through your target in case you miss. Do you understand, Thomas?"

"Yes, sir. Shoot and ride. I can do that."

With a wave of Creed's saber, they were off. They saw the cart some twenty yards ahead, and as they closed, they saw their quarry, a dozen foot men—a Loyalist guerilla band.

"Cowboys!" cried Beall.

"Or Skinners!" replied Creed. "Make no distinction lads, as they have our cart and our friends."

"For Maryland!" cried Creed as the three horsemen crashed into the rear of the Cowboys. He calmly lowered his left hand and discharged his pistol into the rear of the group. A Cowboy fell to the ground with a chestnut sized hole in his back. He ran another through with his saber; slicing the man's shoulder clear through, leaving him staggering as blood spurted out.

A burly ruffian in a fur vest and brimmed hat shouted. "Rebels! But there's only three of 'em, boys. Let's have some fun."

Amid jeers and curses, two marauders assaulted him brandishing their muskets like clubs.

Creed smiled grimly and spurred Finn directly at them. They stepped aside to avoid the horse, but he decapitated one with a backhand slash, then wheeled Finn around and carved open the second man's rib cage with a forehand thrust. Beall fired his rifle into one and then proceeded to smash at the three rowdies who surrounded him. Thomas took up the rear with a veteran's skill, placed the pistol to the neck of one rowdy, and fired. The shot nearly severed the man's head. His two mates tried to flee but Beall pursued them and cut them down with his sword-bayonet.

Then the fedora-wearing leader sprung from behind a stand of bushes and swung his musket butt at the back of Creed's head. "Nobody stops the Kingsbridge Cowboys—nobody!"

He stepped forward, poised to render Creed a death blow, but the flash of leather cracked across his wrists, tearing right to the bone and spinning the Cowboy leader to the ground and under the crushing hooves of Thomas' mount.

Thomas replied. "Ain't nobody stopping Lieutenant Jeremiah Creed."

Creed turned and smiled but had little time to banter. The last three Cowboys were attempting to drive off in the cart, one viciously lashing the Percheron to quicken its pace. Creed spurred his horse, caught the driver on side of his skull with a saber slash, and pulled him from the cart. His body landed with a crack of bone and a dull thud, and rolled into the bushes. Thomas overtook the Percheron and slowed him to a walk while Beall chased the remaining rowdies, who disappeared into the brush. The melee ended in a few minutes and the entire Cowboy band lay dead, dying or on the run.

Beall reloaded his rifle and checked each of the ruffians to make sure he could cause no further trouble. Thomas sat on a rock to catch his breath. He put his face in his trembling hands and sobbed softly. Despite the bravery he displayed, his first taste of combat had unnerved him.

Creed dismounted and quickly jumped onto the cart, still covered in blankets. He pulled the top covers off and found Emily and Parker gagged and bound. He cut their bonds and removed the rags from their mouths.

"Are you alright?" He asked the question of both but focused on Emily.

"We are, Mister Creed, but thank heavens you found us." She replied, gasping for air.

"We also found our friend Braaf; he is dead. What happened?" Creed asked Parker who was rubbing his wrists to get the feeling back.

"Lieutenant, they saw no bounty in a wounded wretch so they dumped him a half mile back. His fever and delirium just worsened with the travel. They tossed him so hard I heard a crack and knew he could not survive the fall."

Creed cradled Emily's head in his left hand and put his canteen to her lips. "Here you go...drink slowly now..."

She sipped slowly at the water, stopping from time to time to purse her lips.

Parker took a large swig of water from Beall's canteen. The heat and humidity were now almost unbearable. He smiled at Beall. "Thank you, farmer boy. You have paid back my seamanship lesson in full."

Creed placed his canteen and only reluctantly let go of Emily. "Think they were after *Mijnheer* Braaf?

Parker shook his head. "No. They were looking for gold, money, and weapons. They took our purses, as well as my musket and bayonet. I hid my knife in my rolled cloak; they were so stupid they never searched there."

"With scoundrels such as these that does not surprise me. We are ever advantaged by their ignorance and cowardice." Creed answered as he rubbed Emily's wrists. She kept a composed demeanor but he could tell that she was frightened and nearly in shock by her experience. He restrained the urge to say she had been warned, but that he cherished getting her back safe.

Beall noticed Thomas sobbing and placed a comforting hand on his shoulder. Beall had questioned Creed's wisdom in enlisting a young black man to the fight but realized his lieutenant's judge of character had once more proved correct. A wave of shame went through Beall.

"It is alright, Thomas. We all cry the first time. Some of us inside, some outside. I reckon outside is better. They were bad men. You helped saved our friends. For that I shall be ever thankful."

Thomas nodded, "I'm alright. I'll go see to the horses now."

They gathered their things and backtracked to Braaf; flies now swarmed across his body like a dark ocean of pestilence.

Creed had them cover their faces while they buried the erstwhile spy. He would lay forever in a shallow grave near a boulder by the trail. Without a pause for prayer or any other formality, Creed moved the party north and towards the Heights of Haarlem. The final evidence of Braaf's demise was gone and they all were safe.

Chapter 31

Brooklyn, Long Island, September 15th, 1776

Cornelius Foch watched the British bombardment and invasion of Manhattan from the quarterdeck of the *Red Hen*. His puffed aggressively on his pipe, chewing on the stem as he seethed with anger. Why had the Americans not made the rendezvous? His assessment of English intentions was almost completely correct. His estimate of the location was precise, although the actual attack came later than he had anticipated.

Foch now considered his next step. Rumor was that Braaf had escaped from his cell and was on the run, possibly in New York or out on eastern Long Island. He thought it strange that Jan did not seek his help, unless he was trying to protect him from the English. Foch was surprised but relieved that Jan had kept his wits about him. To add to his worry, three of his men had suddenly absconded. Well, there would be deserters from both armies looking for work and available to recruit. The others had not been very dependable anyway, disappearing for hours at a time, often unexpectedly. Foch suspected that they were up to no good, but as they had stolen nothing from him he never pursued the matter.

Foch decided he would offer the *Red Hen* and his smaller craft to ferry goods across for the English. He could use the money and they paid in gold. Moreover, through that work he could perhaps determine their future moves. The next scheduled meeting was in a little more than a week, and if Mr. Smythe could attend this one, he might yet have some useful intelligence to provide him. Unlike so many now on Long Island, Cornelius Foch still thought that these English would yet manage to lose the war.

After observing the first British wave at Kips Bay chase the hapless rebels from the shoreline, Foch decided he had seen enough. He went into Brooklyn to visit Marta and Krista, in the hope they had heard something of Jan's situation. Foch planned on spend spending more time with them. They would both need his comfort and support, especially Marta.

He arrived at the Braaf home at in the afternoon. Earlier in the day, the two women had learned of Jan's escape. Since then, they had spent the long, lonely hours in worry over his fate, as well as their own. The head of their household was now a fugitive from British justice.

Foch wasted no time with greetings. "I am glad Jan escaped. Those English swine would have hung him for certain. Now at least he has a chance."

Marta's reply surprised Foch. "*Ja*, I agree. Our Jan is a soft and weak man, but he is also very smart and resourceful. He will hide until these English leave. We have relatives in the North Valley and the Hackensack Valley in New Jersey. Perhaps he will go there."

Krista seemed calm and composed, considering all that had happened. "Yes, I think papa will meet up with Jan, or with Jonathan."

"Jonathan?" Foch was confused.

"I meant–Private Beall." She blushed. The thought of Jonathan almost brought a smile to her face.

Foch gave her a puzzled look but Marta smiled. Foch had no way of knowing that Krista had developed a fondness for the young soldier from Maryland.

"Well ladies, I shall come by every day that I can. If there is anything you need, please let me know. The Tories and their bullies trouble you...I want to know that as well. And, if you hear anything of Jan, I must know immediately. But be discreet, the English and the Tories will surely be watching you."

Marta and Krista murmured their agreement.

Marta then said. "They already are. One of those English dragoons was here earlier to inform us of Jan's escape. He gave me a note from Jan, written shortly before he eluded them."

Foch cocked his head. "That is strange. He came here with a note?"

Marta replied. "Yes, here it is. Read it for yourself."

Foch took the envelope from her hand and read it. "This says little, but it is indeed Jan's handwriting. Why would they bring a letter from a condemned prisoner who has escaped their clutches?"

Marta placed her soft hand on his sinewy forearm. "I do not know, Cornelius."

Foch placed his hand over hers. "I think I do. But for your sake I will not say. Be vigilant, Marta. They likely have people watching this house right now."

Tears welled up in her eyes. "I cannot tell you how much we value your trust and support...and your friendship. Now, we have all missed our midday meal from all this worrying. Krista–go fetch something from the kitchen. We still have some smoked ham..."

When Krista left, Marta slumped into Foch's arms and whispered. "I have lost my son and husband to this awful war, Cornelius. And almost my dear daughter. You take care yourself. I cannot lose you as well. I do need and appreciate your concern and support. It is such a comfort."

He stroked her lustrous hair and replied, "Do not worry, dear Marta. I assure you that I will take care of this business...and of you."

ಶಿಐೞ

From a small promontory near Bushwick, Drummond also watched the British invasion with a rising sense of anger and frustration. He had hoped to lead his squadron to glory once it had landed in New York. Chasing those rebels all the way to Albany would have given him the greatest pleasure. Unfortunately, his knee had not improved enough and he could not ride hard for hours at a time.

General Clinton, who stood beside Drummond, put down his a spyglass. "I know you'd prefer to be there, Sandy, but your work is here for now."

Drummond nodded. "Indeed, I have just received word that a rebel spy was seen landing on the north coast of the island, and was suspected to be somewhere between there and Brooklyn.

Clinton smiled. "You seem less than enthused. Lord Howe appointed you interim Chief Provost for the occupation of Long Island. Now you have a real spy to catch. Once you clean up the rebel pack here you may join the rest of the army to organize espionage and counterespionage activities against the rebels and their sympathizers in New York. Who knows, perhaps by then you will have heard from your Golden Apple."

Drummond nodded. "Despite the Royal Marines' failed efforts, Braaf somehow got onto a rebel boat and over to New York. I believe he will continue with the plan. "

Clinton raised the spyglass and scanned Kips Bay. "Are you so certain he did not expose the plot?"

Drummond shook his head. "The crafty Dutchman could talk his way through any interrogation, if he keeps his head and does not panic. Braaf would not do anything stupid and thereby jeopardize the safety of his wife and daughter. However, to make sure, I shall keep them under my special protection."

Clinton watched watch his men charge from the beaches in pursuit of the few remaining defenders. "It might prove amusing sport for you as well. I have been told both mother and daughter are quite lovely, in the Dutch way, of course."

"In the Dutch way..." Drummond replied.

Just over a mile away they saw more British warships bombard the shoreline, flushing packs of rebels into flight.

"We have them, by God Sandy, we have them!" Clinton exclaimed.

Drummond said. "By your leave, sir, I have important matters to attend. Not the glory of battle, unfortunately, but important all the same...I suppose."

Clinton kept his eye on the spyglass. "By all means...my sloop is waiting. I should crossover now that the landing is cleared."

Drummond retrieved a pen and paper from his saddlebag. Using a large boulder as a makeshift desk, he prepared a short note to General Howe. He requested another week or so to arrange things on Long Island, and then he would proceed to New York City to establish operations there. Unbeknownst to either Clinton or Cornwallis, Drummond was secretly in direct correspondence with the British commander-in-chief. One had to be clever to advance in this army. He smudged the ink on the paper but decided information trumped appearances, even for a general.

Brooklyn,
September 15th 1776

My Lord,

As you are well aware, I hope to return to command of the 17th as soon as my physical condition allows. Until then, I will work diligently to establish Espionage and Counterespionage activities in support of the Campaign. By now, our late Prisoner, "Golden Apple," should be safely ensconced somewhere in the vicinity of the rebel Forces. I hope to have communication from him within the fortnight.

Meanwhile, I am establishing a small network of Agents here on Long Island to secure gains made by His Majesty's Forces. "Golden Apple's" two remaining Associates, code names "Pear" and "Plum," have been paid a tidy sum to establish themselves further east on the Island to report on political Activities and warn us of any attempts by the Rebels to subvert the Populace. I shall also make use of the Brooklyn Home Guard whenever possible. They are our eyes and ears on the populace. For now, they will be of great assistance in helping to root out rebels and assist in the search for the suspected spy now loose on Long Island. I expect to make similar use of Loyalists once I move to New York.

In stark contrast to many of my Colleagues, I feel we must use our Loyal Americans to the full. Therein lies our best hope of crushing this Rebellion, and more importantly, maintaining His Majesty's Peace.

My Lord, I know you have had Calumny and Insult thrown at you from various quarters because of the tempo of this Campaign. I for one now believe that only the measured use of our Forces, provided with excellent Intelligence, will bring the Rebels into submission and assure the Loyalty of the citizenry of these Colonies. The Populace must understand that the Crown is watching out for their Security by rooting out Subversives, Spies, and Traitors.

I Remain as Always,
Your Most Humble and Obedient Servant,
S. Drummond

Drummond sealed the letter in an envelope using a special wax, indicating it was top priority for Howe. He waived to his sergeant, who stood patiently holding Shoe. "Digby, please deliver this letter to General Howe. You must deliver it in person. Do you understand? "

Digby saluted and took the envelope, and slipped it into his tunic. "That I do, sir. That I do."

Digby mounted his horse and made his way down the trail to the Brooklyn ferry. Drummond rejoined Clinton and scanned the shoreline one last time.

Clinton smiled. "Our lads have driven them from every strand and are moving inland. Did you finish your business, Sandy? Hopefully nothing tedious."

Drummond replied dully. "Tedious work is often critical to victory, sir."

Drummond knew his directly communicating with Howe breached protocol but he wanted to ensure full recognition for his efforts. If his military career was going into eclipse, his intelligence career needed to shine. Drummond approached this shrewdly. He would not hide this correspondence from his superiors, but he would condition them to accept the necessity of reporting directly to the commander-in-chief. He would greatly miss leading troops in combat, but was now beginning to appreciate the importance of his new career in espionage.

ఴఛ

The Morris Mansion, Haarlem Heights, New York

Creed found Fitzgerald at the Morris mansion, General Washington's new headquarters on the Haarlem Heights. The mansion was a large white Palladian styled two-story building that commanded a large and prosperous estate of more than 130 acres. Situated on a hilltop with views of Manhattan and Westchester, as well as parts of Long Island and New Jersey, it made an excellent location for a command post.

The parlor and dining rooms on the main floor now functioned as an operations center where staffs and aides de camp conferred, wrote exhaustive memos and letters, or awaited orders. Washington occupied the large bedroom on the second floor as his sleeping quarters and personal study. With the fluidity of action now facing the Continental Army, General Washington wanted his intelligence advisor nearby. Fitzgerald was surprised to learn his room would be on the second floor as well. Just across the hall from the commander-in-chief, its location enabled Fitzgerald to consult with the Washington and update him as needed.

The comfort and style in so many of the homes in America still amazed Creed. Before he came over from Europe, he had pictured a land of hovels, tents and cabins at the edge of a primeval forest. Instead, he found that most middle and upper class homes trumped their European counterparts in comfort, cleanliness, and spaciousness. The Morris Mansion offered just another example of how wrong Creed had been about the quality of life in the New World.

Fitzgerald waived Creed into the room and motioned him to close the door; security was often as simple and direct as that. "I do not have time for a full report, Jeremiah, so please provide me a brief summary of our prisoner's situation."

Creed stifled a laugh. "Why then sir, briefly stated, he is dead."

Not amused at the glib reply, Fitzgerald cocked his head and bore into Creed with his stare. Creed smiled grimly. "Sorry, sir. But *Mijnheer* Braaf, our British spy, is dead."

Creed went on to relay the events leading to Braaf's burial in an unmarked grave. He mentioned the roles of Emily Stanley and Thomas, but omitted his role in saving the commander-in-chief from the British.

Fitzgerald removed his spectacles and began wiping them with a worn silk kerchief. "I am concerned that you would involve this Miss Stanley in our affairs, Mister Creed. The British will soon cut all communication with New York."

Creed lowered his head. "She insisted on helping. She offered her wagon and horse. I could not refuse."

Fitzgerald scowled, but slyly changed the subject. "Meanwhile, I have met with Smallwood. He has agreed that you and your men will be attached to the head-quarters staff. Officially, we assigned you to the commander-in-chief's personal escort, his Life Guards. Unofficially, you work for me. His Excellency has agreed to a more formal structure for gathering information, and for catching spies. This will be the beginning of that effort."

Creed did not take this latest news well, "What about this 'Committee for Detecting and Defeating Conspiracies'? Why not employ them?"

"Never! They are a cabal of civilian amateurs who focus primarily on local political loyalty, searching primarily for Tories who support the British, and the like. Besides, the army needs a special unit reporting directly to the commander-in-chief. One capable of gathering information on the enemy that is both usable and reliable. I need good officers to lead it, officers of the finest intellect, determination, and loyalty."

Fitzgerald placed his hand on Creed's shoulder and looked him in the eye, "Officers such as you, Jeremiah. I will not name the others since their commanders have not yet agreed to their release. They serve as you do, under state commissions. In your case, Colonel Smallwood immediately understood the need. Thank God he is not as parochial as his peers. And His Excellency asked him personally."

Creed stiffened just a bit, partly from disappointment at leaving the First Maryland, and partly pique at being a pawn. "So what are my orders?"

Fitzgerald pushed back his white forelock and placed his glasses back on his thin nose, "The British have all but cut the island in half and continue to reinforce their initial attack at Kips Bay. Fortunately, General Putnam successfully withdrew his division from the southern extreme of the island before they did so. His Excellency called a council of war, to be held tonight. Some want to turn Haarlem Heights into the next Breed's Hill and avenge Brooklyn. I am not so sanguine. Now for the time being, you will to report to Lieutenant Colonel Thomas Knowlton."

Creed pursed his lips. "Knowlton? The name sounds familiar..."

"A superb fellow. From Connecticut. Commands the Ranger Battalion. Some of our best fighters and scouts. Served with great distinction near Boston. His rangers will lead the attack against the British. Your experience could be of great use to him."

Creed looked skeptical. "If you say so, Colonel. Now what about the contents of the valise, and our now late spy? Our plans to use him? I suppose they are now all *passé?*"

"We shall discuss these matters and others, in due course."

Creed became suspicious, "Others?"

"Yes, your services will be required when Misters Smythe and Jons next communicate, and this time, let us pray it will be with a genuine purpose."

Creed gasped, "A genuine purpose? I am confused sir. Did we not cross over to gain information on the British intentions, from your...Mister Jons? Was that not a...a...genuine purpose?"

"Well, umm, yes. However, when Mister Jons requested the meeting, I was unsure that his information would be specific enough to risk it."

Creed's brow furrowed in thought and bewilderment. "Then why were we sent? Why take the risk? Did you know that they were going to stage Braaf's escape?"

"No, that was a surprise. But a most fortuitous one as it turns out. For that, I have you and your men to thank. No, we sent you and your men as a decoy for another mission. A mission ordered by His Excellency. I strongly advised against it, mind you. His Excellency's personal involvement in these matters is both a boon and a curse."

Creed stared blankly at Fitzgerald. "I do not understand..."

"You see, my boy, General Washington wanted another set of eyes on the British, another military man behind their lines to report back on them. When no one else would step forward, a young captain from Connecticut volunteered, one of Thomas Knowlton's men–Nathan Hale. A very brave man, but an amateur, and there was not sufficient time to prepare him properly. Brave Hale departed several days ago. But since the British have landed here, his mission is somewhat pointless. One hopes he will make his way back to our lines soon."

Creed could barely contain himself. He stomped out of the headquarters confused and angry. He and his men had been used in a ploy! By pure luck, the ploy resulted in Braaf's interception and dying confession. Creed was tiring of it all–the secret missions; the half-truths; the deceptions. He toyed with resigning, or at least threatening to resign, if they did not send him back to the Line. However, he soon calmed down, realizing that George Washington, the commander-in chief and "essential man" of the cause, had depended on him and would do so again. His devotion to the commander in chief pulled harder at him than his dismay with the manipulation that came with the world of intelligence gathering.

Creed went to find his men. Their company provided him a semblance of a unit and was now the closest thing to a family that he had. He could relax in with them and forget his troubles for a while. They had set up a small tent in an orchard near the mansion and had scrounged a chicken and some vegetables, which were already boiling in a copper pot. The smell reminded him that he had not eaten in some time. Creed also inquired as to the whereabouts of their recent associates, although he was actually interested in finding Emily.

Beall answered with a frown. "Sir, we thought that you knew. She has returned to New York. Miss Stanley said that she needed to depart before the British army blocked all the roads and passes. Thomas agreed to assist her. He is a likely lad. His good Maryland roots, I suppose. Fear not sir, Miss Emily will arrive home safely with Thomas as her escort."

Creed said nothing. He stared blankly in barely concealed disappointment. Of course, she needed to get home, he was just hoping for some time alone with her first. Maybe it was better this way. The campaign was shaping up to be gruesome and as dangerous for civilians as for the soldiers. As much as he longed to be with Emily, he longed for her safety even more.

Elias Parker guessed what was going through his lieutenant's mind. In the midst of all the danger of the trip north, Miss Stanley had talked mostly about Creed. Both he and Beall saw the affection that had grown between the pair.

Parker cocked his head in a show of sympathy. "She said that she was sorry for the death of our wounded charge, *Mijnheer* Braaf. But she had urgent business to attend at home and was, after all, responsible for the care of her father's home. And she gave me this note for you."

Creed took the note, almost afraid to open it. "Well, thank you. I think I shall have a rest and read this. Well...call me when that chicken is cooked."

Creed settled in under a cherry tree in the orchard. A small fife band assigned to the commander-in-chief's escort was playing "Yankee Doodle," that strangely uplifting song that had become the de facto anthem of the rebellion. The chicken and vegetables were cooking to the point now where a powerful and enticing aroma engulfed their little camp. The sounds and smells blended into the background as he read and re-read the letter. Before even reading it, he analyzed it: the neat flow of her handwriting, the precise arrangement of the words, and of course, and her thoughts.

Dear Jeremiah,

I hope that I may address you as such. I pray that Mister Parker and Mister Beall have informed you of my decision to depart and why.

I would have liked so much to spend some more time with you, Jeremiah. Certainly, there has not seemed enough time to say what I have to say. Under the circumstances this may be for the best, as what I have to say is perhaps best left unsaid. Therefore, I shall keep my deepest thoughts and feelings to myself and will hold them close to my bosom until Providence provides us time and place to reveal them.

I fear now that this war will be long and it will be some time before we speak again. Nevertheless, I know that we shall. I will think of you each day and pray for you. New York needs Patriots as well as Loyalists. I shall be discreet about my views, and deign to help the Cause whenever and wherever I can. Just how, I cannot say. Once more, only time and Providence will allow. Until such time, please do take care of yourself and your good...your gallant men.

God bless you—for everything you do for your adopted Country.

With the fondest Esteem and warmest Affection,
I remain, forever Yours,
Emily

Chapter 32

Haarlem Heights, New York, September 16th, 1776

The faint glow over the eastern horizon meant they had less than an hour before dawn. Lieutenant Colonel Thomas Knowlton folded a crude map as he finished his final instructions to his officers.

He gazed evenly at them. "General Washington is in need of intelligence and by God he shall have it!"

"Hear hear! Hear, hear!" They replied in unison.

Knowlton further exhorted them. "Gentlemen, stealth and speed are critical in this operation if we are to discern the whereabouts of Howe's forces."

"Why, they must be somewhere down there!" A pimple-faced lieutenant pointed south of the Heights of Haarlem.

Laughter erupted and Knowlton joined in. "Indeed, Lieutenant White. But we must be a bit more precise to satisfy His Excellency."

More laughter erupted. A special order from the commander-in-chief had just assigned Creed, Beall and Parker to Knowlton's handpicked force of just over a hundred men. The weary-looking Marylanders became, if only temporarily, members of Knowlton's elite Connecticut battalion, known as the Rangers. They were the bravest, led by the bravest. Many of the officers and men questioned the need for these new additions—as did Knowlton himself. However, Creed professed knowledge of the area so Knowlton assigned them to the advance guard, twenty-five men under the command of Captain Bran Yardley. Yardley, a farmer from Cheshire, had distinguished himself the previous year during the siege of Boston.

Yardley spoke gruffly when Creed reported to him. "Our objective is the Bloemingdale Road. Since you claim to know it, lead the way, Mister Creed."

Creed led Yardley's men at quick pace in single file, the so-called "Indian file," down the road toward the small draw called the Hollow Way. When they crossed the Hollow Way, Creed signaled that they were near the objective. Up ahead they saw a small wooden clapboard farmhouse with peeling gray paint and a black wood-shingled roof. Yardley halted the company and split them into two columns, one on each side of the house. Militia scouts had reported British patrols in the area late the day before. So they proceeded with caution, bending forward slightly with muskets at port arms. The woods were light but the ground rocky, forcing each group to remain in single file on either side of the road. The dawn sun broke through the leafy canopy and began to bathe the woods in a faint golden light.

Creed halted and whispered to Yardley. "Daylight will spoil our surprise. We must move quickly or lose our advantage. I can already make out silhouettes at almost a hundred yards."

"I welcome any suggestions." Yardley replied tersely.

Up ahead they could make out the outline of another house, this one made of stone. Creed remembered the stone house in Brooklyn, and immediately became suspicious. "British could be in that old house ahead. Let me take the left file and circle round it. I suggest you keep the other in the wood line till we clear the house."

Yardley nodded and Creed moved out. After they cleared the woods along the left of the house, Creed pumped his fist to signal Parker and Beall forward to reconnoiter the building. He looked back and saw Yardley leading his file towards the house in a perfect skirmish line. Creed sent one of the Rangers, a short wiry man named Closs, to warn Yardley to stay in place, but he acted too late.

Musket fire erupted and Closs fell from a ragged volley that nearly tore his body in half. In moments the British skirmishers holding the line had Yardley and his men pinned down. As Creed suspected, the British were using the stone house as their forward observation point.

"Up lads, on me!" He yelled.

Creed had his men rushed left and then angled right around the house. He was in luck. The British were all in the house. They had posted no flank security. Now, focused on Yardley's men, they did not see Parker smash the door open with his shoulder. Behind him rushed Creed, Beall and two of the rangers—deafening fire was the last thing the British heard. Creed and his men poured lead into them at point blank range. The three elite British light infantrymen throttled backwards as the lead balls ripped into flesh and bone, staining the walls and floor with their viscera.

However, the volley alerted the rest of the British battalion waiting patiently down the road.

Beall saw them first. "Lieutenant! Lobsters coming up the road toward the house! "

"How many, Elias?"

"Hundreds of them."

Now the British drummers beat the attack, and six hundred feet pounded the dirt in an eerie dance that presaged death.

Yardley saw the column rapidly closing on the house and called out. "Mister Creed, rally your file and fall back!"

Parker muttered to a nearby ranger. "Best damn order we had today."

British musket balls began to rattle the walls of the house like a malevolent hailstorm and a platoon of light infantry rushed the building. Creed's file rushed back to the wood line just as the first British light infantry entered the stone house and began firing through the windows.

Crossing the open space between the house and tree line Creed tripped over a tree root and hit the rock-hard earth with a thud. He felt a twist and pain in his ankle as his foot came loose from the root. Winded, he reached for his rifle. His ankle throbbed but in the excitement he scarcely felt it. Three British musket balls whipped just over his head—so close that one creased his hat. Creed froze, and then rolled twice until he had his rifle firm in hand. With balls zinging just above him, he lay on his back and reloaded.

He synchronized the loading drill with his last prayers. "Hail Mary, full of grace..."

A stray round caught the tip of his shoe and tore a piece of leather. The rifle loaded, he took a deep breath and rolled under a bush and onto his belly. He cocked the rifle and waited for a British face to appear at the window.

Yardley saw Creed's danger. "Keep firing, boys...provide them cover!"

The desperate Connecticut men fired each time a British head appeared at a window or door. Patches of gun smoke began to drift across the field and waft around the house. Others clouded the windows, obstructing the British marksmen's view.

Parker and Beall made it to the wood line just as Creed tripped. They looked at each other then watched their lieutenant as he lay supine, methodically loading while British shots landed all around him.

"The Lieutenant is down! We must help him back!" Beall cried.

Parker nodded grimly. Even with the smoke, both knew the field was now a death trap. Without hesitating, they stepped out of the trees and fired back at the windows to draw British fire from Creed. The light infantry turned on them, but fire from Yardley's file struck two more, sending the remainder ducking for cover. A British sergeant poked his head from the doorway and aimed his musket at Beall. Creed's rifle drilled a hole between his eyes. The sergeant's head flew back and smashed against the doorframe like a pumpkin.

However, the main British column had now reached the house and fanned out on either side to form an assault line. Soon, hundreds of musket balls tore through the air like a swarm of hornets. Beall and Parker helped Creed to his feet and arms locked at the elbows, they raced back staying under the lead that sprayed the trees and brush but otherwise missed their mark.

"Everyone fall back!" Yardley cried out.

Under heavy from the British main body, Knowlton's advanced guard abandoned the woods before the stone house and rejoined the main body.

When Knowlton heard the firing to his front he positioned his men behind a stone wall near the Bloemingdale Road.

Yardley reported the British disposition to their front.

"Very well, Yardley," Knowlton said. "Place your men on our left flank, at least thirty yards behind the wall. Cover our flank and prepare to reinforce us if necessary."

Yardley's men no sooner took up their position and regained their breath when the British light infantry came trotting up the road, followed by the grenadiers in a column six abreast that seemed almost quarter mile long to the rangers.

Knowlton and his men, however, stood their ground and a tremendous firefight ensued. They began by exchanging disciplined volleys, but soon the rough ground with its scattered trees and bushes had both sides resorting to individual fire. Musket balls tore apart tree limbs, eviscerated bushes and splattered into rocks and earth in a constant fire that made it hard to think. Waves of acrid dark gray smoke began to engulf the fifty yard no-man's-land between the two sides, choking throats and stinging eyes. The constant crack of muskets and the buzz from hundreds of lead balls tearing through the air gripped the men on both sides with horror and fear. Each knew that the lead torrent could tear him to pieces at any moment. The battle challenged all their senses and each man, American or Briton, fought desperately to summon courage he never thought he possessed.

Knowlton ran from one end of his line to the other. "That's it, boys! Aim low! The battle is soon ours!"

Several times the British took a bead on the crazed American officer but each time the shot was foiled by bush, rock or smoke. Several cursed the American and vowed to take him, come what may.

Washington heard the firing coming from the head of the Bloemingdale Road as he was forming up the main body of troops. He reached across his saddle and grasped the arm of his aide, Tench Tilghman. "Order Knowlton back to our lines before it is too late."

Tilghman nodded and spurred up towards the action.

Minutes later, Knowlton's men withdrew and he reported to Washington in a fury.

"Sir, we had their advanced guard stopped cold. Why call us back?" He asked incredulously.

Washington maintained a strange calm. "You have led them into a trap, Colonel Knowlton. Now, you have the honor of springing that very trap. Take your detachment plus three Connecticut companies into the woods on the left and envelop the British right as they advance on us. I hope to cut them off entirely. General Nixon will fix the front. Go quickly, sir. Your country's fate is in the balance!"

Knowlton led a detachment of some two hundred men around the right flank of the British, who were now fixated on taking the Hollow Way. The 42d Regiment of Foot, the famous "Black Watch" led the British advance supported by the 33rd Regiment of Foot and the Hessian Regiment of von Donop. As they advanced, one of their officers had the buglers blow the fox chase to once more insult the Americans. One thousand plus of some of the finest infantry in the world descended on erstwhile farmers and shopkeepers who patiently stood their ground.

The toot–toot–toot echoed through the woods and across the Hollow Way. However, the "fox chase" incited a bloody outrage in the Americans defending the heights and stiffened their resolve.

Knowlton was first to anger. "I hear the fox chase called," he cried. "Let us foxes take the hounds!"

With that, his force, now reinforced by several companies, rushed around the British right flank to encircle and cut off the British column. Nixon pushed a small frontal force of over 150 men down into the Hollow Way just as the British column advanced. The foxhunt bugle call had also enraged Nixon's men, who engaged the British head-on in a furious firefight. Muskets blazed up and down the line as men frantically reloaded then quickly stepped forward to take aim at their opponent.

Finally, Nixon pushed the reserve of his brigade into the shallow valley and the momentum of the extra troops, coupled with their growing fury, drove the British back. Nixon's men pursued aggressively–too aggressively. The zeal of the Americans forced the British out of the trap before it could close on them. Washington's plan to encircle the British failed.

But Knowlton's force was still situated along the British flank. As they retreated, his men poured a withering fire into them.

Knowlton raced among his men. "Keep a steady fire, boys! Make them bleed."

And bleed they did, as his men poured a disciplined fire into the fleeing enemy.

Creed's file held the far left flank of Knowlton's force. He used his Jaeger rifle to great effect, downing three British officers during an exchange lasting almost half an hour. Sensing the British were now in disarray, Knowlton signaled the advance. With that, his men moved forward with tomahawks, knives and a few fixed bayonets.

Knowlton was out in front with his adjutant. "Order incline left, we can still cut them off if we move quickly!"

The British responded with steady, accurate fire. Knowlton's adjutant went down before he could pass on the order to incline. Frustration and bitter rage rose up in Knowlton, as he sensed victory slipping away.

He raised his sword high and hollered to his men. "If we cannot cut off the British, we can at least collapse their flank."

A British musket ball struck him in the spine. His back arched, and the Knowlton collapsed, his once powerful body now blood soaked and broken.

Creed was on his way to inform Knowlton of a gap he had seen in the British formation. He watched Knowlton try to aid his fallen adjutant, and then draw his sword and turn to move the rangers forward. Knowlton suddenly dropped his sword and pitched forward, tumbling into the tall grass. Ignoring his throbbing ankle, Creed and ran straight to him. He was the first to arrive and knew immediately that the gallant ranger was not long for this world.

Creed hollered louder than he ever had. "Colonel Knowlton is down! Colonel Knowlton is down! "

Creed then spoke gently to Knowlton. "'Tis serious sir. But I have seen a few survive such wounds. Your lads are on the way. I will see that your men come through victorious."

Knowlton could not answer. Although Creed thought the gallant officer blinked a final affirmation, he would never be sure. Creed gave him some water from his flask, but Knowlton's breathing grew shallow and his eyes began to glaze over as death encroached on the once vigorous man.

As an orderly and two sergeants carried their dying commander to the rear, Creed scanned the front and saw the red coat column retreating out of musket range. Already the narrow window in which they could have destroyed the British had closed. Disgusted, and distraught at the loss of Knowlton, he returned to his men.

"Lads, the gallant colonel is down but I aim to lead those who would follow straight at that gap and shear the column in half."

Parker looked incredulous. "No, sir. Their musket balls swarm like bees. You would bring too many good men to their death."

Creed looked along the line and could see Parker was right. "Very well, Elias. We will hold the line. Tis up to His Excellency to order the next move"

At length, Washington pushed more troops forward in hope of routing the British. But the British retreated in good order and found a safe position under the cover of the guns from their ships anchored on the North River. By three that afternoon, the battle was over. Washington had made his point. He had defied the British, but he would attempt no more that day. He had checked their advance, but this was no Breed's Hill.

శఄఛ

Creed arrived at army headquarters just before dusk. He was limping, tired and ragged, his uniform now torn and covered in dirt, dust and blood from a bitter day of battle. As he entered Fitzgerald's office, he could scarcely contain his anger and despair over the day's events. Fitzgerald, seeing the agitation in the young officer, quietly closed the door and pointed him to a seat at the small table that served as a desk.

"I know what you are thinking, Jeremiah. Another lost victory. And that may well be true, but even a small moral victory at this juncture serves His Excellency's plans."

Creed frowned, "And how can that be, sir? How many more of these senseless skirmishes must we fight? How many leaders like Sullivan, Stirling or Knowlton must we lose? How many good men like Corporal Beall or Private Jorns?"

Fitzgerald reached under his small cot and pulled out a bottle of whisky, nearly half empty, and poured each of them a tin cupful.

"Not the good Irish whisky you are familiar with, Jeremiah, but it has a good Yankee bite."

Creed smiled at the comment, then frowned faintly.

Fitzgerald continued. "Now hear me out, young man. You joined this cause, as most did, expecting it would take only one or two battles for the redcoats to give up their empire. His Excellency is one of the few among our esteemed leaders who understand that it may take years to wear them down. He has a recipe for winning. There are two key ingredients to this recipe: first and foremost is the survival of the army. He will no longer risk all in one grand gambit. He will chip away at the British, hold what he can; give up what he must, and live to fight another day. If we survive over time, he hopes Congress can coax one of the European powers to side with us. Maintaining a viable Continental Army is vital to achieve that."

Creed shook his head. "No sir. I always knew this war would be long in ending—*if* the Cause were to succeed." Then he eyed Fitzgerald suspiciously. "The strategy makes sense, but what is the second ingredient?"

Fitzgerald looked him in the eye. "Why, the second ingredient is intelligence. As I told you earlier, you will have a role in that."

"But I am no spy, nor am I a counter spy. I am a soldier. Yes, I can conduct a patrol or a raid but this other business—I want nothing of it!"

"Your actions belie your words Jeremiah. Recall the valise you purloined and its critical role in saving the army. And...you seem to pass yourself quite nicely as a redcoat—enough to gather more intelligence. And you did excellent work with Braaf—Golden Apple."

"Yes, but that was pure luck and I..."

"Jeremiah, His Excellency needs your services. Full time, not just between battles. This army has few men like you who can do the painstaking and anonymous work of espionage and counterespionage. When the army withdraws from New York, His Excellency will still need information on activities in the city and its environs. New York is the key ingredient in the British strategy. We can find a score of good battlefield officers, but someone who can match the British at the game they have played so well for so many years is worth two score on the battlefield. His Excellency thinks you are just such a man, as do I."

"So the future of our cause relies on my ability to slip into British occupied New York?"

"You will not work alone; your two fine men will support you. And I have two other agents recruited. One is in Brooklyn—our Mister Jons."

"Much good he did us." Creed replied.

Fitzgerald waved a finger. "You missed the meeting with him, not the other way around. Besides, his efforts are only beginning. Now, I have another agent... in New York. I call the second agent Mister Smythe. They report passively, that is, based on what they overhear, observe or read. His Excellency needs to communicate with them from time to time. We have...procedures in place that I will not trouble you with. However, you are to be His Excellency's special arm. You will be used when we cannot wait for their routine reports—not that smuggling information through British lines is any way routine."

Creed sipped at the whisky. He said nothing for a long time. He thought hard about Fitzgerald's words. He reflected on the war and his role. He joined to fight, after all. Although since the battle in the passes on Long island he had done little fighting in massed formations, he realized now that he and his men had seen more action, and faced more British, than any other unit in the army. In seconds, the faces of friends and enemies fallen over the past few weeks flashed before him in a torrent of raw emotion. And he saw the logic of Fitzgerald's argument. The army, and the commander-in-chief on whose shoulders the cause now depended needed intelligence, for they surely lacked everything else.

"I think...I believe...I see your point, sir. What do you call this stuff? It burns like gunpowder when it first hits the palate but then becomes disarmingly subtle."

Fitzgerald smiled. "Rye whisky. The still pots across Pennsylvania are known for turning out some fine spirits. I am glad you like it."

Fitzgerald stood, reached under his cot, and opened up a small wooden box. In it was a chess set, hand carved wooden pieces of very nice workmanship. He opened the small leather board and began placing the pieces on the board, very deliberately, as he continued speaking to Creed in a low voice.

"I find chess relaxing. It takes my mind off things. Do you play?"

Creed nodded numbly. The whisky was having some effect.

"This business of intelligence is very much like a chess match, Jeremiah. Even when you see the board, you do not know what your opponent is planning."

Fitzpatrick, selecting white, began the match. Although it had been some years since he played, Creed was no novice, matching him at every gambit.

Fitzgerald hid his surprise, "Or if you do know what he is planning, you do not know why he is planning it. The real challenge, my boy, is to know what he will do before he does, to create situations that will reduce his options—and force his hand."

Creed's brow furrowed as Fitzgerald took one of his bishops. He was out of practice.

"Still, sure tis a great advantage to see the entire board, sir. Something lacking in our own 'business,' as you call it." Creed said.

Fitzgerald smiled, "Precisely!"

He moved his knight, threatening Creed's king, and declared, "Check."

Creed answered hoarsely, "Not quite, sir."

A surprised Fitzgerald watched as Creed's own knight took his. Creed downed the last drop of the whisky in his mug. He then took Fitzgerald's white knight from the board and placed defiantly in his pocket.

Fitzgerald's response was anxious. "So, are you in the game, Jeremiah?"

"So I am, sir. I believe I have been for some time. I just would not admit it."

"I am glad to hear it my boy! A canny chess player will do well at this game too."

"Canny, sir? I should think not. "Twas simple Irish luck!"

Epilogue

The Continental Army Encampment, Haarlem Heights, New York, September 17th, 1776

With Creed gone to yet another errand at the headquarters, his men took the time to rest before the next call to action. Jonathan had just finished another letter home. Parker sat across the campfire resting his back on his horse's saddle while watching his friend seal the coarse paper in the envelope. "How many of those have you written, Jonathan? Seems as if you always have a quill in hand–if you don't have a rifle."

Jonathan smiled. "Only three, thus far. And have I been able to post only one. I will mail this along with an old one I wrote just after Simon lost his arm. "

He paused a second as he thoughts turned to Simon. "I sure hope the letters reach Frederick before he does."

Parker nodded. "Well, at least they sent him home. Might be worth my losing an arm…if it would get me home to my family."

"You miss them, don't you?" Asked Beall.

"Of course I do." Parker replied tersely.

"I miss my parents and the rest of the family." Beall opined.

"Not the same as missing a woman, if you love her."

"I miss Krista fiercely…though I'll likely never see her again."

"The war won't last forever, Jonathan. Least that's what I keep telling myself.

It occurred to Jonathan that he had never seen Parker write home.

"Have you written them?"

"No, I have not."

"Well, if you wrote them, your wife could write back. Not the same as being with them but a whole lot better than nothing."

"Don't think I will. Might make me more homesick, and besides, I have no writing materials."

"Use mine then. I will even pay the postage."

Parker lowered his head. "Truth is Jonathan…I cannot write. Oh, I can read some, and do numbers. Even manage a word or two–mostly regarding my fishing and all. You know…business. But write a sentence–I never learned."

"Then let me help. You sit there and say what you want–I will write it and you can make your mark at the bottom."

"Say, I am no ignoramus! I can sign my name at the end. Sort of."

The both laughed.

ΒΟΩ
The Stanley House, New York, September 26th, 1776

Emily winced as Nancy helped tighten her stays. Tall and slender, Emily had little need for stays but the fashion of the day required a tight fit below the bosom.

Emily said. "Is the carriage ready, Nancy? You know how papa complains when he is late. We must be at Lady Dunning's by seven, sharp. The ball starts at eight, sharp."

Nancy nodded. "Your daddy is getting the carriage himself. Would have been better if that nice young Thomas had stayed on as stable hand and driver. Where did you meet him, anyway?"

Emily startled at the question. She was getting jittery these days. "He was a friend of Jeremiah's, uh...Lieutenant Creed's. Helped us move that sick man out of harm's way. Guess he was needed at home, wherever that is."

Nancy stepped back and eyed her mistress approvingly. She wore a gown of deep burgundy trimmed in black lace. Her only jewelry consisted of simple pearl earrings and a tight pearl choker that embraced her slender neck. Her honey colored hair was piled high on her head.

"I say, Miss Em, you don't need no powder or wig. Your hair is perfect just like it is now. "

Nancy was proud of her employer's daughter and not just her looks. She thought Emily ran the boarding house better than her father, and since the occupation started had already attracted an exclusive coterie of eligible young officers, both British and Loyalist.

Emily tilted her head and looked approvingly into the mirror. "I believe you are right, Nancy. Let us hope Major Butler and his officers agree."

Nancy smiled. "I am sure they will, Miss Em."

Both women giggled but Emily's display was purely pro forma. Her giggle stifled a choke that tore at her heart, for it belonged to a Yankee officer whom she would likely never again meet. Her efforts to impress the British officers at lady Dunning's were aimed at helping her father's social and professional connections and to enable her to learn more about the expected long term occupation of the Island of New York.

Downstairs, the door to the parlor abruptly flew open and Doctor Stanley called up to his daughter. "Emily! Are you powdered and primped yet? It is past time we go."

Emily took one last look in the mirror and nodded at Nancy. "Yes, papa, I shall be right down."

The aftermath of the battle before Haarlem Heights proved vexing to Washington. Despite his evolving strategy of victory through survival, he had hoped for a version of Bunker Hill to prop up the morale of his army, the populace and most importantly, the Congress. Already both supporters and detractors in Congress bombarded him with letters. Some favored another attack; others that he defend in place, even if it meant the army's destruction. Still others favored a retreat over the Kings Bridge into the Hudson Highlands. He tossed one such letter into the basket marked for burning. It urged negotiations once more. The name of the congressman was disturbing. Washington had thought him a good friend and a steadfast Patriot but such was the state of politics.

A knock on the door brought Washington from his thoughts. The heavy oak door opened slowly and Tench Tilghman peered into the room.

Tilghman announced. "Colonel Fitzgerald has just arrived, sir."

Washington nodded. "Ask him to come see me."

A few minutes later, Fitzgerald arrived with a sheepish grin on his face.

Washington pointed to a seat just across his desk. "I hope your exuberance is transferable, Colonel. I could use a shift in mood right now. Most of my correspondence has given me little cause to smile."

Fitzgerald held a heavy envelope of light brown kidskin. He opened it and examined the contents under the commander in chief's watchful eye. Fitzgerald's face evinced nothing as he read.

Finally he looked up and smiled again. "Well Your Excellency, it seems our scheme is working. I dispatched Creed to one of Mister Jons' appointed sites, from which he retrieved this packet. Our good Mister Smythe has delivered as promised. Mister Smythe dropped the packet at one of the appointed locations near the city. Mister Jons retrieved the packet and delivered it to a point north of here, where Creed fetched it."

Washington grew uncomfortable. "Does Lieutenant Creed suspect anything?"

"No. As far as he is concerned, he serviced a delivery for me. It could be from anyone."

"Anyone engaged in spying, you mean." Washington corrected him.

Fitzgerald chuckled. "Well, yes, of course. However, I send him out every few days to check one or more locations stipulated on Mister Jons' very excellent map. He likely thinks we have a trove of spies in British-occupied New York."

Washington nodded. "When we have but one. And, this being the first communication from Mister Smythe, who can tell its value? Yet withal, it is a start."

"We have Mister Jons' on Long Island as well. The British quartermaster provided him with a lucrative contract to ship goods along the littoral. So long as we maintain a foothold along the Hudson Highlands or the Connecticut shores we should be able to maintain the link, if only sporadically."

Washington nodded. "Now it is I who stand corrected, Robert. Mister Jons is just one key piece to this enterprise. Your Mister Smythe is the other. How did you link the two?"

"As you know, back in July, Mister Smythe volunteered to serve in the event the army left New York. A very perceptive bit of judgment, I might add."

Washington frowned. "So little faith in your commander..."

Fitzgerald smiled wanly. "Merely planning for any eventuality, Your Excellency. Anyway, when the army returned from Brooklyn I had several meetings with Mister Smythe, the last one here in Haarlem, where we made our final arrangements with regard to communicating. I told Mister Smythe to refrain from taking...undue risks."

"This entire enterprise involves great risk, to all involved." Washington said. "To Mister Smythe, Mister Jons, to young Creed and his men...to the Cause."

Fitzgerald replied. "Well, true enough. We too have assumed no small measure of risk in using both Mister Smythe and Mister Jons. Both are volunteers whose ultimately loyalty we cannot ascertain, but must nevertheless trust in. As for personal and physical risks—that is what we have engaged Creed for, and I do believe, despite his protests, he now thrives on them."

Fitzgerald suddenly thought better of his levity. "Poor of me to mock Creed. He is a gallant lad and will prove to be our knight rampant, however..."

Washington eyed Fitzgerald. "However, what?"

Fitzgerald lowered his eyes. "He can never learn the true identity of either Mister Smythe."

Washington nodded and lowered his voice. "That decision is for the good of all. What good do you think he would be if he knew the truth? The only persons who know...who can ever know...the true identities of Mister Smythe or Mister Jons are in this room. This secret is one of the most important of our new nation. It must remain, how should we say, under our four eyes..."

৪০৩

The Stanley House, September 27th, 1776

The parlor clock struck two. The chimes could be heard up in Emily's room. The party at Lady Dunning's had been a success. A bevy of the more socially acceptable women in New York, of all ages, mingled with some of the finest officers on Lord Howe's staff. The food was excellent, not that she ate much. However, she did dance with at least eight officers, half of whom pledged their undying affection for Americans...at least of the female sort. A few invited her for discreet walks in the garden but these she declined for now. Not good to appear too eager and easy to get. No, any would-be suitor must work his way into her good graces.

A knock on the door was followed by a whispering voice. "Miss Em, you still up? Your daddy's been sleeping for over an hour. You need your rest too. Maybe I should bring some warm milk?"

"No need to worry over me, Nancy. Please go to bed yourself. I want to capture my innermost feelings for my journal before I retire. This proved a most romantic night and I wish to recount every moment."

Nancy smiled knowingly. Her young mistress was becoming a real lady. "Alright then. Good night, Miss Em."

After she heard Nancy's footsteps descend the stairs, Emily removed a small valise from a crawl space in the floor under her commode. She had loosened the slats when she was a young girl to hide all sorts of contraband—candies and other sweets. Now it provided her a secret compartment for contraband of a very different sort.

Opening the valise, she removed several paper sheets, her quill and ink. For nearly two hours, she worked by the light of a solitary candle, carefully arranging her thoughts, her impressions of the British officers; the state of Howe's army; civilian morale and the like. New to military talk, she had bombarded her suitors and the other guests with simplistic questions aimed at extracting detailed if bombastic answers. By the evening's end, she had learned the approximate number of regiments on the Island of New York. She gleaned from the ruminations of several officers, the latest British plans to reverse their check at Haarlem.

An eager naval officer confided that the Royal Navy would play a role in the next phase of Howe's campaign. Although she could not ascertain the specifics, she got a sense that several small landings were in the offing, more as a probe and test to pry the rebels from their defenses than as a serious offense. One officer even boasted of leading a "flying column" to sever the Kings Bridge connection and cut Washington off from Westchester.

Emily finished committing her recollections to paper. She was proud of her work, and how relatively easy it had been. She paused, thinking of Jeremiah Creed and the brave men who served with him. It gave her no small satisfaction that, in some way, she was helping them serve the cause they all held dearly. The act of committing this information to paper somehow, in her heart and mind, bound her to Creed as well as her new nation. For this, she was grateful–even joyful, and not the least bit apprehensive. For in the short time she knew Creed she had learned that care, caution and preparation would reduce the danger of discovery and provide the difference between success and failure.

The finished note was three solid pages long, even with her fine, neat print. Before she folded them, she made her special mark at the bottom and signed the correspondence to Colonel Robert Fitzgerald....

I remain as ever,
Your Loyal and True Patriot,
Mister Smythe

The End

Author's Notes

This is an adventure story. However, this adventure tells a part of the history of the American War for Independence and the struggles of a few individuals who, through the fortunes of war, play a part in the seminal intelligence organization of the Continental Army. The backdrop is the War for Independence, a political struggle that turned into an insurgency, which evolved into a civil war and eventually a world war. The military strategy and tactics, and the espionage and intelligence activities adhere as closely as practical to the practices of the 18th Century.

The Patriot Spy is a mix of historical and fictional characters. The central historic figure is Lieutenant General George Washington, the often harried and burdened commander in chief whose determination, leadership and faith in the 'Cause' was largely responsible for its success, despite overwhelming odds. The story's other fairly well known historical figures include Nathaniel Greene, Nathan Hale, Aaron Burr, and the British Generals Cornwallis, Clinton and Howe. Less well-known figures such as Benjamin Tallmadge, "Lord Stirling," John Sullivan, William Smallwood, Israel Putnam, Charles Pickering, Thomas Knowlton, John Glover and Mordecai Gist play important but less celebrated roles in the story, just as they did in real life.

The fictional characters in the story are purely the product of my imagination, and are not based on actual historic persons. Jeremiah Creed, Robert Fitzgerald, the Beall cousins, Elias Parker, Cornelius Foch, Thomas Jeffries and Emily Stanley represent average people who sacrificed so much for America's independence. Sandy Drummond, Stanislaus Kuyper, and others, represent those who sacrificed all for their King. The Braafs represent the many conflicted families that were torn apart and often destroyed by the struggle.

Finally, some factoids aimed at providing background to certain historic events contained in this story: British Loyalists did lead the British under the Generals Clinton and Cornwallis to an undefended pass near Jamaica. There in fact *was* a heroic counterattack against the British by Smallwood's Maryland Continental Line and Haslett's Delaware Line. William Alexander, known as Lord Stirling, did lead the grand attack that allowed other Americans to escape back to the main American defenses. He was captured. General Sullivan, failing to live up to expectations in everything but heroism, was captured on the field of battle along with many of troops. Lieutenant Benjamin Tallmadge did make a mysterious return to Brooklyn to retrieve his horse. He never explained if there were any ulterior reasons. We can only wonder what they might have been.

The British officer corps was not pleased with General Howe's sluggish and methodical approach to fighting the rebels, a theme that tore at their command structure until Howe gave up command. Howe felt sympathy towards the Americans as a whole, although obviously not for the rebellion. He sought a peaceful resolution to the "family feud." Howe did have an American mistress named Elizabeth Loring whose husband acquiesced in their relationship in return for a lucrative posting. There was a Lieutenant Colonel Knowlton who led his Rangers in a gallant but ultimately futile attempt to cut off the British at Haarlem Heights. He died in the attempt and is honored today by the Military Intelligence Corps' famed "Knowlton Award" for excellence in Army intelligence service. And, of course, Captain Nathan Hale, of Knowlton's Rangers, volunteered for a mysterious and ill-fated espionage mission behind British lines.

S. W. O'Connell
Leesburg, Virginia

About the Author

S. W. O'Connell holds degrees in both History (Fordham University) and International Relations (University of Southern California). He is a retired US Army intelligence officer who spent the majority of his service in the field of counterintelligence. Most of his time was spent overseas in US Army Europe and Allied Command Europe, but he does admit to a tour in the Pentagon and a stint at the John F. Kennedy Center for Special Warfare at Fort Bragg.

A native New Yorker, S. W. O'Connell settled in northern Virginia when he returned from his last overseas tour. His long-held love of history made it only natural that he would turn to the historical novel when he finally succumbed to a decades-long urge to craft fiction.

The Patriot Spy is his first novel in the Yankee Doodle Spies series.

CPSIA information can be obtained at www.ICGtesting.com
Printed in the USA
BVOW021630031012

302033BV00002B/192/P